FOREVER FANTASY ONLINE

BOOK 1 OF 3

RACHEL AARON / TRAVIS BACH

IT'S NOT A GAME ANYMORE...

In the real world, twenty-one-year-old library sciences student Tina Anderson is invisible and under-appreciated, but in the VR-game *Forever Fantasy Online* she's Roxxy—the respected leader and main tank of a top-tier raiding guild. Her brother, James Anderson, is a college drop-out struggling under debt, but in FFO he's famous—an explorer known all over the world for doing every quest and collecting the rarest items.

Both Tina and James need the game more than they'd like to admit, but their favorite escape turns into a trap when FFO becomes real. Suddenly, wounds aren't virtual, the stupid monsters have turned cunning, NPCs start acting like actual people, and death might be forever.

In the real world, everyone said being good at video games was a waste of time. Now, separated across a much larger and more deadly world, their skill at FFO is the only thing keeping them alive. It's going to take every bit of their expertise (and hoarded loot) to find each other and get back home, but as the harshness of their new reality sets in, Tina and James soon realize that being the best in the game might no longer be good enough.

Aaron Bach, LLC
"Writing to Entertain and Inform."
Copyright © 2016 Rachel Aaron & Travis Bach

ISBN Paperback: 978-0-692-17162-2
ASIN eBook: B07D8QTWJM

Cover Illustration by Tia Rambaran,
Cover Design by Rachel Aaron,
Editing provided by Red Adept Editing.

Acknowledgements

As always, this book would not have been nearly as good without my amazing beta readers! Thank you so, so much to Kevin Swearingen, Eva Bunge, Beth Bisgaard, Christina Vlinder, Hisham El-far, and the ever amazing Laligin. Y'all are the BEST!

Content Warning

A note from Rachel Aaron

This a book about gamers. The characters talk like gamers, think like gamers, and act like gamers, which—as any gamer knows—is sometimes not very well. As such, this book will contain far more cursing, sexual situations, prejudice, and blood than my novels usually do.

That said, it's still us. Travis and I do not tolerate hate in our fiction any more than we do in real life. Just because a character says/does something awful does not mean that we agree with it, or that that person will not have to pay for their actions. This book deals with difficult issues many real people face, and we tried our best to give those issues the gravitas and realism they deserve. We might not have done everything perfectly, but Travis and I did our best to get it right.

Forever Fantasy Online is our love letter to the online games we played obsessively for years. We wanted to show the amazing strength and resourcefulness of the gaming community without painting over its pitfalls. This book reflects that, and we hope that you love it as much as we do.

Thank you for reading and enjoy the story!

CHAPTER *1*

Tina

Tina Anderson, aka Roxxy, aka guild leader and main tank of the Roughneck Raiders, aka the poor person in charge of tonight's raid, was trying to drum up a few more seasoned fighters and not having much luck.

"Where the fuck is everyone?"

Tina propped her character's elbow on the edge of her massive tower shield, scowling at the glowing menus. The game's fully immersive VR engine made it look like they were floating right in front of her, rubbing the long list of grayed-out, offline names in her face. "We had eighty-five people begging for raid slots yesterday, but now that I need volunteers to help with tryout night, everyone's mysteriously gone." She glanced down at the deadly-looking elf wearing a killer's suit of black-and-red armor beside her. "You got anyone?"

SilentBlayde, her second-in-command and the only Roughneck who *never* missed a raid night, shook his head. "Sorry, Roxxy. It's Golden Week here in Japan, and all of my friends are busy."

"Damn," Tina said, pinching the bridge of her towering character's stone nose. "Thanks for trying. I just can't believe this bullshit. Look."

She waved her hand through the cluttered floating interface, bringing up her browser window showing the tryout-night sign-up sheet she'd posted on their guild forums over a week ago. "We had a full group lined up! Now that it's actually go time, though, five people suddenly have connectivity issues, four are down with the flu, two have work emergencies, and Chris is claiming he's got food poisoning for the third damn week in a row."

"Chris *does* eat a lot of weird stuff," SilentBlayde hedged. "Maybe it's just bad luck?"

"It's lies. *That's* what it is," Tina snarled. "I don't know what's worse, the shirking or the fact that they think I'm dumb enough to believe this crap." Her eyes narrowed. "I should kick them all out."

"Hey, it's only tryout night," SB said, his slightly accented voice cajoling. "Let's go in anyway! What's the worst that could happen?"

"Are you crazy? We're eleven short!" She pointed at the truncated raid list floating in the left of her heads-up interface. "If they were all Roughnecks, that wouldn't be an issue, but these are newbies. I don't even know what gear they're wearing." She sighed. "If we didn't need new recruits so badly, I'd cancel the whole thing."

"Yeah," SB said, the good humor draining from his voice. He knew as well as she did how many A-list players they'd lost over the last few months and what that meant for the guild. "It's the stupid Once King fight," he said bitterly. "It's too hard."

"He's the final boss," Tina said with a shrug. "He's supposed to be hard."

"Not *that* hard," SilentBlayde said. "He's a guild killer. His fight broke *Six Ways from Raiding* and *Richard's Inferno*, and they were the top two raiding guilds in the world. People are starting to say that the Once King *can't* be killed."

"Fuck that," Tina said. "Why would they put a boss who can't be killed in the game? If other guilds couldn't handle it, that just means there's room at the top. We are *this close* to figuring the Once King out. We got him to thirty percent last week. Just a little bit farther, and we'll be the new number one!"

Just thinking about that pumped her up. The Roughnecks had scored a world-first kill earlier this year, and it had been the best night of Tina's life. But that was just the Blood General, a lesser dungeon-boss who was now on farm status for most of the top guilds. The Once King was different. He was the final boss of the Dead Mountain, the hardest raid dungeon Forever Fantasy Online had ever released. His fight was so famously unfair, even non-FFO gamers had heard about it. If Roxxy and her Roughnecks could kill him, they'd be legends.

Assuming she could ever fill a raid again.

Armored shoulders slumping, Tina shoved the browser window full of excuses, laziness, and lies to the far side of her interface so she could see her clock. 9:30p.m. She'd been trying to fill this group for two hours now. Two damn hours *wasted* playing the obnoxious Guild-master-game-of-bullshit-menus instead of Forever Fantasy Online, the most beautiful full-immersion VR game ever made. The game she'd played obsessively for the last seven years. The game she used to love before it had turned into a weekly cycle of nagging and brow-beating a hundred players into acting like the hardcore raiders they claimed to be.

"Hell with this," Tina muttered, punching her gauntleted hand through the "Close All" command. The interface chimed when she touched it, and the sphere of guild-management menus, chat boxes, and windowed browser plug-ins surrounding her vanished to reveal the ancient flagstone road leading to the Dead Mountain.

Even a year after release, the dungeon still looked damn impressive. Now that Tina's vision was no longer cluttered with floating boxes, it really did feel like she was standing at the threshold of a dreadful mountain of death. The Once King's stronghold rose from the dusty gray valley like a giant black thorn. There were no plants on its slopes, no life. Instead, the barren stone was stitched with battlements where skeleton archers, zombie hounds, and other undead roved in huge packs, their eyes glowing like ghostly blue-white candles.

At the base of the mountain, where the broken road ended, a giant arched gate stood open in invitation, its four-stories-tall iron doors filled with the vortex of swirling purple magic that marked the entrance to the Dead Mountain raid dungeon. It was all beautifully detailed, a masterpiece of atmospheric game design, which only made it more obnoxious that the rest of the Once King's zone was a whole lot of rolling gray nothing.

Tina hated the Deadlands. Unlike FFO's other zones, which were filled with beautiful elven forests, glowing volcanoes, and endless golden fields, the view here was gray, gray, and more gray. There were dead gray trees, gray roads, gray boulders, gray rocks, and fields of gray dirt spread out below a cloudy gray sky. Even the air smelled of ash and tasted like road grit, which was a total waste of FFO's revolutionary Sensorium Engine technology. The game automatically muted sensory input that was deemed painful or unpleasant, so at least the dust that was constantly blowing into her eyes didn't sting, but it was still ugly and depressing. Sometimes, Tina couldn't believe she'd spent a year in this damned place. When she looked up at the pinprick of blue-white light shining from the Dead Mountain's peak, though, it all came back. The Once King was up there, and she'd eat all the gray crap in the world if that was what it took to claim the prize of his defeat.

Burning with renewed determination, Tina turned on her

armored heel and marched down the road to address her raid, such as it was.

A few dozen feet from where she and SB had been standing, thirty-seven players stood out from the gray landscape like neon stars. The glow of their enchanted weapons and armor transformed the Deadlands' dusty air into a rainbow prism, and their wildly colored hair, hats, and vanity decorations showed no sign of the dirt that clung to everything else. But while they looked like an army of radiant gods, they acted like a bunch of bored teenagers.

The players stood in small packs, some chatting, others dancing half-heartedly or fiddling with in-game toys. One group was sitting in the dirt with their weapons discarded around them, blatantly watching anime on a giant floating screen someone had projected into the shadow of a destroyed catapult. Tina couldn't believe no one was complaining about such an immersion-breaking faux pas, but what else was there to do? All the other raiding guilds had long since gone ahead into their own private versions of the Dead Mountain dungeon, yet her crew was still standing around, doing nothing.

Tina ran a metal-gauntleted hand over her character's face. Everyone in front of her met the minimum requirements for the dungeon—she wouldn't have invited them otherwise—but this was a shit group. Other than the pack of Roughnecks hanging out together in the back and a few regulars who weren't in the guild but always came to Tina's raids when she invited them, no one had end-game gear. Taking a raid like this into the hardest instance in the game was just begging for an ass kicking, but giving up meant another week without bringing any new blood into the guild, putting them even farther away from a Once King kill.

That was too close to defeat for her to stomach. Gritting her teeth so hard she could feel the pressure in her real head beneath the VR helmet, Tina waved her arm for the raid announcement command. The second she finished the gesture, a gleaming silver megaphone appeared in her character's fist. She was raising it to her mouth to order everyone into the mountain, ass kicking be damned, when she heard SB calling her name.

Tina looked over her shoulder to see the elf running toward her, and she felt her real face again as a blush spread over her cheeks. Watching SilentBlayde move was one of her guilty pleasures. As an elven Assassin, his character model had fluid animations that the less graceful classes, even those played by elves, simply couldn't match. She'd actually tried the combo herself back when she'd first gotten into FFO and had a pretty fun time.

Then she'd made Roxxy.

It had taken less than five levels before Tina was hooked. Her stonekin Knight was eight feet tall and seven hundred pounds of armored elemental fury. With granite for skin and copper for hair, Roxxy was striking rather than pretty as her elf had been, but Tina didn't care. Playing her stonekin felt titanic. Even when the game's Human Analogue Translation System made it feel as if she was walking on stilts inside her giant character, it was worth the inconvenience, because that size was *power*. Unlike her real-life self, people paid attention when Roxxy spoke, and Tina loved it. Even better, stonekin didn't blush, which meant her character's face at least was fine when she turned around.

"*Please* tell me you've found eleven geared players to come and save us," she said as SilentBlayde slid to a graceful stop beside her.

"Not eleven, but I might have one," he said, blue eyes shining above the ninja mask that covered the lower half of his face. "James just came online."

What little of Tina's good mood watching SB had brought back evaporated at the mention of her brother's name. "So?" she said sourly. "James never says yes when I invite him."

"He does sometimes, and he's always top notch when he shows up." SilentBlayde gave her a warm look. "Just try him. The worst that happens is he says no."

That was *not* the worst that could happen, but she wasn't in a position to be picky, and they could use another healer. She was weighing the salvation of her raid against the emotional minefield that was spending time with her brother when the inside of her head began to ring.

"Speak of the devil," Tina said, glancing up at the corner of her vision, where a green phone icon was pulsing next to a picture of James's tired face. "Hang on, SB. Looks like he's calling me."

SilentBlayde stepped back politely, and Tina tapped the icon to pick up the call, trying her best to inject some enthusiasm into her voice as she said, "Hi, J. You logging in soon?"

Her older brother's reply spoke directly into her head. "Hi, T. Yeah, I'm on the character-selection screen right now." She could hear the nostalgic FFO login music through his speakers as James's voice took on a suspicious level of charm. "You want to ditch raiding for a night and come get something amazing with me?"

Tina snorted. "Amazing like that stupid fire rabbit pet you spent twelve hours grinding for last Saturday?"

"Hey, that drop normally takes a year to get!" James said defensively. "And I did it in *eleven* hours because I saved up all those luck potions from the April Fools' Day event. But forget the fire rabbit. I found something way cooler. Get this: there's a place in the Verdancy where the game developers are building part of the next expansion. We can sneak inside if we wall-walk just right, and—this is the best part—it says on the internet there's an active quest giver who awards some kind of giant-lizard mount! Wouldn't it be cool to be two of the only people in the world riding it?"

"Sounds like asking for the ban hammer to me," Tina said, glancing at her wilting raid. "I have a better idea. Why don't you come raid with me for once? We're short for the Dead Mountain. If you help us out, I'll guarantee you one piece of loot if we kill anything."

"Thanks," James said, the excitement draining from his voice, "but I'll pass."

"I can't believe you're turning down free loot," Tina said angrily. She was being dangerously generous bribing him like that, and she knew that he knew it.

"Dying all night is not free," James countered. "And it's not fun, either. I appreciate the offer, but I just want to kick back and explore tonight, not slave away in a raid."

"No, I get it," Tina said. "You're good for messing around with some buggy wall walking but not for helping me."

Her brother heaved a long sigh. "Tina, this is a *game*. It's not supposed to be work. I'm already working three jobs to pay my student loans. More hard stuff is not what I want right now."

"And whose fault is that?" Tina snapped. "If you'd finished college instead of slacking off for five years, maybe you wouldn't have to work three jobs."

"Tina—"

"Don't 'Tina' me," she said, probably sharper than she should have, but she couldn't help it. As always, her brother's complaining pissed her off more than anything else ever could. "That's your entire problem! You *never* want to do the hard work. I had to pay for college all by myself, but I'm leading a world-first raiding guild *and* on track to graduate on time because I'm not lazy."

"It's not like that."

"Whatever you need to tell yourself," Tina said with a sneer. "I knew you wouldn't come. You always flake out when I need you. Have fun doing your bullshit alone."

James started to sputter more excuses, but Tina had already jabbed her finger into the silver *X*, closing the voice chat. She was still fuming when she noticed the concerned look SB was shooting her from above his ninja mask.

"What?"

"Nothing," he said. "It's just...that was a little harsh. Don't you think?"

"That's why I didn't want to talk to him!" Tina cried. "It royally pisses me off. He's one of the best healers in the game, yet he wastes all of his time on meaningless *crap*. It's the story of his life. I'd feel almost sorry for him if it wasn't also the story of *my* life due to all the shit I've had to go through because of him!"

SilentBlayde winced as she finished, and Tina realized belatedly that she was yelling, which made her feel awful. SB didn't deserve her temper. Her guilt intensified when he turned away, wrapping his arms around his waist in a sign she recognized as maximum SilentBlayde upset.

"I'm sorry, 'Blayde," she said, running her hand through Roxxy's copper dreadlocks. "I'm just stressed. It's been an awful night. I didn't mean to take it out on you."

She paused, waiting for him to reply. When he didn't, Tina winced. She was trying to think of what else she could say when the elf collapsed right in front of her.

"*SB!*"

Tina lunged to catch him but stumbled instead when a horrible pain stabbed into her chest. The agony quickly spiraled outward, spreading down her torso and into her limbs until her whole body felt as if it were being crushed. As she gasped for air, her first panicked thought was that she was having a heart attack. It had to be *something* in the real world, because this pain was way worse than anything the game allowed for. But when she forced her violently shaking hands up to cover her ears in an attempt to trigger the emergency logout command, something new slammed inside her.

It felt like hitting a wall at full speed. Her head went WHAM, then SPIN, then WHAM again as the world turned to blurry Jell-O. She could dimly hear the other players screaming as their hazy figures dropped like cut puppets. A second later, Tina went down too, pitching onto her face next to the inert form of SilentBlayde.

The blackout couldn't have lasted more than a few seconds. Tina almost wished it had been longer, though, because the moment she regained consciousness, all of her senses started trying to kill her. Her eyes were burning and blinded, and her body just felt *wrong*. It was too gigantic, too heavy. The sound of her own blood pumping was like hammer strikes in her ears, and her mouth was full of the gritty, acidic dust of the Deadlands.

It was overwhelming. Tina had never realized just how much FFO's engine muted her in-game senses until they'd all kicked into overdrive. Even when she managed to roll over onto her back, the sullen gray light of the Deadlands scorched her eyes like she was staring straight into the sun. She threw an arm over her face to block it as she waited for the pain to fade, but that just let her focus on the roaring in her ears and the heaviness of her armor as it crushed her limbs. No matter what she did, the torment just kept going, rolling on and on without any hint of why it was happening or when it would stop. Then just when Tina was sure she was going to crack under the pressure, the hand she'd dug into the dirt beside her bumped something blessedly familiar.

Multiple small glass vials were strapped into loops on her belt. It was her potion holster, the place she kept her healing items for quick access while she was tanking. They were all still there now, and Tina grabbed one automatically, yanking a pan-elixir from the first slot. She knew it was stupid. Whatever was happening, it was obvious that the Sensorium Engine—the kinesthetic feedback system that allowed FFO to mimic physical sensation in virtual reality—was catastrophically broken. Hell, it was probably cooking everyone's brains right now. A healing potion, even the most amazing cure-all in the game, was just a digital item. It couldn't actually help her, but Tina didn't care. She was willing to try anything to make the hurting stop, so she grabbed the potion and popped the cork, relying on years of habit to bring the vial to her mouth and dump it down her throat.

When she promptly choked on it.

Rather than simply vanishing as usual, the rainbow liquid of the pan-elixir splashed wetly against her tongue. Equally astounding was how *good* it tasted—like the freshest, sweetest strawberry smoothie that had ever been. It took a few coughs, but once she got it flowing down the right pipe, the magical ambrosia washed away her pain and confusion, replacing them with glowing warmth as Tina's broken senses slammed back into place.

Strength surged through her limbs, causing the coffin-like weight of her armor to vanish. Light and free, Tina shot to her feet with such vigor that she missed her new center of gravity and nearly fell over again. Swaying from side to side, she wondered what the hell the Human Analogue Translation System was doing. Operating Roxxy had always felt a bit like walking on poles, but at least the game had more or less matched Tina's real five-foot-tall body to that of the hulking stonekin. Now, though, she felt as if she was something else entirely.

Flailing for support, Tina grabbed one of the road's crumbling stone signposts. Grabbed and missed, because her arms were now three times longer than she was used to. Off guard and off balance, Tina lurched forward to wrap the entire post in a bear hug. She was leaning on the stone to steady herself when the post cracked in half under her tremendous weight, sending her right back toward the ground.

She caught herself at the last second, narrowly avoiding another face full of dust. In her rush to stay upright, though, Tina accidentally took the top half of the broken post with her. The huge chunk of stone had to weigh a hundred pounds or more, but it felt like nothing in her arms. Surprised, Tina gave the stone a squeeze, grinning when the gray rock crumbled beneath her colossal strength.

It was incredible. All the previous sensory trauma was gone, forgotten in the power-drunk euphoria of the pan-elixir. As she steadied herself at last, Tina could feel the astounding strength of Roxxy's body, *her* body, running through every muscle. She could smell the earth on her stone skin and taste the cool smoothness of her white marble teeth. The stonekin's senses had completely overwhelmed Tina to the point where she couldn't even feel her real body lying in bed at home anymore. She was still marveling at the way her stone hands moved like actual flesh inside her armored gloves when a loud, persistent, and terrifying noise finally beat its way through her magical high.

Tina looked up with a start. Someone was screaming. Lots of someones. Shaking her head to clear the last of the pan-elixir's effects, Tina turned to see the rest of her raid thrashing on the road like an entire school of fish out of water. From the way their hands were covering their faces, she knew that they were going through the same sensory hell she'd just escaped. She still didn't know what had caused the disaster—if it was a bug or some horrible new hack—but the pan-elixir had worked on her, so she grabbed another off her belt and dropped down beside the spasming SilentBlayde.

He cried out when she touched him, screaming in pain as her huge hand crushed his shoulder. Tina let go with a curse and eased up on her strength until she was cradling him like an egg. Next, she pinched the small potion bottle delicately between her giant stone fingers and popped the cork. When it was ready, she pulled down SB's special-edition Fukumen Festival 2060 ninja mask and gently pried his clenched jaw apart just enough to shove the pan-elixir into his mouth.

After a few sloppy chugs, the elf's hands flew up to cup the potion bottle. SilentBlayde finished the rest of the elixir in one gulp, then his bright-blue eyes snapped open as he slipped out of her grasp. He moved so fast, Tina didn't even see him stand before he was on his feet in front of her, hands raised high over his head.

"Woooooo!" he cried, doing a perfect double back-flip. "That was *amazing*!"

"SB!" she snapped as he did a cartwheel. "Get a grip!"

Her voice—huge and deep now to match her body but still female—boomed across the dusty plain, and the frolicking elf covered his long ears in pain.

"Sorry," she said at a much more reasonable volume. "But we've got problems."

She pointed at the convulsing players, and the Assassin's blond eyebrows shot up.

"Whoa," he said, pulling his ninja mask back over his nose. "What's going on, Roxxy? I felt like I was dying, but now I feel amazing. Never better in my life." He reached up to touch his delicately pointed ears in wonder. "What'd you do?"

"Gave you a pan-elixir," Tina replied, pulling off her backpack. "No idea what's going on, but it worked for me, so I tried it on you. We need to get everyone else up or at least not in seizures. Got any pans on you?"

"Two on my holster plus a full stack of twenty in my bags," SB said proudly.

Tina whistled. "Damn, dude, you've been working hard." Pan-elixirs were stupidly expensive to make. "I've got the main tank's allotment in my pack, which is another twenty. Go get started administering yours, and the guild will pay you back. Get the healers first so we don't all get slaughtered by some random monster."

SilentBlayde saluted then popped the first of two elixirs off his belt holster as he moved toward the closest healer, a white-robed, fish-faced ichthyian Cleric who was curled up in a ball. Meanwhile, Tina turned her attention to her backpack. Between her and SB, they should have enough potions to get everyone up, but when she flipped her bag open and made the hand gesture to bring up her inventory, nothing happened.

"What the hell?"

She made the gesture again with the same result. Her backpack was no longer a void of floating icons representing her stuff. It was just an ordinary cloth rucksack filled with squashed bread. Grabbing the strap, Tina turned her bag upside down and shook it. Twenty loaves of bread, some gold coins, and three large iron bars fell out. She was staring in horror at the sad pile when she realized it wasn't just her inventory that was broken. The *entire* interface was gone. Her health bar, defense points, ability icons, mini-map, chat log, raid list—everything she normally kept up was missing. Her vision was perfectly clear of all information overlays, including the level icons and player names for the raid in front of her.

Bag forgotten, Tina shot to her feet, swiping her hands through the menu gesture as she went. Just like with her backpack, though, nothing happened. She made the gesture to bring up the system menu next, but all she saw were her own giant steel-gauntleted arms waving in front of her.

She stopped, stone body shaking. As alarming as this situation had been so far, Tina had never questioned that it was caused by something explainable—a bug, a hack, a horrible malfunction—something that made *sense*. Now, every instinct she had was screeching at her that this was different. This wasn't just an interface screwup. Something fundamental in the game had changed, something *bad*. She was struggling to make a list of everything that was broken when a wind blew down from the Dead Mountain's battlements, carrying the faint sound of hundreds of screams.

Her head shot up, then she took a step back. Maybe she was just seeing things differently without the interface, but the Dead Mountain fortress looked... bigger. *Much* bigger, like an actual mountain. With the wind blowing down it, she could hear screams coming from the upper levels, but she didn't see the undead patrols on the battlements anymore. She also didn't see the purple swirl of the instance portal. The giant gate was now just empty, standing wide-open to reveal the huge, dark hall of the dungeon's first wing and the things moving in the dark inside it.

"SB?" Tina called, voice trembling. "I think we need to get out of here. How's that healer coming?"

When the Assassin didn't answer, Tina turned to see he was still wrestling with the Cleric. Trapped in sensory overload, the blue-scaled ichthyian thrashed at every touch, wrenching his mouth away whenever SilentBlayde tried to cram the pan-elixir between his fish lips. Tina was about to go help hold him down when a harsh metallic screech pierced the air.

She whirled back around with a curse. Every Dead Mountain raider knew that noise. It was the sound the skeleton patrols made when they detected a player. Wincing at the bad timing, Tina drew her sword and started searching the gray landscape for the enemy, but all she saw was the empty road.

Confused, Tina squinted down the gray road toward the mountain. As she'd noted before, the swirling purple vortex that used to mark the start of the dungeon was gone. Without it blocking her view, she could see undead moving inside the Dead Mountain's grand entrance hall, but they were hundreds of feet away, much too far to have been triggered by the raid.

No one must have told them that, though. No sooner had her eyes adjusted to the dark than Tina spotted a pair of enormous armored skeletons as they ignited their flaming swords and rushed forward, bones rattling as they charged through the hall and out the mountain's gate.

Straight toward her.

Scrambling, Tina bent down to grab her massive tower shield off the ground where she'd dropped it. By the time she'd gotten it back onto her right arm, the first skeleton was on top of her. It was even bigger up close, ten rattling feet of dusty bone, tarnished armor, and blue-white ghostfire filling her vision as it raised its flaming sword with both hands to chop at her head.

For an eternal second, mortal terror froze Tina in place. Then years of habit kicked in, and her body moved on its own, snapping her shield up just in time to catch the burning blade before it could land in her scalp. The impact sent Tina's feet sliding backward down the dusty road, but she managed to stop the monster's rush. She shoved the skeletal knight back next, swinging her own oversized sword to smack its blade off her shield with a ringing *clang*.

The parry was pure instinct. The undeads' chopping attacks had always been repetitive and predictable, and Tina had spent so many years battling skeletons, bandits, dragons, and so forth that the motions of FFO's active combat system had long since become second nature. But while all of those battles had felt as real as the game could make them, they were nothing like this. With the gritty wind blowing in her face and her muscles aching from deflecting the skeleton's attack, Tina had never felt more heart-poundingly "here." The rattle of animated bones, the cobblestones sliding under her metal boots, the so-cold-it-burned heat of the ghostfire rising from the monster's blade—it all felt *real*, and the fear that brought was real as well, slowing down her practiced motions as the skeleton threw its sword up to hammer into her shield again.

Focused on the enemy with the blade over her head, Tina didn't even notice the second skeleton rushing past her until it was several feet down the road. Confused and frantic, she considered letting it go until she realized it wasn't trying to flank her. As the tank—the player in the party who taunted monsters into attacking them instead of going for smaller, squishier prey—Tina was used to being the only target, but the second skeleton hadn't even glanced in her direction. It was going for the downed raid *behind* her, its sword already lifted to strike the helpless body of a human player lying on the ground.

By the time Tina realized what was about to happen, it was too late. She watched in horror as the skeleton's blue-white flaming sword swept down, slicing the incapacitated player's head off in a single strike. The head bounced away like a rotten melon while the neck stump pumped blood onto the gray rocks of the road.

As she watched the viscous red liquid soak into the dust, Tina forgot that there was a skeleton over her head as well. She forgot about the fight, forgot about the raid. All she could see was that red liquid pouring from the stump of what had once been a person.

There was no dismemberment in Forever Fantasy Online. Getting hit with a sword caused a stagger animation and lost hit points. There wasn't even blood. Certainly nothing like this. This wasn't just a new graphic. She could *see* the bright white vertebrae sticking out of the dead player's neck. See the blood dripping down the sundered flesh to the ground where it sank like an oil spill into the gray dust of the—

The skeleton in front of her brought its blade down on her shield with enough force to make her stagger. The deafening crash of cursed metal on sunsteel snapped her out of her shock. Blinking frantically, Tina tore her eyes away from the corpse and shoved her shield at the skeleton attacking her to buy some room. While it was recovering, she looked frantically over her shoulder to get an eye on the skeleton behind her, which was already moving toward the next unconscious player.

Tina moved on instinct, slamming her foot down to activate her wide area taunt. The only way to prevent another disaster was to get the runaway skeleton focused on her, so she stomped as hard as she could, yelling for good measure. With no ability interface, she had no way of knowing if the ability would work, but the moment her boot landed, a brilliant shockwave pulsed out from her foot, running up the skeletons' legs and through their bodies until the blue-white ghostfire in their eye sockets flashed red.

That was exactly what was supposed to happen. But before Tina could feel relieved about activating the right taunt by gesture alone, everything else went wrong.

Normally, the environment in FFO wasn't collapsible. That must have changed too, though, because unlike every other time she'd used her taunt on this exact stretch of road, her stomp now sent a spiderweb of cracks through the ancient cobblestones. The ground fell apart a second later, toppling Tina and both skeletons over as the road collapsed into a wide crater of loose dust and rolling stones.

To Tina's dismay, the skeletons were the first to make it up. They rolled back to their feet in unison, chopping at her with their swords while she was still scrambling to get her legs under her. She lurched backward just in time to avoid getting filleted, throwing out her arms for balance, which was a nearly fatal mistake. The moment her shield was out of the way, the first skeleton's blue-white flaming sword shot through the gap in her defenses.

Tina gasped in terror as seven feet of flaming steel crashed into the heavy armor that guarded her neck. As expected of top-level raid gear, the runed metal deflected the blade with barely a scratch, but the ghostfire that coated the skeleton's weapon flashed an angry white. As the light pulsed, Tina felt burning cold bite through her armor, down her neck, and into her collarbone on her right side. It wasn't a dangerous hit, but the burn still hurt a hell of a lot more than the game should have allowed, and the unexpected pain destroyed what was left of Tina's stability.

She went down with a pained yelp, smacking her head on a rock as she landed, which was how Tina learned that the "don't show helmet" setting she used so she wouldn't have to play the game while staring through a realistic-style visor now meant "you have no helmet." The only things that saved her from an instant KO were the weird metal-but-not-metal copper dreadlocks of her hair, which softened the blow. Still, all Tina could do for the next several heartbeats was lie dazed on her back with her sword arm flung out and her shield over her chest as she stared up at the flat gray clouds of the Deadlands. Then the sky vanished as the two skeletons appeared above her.

The skeleton on her left stomped her sword flat to the ground with its boot. Meanwhile, the one on the right bent down to grab her shield and wrench it away. Tina strained with all her might, but since she was stuck on her back at the bottom of the crater, their combined strength, weight, and superior angle were more than she could match. No matter how she fought, she couldn't free her sword or stop the skeleton above her from yanking her shield to the side, leaving her body exposed to the sword the left skeleton was now raising over her.

Staring up at the executioner's stance, the fear Tina had felt earlier came back with a vengeance. She still didn't know what was going on, if this was even a game anymore, but her body was completely, one-hundred-percent convinced it was about to die. Her panicked brain raced in circles as she tried to remember which ability she needed to use to save herself, but without her interface, she had no idea what still worked. The sword was coming down, though, so Tina decided that if all bets were off for her enemy, she might as well try something crazy, too.

Letting go of her sword and shield, Tina grabbed a basketball-sized piece of rubble and hurled it with all her might at the left skeleton. The improvised move wouldn't have been possible in normal FFO. Now, though, the mini-boulder flew like a meteor right into the skeleton's face, exploding on impact and knocking the monster flat onto its back.

A sword flashed on Tina's right as the other skeleton tried to stab her, but its grip on her shield forced it to attack from an awkward angle, and Tina easily smacked the blow away with her armored hand. As the skeleton reeled, Tina grabbed the shield it had tried to rip away from her with *both* hands and rolled backward. The skeleton clung desperately to its prize, but now that it was alone, *she* was the one who was stronger and heavier, and she yanked it off its feet, ending up on her back again with the massive skeleton on top of her and her shield in the middle.

It was a dangerous position, but now that she was no longer trying to hold on to her sword, Tina's left hand was free to shove herself up. Once she got her legs underneath her, she pushed up with her entire body, hoisting the shield—and the skeleton on top of it—over her head. Then roaring with fury, she turned her shield and slammed it back down again, crushing the skeleton that was now beneath it into the shattered road. Since her legendary shield, forged during the Age of Skies, could take a beating, Tina stomped her boot down on it next, smashing the trapped skeleton several inches into the stony dirt. She was about to stomp again when she heard retching noises followed by SilentBlayde's cry of distress.

"Oh shit, David! You're not allowed to choke to death on a *healing* potion!"

The shout made her cringe. She was turning to ask SB if that was pan-elixir number one or two being barfed all over the road when the skeleton she'd knocked over with the rock clambered back to its feet. Her dropped sword was right beside it, just a few feet away, but if Tina took her weight off her shield, the skeleton she'd trapped beneath it would get up, too. That left her with no weapon and no door-like shield while facing an end-game monster meant to be fought by 3 or more players.

Tina wanted to run, or panic, or do anything other than fight this terrifying, un-winnable battle, but the image of that unknown player's head bouncing across the broken cobblestones was seared into her memory. The blood was still on the ground, bright red and accusing, reminding her that it was her fault. She'd let the skeleton slip by. If she messed up again, someone else would die, so Tina swallowed her fear and raised her empty hands instead, curling them into metal-gloved fists as the monster charged.

Screeching like a band saw, the huge skeleton brought its curved sword down on her with both hands. It was an easy-to-follow attack, but when Tina raised her arm to knock the sword aside, she discovered that the injury she'd taken earlier wasn't as minor as she'd thought. The burn from the ghostfire no longer hurt, but it was still there, sending a deathly numbness down her shoulder and into her arm as the skeleton's sword slammed down.

She didn't have the strength to block it, so the attack smashed Tina's raised arm into her own face. Still unable to cut through her god-forged armor, the giant blade slid down her gauntlet in a shower of sparks and dropped to land between the knee and thigh plates of her left leg instead. No longer hampered by inch-thick rune-forged metal, the flaming sword chopped clean through the relatively thin chain that guarded her joint and into the stony flesh below.

Roaring in pain, Tina kicked the monster away and scrambled back, looking down to assess the damage. Sure enough, silver blood was welling up from the wound like a faucet, but terrifying as it was to see herself bleeding, part of Tina felt like laughing at how she only had a narrow gash instead of a whole missing leg. Just like the earlier wound in her shoulder, the ghostfire burned like crazy, but while she could already feel her leg going numb, it still worked. Not that that mattered.

In her rush to get back so she could check her leg, she'd stepped off her shield, which meant the other skeleton was now free to climb back to its feet. It didn't even look damaged from its time in the dirt, its ghostfire eyes as bright as ever as it shook the gravel from its armor.

As two pairs of white-fire eyes floating in empty skulls locked onto her, Tina had no choice but to back up again, climbing out of the crater and back up on the road. Her right arm was now completely numb thanks to the spreading ghostfire, and her bloody knee burned like acid where the sword had cut through. She desperately needed to take control of the situation, but she had no sword or shield. She couldn't even see her available skills without her interface, but all of Tina's experience said that this was big-ability time.

The skeletons advanced slowly until they reached the edge of the crater. The moment they stepped up on solid ground again, they charged in unison, the tongues of ghostfire in their eye sockets dancing as they hurtled toward her, swords raised high. Wincing, Tina turned her back on them and slammed her arms together, activating her race's Earthen Fortitude ability.

For a terrifying second, nothing happened. Just the whistle of giant swords streaking through the air toward her undefended back. Then Tina felt the kiss of earth on the soles of her feet as the blessing of the Bedrock Kings flowed into her. Strength and stability settled in her bones, her skin, her armor, and even her metal hair. She felt colossal in its grip, a mountain that could take any storm. But with the power of bedrock came the immobility of it as well, and as her body hardened into position, Tina gritted her teeth for the beating.

Sparks flew over her shoulders in rivers as both skeletons hammered their swords into her back. The normally crushing blows felt like bee stings compared to the mountain within her, but it wouldn't last forever. She couldn't see the cooldown with the interface, but Tina knew she only had eight seconds before the near-invulnerability of Earthen Fortitude wore off. After that, she'd be mincemeat.

Unable to move, Tina used those precious seconds to look for help. She spotted SilentBlayde giving a Cleric the Heimlich maneuver. The white-robed healer was gagging and barfing rainbow-colored pan-elixir everywhere. That was no good for her, but surely someone else was up. SB had had two pan-elixirs on his belt, after all. The Cleric couldn't have barfed them both up.

With her time rapidly running out, Tina desperately looked around for someone else. Aside from SB and the healer he was keeping from choking, though, there was only one figure who wasn't sprawled on the ground. A dozen feet down the road, an ichthyian Cleric who looked almost exactly like the one SB was helping was cowering behind a rock. Hopes soaring, Tina opened her mouth to yell his name only to realize she had no idea who he was. She *had* to know him—all the healers in tonight's raid were Roughnecks—but without a nameplate over his head, she couldn't identify him by character model alone. It didn't help that all the best-geared Clerics wore the exact same white robes *and* there were four in tonight's raid who were ichthyians, scaly fish people whose bug-eyed character models all looked nearly identical.

He was all she had, though, so Tina yelled anyway, screaming at the Cleric to heal her, but the fish-man just turned away.

"It's just a dream," he said, placing his webbed hands over his ear holes. "You aren't real. I'm just having another lucid dreaming episode, that's all. There's no way this is real. It's never real."

There was more, but Tina didn't bother listening to the rest of his babbling. "SB!" she cried instead, looking frantically at the elf since she was unable to lift her arms. "Help!"

Far down the road, SilentBlayde stopped flicking rainbow-colored puke off his leather armor and glanced up in surprise, his blue eyes widening into an *Oh shit* look as he realized her situation.

The mountain within her was starting to fade now, the magic falling out of her like the stone it was. As it left, Tina knew she was screwed. SB was on the opposite side of the raid group from her. Even if he was strong enough to stop the swords falling toward her back, he'd never make it in time. Once she was dead, the Assassin would be outmatched. The skeletons would kill him and everyone else, and it would be all her fault.

The moment Earthen Fortitude released her legs, Tina wheeled around. She might be outmatched, but it was her responsibility as a tank to be the wall between these things and the other players for as long as she could. If nothing else, maybe her blood spraying across the ground would snap that idiot healer out of his shock long enough to save the others.

The skeleton on her left went first. As it swung down, Tina lifted her right arm, choosing her numb limb for the first sacrifice. But even though she was anticipating the blow, the lingering ghostfire left her too slow by miles. She'd barely managed to get her hand up before the massive sword swept right past. It was about to land in her skull when its owner's head was engulfed by a cloud of dark-purple powder.

The sword flashed past Tina's face, cutting so close it flicked a single drop of silver blood from the tip of her nose. Reeling from the powder, the huge skeleton staggered backward, but the cloud surrounding its head followed every move, obscuring even the white ghostfire of its eyes.

With its ally blinded, the second skeleton took its chance to attack. When it raised its sword to chop at Tina, though, SilentBlayde appeared from thin air at its side, one of his gleaming silver swords already wedged perfectly into the joint of the monster's arm. The flat of the blade prevented the ball from rotating fully in its socket, locking the monster's arm comically over its head.

"I've got you, Roxxy!" SB said, keeping his eyes on the skeleton he'd just locked down. "Sorry I'm late. Anders was supposed to heal you while I got David up, but the A-man flipped out on me."

Tina rubbed her numb arm in relief, glad it was still attached. "You got here when I needed you, Blayde. Thanks."

SB took his eyes off the enemy just long enough to give her a wink. "Here," he said, plucking something from his belt pocket with his free hand and tossing it at her. "Drink!"

Tina scrambled to catch the glass vial before it shattered on the ground. Fumbling with the cork, she didn't look at what it was before she downed the contents in one gulp. The half cup of liquid tasted like normal water when it hit her tongue, but it washed away all the weakness in her arm and leg.

"What was that?" she asked, looking down at her once-again functional hand in wonder.

"Unfallen Water from the Age of Skies," SilentBlayde replied proudly. "Ghostfire is purged with water magic, so—"

He cut off as the skeleton he'd trapped suddenly gave a violent shake. It didn't look like much to Tina, but the force of the motion sent the wiry elf flying over her head. She was moving to catch him when he flipped in midair and landed on his tiptoes on top of the ruined catapult.

"Did you see that?" SB cried, pointing at his pose. "I'm like freaking Legolas here!"

Tina laughed. "Thanks, SB," she said, pointing at the skeleton that wasn't currently reeling blindly with a purple cloud over its head. "Play with that one for a minute. I need my sword and shield if we're to have any chance here."

SilentBlayde saluted and leaped at the towering undead knight, smacking the skeleton across the knees with his left-hand sword as he landed. It looked like a solid hit, but the ten-foot-tall monster barely noticed. It was still locked on Tina, almost trampling the slender elf in its rush to get to her.

"Umm, Roxxy?" SB said nervously as he danced back. "You kinda still have its attention. Looks like aggro system still works."

"Just stun lock it," Tina ordered, looking longingly past the skeleton at the crater where she'd gone down earlier.

The ninja mask hid his expression, but Tina could hear the panic in SilentBlayde's voice. "I'm *trying*, but there's no interface! I'm used to having all my macros and mods for abilities. I don't remember how to activate everything by gesture only!"

Tina gaped at him. "*What?* How'd you use the blinding night powder, then?"

"It's just a packet I throw! There was one in my belt!"

"I told you running all those mods was a bad idea!" she cried, ducking the skeleton's sword as it swung over SB's head. "This happens to you every expansion!"

They danced back and forth, with the monster striking at her while SB harassed and parried in between. A few feet away, Tina could already see the night powder's purple haze thinning around the other skeleton's head. Losing her patience, she leaned down and wrenched the lower half of the old stone signpost she'd cracked when she'd first woken up out of the ground. She was about to throw the hunk of rock at the skeleton's face when SB sheathed his left sword.

Pausing with her rock held high, Tina watched in amazement as SilentBlayde pulled a glowing crystal bolo out of one of his many pockets and whipped it at the active skeleton. As the bolo twined around the monster's exposed ribs, the crystal ends crashed together, and electricity coursed over the skeleton, immobilizing it.

"Three seconds!" SB yelled as he pulled his sword back out.

Tina dropped her rock and dove, sliding past the immobilized skeleton to scoop up her sword from the broken ground behind it. She was going for her shield next when the crackling lightning went quiet, then the leather cord of SB's bolo snapped like a whipcrack as the skeleton broke free.

The night powder keeping the other skeleton at bay ran out at the same time. As the air cleared, the skeleton whirled on her and charged, screaming that horrible scream. Wincing at the sound, Tina dropped and rolled, sliding her arm into the straps of her shield. The moment the comforting weight of the wall of metal was back on her arm, she pushed herself up and leaped to the edge of the gravel pit she'd created with her stomp. Too simpleminded to go around, the skeletons both charged directly into the pit again, floundering when they hit the loose soil. Tina was bracing to meet them when SB appeared at her side.

"What's the plan?" he asked, gripping his blades as the skeletons struggled to climb up the rolling gravel toward them. "These guys are both two-skull rated. We've never beaten a pack like this with only two people."

"Forget the game," Tina said, gripping her beloved sword and shield tight. "We've got to fight for real now."

SilentBlayde's confused look was lost as the two monsters reached the top of the pit and slammed into her guard. Tina grunted at the impact, but this time, her feet stayed firm, stopping them cold.

"Sorry, assholes," she said through gritted teeth, glaring over the top of her shield into the burning eyes of her enemies. "We're not dying today. *SB!*"

The elf was moving before she said his name. In a single graceful motion, he leaped over her head to land on the closest skeleton with both swords, sending bone chips flying as he began carving into it from behind.

CHAPTER *2*

James

James Anderson should not have been playing FFO tonight.

Work had been worse than usual. He'd pulled his shoulder saving a student from a bad throw at beginners' jujitsu class, and now his whole arm was on fire. It was his fault, too. He never should have agreed to teach four classes in a row, but the money had been too good to pass up. Now, ten hours later, his muscles were shot, his brain was fried, and the dread of having to get up and do it all over again tomorrow was throbbing like an ulcer in his stomach. A smart man—a *responsible* man—would have gotten his sleep while he could, yet here James was, sitting on his futon, staring at his VR helmet like a fucking addict.

His calloused fingers tightened on the sleek black plastic. He'd ripped it off his head after Tina had hung up on him mid-apology, not that that was new. He'd apologized to her a million times over the years, and she hadn't listened to any of those, either. Yet another reason he should put the helmet down. If he logged into the game, guilt would eventually drive him into raiding with the Roughnecks. Staying up late running a super-stressful dungeon was the last thing he needed, but he couldn't stop looking at the inviting glow of the Forever Fantasy Online screen shining inside the helmet's visor.

He wanted to play. Bad idea or not, he wanted to escape to the beautiful world in which the disaster his life had become didn't exist. The one place where he could pretend he wasn't a failure, if only for a few hours.

"Addict," he muttered, shoving the VR helmet over his head.

The moment the warm plastic covered his head, his tiny bedroom vanished, replaced by the endless blue-black expanse of the character-selection screen. As his eyes adjusted to the sudden change, bright 3-D images of all his characters appeared in front of him and immediately started jumping and waving, pointing at their chests in a "Pick me!"

gesture whenever James turned his head in their direction. After considering his options for a moment, James lifted his arm to point at the first in the line, his main character. The motion sensors on his helmet detected the movement, and the tall, catlike jubatus Naturalist pumped his fist in victory. Bad decision made, James lowered his body carefully onto the bed as his characters vanished, leaving him staring into the swirling dark of the loading screen.

"Initiating Sensorium Engine," said a soothing female voice. "Please relax. Full immersion in 10... 9... 8..."

The countdown moved from the helmet's speakers to inside James's head as the virtual reality expanded to take over his senses one at a time. By the time the countdown hit "1," he was barely aware of his body or the hard bed beneath it. Then the soothing voice reached zero, and James sucked in a breath as he fell into complete sensory deprivation.

He was no longer in his bedroom. He was standing in a translucent white bubble surrounded by a vast starscape that stretched to infinity. It was unspeakably beautiful, but the anti-deprivation loading sphere was actually James's least favorite part of the entire FFO experience because he couldn't move. He supposed a few moments of paralysis were a small price to pay for the miracle that was full-sensory VR, but it still felt terrifyingly like being trapped inside his own body, held down by a force he couldn't understand or fight.

Thankfully, the servers were on the ball tonight. After only a few seconds, the Sensorium Engine succeeded in taking over his kinesthesia, and James's body was returned to him. He was hopping from foot to foot just for the sake of moving again when the soothing system voice spoke his favorite words.

"Loading world."

James's face split into a grin. No matter how many times he logged in, this part never got any less cool. As the game connected, the FFO servers took over control from his helmet, and the endless stars vanished as the inside of the transparent loading bubble became mirrored. Smiling like a doofus, James watched as his reflection grew taller. His face flattened, and his eyes became slitted. Claws and fangs appeared, followed by fur, ears, and a tail. The sequence was accompanied by a full orchestral score complete with martial brass and pounding drums. A dazzling show of bursting golden lights completed the celebration of his log-in, and James silently thanked whichever developer had decided to make this happen inside the privacy of the loading sphere. If anyone saw how happy the transformation into his character made him, he'd have died of embarrassment.

"Connection complete," the system voice said proudly. "Good luck, hero!"

As the words faded, the mirrored ball of the loading sphere vanished, and the world of Forever Fantasy Online blossomed around him.

It was morning in the game. Bright sunlight streamed through the white hide walls of the large yurt he'd logged out in yesterday. It was just an empty tent in a low-level quest hub no one went to anymore, but in his own mind, James liked to pretend it was his character's home. He could have bought an actual place on the player housing islands, but the disconnected dimension of floating mansions felt too artificial. As part of the game world, the yurt felt much more real, even if it wasn't actually his.

Smiling, James stretched his long arms over his head to settle himself into his character's catlike body only to stop again when the movement made his injured shoulder twinge. Pain in full immersion was a bad sign. Yet another reminder that he needed to take it easy tonight. A quick glance at his friends list showed that Roxxy and SilentBlayde were both still in the Deadlands, but neither had messaged him yet. He was reaching for the tent flap to head outside and catch a flight to the Verdancy to see if he couldn't sneak his way into that unfinished zone before they did when a sudden pain stabbed into his chest.

Gasping, James dropped to his knees, clutching his ribcage, which felt as though it were full of knives. The agony quickly spread down his limbs, filling his entire body with pain. He was trying to breathe through it when his head went WHAM, then SPIN, then WHAM again, making everything go blurry as he pitched forward onto the floor of his tent.

When he came to again, every perception he had was ratcheted up to eleven. His skin burned, tickled, and itched all at once. Every fine hair of the hide rug he'd fallen on stabbed like a needle, and his ears were being hammered by the cavernous whooshing of his own breath. Even the normal dustiness of the yurt was like a sandstorm crammed up his nose, drowning him in the musty scents of earth, leather, and grass.

Cracking his eyes open was like looking straight at the sun, but closing them didn't help, either. Even with his eyelids shut, there was a world of dazzlingly colored streamers drifting in the dark behind them. While not as bright as actual sunlight, the luminescence still overwhelmed James's vision, making everything blur together into a swirling, prismatic soup.

Chest heaving in panic, James frantically waved his hand in the log-out command, but instead of hearing the familiar *bing* of the interface, he felt his arm collide with the tent's wooden support pole, causing him to yowl in pain. Desperate and confused, he tried again, going slowly this time to make sure he did it right. But though he was certain he hadn't made a mistake, there were no familiar chimes of his fingers passing through the virtual buttons of the interface. He didn't even hear an error.

"Help!" he yelled, thrashing on the ground. "GM! Stuck! Report! Emergency! 911!"

James tried every voice command he could think of, but nothing and no one responded. That left only one option. It took a long time—he couldn't see, and it was hard to tell where his too-long arms were now—but eventually, he managed to cup his hands over his ears to trigger the emergency logout.

Hard-quitting out of full sensory immersion would leave him barfing on his bedroom floor, but James would gladly take a few hours of dump shock to escape whatever was going on. Unfortunately, triggering the emergency log-out required absolute stillness, which was difficult when all you wanted to do was writhe on the ground. There was no other way out, though, so James forced himself to concentrate, clamping his hands tight over his ears as he silently counted to twenty. Then thirty. Then sixty.

When he passed a hundred, James dropped his arms with a curse. Whatever malfunction had caused the interface to disappear must have disabled the emergency log-out as well. Good for him there was more than one way to dump out.

"Start Console," James said in a croaking voice then paused. Normally, the game would ding to let him know the voice command had worked. Now, of course, there was nothing, or maybe he just wasn't able to hear it over the deafening rush of his blood in his ears. Either way, James didn't know what else to try, so he kept going.

"Command. New macro," he said, pausing carefully after each statement. "Name, GTFO. Script start. X equals five divided by zero. Script end. Save."

There was no way of knowing if the system had gotten all of that, but James had made a lot of macros over the last eight years, and this one was as famous as it was simple. The UI0013 script bug had haunted FFO since launch. Certain errors in the ability macro system, like division by zero, would crash the whole damn game. He and other players had complained about it for years, but since only a tiny portion of the player base was advanced enough to care about writing their own ability scripts, the developers had never bothered to fix it. Hoping that laziness was still in play, James pressed his hands over his eyes and took the plunge.

"Command, Run GTFO."

He held his breath as he finished, bracing for the dump. When nothing happened, he slammed his hands down in frustration then cried out in pain when the sudden smack of his fingers against the ground sent his heightened pain awareness into overdrive.

Clutching his hands to his chest, James curled up into a ball on the needle-sharp rug to wait this out. It *had* to end sometime. He was still logged into the game, which meant someone would find him eventually. It might be his roommates tomorrow once they realized he hadn't left his bedroom all day, but this couldn't last forever. To boost his chances of survival until then, James focused on counting his breaths. With each intake and exhalation, he sought to make his breath the center of the universe. It didn't decrease the sensory agony, but it did help him ignore the worst of it, pushing the pain to the sides of his consciousness as he waited for this to pass.

After three hundred breaths, James began to wonder if it *was* going to pass. He wasn't sure how long this had been going on now, but it couldn't have been more than thirty minutes. The thought of spending *hours* like this was almost enough to make him hyperventilate, but he caught himself at the last second, forcing his mind back to his breaths.

By the time he reached six hundred, he thought his heart was beginning to slow down. By eight hundred, his chest definitely hurt less. His skin felt less sensitive, too, the hide rug poking him less like needles and more like normal scratchy hairs. By a thousand, the dancing lights behind his eyes were more pretty than painful, and James decided to take a chance.

Gingerly opening his eyes, he pushed himself to a sitting position, keeping one hand in front of his face to limit the glare. Everything was still way too bright and intense, but his senses seemed to be drifting back toward normal, and he wasn't dizzy. Encouraged, he opened a crack in his fingers, squinting into the bright-white glare until, slowly, shapes began to emerge.

He was still in the game. Still in his yurt, even. But while that much hadn't changed, everything else had.

The tent's walls were still white, but they were no longer bare. The stretched hide was now lovingly decorated with paintings of animals being hunted by jubatus: the cheetah-like people native to the savanna zone where he'd logged out. The tent's wood support poles were also carved with intricate scenes of jubatus hunting and battling the gnolls, the other major race in the zone. Similar themes decorated the rest of the furniture that was now scattered around the once-empty tent. There was a bed now, and a bench, and woven baskets holding carefully folded stacks of lovingly mended soft-hide shirts and pants with holes at the back for the jubatus's tails.

The decor wasn't all that had changed, either. The yurt was now easily twice as large as it had been when James had logged in. Before, it had looked like a single tent for a scout. Now, it looked like a home for an entire family. There were even some straw cat-people dolls tucked away in the corner next to a rack containing bundles of dried herbs. Now that his nose was calming down, James discovered he could smell them strongly, which was how he learned that Plains Rose smelled a lot like rosemary.

Breathing the familiar scent in deeply, James rose to his feet to take stock of his situation. He still had no idea what was going on—if he'd been the victim of a hack or if a new art patch had just gone horribly awry—but now that he had control of his sight and limbs again, it was time to log out and go to the hospital. There was no way that much sensory nerve pain didn't have serious consequences. At the very least, he wanted a doctor to tell him he didn't have brain damage for his own peace of mind. But when he made the motion to bring up the system menu, all he saw was his own hand moving through the air.

Scowling, James made the motion again. Slowly this time, to be sure he was doing it right. Again, though, nothing happened. The menus must still be busted. He was wondering what to do about that when he realized with a start that *none* of the user interface was present.

Normally in the game, critical information like his health, mana, level, mini-map, status effect, the time, and so on were all discreetly visible at the corners of his vision. Now that his eyes were working again, he was able to look all around, but no matter how far he craned his head or moved his eyes around his field of vision, it stayed empty. There was no user interface, no floating text, not even an internet connection icon, and the more James stared at the blank places where all those things should have been, the bigger the lump in his stomach grew.

"Command," he said, voice trembling. "Message player Tina Anderson."

Nothing.

"Message character Roxxy."

Still nothing.

"Command, join general chat."

Continued nothing.

Each voice command was met with deafening silence. He didn't even hear an error beep, leaving James feeling like he was talking to empty air.

Shaking harder than ever, he rubbed his character's clawed hands together, marveling at the rough and now incredibly realistic-feeling catlike pads on his otherwise human fingers. He couldn't comprehend how much work it must have taken to put this new level of detail and sense-mapped information into the game. James hated the legendary recklessness of the FFO developers, but surely even they wouldn't push through a change like this while the servers were live. That was the only explanation he could think of, though. Unless...

James went still. He still didn't know what to make of this situation, but he had to consider the possibility that maybe this wasn't a hack or a patch. When he mentally tallied the development time and server resources needed to achieve the level of realism his five senses were currently showing him, it didn't seem technically possible. There was just no way the game could have changed this drastically without a massive hardware upgrade. He, on the other hand, had been playing a lot lately. Other than his jobs, FFO was the only thing James did. If the game itself hadn't changed, then there was another, much more likely explanation for what had just happened—lucid dreaming.

The more James thought about it, the more sense it made. Lucid dreams were a pretty common issue for FFO players. At the game's height a few years ago, the FCC had actually commissioned an entire guild to play fourteen hours a day so they could study the phenomenon. He'd played almost that much this weekend, so it made sense he was having the same problem, especially since his shoulder didn't hurt anymore. Given all the rolling around he'd just done on the floor, the joint should have been throbbing, but it felt fine.

James breathed a sigh of relief. That *proved* he couldn't actually be in the game. He must have fallen asleep with his helmet on. He'd pay for that with a splitting headache in the morning, but that was far better than actually being trapped in some kind of catastrophic virtual-reality system failure. Hell, if he was lucky, maybe the fight with Tina had been part of the dream, too.

Smiling at the hope, James wobbled across the yurt on his character's too-long legs toward the long wooden bench set against one side. There was only one surefire way out of a lucid dream, so he positioned himself right in front of the low wooden seat and took careful aim as he pulled his leg back then slammed his shin straight into the bench's sharp corner.

Pain exploded through his limb, and James snatched it back with a hiss. The tail he wasn't used to lashed at the same time. He was standing on only one foot, so the unaccustomed movement threw off his balance, and James toppled to the ground, smacking his head against the central support pole on the way down.

Well, he thought, reaching up to rub his throbbing skull, *that should have been enough to wake anyone.* He just hoped he hadn't broken his helmet when he'd fallen off his bed. But when James opened his eyes, he wasn't on his floor at home. He was still on the hide rug, staring up at the yurt's sun-drenched painted walls.

A cold sweat prickled under his fur. He was still here. He hadn't woken up. There was only one explanation for a lucid dream you couldn't wake up from. It was the most terrible possibility, too. Even worse than his helmet going haywire and giving him a lobotomy.

He might have Leylia's Disease.

Like most FFO players, James had heard plenty of horror stories about the VR-induced mental disorder. People with Leylia's suffered from random involuntary *waking* lucid dreams. The smoking gun was when they couldn't wake themselves up during an episode. No matter what they did, they were trapped in the delusion, moving in reality just as they did in the dream. Like sleepwalking but a thousand times more dangerous, because people with Leylia's had no way of knowing what was real and what was a hallucination.

"Oh no," James moaned, covering his face with a clawed, padded hand. "No, no, *no*."

Leylia's was as bad as it could get. He didn't even know when the episode had started. For all he knew, he'd started dreaming the moment he got home and only imagined logging in. Maybe the sensory overload he'd experienced earlier had just been him freaking out on his apartment floor. If that was true, he didn't dare move from this spot. Anywhere he went in this place, his body would also go in real life. If he started walking, he might walk right out his window and not notice until he hit the ground.

Panting, James looked around the yurt, trying to estimate if its new larger size matched his bedroom. Perhaps those beautifully carved wooden shelves were actually his Goodwill bookshelves. The bed was definitely in the wrong place, but the bench he'd banged his leg on sort of matched his desk.

He was tilting his head to see if he could make things line up better when he heard someone cheering outside. A *lot* of someones. The noise got louder by the second, rising up until it sounded like his yurt was in the middle of a stadium.

James flicked his eyes toward the closed tent flap, a tantalizing few feet away. Moving was a terrible idea. He still had no idea where his body was in real life. If he left this spot, he could walk straight into a wall or fall down his apartment stairs. But those dangers were being crushed by a growing desperation to escape the prison of the yurt and his fear. He had no idea how much of the real world bled into Leylia's waking dreams, but if there *were* people out there, he might be able to get help.

It was a risky gamble, but being trapped here felt even worse, so James cautiously pushed himself to his feet. Standing up again, he was surprised to discover that not only was the dizziness from earlier completely gone, but he actually felt better than he had in years. Nothing hurt, and he wasn't exhausted for once. A cruel mockery considering he was trapped in a mental delusion, but at least he felt ready to roll with whatever was waiting as he eased his way across the tent and pushed aside the hide flap that served as a door.

James's jaw dropped. Up till now, he'd assumed his hallucination would line up with reality, at least a little bit, but this was like nothing he'd ever seen. The dirt street outside the yurt was flooded with jubatus. Like his character, the cat-people were as lithe and muscular as the cheetahs they'd been modeled after, complete with unique spotted patterns on their sand-colored fur. They all had whiskers, tails, claws, and other animal features, but they walked on two legs and had five-fingered hands, just like humans. Their catlike faces had human expressions, too, and right now, every one of them looked overwhelmed by emotion. Some were weeping. Others were shouting with joy, the sound he'd heard. Still more just looked stunned, staring at the village as though they'd never seen it before.

It certainly didn't look how James remembered. The village of Windy Lake was the main town for the mid-level savanna zone. It was a small town with a few quest-givers, some trainers, and just enough yurts to make it look lived in. Now, though, the village looked more like a city. The tents were still laid out in the same orderly grid he remembered from the game, but there were ten times more than there had been. Likewise, the lake he could see glittering in the distance between the tent lines was huge, far bigger than the blue pond it had been before. The only thing that hadn't changed was the land itself. It was still completely flat, a problem since he lived in a third-floor apartment. The stairwell could be right in front of him, and he wouldn't know until he took a step on what looked like flat dirt road and fell to his death.

Swallowing, James looked again, scouring the street for any match to the real world. The more he looked, though, the weirder things got. The sun blazing down on the dirt road and the dry yellow grassland beyond was augmented by lights he had no explanation for. Bright-green glowing ribbons—the same ones he'd seen earlier behind his closed eyelids—drifted up from the ground to mix with sharp white streamers in the sky. If he hadn't been so concerned for his sanity, they would have been beautiful, but James had no time for more weirdness right now, so he put the dancing lights out of his mind and focused on moving without killing himself.

Assuming he was still near his bed, he thought the stairs should have been outside the tent and to the left. Clenching his jaw, James took a cautious step into the road, sliding his bare foot along the ground, but all he felt was hard, warm dirt, which didn't make any sense. Even if he couldn't see it, there should have been a drop. He must have gotten turned around somehow, but there was no correcting it. The neat grid of tents didn't translate to his apartment in any way, and he didn't see anything that might represent objects in the real world. No blocks that could have been a door or their apartment couch. It made an infuriating lack of sense even for a dream, and the continued strangeness of the cat-people's behavior was starting to annoy him as well.

The crowd he'd heard earlier was all around him now. Across the street, an old feline man was sitting on the ground, laughing and crying at the same time. Farther down the road, a pair of warriors had fallen over and were singing enthusiastically at the sky, their yellow eyes shining with wild, reckless joy. There were just as many people weeping as rejoicing, and more were appearing all the time. Watching them stumble out of their tents into the street, James had to wonder if this wasn't Leylia's after all. Maybe he'd just gone plain old crazy.

Hands shaking, he reached up to poke the tall, catlike ears on top of his head. In game, they were normal for his character model to have, but he'd never felt them before since FFO's Human Analogue Translation System didn't convey sensation from nonhuman features. The same went for his tail, which had always been more of an accessory than an actual part of his body. Now, though, James could feel the weight of the long, furred appendage behind him, helping him balance. Moving his tongue around, he found an entire mouthful of sharp, predatory teeth, none of which had been there before, and the wind that made his whiskers twitch was the freaky icing on the freaky sensory cake.

If the additions hadn't been so clearly part of him, it would have felt alien. People with Leylia's always described their episodes as highly realistic, but James was certain he'd never, *ever* felt something like this before. This wasn't like dreaming you had long hair or were eight feet tall. This was entirely new sensory input, like seeing a new color. James didn't even know if he could effectively communicate his problem to a stranger right now. What he needed was to wake up, which meant it was time for the nuclear option, personal safety be damned.

Though much bigger, the dream town still resembled Windy Lake village. The park near his apartment also had a lake, and James was willing to bet that its lake and the Windy Lake lined up. It was late April in Seattle, so the water would still be frigid, definitely cold enough to snap him out of whatever was going on. If nothing else, throwing himself into a lake might result in rescue and a trip to the emergency room, where he could get professional help.

That sounded like a win-win to James, so he swallowed his fear and started striding down the road, walking past the weeping and laughing cat-people without a word. Now that he was moving, he saw again just how much larger this town was than the one in the game, giving him hope that what he saw might line up with reality. The park was at least half a mile from his apartment, and so seemed to be the Windy Lake.

Encouraged, he picked up the pace, keeping to the side of the road in the hope of avoiding the cars he couldn't see. He was trying to figure out if the acacia trees he could see in the distance matched the large oaks by the lake path he sometimes jogged down when the air was split by the enormous booming of a drum.

All around him, the frantic cat-people went silent, their large ears flicking in the direction of the drum. Then as if that had been a signal, they all stopped what they'd been doing and started walking toward the center of town. Since he had to go that way to get to the lake anyway, James joined them, hoping that following other 'people' might protect him from getting hit by a bus.

A minute later, he reached the edge of the plaza at the middle of the village. The open square looked identical to the one he remembered from the game, complete with the iconic giant war drum at the center. Behind that was the two-story Naturalists' lodge, the only all-wood structure in the village. The crowd stopped when they hit the square, but the lake was still a good distance away. Sniffing, James smelled water on the wind. He was about to leave the crowd and follow it to the shore when someone started hammering on the war drum like they were trying to break it.

He looked up in alarm. The five-foot-wide wood-and-hide drum was elevated above the crowd of swishing tails and flicking cat ears by a large wood platform. Standing on it, pounding the drum with heavy mallets, was a muscular jubatus decked in feathers, fangs, and a painted suit of plate armor that, to his enormous surprise, James recognized. It was the village's head warrior, Arbati.

The sight made James rub a hand over his face. Here he was, going as mad as a hatter, and the first person he "knew" was the most obnoxious non-player character in all of FFO. Every new jubatus character had to spend hours here, completing quests that mostly involved repeatedly rescuing Arbati from his own impatience and poor judgment. If James thought Tina had a temper, Arbati could take anger management lessons from the Hulk. He was so famously annoying, he even had his own internet meme called Angry Cat.

James didn't know what Arbati the Angry Cat's appearance in his dream meant, but he'd already decided he didn't care. He turned back toward the lake and tried to push through the crowd only to discover that he was trapped. In the few moments he'd been gawking at Arbati, so many jubatus had arrived in the square that what had been the edge of the crowd was now its center, and James was in the middle of it.

Cursing under his breath, James rocked back on his heels to consider his options. He could try pushing his way through, but he didn't want to accidentally hurt anyone who might be real. He definitely didn't want to risk starting a fight. Of course, for all he knew, these "people" were just bushes, but James didn't want to risk hurting others unless he absolutely had to. Looking up at the warrior, who was still banging the drum, James decided to bide his time. If they moved on their own, he'd continue to the lake. If he stayed here, maybe someone would notice him acting crazy and call the cops, saving him from potentially drowning.

That was as good a plan as any, especially since he didn't have a choice. Fortunately, he didn't have to wait much longer. The square was already nearly full. When the crowd was packed all the way to the tents, the person James's delusional vision saw as Arbati stopped drumming and turned around to assist a gray-furred old cat-lady in a feathered headdress onto the war drum's platform. When she reached the top, James realized with a shock that he knew her, too. It was Gray Fang, the stern old battle-ax of a grandma who served as the spiritual leader of Windy Lake.

Seeing her sent James's worry into overdrive. Arbati was the subject of a famous meme, which made him easy to remember, but

Gray Fang was just a normal NPC. James only recognized her because his character was a Naturalist, and Gray Fang was the Naturalist class trainer. But seeing Non-Player Characters was a *textbook* symptom of Leylia's. He was working himself into a panic again when Gray Fang—or the poor person he'd hallucinated was Gray Fang—swept her hand over the crowd.

"It has happened at last," she said when they fell silent. "The Nightmare has finally broken." She lifted her clawed hands in blessing. "We are free!"

The crowd roared in reply. Even now that his hearing was more or less back to normal, the noise was deafening. James was rubbing his ears when a potbellied cat-man grabbed his shoulder and started crying on him in joy. James was desperately trying to wiggle free when the elder motioned for silence again.

"Our world returns to normal, and we are able to move once more," she said. "But we know not how or why we were imprisoned these last eighty years. We know not where the 'players' of the Nightmare came from, where they went, or if they'll return."

The way the grandmotherly old cheetah said "players" made James's ears flatten. It wasn't just the hatred in her voice. It was the emotion that word drew from the crowd. All around him, jubatus were flexing their clawed hands and flashing their sharp teeth. Even the children looked murderous, snarling around their baby fangs. Suddenly, it didn't matter if this was a delusion. The crowded square was now somewhere James very much did *not* want to be. But as he started to push his way through the mob, a bloodcurdling scream ripped through the air.

"*Player!*"

He, and everyone else, whirled around to see a tall old jubatus at the back of the square, pointing a shaking claw at James. "I see you! You're not one of us! You're a player! *Player!*"

The jubatus around him scurried away, leaving James standing alone in a widening circle. The entire crowd was looking at him now, hundreds of slitted cat eyes tightening in rage. Then as if answering an unheard signal, the angry mob surged toward him, their clawed hands grabbing his clothes, his fur, his skin—every part they could.

"*Monster!*" they screamed. "*Slaver!*"

"I'm not!" James cried, putting his hands up. "I didn't—"

A rock smashed into his head. James staggered back, blinking as hot blood began to trickle through his fur. As it dripped into his eyes, he noticed that the strange glowing streamers that had haunted his vision since this madness had started were getting brighter, their curling lengths twitching above him like a rope tossed to a drowning man.

Desperate and terrified, James reached up to grab the closest one—a gray-white tendril that glowed like the inside of a cloud. His fingers passed right through it—no surprise there since this whole thing was a hallucination—but what *was* surprising was that the moment he touched it, James knew what the glowing ribbon was. Lightning. He couldn't explain how even to himself, but something deep inside him was certain the floating light was *lightning*. Air magic in lightning form to be specific, and he knew how to use it.

Clutching a hand to his chest, James pulled up the deep-blue mana from inside himself. It was the same motion he'd used to cast spells in the game, but unlike every other command he'd tried, this one worked. When he felt his own magic rising, he reached up to grab the ribbon of lightning again. This time, with his hands filled with his power, the white light stuck fast to his fingers, letting him yank it down into his fists. It was the same motion he used to cast lightning spells in FFO, a motion he'd done a thousand times. Bright-white electricity arced from his fingers as James brought the power together, and the attacking crowd began to back away.

James smiled as they retreated. He was wreathed in lightning now, and the power was glorious but also comfortingly familiar. He'd never been this close to it, but he'd played long enough to recognize the shape of the electricity arcing between his hands. It was chain lightning, the Naturalist class's staple attack spell.

His smile turned into a triumphant grin. As he was a level eighty in the low-level Windy Lake, one spell would be enough to kill anyone in the crowd. Even better, chain lightning jumped between targets, and the jubatus were nicely clumped together. With this kind of target density, the magic that was already in his hands could devastate the entire square, leaving him free to run. If he could get to the lake, maybe this horrible hallucination would finally end, then he could apologize for whatever the hell had *actually* happened here.

The finished spell was throbbing in his hands, and James decided that the warrior holding the rock that was red with his blood would be a fine opening target. But as he began the motion to let the spell go, people turned and started to flee.

An old jubatus lady scrambled backward on all fours, tears streaking down her dusty face. Beside her, a man grabbed his young son and turned around, shielding the boy from James with his body. Others simply ran, crashing into the people behind them in their rush to escape. Even though he knew it was a dream, the fear on display in front of him was so *real*, James felt it echoing in his body, making him wonder for the first time if maybe, just maybe, this wasn't a hallucination at all.

Sweat drenched his fur as he clutched the magic tight, fighting the spell as he scrambled to think things through. This couldn't actually be the game. He could smell his blood and the hot hate of the mob in the dusty air. Feel the intense, throbbing pain from the rock that had struck his head. None of that was possible in FFO or in life as he knew it. Pain was common enough, but the wild lashing of his tail and the instinct that kept his catlike ears flat against his skull were utterly alien. Even with Leylia's, it didn't seem possible that he could dream entirely new sensations. No theory he'd come up with could properly explain what was happening, and if he couldn't explain it, then James needed to make a decision fast. The lightning in his hands had to go somewhere soon, but if he released it without knowing the consequences, there was a chance that "target density" might translate into real lives. Because if this wasn't the game and it wasn't a lucid dream, the only explanation left was that this was *real*, which meant he was about to become a mass murderer.

That was a risk he couldn't stomach, so James thrust his hands into the air, loosing the lightning he'd built into the clear blue sky. The tree-trunk-sized bolt left his hands with a thunderclap that flattened the crowd. Then there was complete stillness. No one moved. No one shouted. Everyone, James included, stared fearfully at each other, waiting to see what came next. The standoff was still going when weakness crashed into James like a wall.

He staggered, clutching his chest as his head began to spin. He was worried he'd damaged something inside him with the lightning when he remembered that he'd taken off all his gear before he'd logged out last time and hadn't yet tried to reequip anything. Chain lightning didn't normally take much of his mana, but without his magical armor and staff, one casting was enough to drain him nearly dry.

James closed his eyes with a wince. That had to be it. He wasn't hurt. He was low on mana, yet another sign that things weren't what he'd thought. Nervously, he looked around at the crowd he'd just spared, debating if he should run for the lake anyway. He was already edging toward the scent of the water when a yell broke the silence.

"*Enough!*"

The terrified crowd parted as the tall cat-warrior, Arbati, leaped off the drum platform. There was no hint of fear or hesitation as the jubatus marched toward him. James was opening his mouth to say... something. He wasn't sure what, but before he could get a word out, the warrior decked him in the jaw with a gauntleted fist.

The stinging blow smashed him straight into the dirt. He was trying to push back up when the warrior kicked him in the ribs.

"Bring me rope and a sealing mask!" Arbati called, planting his boot on James's neck to keep him down.

Reeling from the attacks and still weakened from the spell, James didn't even manage to get his hands up before someone brought Arbati what he'd asked for. The warrior rolled James onto his stomach and tied his hands behind his back with what felt like a strip of leather. The binding bit painfully into his wrists, but things got even worse when the elder jubatus, Gray Fang, shuffled down from the drum platform and began smearing James's face with what felt like cold mud.

It was so sudden, James didn't even think to struggle as the old lady smashed the dirt into his fur. He'd never seen anything like this in the game before, but her rough claws painted his face with practiced ease, layering the mixture on until only his eyes, nose, and mouth were left uncovered. When she was finished, the old Naturalist reached up to snag a handful of the glowing magical lights James had been watching all morning.

She wound the magic between her wrinkled fingers like a cat's cradle then pressed the strands into the drying mud on James's face. When she was finished, the mask hardened into something much stronger than clay, and the colorful floating lights faded from James's vision. He was still blinking at the loss when Arbati hoisted him off the ground using only one arm.

"Our revenge starts with this one!" the head warrior proclaimed, holding James up like a trophy. "How shall we kill it?"

"Drawn and quartered!" a woman yelled.

"Stake it out to dry!" cried another.

"Skin him alive!" screamed an otherwise adorable little girl with big, poofy ears.

James shook his head frantically, but the mask prevented him from fully opening his mouth, so he couldn't speak loudly enough to be heard. He was frantically kicking at Arbati's legs in a last-ditch effort to get free when Gray Fang straightened up.

"We will not be killing this one," she said, dusting the dried mud from her fingers. "At least not yet."

The crowd roared in fury at that, but Gray Fang silenced them with a hiss.

"I hear your anger," she said when they'd quieted. "I would also like nothing more than to see his blood on the ground. But we know nothing of why we were imprisoned, who the players are, or if it will happen again. I have eighty years of questions this one might be able to answer. We must know more before we execute him, if only for our peace of mind."

The other villagers growled, but Gray Fang's word must have been law, because no one spoke again as Arbati threw James over his shoulder and carried him toward the lodge.

"That's enough anger for now," Gray Fang said as James was hauled away. "We are still free this day! Go back to your families and homes. Warriors, see if there are any other players hiding in the village and bring them to me."

The crowd lowered their heads and began to disperse. Once they were moving, Gray Fang turned and followed the warrior into the large wooden building at the village's center, where Arbati had already hurled James as hard as he could onto the board floor.

"This player greatly angers you, doesn't he?" Gray Fang said as she closed the door flap.

"More than I have the words for, Revered Grandmother."

The old woman placed her hand on the warrior's shoulder. "The Nightmare is over, my child. *That* is what matters. We are finally free to deal with these monsters on our own terms. A path that was denied us all these years."

"For how long, though?" Arbati growled, never taking his eyes off James. "I'm as happy as any to no longer be stuck in place, reciting the same foolish words about gnolls and undead to every new 'hero' who walks into town. But seeing this one still here makes me worry our reprieve is only temporary. How many more players are hiding in our midst? Could they bring the Nightmare back?"

Gray Fang nodded. "Those uncertainties are why we must use this one to get answers. You have more reason to hate the players than any other in our village, but you cannot take your revenge yet."

Arbati's whole face ticced at that. James winced as well. He was pretty sure they were talking about the scripted event where Arbati was captured, tortured, and if no players arrived in time to save him, sacrificed. The event had run once a day in the game, resetting every morning with Arbati back in position to hand out quests whether he was saved or not. It was one of the repeating story scenarios FFO was famous for, but now that he was facing the warrior's thousand-yard stare, James had to wonder what it would be like to be a helpless victim of some quest writer's plot, forced to repeat the same mistakes over and over, to feel the pain of your own death every single day.

It would certainly explain the mix of pain and fury on the warrior's face. In fact, the more James watched the two jubatus interacting with each other, and reacting to *him*, the more certain he became that this had never been a dream at all. Now that the possibility of everything being real had been breached, it felt more and more like that was the only explanation. It sounded crazy even in his mind, but if he really was *here* and FFO was no longer just a game, then he needed to get serious about his situation before Gray Fang made good on her promise to kill him.

Taking a deep breath, James pulled his eyes off his captors and started looking for an exit. Like the tent he'd woken up in, the Naturalists' Lodge was much bigger and far more ornate than he remembered. The large, open wooden building was lavishly decorated with paintings, masks, hides, and antlers. The layout was also different from how it had been in game. Before, the lodge had just been a big room where the Naturalist trainers stood waiting for players. Now, it looked like a place where people might actually live. There were sleeping rooms off to the sides for the elder and her apprentices as well as a kitchen and a small common area. He even spotted an outhouse through one of the building's rear windows, which almost made him laugh. All those times he'd joked about there being no proper bathrooms in FFO, and there they were. He was still reconciling all the changes when Arbati grabbed him again.

There was no throwing over the shoulder this time. The warrior simply tossed him onto the rug in the middle of the ring of pillows at the lodge's center. Gray Fang took a seat on one of them, arranging her graying tail across her lap while Arbati took the pillow directly in front of James. He expected them to get right to his interrogation, but surprisingly, neither the elder nor her warrior grandson said a word. They both just sat on their pillows, staring into space as though they were searching for something he couldn't see.

"I guess the others aren't coming back," Arbati said at last. "I'd hoped that when the land returned to normal, they'd reappear, but..."

"We've been free for less than an hour," Gray Fang reminded him, pulling a long-stemmed pipe from inside her robes. "It's too soon to give up on our vanished families yet. Perhaps they've respawned somewhere in the world and are still making their way here."

"'Respawned,'" the warrior repeated, lips curling in a sneer. "I wish you would not use the players' words, Grandmother."

"There's no other way to say it," Gray Fang said, lighting her pipe with an ember from the nearby brazier. "Our language has no words for what they did to us, so we must use theirs. It's the only way we'll get answers."

"But we know so little!" Arbati cried. "Lilac is among the missing! The questl—" James thought he heard "questline," but Arbati struggled for another way. "The situation with the gnolls that started with the Nightmare might still be happening. If that's true, then my sister is trapped in the middle of it."

"We can know nothing until we have more information," the elder said, her gentle features growing savage as her yellow eyes slid to James. "We'll start with this one. The mask seals its magic, but I saw this player in our village many times during the Nightmare. It was level eighty then, as powerful as they get." She smiled. "It will know things."

James's ears pressed flat against his head. He certainly didn't feel powerful with no weapon, no armor, and the mask binding his spells, which he couldn't cast anyway since he was still desperately low on mana. All he had was his white linen undershirt and the leather pants that all jubatus characters started with by default. He didn't even have his backpack. He didn't even have *shoes*.

Growling, Arbati rose from his pillow and prowled forward,

drawing a long knife from his belt as he leaned down to peer into James's face. "Can it speak through the mask?"

Gray Fang nodded, the bone beads of her headdress clacking together, and Arbati frowned. "Perhaps it doesn't understand us anymore?"

"Try English," Gray Fang suggested, causing both James's and Arbati's eyebrows to shoot up.

"How did you know I can speak the players' language?" the warrior demanded.

"Because no family of mine would be stupid enough to stand surrounded by the enemy for eighty years and not learn something useful," the elder replied matter-of-factly.

Arbati made a huffing noise and turned back to James. Given all the talk of talking, James was pretty hopeful about finding a diplomatic way out of this. Or at least, he was until the cat-warrior casually stabbed him in the leg with his knife.

"*Ow!*" James cried, wiggling away. "Stop, dude! I understand you!"

A look of supreme disappointment crossed Arbati's face, but at least he pulled the knife back. "What is your name, player?"

"James Anderson," James said automatically, struggling into a sitting position.

"*Lies!*" Arbati hissed. "I know you! You are the Naturalist known as 'Heal-a-hoop,' and you have squatted in our village for the last eighty years!"

"I'm not lying!" James said frantically. "James is my real name. 'Heal-a-hoop' is just the name of this character. It was supposed to be a joke!"

Arbati's scowl deepened. "A joke?" When James nodded, the warrior crossed his arms over his chest. "Explain."

James looked down at the rug, scrambling to think of how to explain a pun involving a toy that didn't even exist in this world to a giant, angry cat-man. But while most of him was now convinced this was all real, the hope that it wasn't hadn't fully died yet. There was still a chance he had Leylia's and this wasn't some bizarre real version of FFO at all. For all he knew, Angry Cat there was actually a police officer trying to restrain a crazy person in a park, which meant James still had a shot.

"Look, dude," he said, trying to sound calm. "I'm hallucinating real

43

bad." His voice choked. "If I'm making any sense to you, can you please take me to the hospital? Or call 911? Because I need serious help."

He finished with a pitiful look, but Arbati seemed angrier than ever.

"More lies!" the cat-warrior roared, grabbing James by his shirt. "You seek to deceive us so transparently, demon? You claim madness, yet you plainly speak the language of Wind and Grass. Now tell us who and what you are before I make you bleed!"

He brandished his knife to finish the threat, but James could only gape at him.

"Wait," he said at last. "You mean I'm *not* speaking English right now?"

"What do you mean?" Gray Fang asked, her yellow cat eyes sharp. "You haven't spoken anything but our language since you appeared."

James fell back on his heels, replaying her words in his head—the slippery, beautiful, foreign-sounding words he hadn't even realized he was saying until she'd pointed them out—and he knew Gray Fang was right. They *weren't* speaking English, and James had no clue what that meant for any of them.

CHAPTER 3
Tina

Tina didn't have a clock in her vision anymore, so she wasn't sure how long it took her and SB to finish the skeletons off, but it felt like years. When her giant metal boot finally crushed the last skeleton knight's head to powder, the first thing she did was whirl to look at the unnamed human player who'd been killed at the start.

Or what was left of him.

The body had finally stopped bleeding and was now lying pale and limp at the edge of the broken road. His severed head had stopped a few feet away, resting beside a small pile of rocks like a discarded ball. From his robes, Tina guessed he was a Sorcerer, but his generically handsome face looked like every other male human model. Without nameplates, she had no idea which of the raid's Sorcerers he was, but the image of his vacant eyes frozen wide in shock and pain was something Tina didn't think she would ever be able to get out of her head.

"Fuck," she said, voice shaking. "This is bad. This is really bad. That guy looks hella for-real dead."

Sheathing his silver swords, SilentBlayde put a hand on her arm. "Are you okay, Tina?"

"How can I be okay?" she snapped. "He's dead, and it's my fault. I'm the damned tank! I was up, I had my shield, I even had the monsters in front of me, and I just…" Her voice broke, forcing her to stop and take a breath. "I fucked up," she said at last. "I hesitated, and his life slipped through my fingers. I don't even know his name."

"It's not your fault," SB said. "There was a lot going on, and you pulled it together quicker than anyone else. You're the reason the rest of us are still alive. No one else could have handled a Dead Mountain patrol without any healing."

"We have to get him a rez," Tina said desperately, looking around at the still-unconscious raid. "His body is still here, which means he didn't revive at the graveyard. A healer might still be able to get him up."

She didn't have much hope of that. The fight had been long, and the Raise Ally spell had a six-minute window. After that, you were just dead. In the game, that meant you were forced to respawn at the nearest graveyard or shrine. Now...she had no idea.

"Let's get a healer and try," SB said, kindly not mentioning the fact that it had been much longer than six minutes. "David barfed up the potion I gave him, but my other pan elixir worked on Anders." He reached up to rub his battered shoulder. "We could both use healing anyway."

Tina nodded and turned to yell at the cleric she'd seen earlier, but he was no longer crouching behind his rock. When Tina looked around to see where he'd run off to, she saw something that made her blood boil.

"What's wrong?" SB said when he saw her murderous expression.

Tina didn't answer. She just shot to her feet and charged down the gray stone, hurdling over the downed players toward the only one who was moving.

Her target was "Fishface," the white-robed ichthyian Cleric she now recognized as her guildmate, Anders. He'd been a babbling mess the last time she'd seen him, but he must have pulled himself together, because he was now all the way over at the far edge of the staging area, kneeling over an unconscious jubatus Naturalist. A *female* Naturalist with an impressive chest, which Anders had just finished ripping open her silk robes to grab.

He was pressing his webbed hands against the catgirl's exposed breasts when Tina bulldozed right into him. He bounced off her shield like a pinball, flying through the air before crashing into gray dirt a dozen feet away. He hadn't even managed to lift his head before Tina was on him again, grabbing the bastard by his robes and hauling him up until his webbed feet were dangling two feet off the ground so she could yell in his face. "What the *fuck* are you doing?"

"*Ow!*" the fish-man cried, pawing at her armored arm with his slimy, webbed hands. "Jesus, Roxxy! Even in my dreams, you're a bossy bitch."

"This isn't a dream, asshole!" Tina screamed, shaking him. "You were about to molest someone for real!"

The fish-man rolled his bulbous eyes. "I hope this isn't gonna be one of those dreams where I keep getting interrupted and never get to have any fun." He turned to leer again at the half-naked jubatus. "Let me go, would you? I want to get back to business before something else gets in my—"

Tina punched him hard with her free hand. The Cleric gasped in pain as her fist connected, but he still didn't look at her. Instead, he closed his eyes, rocking back and forth in her grip.

"Okay, me, don't panic," he muttered. "This is just an unruly dream. Ignore her, and she'll go away." He waved his webbed hands at Tina. "I banish you bad parts! Only good dreams for me!"

Tina stared at the fish hands waving in front of her face. It was all so weird, she didn't know what to do. She was still boggling at the guy when SilentBlayde ran over.

"Roxxy, what's going on?" he asked, standing on tiptoe to stare at the fish-man dangling from Tina's hands. "What are you doing to Anders?"

"You should ask him that," Tina growled, catching SB's eyes before looking back at the half-naked female player splayed by the roadside.

For a moment, the Assassin looked confused. Then his pale face went even paler as he realized what must have happened. "That's NekoBaby," he said, voice shaking.

Tina's eyes grew wide. "Shit, for real?" She hadn't even recognized Neko. Like the fish-men, all the cat-girls looked the same to her without their nameplates. Now that she knew who he'd gone after, though, it only made her angrier.

"You fucker!" she yelled, shaking the Cleric. "You did that to one of your guildmates! A fellow Roughneck!"

Her angry voice bounced off the hills, but the fish-man just waved his hands at her faster.

"SB," Tina said through clenched teeth, "can you go cover NekoBaby? I'd do it, but my cape's gone to the same place my helmet vanished to."

SB nodded and darted back to the road, pulling off his crimson half cape to cover the exposed form of NekoBaby. The fish-man, Anders, cried out in dismay when the cat-girl's form vanished from his view, and he turned on Tina in a rage. "No fair!" he cried. "That was mine! I was finally having a happy, sexy dream, and you ruined it!"

He lashed out after that, smearing his slimy webbed fingers frantically across her face like he was trying to scratch her eyes out.

Tina leaned away from his flailing hands in disgust more than defense.

"Poor Anders," SB said quietly, looking at the fish-man in pity.

"Poor Anders nothing! Dude's a total creep! Ugh, and here I thought I knew the guy."

"What he tried to do was horrible," SB agreed. "But please don't be too hard on him. He has Leylia's Disease."

Tina's copper eyebrows shot up. "Anders has *Leylia's?*"

SilentBlayde nodded. "We've all had lucid dreams of the game. Remember when the Deadlands first opened and we played for seventy hours straight?"

Tina winced. "I had some weird episodes."

"So did I," he said. "Now imagine having those weird episodes *all the time*, including when you're awake, and you can't snap out of them no matter what you do. That's what it's like for people with Leylia's." He gave Anders a sad look. "Poor guy has serious trouble telling what's real on a normal day. Can you imagine how bad he must be freaking out now?"

Tina turned back to the fish-man, who was still trying to claw her face. "He does look pretty gone. But I thought people with Leylia's were banned from VR for life. How's he been coming to raid nights?"

"He said the game was too important to him to lose," SilentBlayde replied, nervously adjusting his mask. "I can sympathize with that, so I agreed to keep his secret."

"Do you think that was a good idea?"

SB shrugged. "I don't know. But Anders always said it was safer for him to be in the game than in real life. At least there he knew he wasn't dreaming. It'll make his condition worse in the long run, but it's not like there's a cure for Leylia's, so what does he have to lose?"

"Not a lot, I suppose," Tina said, then her jaw tightened. "But having Leylia's does *not* excuse being a rapey creep!" She glanced back at the other players, her eyes catching on the dead one. As always, the corpse stuck in her mind like a barb. She had to fix this, had to make it right, and disgusting and crazy as he was, Anders was the only healer they had.

Ignoring the bile rising in her throat, Tina dragged the struggling Cleric by his collar over to where her failure lay headless in the road. "Anders," she said using her raid-leader voice, "rez him."

For a moment, the everyday nature of the command worked. The fish-man stopped flopping in her grasp, and Tina's hopes soared until he crossed his arms. "No," he said stubbornly. "I'm still mad at you."

"I'll kick you from the raid if you don't," she lied, hoping that pretending they were still in the game would have some sway on the delusional idiot.

"Nice try, dream," Anders said, shaking his head so vigorously his spines swayed. "But you can't trick me. I do whatever I want here."

"You motherfucker," she growled, leaning down into Anders's fish face. "This guy is *dead*, and you're the only one who can save him. Cast Raise Ally on him *now*, or I swear to god, I'll—"

A mournful sound cut her off. Somewhere behind them, a discordant horn was resonating through the dry, cold air. More horns joined it moments later, followed by the heavy clanking of massive chains.

Forgetting Anders for a moment, Tina and SB both turned toward the Dead Mountain. "Whoa," the Assassin said, stepping back. "Is it just me, or did the Once King's fortress get a *lot* bigger?"

Tina said nothing. She was too busy squinting through the gates where the instance portal had been before it had vanished. The enormous stone hall that started the dungeon was just as dark as it had been when she'd spotted the skeleton patrol inside thirty minutes ago. Now, though, there was a *lot* more movement. Instead of just one pair of skeletons, Tina spotted dozens, maybe hundreds, their ghostfire eyes burning like blue fireflies in the dark. As terrifying as that was, though, it was the still-blaring horns that frightened her the most. They were louder than they'd been in the game, but she'd know that haunting cry in her sleep. It was the sound effect that signaled the start of the Grel'Darm encounter, the Dead Mountain's first raid boss.

"Shit."

"Those are Grel'Darm's horns!" SB said at the same time, staring at the open gates in new horror. "He can't come out here, right?"

"The skeleton pair did," Tina said. "They're clearly not dumb mobs stuck on patrol paths anymore."

"And they know we're here," SilentBlayde said, cringing at the dozens of ghostfire eyes that were now staring at them from the dark. "What do we do? We can't take that many. We barely handled two."

"Hell no, we're not fighting that," Tina agreed. "We're gonna run."

With that, they both looked at the rest of the raid, still down on the ground.

"I don't suppose you miraculously found more pan-elixirs?" Tina asked hopefully.

"I only had the two," he said sadly, and then his blue eyes brightened. "Cleansing magic might work! That's all the pan-elixirs do. Too bad Anders isn't in his right mind."

"Too bad for him, you mean," Tina said. "Because he's what we've got."

She turned back to the fish-man dangling from her hands. It was clear by now that Anders was not going to rez the player she'd gotten killed. At least not voluntarily. If they could get the rest of the raid up, though, she wouldn't need him. She could get a non-crazy healer to cast Raise Ally, and then they could all GTFO together.

That was the best idea Tina had had all day. Tightening her fists on the Cleric's robes, she gave the still-struggling fish-man a hard shake. "Anders!" she barked in his face. "We're all down with a status effect. I need you to cleanse the raid *stat*!"

Anders tilted his head lopsided and laughed at her. "No way! I'm not doing work in a dream. Now let me go so I can fly!"

He started flapping his arms and making chirping noises. Tina was shaking him back into submission when a thundering clatter like thousands of pieces of metal tumbling down a hill rose from the fortress behind her.

"The skeletons are starting to move," SB reported, his face pale above his mask.

Tina gritted her stone teeth. "Dammit, Anders!" she shouted. "Do you hear that? We're all going to die if you don't start casting!"

"Chill out, Roxxy-boxxy," the Cleric said with a grin. "We can't die. We're in my dream! It's all fine." His eyes brightened. "Maybe they're delivering pizza!"

"Dude, *please*," she begged. "Just start casting! One other healer, and we're good. How about David over there? Once he's cured, he can do all that healing work you don't want to do. Okay?" She turned Anders toward the other blue-scaled ichthyian Cleric, who was lying on his back, covered in rainbow barf.

"Nope!" Anders said, crossing his arms. "Nopey nope nope noppity! I'm not doing a thing you say. You're mean dream Roxxy, not hot dream Roxxy."

If she hadn't needed the Cleric so badly, Tina would have thrown him into the gathering undead army for that one. She was seriously considering doing it anyway when the ground shook beneath her feet. Stones began sliding from the barren hills behind them, but the crashing rocks were drowned out by the giant groan that came from inside the fortress. A sound so huge and deep, it was more vibration than noise.

"Um, Roxxy?" SB said nervously. "I think Grel'Darm the Colossal might be coming this way."

His words were followed by another crashing footstep, and bile rose in Tina's throat as she realized what she was going to have to do. Grel'Darm was a raid boss. If he caught them on the road like this, it wouldn't be just one dead player. It would be all of them. They were *all* going to die if she couldn't make Anders do his damn job.

With that, Tina swallowed her bile and dug down to her rage. It wasn't hard to find. Anders may have been a guildie, but he was also a man who, when he thought he could get away with it, had chosen to try to rape an unconscious friend. Whatever she did to this bastard was fine. The creep deserved it.

"We're out of time for your crazy," she said in a low, cold voice. "You are going to start cleansing people *right now*, or I am going to turn this into a real nightmare for you."

Anders stuck out his green tongue at her. "Whatever. This is my dream. You can't do anything."

"Oh yeah?" Tina said, then she punched him. *Hard.*

After her and SB's battle with the skeletons, Tina was fairly confident that FFO's hit points system was still around in some form. That meant a raid-geared healer like Anders should have the health to take plenty of abuse, so Tina didn't hold back. She punched him hard, driving her metal-gloved fist into Anders's face with a wet crunch that sent green blood splattering across the ground.

"Ow!" he screamed, his confident voice finally cracking as actual pain got through.

"Does *that* feel real to you?" Tina shouted. "Ready to cast some healing now?"

Instead of doing as she asked, the Cleric began to panic, his slippery blue fish-skin sliding through her fist as he fought to get free. Cursing loudly, Tina redoubled her grip and hit him again, slamming her fist into his face until his wide fish jaw was broken and his double eyelids were fluttering.

"*Cleanse the raid now!*" she roared.

"*Screw you!*" he roared back, spitting green blood in her face. "News flash, bitch! There's no interface. Therefore, this. Is. A. *Dream!* But feel free to keep hitting me. Maybe it'll wake me up, which would be *great*, because this is the worst hallucination I've ever had!"

"I can do worse than hitting," Tina promised. "I don't care about your delusions, and I don't care if I break your skull. There's three dozen *not*-crazy people here who are all going to *die* if you don't cast that spell!" The ground rumbled again as she finished, and Tina yanked Anders forward until they were nose to broken nose. "Last chance, asshole," she said through clenched teeth. "Heal the raid, or I'm gonna get real ugly on you."

"No," Anders said, petulantly turning his head away.

As he turned up his squashed fish nose at her, something inside Tina snapped for real. Whatever friendship she'd felt for Anders when they were guildmates was forgotten. She just couldn't take that this crazy idiot—this *molester*—was going to get them all killed out of delusional belligerence. The rage was boiling so fiercely inside her, she didn't even realize she'd drawn her sword until she was holding it to his throat.

"Heavenly Salvation," she said, slow and deadly. "Your raid-wide cleanse. Cast it now."

When he didn't start making the casting motions, Tina stabbed him in the shoulder.

Anders screamed as the blade slid into his flesh. He grabbed the sword to try to pull it out, but Tina was much too strong for him.

"Cast the goddamn spell, Anders!" she yelled, holding her blade steady in his shoulder as his white robes turned green with fish-man blood. "Do it now, or you'll be learning to cast with one arm!"

"Roxxy, stop!" SilentBlayde yelled. "He's got a mental disorder! It's not his fault he's acting like this!"

"No, it's yours for wasting that potion on this basket case!" she shot back. "Seriously, 'Blayde. Did it ever occur to you that maybe, just *maybe*, the guy with Leylia's wasn't going to be useful? There were five other healers to choose from!"

"I'm sorry!" SB cried, his voice panicked. "I confused him for David! I don't know everyone perfectly by sight without nameplates!

Everything would have been okay if David hadn't choked!"

"Whatever," Tina said, keeping her eyes on Anders, who was now a sickly shade of gray. "If you don't like this, you can run, but the enemy is on its way, and this idiot is the only chance we've got at saving the raid. I don't care what I have to do so long as he blows that ability and gets our people up."

"But this is *wrong*," SilentBlayde pleaded, his face horrified as he stared at the panting fish-man. "There has to be another way. Maybe we can hide everyone while they get it together?"

"The two of us can't move thirty-seven people before that army gets here, and you know it," Tina snapped. "If we're going to make it, we all need to run together, and Anders here is gonna make that happen. One way or another."

She removed her sword, dropping the Cleric into a gasping, bloody heap on the ground. "You ready to cast that spell yet?" she demanded, kneeling beside him. "Because I *will* cut you into itty-bitty pieces before the undead get here if that's what it takes."

Anders lifted his head, green blood trickling from his mouth. "Screw... you..." He panted. "This is a *dream*, you crazy *bitch*."

"You know, I'm not even going to argue with you anymore," Tina said, raising her sword. "Dream or not, it still hurts. Now cast, or get ready to lose some scales."

Anders looked at her like she was a monster then, and underneath the rage, Tina felt like one. Creeper or not, a small part of her knew her desperation was getting the better of her. Anders had always been a little weird, but current attempted molestation aside, he was normally a peaceful, together sort of guy. Unfortunately for him, he also had the one thing Tina needed to save everyone, so friend or not, monster or not, she would do whatever it took to make him use it.

When he still didn't raise his webbed hands to cast the spell, Tina swung her sword and sliced off the webbed ridges from his upper arm. She was turning to do the same to his other arm when SilentBlayde was suddenly there.

He appeared between blinks, standing between her and Anders. Tina barely managed to stop her swing before she cut into his back, but the Assassin wasn't even looking at her. He was kneeling in front of Anders, grabbing the fish-man's limp arms and moving them in the circular motion all Clerics made when they cast.

"You see, Anders?" SB said nervously. "When you start casting, she stops stabbing. Easy!"

SilentBlayde was speaking to Anders, but he was looking over his shoulder at Tina, his ice-blue eyes begging her. Unable to keep going with him looking at her like that, Tina stepped back, watching suspiciously as the white-robed Cleric began experimentally going through the motions SB was leading.

"Look! It's working!" the elf said excitedly. "Maybe if you cast the spell, Angry Roxxy will vanish!"

This suggestion seemed to please Anders very much. The blue-scaled ichthyian rose to his feet, waving his arms in circles with more certainty. As he moved, Tina felt power rushing past her to gather in the Cleric's hands.

She'd seen the Heavenly Salvation spell many times in-game, but she'd never paid much attention to the graphics. Now, as Anders stepped through the casting motion, the gray clouds of the Deadlands parted, and a shaft of brilliant golden light shot down to bathe them all in dazzling warmth and radiance. A heartbeat later, the spell went off in an explosion of angelic wings and white illusionary feathers.

As the spell exploded around them, Tina swore she felt an unsettling presence looking down at her from the suddenly clear sky. Fortunately, the feeling—both the sense of being watched and the warm radiance—faded almost as soon as it began. As the feathers vanished, the Deadlands returned to its normal cold gray, leaving her half-blind and shivering with loss. When her vision cleared, though, the first thing Tina saw was all the unconscious players sitting up. She was watching them blink their eyes open with heart-pounding relief when she realized that SB was standing beside her.

"Thank you," she said quietly.

"Don't mention it," he whispered back, sounding just as relieved as she was. "But we're not in the clear yet." He nodded at the dark gate, where the clamor of the undead army was getting louder by the second. "They haven't come out yet. I'm not sure why, but my best guess is that they're waiting for Grel'Darm. If that's the case, then we've got maybe five minutes to convince *everyone else* that this isn't a dream before he finishes walking from his boss room to the front gate and we get crushed under skeletons."

The idea of facing a raid boss in their current condition was enough to make Tina's new stone heart stutter. "Then we'd better get to it," she said, breaking into a run as the two of them rushed into the crowd.

■ ■

"We're saved!"

"What the hell?"

"I'm a *girl?*"

"I'm a guy! And I have a...oh god."

"Why is the dungeon so big now?"

"Did anyone else get that *wham-spin-wham* feeling?"

"Did we get hacked?"

"Guys? Where'd the interface *go?*"

"I can't log out! Someone call a GM!"

"People!" Tina bellowed, slamming her shield down to get their attention, but no one was listening. Everyone in the raid was freaking out in their own special way. Some stared blankly at the gray Deadlands. Others waved their hands and staffs, their eyes growing wide as magic lit up around them. One of the giant muscular Berserkers just cackled and started doing one-armed push-ups, yelling for the others to come and look at him. Mostly, though, people seemed to be obsessed with checking out their new bodies. Particularly the nonhuman races.

"SB," Tina said quietly, tilting her head toward the cat-girl Anders had attacked, who was just now sitting up. "I need you to secure NekoBaby before she freaks and starts a shit storm. We can't afford another crisis right now."

"Secure how?" the Assassin nervously asked.

"Sweet talk? Move to the side? Crowd-control?" Tina shrugged. "I'm not asking you to black-bag her. Just no screams, and make it fast. And get her to try Raise Ally on the Sorcerer."

When he nodded and ran off, Tina drew her sword and started to bang the flat against her shield, getting louder and louder until she'd finally annoyed the road full of players into looking at her.

"Listen up!" she shouted, her new deep voice bouncing off the rocks. "I know you've got questions, but we're in serious danger." She pointed her sword at the looming shadow of the Once King's fortress. "The raid mobs are intelligent now, and they know we're here. They're

already massing to come out, and if we don't get away pronto, we're all going to die."

That was the type of dire announcement one would expect to be met with instant obedience or at least major hustle. Instead, Tina got dazed looks, a jumble of questions, and a whole lot of not running for their lives. And other than the obvious immediate problem of impending death, that seriously pissed her off. Her Roughneck Raiders would have fallen in line instantly.

"What is wrong with you?" she cried, stabbing her sword toward the mountain. "Death, that way." She swung her sword around to point up the road. "Not dying, *this* way. Now march!"

Again, no one moved. "I know what's going on," said someone in the back. "I must be having another one of those lucid dream—"

"*No!*" Tina shouted. "Don't even start with that shit! You're not dreaming, and you don't all have Leylia's. It's a *rare* condition, people!"

"If we're not dreaming, then how do you explain this?" one of the Rangers yelled.

"I don't know," Tina said honestly. "But we'll figure it out later. Right now, we need to move."

"Wait, so does this mean we aren't raiding tonight?" asked a human Naturalist.

Tina put a hand over her face. "No," she said. "Raid's canceled so we can focus on getting out of here before we *die*."

"Why don't we just teleport out?"

Tina blinked in surprise. Of course. Why hadn't she thought of that? "Good call!" she said, face splitting into a grin. "Sorcerers, get on it! One portal to Bastion, and let's get the hell out of here."

One of the Sorcerers in the front nodded and started to wave his hands around his staff. Tina watched impatiently, comparing his movements to the portal spell she remembered from the game. It was only supposed to take fifteen seconds to open the magical hole through reality that would let the whole raid step right into the continental capital of Bastion, but when her count hit fifteen, the Sorcerer was still gathering glowing magic into his hands. He kept it up for nearly a minute, gathering more and more magic until Tina could feel it humming in the air. Then all at once, he let the power go, sending a wave of loose magic crashing over the raid as he collapsed on the ground.

"I can't!" He gasped. "It's taking all my mana, but it won't come together."

Tina kicked a rock. So much for the easy way. Still, there were thirty-seven players here, not counting her and SB. If they were lucky, maybe someone's inventory still had a summonable riding mount.

"Check your bags," she ordered. "If we can't open a portal, we'll do it the old-fashioned way. I bet a dragon or a Phumbar lizard could ferry a ton of us."

There was much scuffling as the whole raid dug into their backpacks. This was followed by much cursing as everyone realized, just as Tina had, that what had once been hundred-slot magical Bags of Holding were now just ordinary old bags, and they hadn't gotten to choose what got tossed when the size shrank.

One person had a bag full of nets. Someone else had nothing but rocks. Another had eight severed heads. Two people had nothing but fingers, and one of the Rangers had an entire collection of ooze blobs in various colors. Then just when Tina was beginning to despair that all they had was junk and useless quest items, someone whooped in triumph and held up a set of leather riding reins.

The whole raid started clapping, and the Berserker who'd found the reins bowed before waving his arms dramatically to cast the Summon Mount spell. He finished it with a flourish, but nothing appeared in front of him. Blinking in confusion, he tried again, but the result was the same, and everyone's eyes fell in disappointment.

"Crap," Tina said, rubbing her stone temples. Apparently, this new version of FFO was dead set on dicking them over. But while portals and mounts seemed to be out, they still had their legs, which meant they weren't screwed yet.

"All right," she said loudly, getting the raid's attention. "Looks like we're hoofing it. Everyone get moving, and do it fast. Grel'Darm the Colossal is on his way."

"Grel?" asked a raider. "Doesn't he de-spawn if he leaves his room?"

"Welcome to the new world," Tina said grimly. "There's no more de-spawning or resetting or monsters patiently walking in circles while we figure out how to kill them. Everything can move however it wants to now, which means if *we* don't move, we're going to have even *more* bosses on our tail, so let's *go*."

Trusting survival instincts to take care of the rest, Tina turned and started marching up the road double time. When she looked over her shoulder, though, only the actual Roughnecks were picking up their bags to follow. The rest of the raid was still hanging back, their faces surly, and Tina clenched her fists.

"Do you not hear the *undead army* getting ready to march through that gate?" she bellowed, pointing at the mountain, where the pounding of boots and rattle of bones were echoing like a distant avalanche. "You got problems, we'll handle them later. Now *move!*"

By the time she reached the last word, her stonekin's deep voice was loud enough to rattle the paving stones. It was the most impressive sound she'd ever made, and it worked. No one looked happy, but all the raiders picked up their things and started trudging down the road. Tina waited until every single one had walked past before falling in behind to bring up the rear, constantly looking over her shoulder at the terrifying army she could hear but not yet see.

The last players to pass her were SilentBlayde, leading NekoBaby behind him. She opened her mouth to ask about the dead Sorcerer, but SB just shook his head.

There was no need to say more. She'd known there wasn't much of a chance, that they had to be well past the six-minute window where Raise Ally worked, but she hadn't completely given up hope. The moment she met SB's eyes, though, she knew it was over. The unnamed Sorcerer was dead. Really dead. Never-coming-back dead, and she was the reason why.

A horrible tightness formed in Tina's throat. She tried to tell herself the unknown player might still be alive in the real world. Maybe he was waking up right now and letting people know about whatever the hell that *wham spin wham* was. Maybe he was getting help.

Those were the happy thoughts she tried to think, but the chokehold on her neck didn't go away, leaving her shaking and empty as she turned to bring up the rear, following SB and the huddled form of NekoBaby up the dusty, broken road.

■ ■

For the next hour, Tina committed herself to playing the devil for everyone's sake.

She kept them walking at a pace any normal person would have called a run. When a Naturalist stopped to sort through his backpack, she took one glance at the worthless contents and threw the entire bag into a grove of dead trees. A few minutes later, two jubatus tried to detour over to an old quest tower. She dragged both back by the literal scruffs of their necks, throwing them back into line with a deadly glare.

When a Sorcerer started juggling fire in the middle of the raid, she learned that she could use her casting interrupt—the aptly named "Gut Punch"—to shut down friendlies as well as enemies. Tina followed this up by ordering everyone not to kill themselves or others with friendly fire since abilities now seemed to obey the laws of physics rather than the targeting system.

By the time they'd cleared what she estimated was about five miles, the entire raid was giving her nasty looks, but Tina didn't ease up. It was clear from the goofing off that they weren't properly afraid of the army behind them. Tina supposed that made sense seeing how they'd all been unconscious during her and SB's terrifying fight with the skeletons, but she also didn't give a shit. If they weren't afraid of the Dead Mountain's monsters, she would be what they feared instead. She was determined that there'd be no new tragedies on her watch.

It didn't help that her own fears were riding higher than ever. Tina glanced over her shoulder every five minutes, peering down the dusty gray road for signs of the enemy. Thanks to the hills, slight curves, and dips in the landscape, she never actually saw the army chasing them, but she knew they were coming. Whenever she stopped walking, she could feel Grel'Darm's giant footsteps rumbling through the ground, blending into her frantic heartbeats as she pushed the raid to move ever faster.

It never seemed to be enough, though. The Deadlands was a long, narrow zone walled in by jagged, knife-sharp mountains that—just like the Dead Mountain itself—were a lot bigger now than they'd been in game. The road was longer, too. In FFO, a fifteen-minute jog would take you all the way from the Once King's fortress at one end of the zone to the Order of the Golden Sun's fortress at the other. But they'd been moving as fast as they could for an hour now, and the Dead Mountain still loomed behind them, poking up from the gray landscape like a ragged black spike. Tina was watching it nervously over her shoulder when, without warning, several of the players in front of her stopped.

"What?" she demanded. "Is something wrong?"

"Yeah, something's wrong," said a black-haired human. "*You.*"

Tina narrowed her eyes. "Excuse me?"

The man crossed his arms over his chest. His very *large* chest. He'd clearly maxed out the character customization settings for both height and muscle, though since he was human, this meant he still had to look up at Tina's stonekin. The two-handed ax on his back marked him as a Berserker, a melee-fighting class like Tina's Knight, albeit one meant for dealing damage rather than taking it. He certainly looked ready to hit something as he glared up at her with an ugly sneer on his generically handsome, made-in-the-art-department face.

"I'm sick of your shit," he spat. "You've had us on a death march for an hour now, ordering us around like you're a goddamn general, but I don't see any undead army." He pointed at the empty road behind them. "For all we know, this whole mess is just a hack someone wrote for the lulz."

"A hack?" Tina repeated, incredulous. "Seriously, that's what you think this is?" She pointed up at the now-massive mountains surrounding them, their sharp peaks dusted with ash-colored snow. "Does *that* look like a hack to you?"

"Makes more sense than your bullshit," the Berserker said with a shrug. "You've got us running around like this crap is real, but I think you're the one who's full of it. I bet this whole running-for-our-lives thing is just you getting your rocks off ordering around a bunch of people who aren't in your guild."

Tina stared at him, unbelieving. "You think I've just been *making this up* to screw with you? What the fuck, man? Did you not hear the horns?"

The Berserker shrugged his huge shoulders. "I've never done the Dead Mountain before. For all I know, that's how the encounter starts."

Tina gaped at him. "This is *not* the normal Dead Mountain!"

"Whatever," he said, sneering. "I joined your stupid raid to kill some bosses and get some loot. We waited two hours for this shit before you made us run away! But I ain't afraid of some skeletons, and I'm not taking another step down this damn road."

She clenched her teeth. "We are *not* stopping."

The Berserker lifted his chin defiantly. "Try to move me."

Tina didn't bother replying. The man had an open-front helmet, so there was nothing in her way as she decked him in the face with her massive fist.

It was a solid hit, but unlike the frail, cloth-wearing Anders, the Berserker was a mountain of muscle. Her punch only made him stagger, but she still got what she wanted when his eyes grew wide at the pain. Hands shaking, he reached up to dab at the trickle of blood coming down from his lip, and Tina smirked. Maybe that would finally convince him that this shit was serious. But when she opened her mouth to order him back into line, the Berserker's face twisted in rage.

"So that's how it's gonna be?" he roared, flinging the blood from his fingers. "I don't take that crap from anyone! Step and you get pwned!"

He reached for his weapon only to fumble as he discovered that ridiculous, seven-foot-long axes didn't just "come loose" from a back harness in real life. As he struggled to get his weapon out, Tina grabbed him by the shoulders and drove her rocky knee into the chain armor covering his stomach.

He doubled over in pain, and the whole road fell silent, all the players staring in horror at the sudden violence. Tina let them look. She had a point to make.

In front of her, her victim straightened up just enough to puke. The putrid stench of his vomit filled the road, causing people to cover their mouths. That was the reaction Tina wanted, but she forced herself to keep waiting, letting the horror sink all the way in before she hammered it home.

"Does this feel like a game to you anymore?" she asked at last, her voice stony. "Does it *smell* like a game?"

A few players shook their heads, and Tina nodded. "That's right. It doesn't, because it's *not*. Whatever this is, it's real, and it's painful. Now, we've got an army behind us coming for our blood. I don't think the respawn system works, like it did in the game, and I don't want to be the one who finds out. If you don't either, then you'd better start marching again. Because I am getting us out of this, and anyone who's too slow is gonna have to deal with *me*."

Her words echoed across the silent pass. In front of her, the entire raid was frozen, their angry, fearful eyes locked on her. Tina fought the urge to cringe under their glares, to say she was sorry, that she didn't like acting this way, either, but her mouth stayed shut.

She couldn't show this mob of players weakness or hesitation. From the moment she'd decided to save these people, they'd become her responsibility. This was her raid, and if she didn't want to lose another person, she had to keep them moving. Eventually, the others would realize this and thank her for saving their asses. Until then, Tina would do whatever it took to keep the group from falling apart.

She was still glaring the crowd into submission when SilentBlayde stepped forward.

"Come on, everyone," he said cheerfully, clapping his hands. "Rule one of the Roughnecks: you can't stop the Roxxy! Now let's get rolling before she rocks someone else's socks off."

To Tina's relief, people groaned at the terrible puns, and the horrible tension broke. They were still glaring at her, but with SB's expert cajoling, the raid started moving again. Even the Berserker picked himself back up, spitting blood on the ground at Tina's feet before shuffling down the road.

■ ■

The next mile was relatively quiet. They still weren't moving fast enough for Tina's liking, but at least people had stopped trying to do things other than hike down the road. As the escapades subsided, they started to make better time. She was starting to hope they might actually reach the Order's fortress before nightfall when she heard yells followed by an explosion from the front of the line.

"Son of a *bitch*!"

Tina broke into a run only to skid to a halt a few seconds later. At the front of the group, a pack of skeleton cavaliers—one of the random patrols that roamed through the Deadlands—were down on the ground being chopped to pieces by the raid's hulking Berserkers. Axes, dirt, and bones were flying everywhere, but that wasn't the problem. The *problem* was the people who were on fire.

"*What happened?*" she cried, staring at the two Knights and SB, who were rolling around in the gray dirt, trying to put themselves out. Her first fear was that they'd been consumed by ghostfire, but the bright orange-and-red flames rising from their clothes were the wrong color to be the undead's doing. Then she noticed the elven arrows sticking out of the Knights' backs, and Tina's hands curled into fists.

"Healers to the front!" she bellowed. "Get those fires out!"

A pair of white-robed Clerics stepped forward timidly. A few moments later, a shower of golden magical light fell on the road, putting out the fires and healing the players' burns before Tina's eyes. She was still appreciating the miracle when one of the Knights surged forward. Tina had her shield up before she realized he wasn't going for her. He was going for the short elven Ranger who was hiding in her shadow.

"You team-killing asshole!" he yelled, grabbing at the girl. "I'm gonna stab this arrow into *your* back and see how you like it!"

"That's enough," Tina said, smacking his arm away. "It was an accident."

"She shot me in the back!" the Knight cried, lifting his steel visor.

Tina turned to glare at the terrified elf. "What were you told about friendly fire?"

The Ranger gulped. "That it isn't friendly?"

"Exactly," Tina said. "We can hurt each other now, so we all have to *be careful.*" She said that last part extra loud, glaring at the Sorcerer who was trying to hide his smoking hands behind his back. "No big spells if friendlies are in the area, and no shooting at things when someone else is in front of you. Got it?"

The Ranger nodded rapidly, vanishing into the raid with the amazing speed possessed only by the Agility-based classes. The guilty Sorcerer nodded as well, shooting the angry Knight an apologetic look. The Knight took a menacing step toward him before Tina grabbed his shoulder.

"Lesson's learned," she said firmly, glaring down at him from Roxxy's massive height. "Got it?"

The man opened his mouth but then thought better of it. When Tina was sure he wasn't going to try anything stupid, she let him go. He was walking back to the other Knights in a huff when SilentBlayde appeared beside her.

"I'm sorry, Roxxy," he said, dusting the ash off his armor. "That patrol was one-skull rated back in the game. I figured we could just nuke them and move on. It worked great, until it didn't."

"It's cool, dude," Tina said. "I'm just pissed that Ranger"—she glared pointedly at the scorch marks on SilentBlayde's irreplaceable top-tier red-and-black armor—"and *certain fire Sorcerers* completely forgot what I said not half an hour ago."

The Ranger and "certain fire Sorcerers" looked properly ashamed, and Tina shook her head. She was opening her mouth to get them marching again when she realized someone was missing.

"Wait," she said, looking around. "Where's DarkKnight? I told him to be the tank up here."

"Good question," SB said. "He wasn't in the fight just now, so I guess it's tanks for nothing!"

Tina rolled her eyes. She was about to organize a search party when she spotted a plate-armored shoulder sticking out from behind a dead tree just off the road. "Hang on," she muttered angrily. "I'll be right back."

Her footfalls stirred up puffs of ash as she stomped toward the player in hiding. "Dammit, Jake," she said as she rounded the tree. "You'd better have a damn good reason for deserting the front line like—"

She stopped cold. The Knight she'd assigned to be their forward tank was sitting with his back to the dead tree, visor up, tears running down his stocky face.

"Oh shit, dude," Tina said awkwardly, her anger vanishing. She looked over her shoulder at SB, who was watching curiously from the road. "Get the raid moving! I'll deal with this."

The elf gave her a jaunty salute and started shooing people forward. When everyone was moving again, Tina crouched on the ground in front of the other tank.

"It's okay," she said gently, putting a hand on his knee. "I'm not mad. I know we're all still trying to cope with this. You want to talk about it?"

DarkKnight was one of the few raiders Tina knew by sight alone. As the Roughneck's second main tank, he'd stood shield to shield with her for years. He was a solid guy and a good friend, and current situation notwithstanding, she'd never seen him lose his cool.

"Come on," she said gently, smiling at him. "Talk to me."

DarkKnight shook his head. "Just tell me how to logout, please," he said in a soft, very un-Jake-like Southern accent. "I shouldn't've tried this."

Tina jerked back. "Holy crap," she said, her voice sharpening. "You aren't DarkKnight!"

The man wiped his eyes before looking up at her. "I'm sorry, is this not a dark knight?"

"DarkKnight isn't a class in FFO," Tina said. "It's your name. Or it *was*."

"My name's Frank," the Knight said in a shaky voice. "I—"

"Where's my friend?" Tina demanded. "You aren't the guy who owns that character, so why were you playing it? Jake would never let someone else play his account on a raid night!"

Not-DarkKnight frowned. "I'm afraid I don't understand. I just bought this character a few hours ago so I could play with my great-grandson. I was waiting for him to get home from school when you invited me to your party. A party sounded like fun, so I said yes, and here I am."

Tina looked away with a curse, and the man winced.

"I'm very sorry, young lady," he said sincerely. "If you could just tell me what I've done wrong, I'll try to make it right."

"Okay," she said, rubbing the bridge of her nose. "Since you clearly know nothing about video games, I'll spell it out. That body you're in, the one with all the legendary gear, belongs to one of my best friends. I can only guess that his account got hacked, and you happened to be the dope who bought it."

This earned her a relieved chuckle. "Well, don't that beat all? Can I just give it back to him then? Because, I'll be blunt, you kids are *way* too into this for me. All this acting like the game is real and we're actually running for our lives." He shook his head. "Y'all need to chill out, 'cause this isn't fun at all."

"Wait," Tina said, confused. "Have you been going along with everything up till now because you thought this was the *game?*"

He nodded, and she gaped at him. "Seriously? Why are you hiding behind a tree, crying, then?"

The Knight, Frank, blushed. "Em... well, you see, I've never done full sensory VR. It's amazing stuff! Aside from that horrible *wham-spin-wham* bit at the beginning, I've never felt better in my life! I'm eighty-six years old, but I feel young again in here. It's pretty hard to handle all these young emotions, though. Real nice—don't get me wrong—but hard. When that skeleton hit me, I guess I just got overloaded. Too much unfamiliar stuff to deal with all at once."

As he talked, the excitement spread over his features, making his square-jawed face with the handlebar mustache she'd given Jake so much shit for over the years look like a kid's. "I had no idea full sensory would be like this! If I'd known, I'd've come in here ages ago just to hang out. I don't care about sword fighting or punching skeletons, but this sure as hell beats sitting in my chair all day, being a burden to my kids. I bet they're super happy I've been zonked out in a VR helmet all evening, but I really do need to get to bed, so if you could tell me how to unplug, I'd be very appreciative."

Tina's heart sank further with every word. "Oh man," she said, running a hand over her face. "Dude, you have the world's worst luck."

Frank laughed. "Nonsense! I told you, I'm eighty-six. It takes a lot of luck to get that old. So I got scammed. No biggie. I was a chemical engineer and a plant manager for forty years. Got a nice big retirement fund I won't live to spend. What's a few bucks lost on a game?"

"That's not what I meant," Tina said gravely. "You're unlucky because you logged in just in time to get caught in the worst disaster FFO's ever had."

He gave her an annoyed frown. "You ever gonna break character on me, girl? Because I'm done pretending for tonight. Now tell me how to log off, and I'll give your friend his account back. Just give me his email, and I'll take care of everything. Scout's honor. Once that's settled, I'll go and get me a proper account from the company store so I can hang around in here and not feel my hips ache all day."

He finished with a wide grin, but Tina's mouth stayed flat. "There is no logout anymore."

"That's enough, darlin'," he said, his tone turning serious. "I'm not playing your game anymore."

"For the *last time*, it's not a game!" Tina shouted at him. "That's the entire problem! We're *not* playing, and *there is no logout!*"

The Knight cringed away from her, and Tina immediately felt terrible. She didn't want to yell at the nice old man who didn't know any better, but having to spell things out over and over again just reminded her of how trapped she felt.

This raid wasn't going to end when they got tired or killed a boss. She had nearly forty people, most of whom acted like children, that she had to yell at and beat just to keep alive. Most of them weren't even her friends. They were tryouts, strangers. If this had happened while she was raiding with her Roughnecks, the last hour and a half would have gone completely differently. Hell, it might even have been fun. But this wasn't. She was just as trapped as poor Frank, fighting tooth and nail to keep random strangers alive. Possibly until she died, which at this rate wouldn't be too long.

Sighing at the hopelessness of it all, Tina lifted her heavy head and focused on the stranger in DarkKnight's body, who was still looking at her with blatant skepticism.

"Listen, Frank, the game you thought you were playing is gone. You say you feel young here, but full-immersion VR doesn't do that. You log in with aches and pains, they stay around. If you're not feeling your hips hurt anymore, the only explanation is that somehow, some way, you're no longer connected to your real body."

His eyebrows shot up at the words *real body*. "You're puttin' me on."

"I swear I am not," Tina said solemnly. "Though I wish to hell that I was. We've been death-marching our way through a dust bowl for an hour now. Did you really think we did that shit for fun?"

"But this is crazy!" Frank protested. "You're seriously telling me that we're in another world, one that's like the game but not? Doesn't that sound nuts to you?"

Tina nodded. "I know how it sounds. Believe me. But I've been playing Forever Fantasy Online for seven years now. My play time on this character alone is over twelve *thousand* hours. I know Forever Fantasy Online, and whatever this is, it's not it. Not by a long shot."

Frank's face turned pale. "So it *was* real," he whispered, looking down at his shaking hands.

"I'm not sure what this is, to be honest," Tina said with a shrug. "But it isn't the game, and it isn't a dream, and it hurts like hell, so I'm going to call that real. Unless you have another explanation."

Frank shook his head, and Tina smiled. "Welcome to the raid," she said, putting out her hand. "I'm Tina Anderson, by the way."

"Frank Gilmore," he replied, gripping her dinner-plate-sized stone palm. "But why does everyone call you Roxxy if your name's Tina?"

"Roxxy is my character's name."

Frank chuckled. "Is that 'cause you're a giant stone lady?"

Tina's smile turned sheepish. "Yeah. I originally made this character as a joke to troll one of my friends, who couldn't stand corny names, but I liked tanking so much that Roxxy became my main character, so joke's on me, I guess." She shrugged. "I could've name-changed her, but you play a character long enough, and it sticks, you know?"

"I suppose," Frank said as she hauled him to his feet. "So what now?"

Tina looked back down the road. Several miles behind the raid, a large white-gray dust cloud was rising behind the hills. It was hard to see against the endless gray clouds of the Deadlands, but there was a darker shadow inside the swirling dust. A huge humanoid one, steadily plodding toward them.

"You see that?" she said, pointing at the shape in the dust. "That's Grel'Darm the Colossal, first boss of the Dead Mountain raid dungeon. He's a five-skull monster, which means it takes at least fifty players of the same level to kill him. Also, since he's the start of the current end-game content, he's *way* harder than other five-skulls. Only the best-geared, most skilled, and well-coordinated groups can hope to beat him."

Her voice rose with pride. "My guild, the Roughneck Raiders, is one of the top raiding guilds in the world. We were the fourth group *ever* to kill this guy, and that was only after he wiped us out forty-five times. That was months ago, though. At this point, we've downed Grel so much, he's actually boring to fight. The only reason we still bother is because we have to kill him in order to get to the other bosses in the dungeon."

"Wow," Frank said, clearly not understanding much of that but politely trying to look impressed anyway. "But if you're so good at killing him, why are we running?"

"Because most of my best people aren't here," Tina said bitterly. "Almost everyone in the group tonight was a tryout—basically a job applicant for my guild. Some of them have very little raiding experience, but since Grel's such an easy fight for us, I only brought my good healers and the tanks so I could access as much new talent as possible." That, and no one else had showed up. "Anyway, it would have been rough, but we probably would have downed Grel eventually. Now, though? With no interface and actually having to fight with our physical bodies?" She shook her head. "I wouldn't want to face him like this even if I had all my A-string raiders, which I definitely do not. Also, we don't know what happens when we die yet. Death is starting to look pretty permanent now though, and like hell are we going into a fight that routinely kills several people without knowing if we'll get them back."

"Oh," came Frank's tiny reply.

"I'm *really* glad we didn't try to fight now, though," Tina continued.

"The real DarkKnight and I might have been able to handle it since we're so used to working together, but if we'd tried to fight Grel with a rookie as the secondary tank, we'd all be dead."

"Good thing we ran, then," Frank said, looking relieved.

"Yep," Tina said. "Fortunately, we won't have to run forever. There's a big fortress full of badass holy-warrior types at the other end of this zone who should be able to help us. In the meanwhile, though, you're going to have to learn how to play, because until we reach safety, you're the only other tank-specialized Knight we've got. So pick up your shield and let's move."

Frank's face went ashen. Tina flashed him a helpless smile and turned away, jogging to catch up with the raid, which was now nearly half a mile ahead.

CHAPTER 4
James

"**I** know thirty different words for wind," James said, dumbfounded.

He was certain he'd never learned them. The knowledge was just there in his head, words for weak breezes and strong ones, for winds from the south, which meant storms, and the steady gale from the west that promised gentle weather. Each word was unique and nuanced, just as a real language would be. The grammar of the language of Wind and Grass was substantially different from English as well, yet James knew it all, even the stupid exceptions and contradictions that would trip up anyone who wasn't a native speaker. He was still marveling in wonder at the entirely new way of thinking the new words presented when Arbati cuffed him upside the head.

"We will no longer tolerate your disguise, demon," the warrior hissed. "Tell us how and why you inhabit that body, or I will stake you out for the vultures to eat!"

James was eager to tell the truth, if only to make the angry cat-man stop hitting him, but he had no idea how to explain a virtual-reality game to people who lived in a medieval-level fantasy world. "Okay," he said cautiously, struggling to keep things as simple as possible. "You're right that this isn't my real body, but I'm not a demon. I'm actually human. I, um, I put on a special helmet in my world, and it lets me be here. It's a game. I've been playing for about eight years now and—"

That was the exact wrong thing to say.

"A *game?*" Arbati roared, grabbing him by the throat. "The hell you put my people through was a *game* to you?!"

"No!" James said quickly. "Well, technically. Kind of. It's hard to explain. We were all told this was a game. That's why we're players. I didn't know this world was real!"

Arbati threw him back to the floor. "A game," he snarled, kicking James in the ribs. "It was not *eight* years! We were forced to live in a timeless hell, repeating the same terrible day over and over for *eight decades.*" He kicked James again, his eyes wild. "You destroyed our world! Our people are a tenth of what they once were! Whole families have vanished! Evil is everywhere in our lands! I've died *thousands of times*, and you're saying it was all for some other world's *amusement?*"

The warrior's boot slammed into James with every yell, kicking him in the chest, the ribs, the legs, and finally, the head. It should have been a fatal beating, but other than the pain—which *did* hurt quite a lot—James didn't feel anywhere near as bad as he should have, which made no sense. With all the stabbings, slashings, and brutalization he'd suffered since being discovered in the square, he should have been in the hospital. But while each of Arbati's blows hurt worse than the last, they did no crucial damage.

Probably because he was still level eighty, James realized with a start. Even if he couldn't see his stats, the hit point system must still be working in some capacity to let him take a beating like this without broken bones. Unlike damage in the game, though, this *hurt*, and he couldn't stop it. Every time he tried to say something, Arbati would just kick him again. He didn't even seem to see James anymore. He was just blindly taking out his fury, all eighty years of it.

Desperate, James cast a pleading look at Gray Fang. She was the spiritual leader of the jubatus, and the FFO wiki described her as wise. Maybe she could stop this? When he met her eyes, though, his hopes sank. The rage on her face was every bit as terrible as Arbati's. Like her grandson, Elder Gray Fang had also been trapped by the game, stuck in place and forced to repeat the same actions over and over for decades. She probably wouldn't let Arbati beat him to death since she still needed James for questioning, but she looked perfectly happy to watch the warrior bring him as close as possible, which was not where James wanted to go. He was wondering how he was going to get out of this while there was still some of him left to get out when one of the warrior's increasingly frantic kicks hit the binding mask covering James's face.

The hard clay cracked under the blow. Not much, but the hairline fracture was still enough to bring back a sliver of James's magical sight. All at once, the air was full of glowing lights again, but the magic was still too hazy to tell apart due to the interference of the remaining mask. If he finished the break, though, he might be able to use them.

Now that he had a goal, James's years of martial arts training kicked in. The next time Arbati pulled back his boot to kick him, James rolled onto his back and kicked up to his feet. The moment he was standing, he turned away from the astonished Arbati to face the huge support beam that held up the lodge.

The warrior growled like a lion behind him, sending chills down James's spine. Even with the level difference, putting his back to a vengeance-crazed warrior felt like a *bad* idea, but James stuck to his plan. He was rearing back to smash his face into the pole—and hopefully shatter the rest of the mask—when a young warrior jubatus burst into the lodge.

"Elder Gray Fang! Ar'Bati!" the young man cried. "It's an emergency!"

The words splashed over the room like cold water. Arbati skidded to a halt inches from burying his claws in James's neck, and James aborted his headbutt, turning instead to look at the newcomer, who was staring wide-eyed at the full-out prison brawl happening in front of him. For several moments, no one moved a muscle, then Elder Gray Fang turned around on her pillow with a sigh.

"Please tell us what is going on," she said then took a draw off her pipe.

"Yes, Elder," the young warrior said nervously, looking sideways at Arbati, who had not lowered his claws. "Scout Lilac's squad has returned, like they always do."

Behind him, James heard Arbati curse. "Lilac is poisoned from a gnoll's arrow, isn't she?"

"Yes, sir," the warrior said, his voice bleak. "It's still the same. Her patrol was ambushed, and she was struck with a poisoned arrow, just like always."

James blinked in surprise. He knew exactly what the warrior was referring to. The Poisoned Patrol was a scripted event that kicked off the Red Canyon questline. It happened every morning. Or at least, it had when this was a game.

"The Nightmare still has momentum, it seems," Gray Fang said bitterly. "But *we* are different. Now that I am no longer trapped in this lodge, I will simply cleanse the poison. Bring Scout Lilac to me."

"Yes, Elder," the young warrior said, bolting out of the lodge.

In the silence after he was gone, James turned to see Arbati wasn't

72

looking at him anymore. His sharp eyes were fixed on the elder with a wild hope. "Can you truly break the cycle?"

"I don't see why not," the old cat-woman said. "The gnolls use the same herbs in their poisons as we do." She looked up at the roof of the wooden lodge. "I was helpless before, bound to this building by the Nightmare just as Lilac was bound to her doomed scouting mission and you were bound to do nothing. But the Nightmare is broken. We are free again."

"We will take our lives back," Arbati agreed, fists tightening. "Then we will make them pay for what was done to us."

James swallowed. The warrior wasn't even looking at him, but he didn't have to. The raw hatred in his voice had only one target. But before Arbati could go back to taking it out on him, the young warrior returned with several others, bearing a young female jubatus on an improvised stretcher of hide and branches.

Gray Fang stood up at once. "Bring her here," she said, pointing to a circle of markings carved into the lodge's wooden floor.

The warriors obeyed, placing the unconscious jubatus—whom James could only assume was Scout Lilac—on the floor at the elder's feet. With a final poisonous glare at James, Arbati rushed to the girl's side. "Sister," he said, falling to his knees. "Hang on. It will be different this time. I swear it. We will save you!"

Elder Gray Fang made no such promises. Her old face was locked in a dour scowl as she leaned down to examine the wound in Lilac's arm. The arrow itself had broken off, but the shaft was still sticking out of her bicep, and the flesh around it had turned a sickly blackish purple.

The elder's face was more serious than ever as she straightened up and began moving her hands over Lilac's body. Through the crack in the mask, James could see her weaving the glowing magic together. Greens and blues and amber browns—which the same part of his brain that had suddenly learned an entirely new language now recognized as the colors of life, water, and earth—came together in a glorious tapestry between her hands. It looked incredibly impressive, but no matter how many of the beautiful lights the elder wrapped around Lilac's body, the scout did not stir, and eventually, Gray Fang dropped her hands with a bitter sigh.

"It does not work," she said as the magic faded, leaving the ugly black of the wound unchanged. "This is no normal poison."

"What do you mean?" Arbati demanded. "Why can you not

cleanse her?"

"I *did* cleanse her," the elder snapped. "But the poison is still here, and I do not know why."

"I do."

Both of their heads snapped around to look at James, who did his best to look confident and too knowledgeable to kill. "You can't cleanse the poison because it's not really a poison," he said authoritatively. "I'm a Naturalist healer, too. I tried the exact same thing you just did when I did the Poison Patrol quest years ago. It didn't work then, either."

"Why not?" Gray Fang demanded.

Because the quest would be too easy if players could just heal the NPC. James didn't think they'd like that answer, though, so he went with the explanation he remembered from the quest text. "Because the poison isn't actually the problem. It's the curse inside it. The undead have infiltrated the gnolls. They have a dark orb in the canyon below the gnolls' village that they use to empower tainted poisons into something normal nature magic can't touch."

"How do you know what goes on in the gnolls' filthy camp?" Arbati asked suspiciously.

"Because I'm a player," James said with a shrug. "I've done this questline on five characters, and—"

He cut off with a gasp as Arbati grabbed his collar. "*Tell me how to save my sister, demon!*"

"I was getting to that," James choked out.

"Then speak," the warrior snarled in his face.

James narrowed his eyes. "No."

The dry, hot air in the lodge grew glacially cold. "No?" Arbati repeated, his tail lashing. "*No?*"

"No," James said again, setting his jaw stubbornly beneath the mask. "It's painfully obvious that you both hate me and want me dead, so I'm not telling you a damn thing unless you agree to let me out of here."

By the time he finished, Arbati was growling loudly enough to rattle the floorboards. "You will tell me what I need to know," he said, moving his hands to James's throat. "Or I will—"

"What?" James taunted. "Torture it out of me? Beat me even more than you were already doing?"

"I can do worse," the warrior promised.

"But can you do it in time?" James said, tilting his head at the deathly-still Lilac. "Your sister's only got twenty-four hours before the curse spreads through her entire body. Once she's completely infected, the lich beneath Red Canyon will be able to open a conduit to fill her soul with ghostfire, and she'll become undead forever."

The look on Arbati's face when he finished chilled James to his bones, but he couldn't afford to show weakness. Trading Lilac's life for freedom felt uncomfortably like taking a hostage, but it was the only escape James could see from this situation. He would happily tell them the entire questline if they'd just agree to let him out of this stupid lodge. Until then, his knowledge of the game was his most valuable resource, and he meant to leverage it as hard as he could.

"I'll tell you everything you need to know," James promised. "But only if you agree to let me go. So what's it going to be? Beat me up some more, or save your sister?"

Arbati actually seemed to consider it for a moment, then he let go of James's neck with a curse. James grinned behind the mask. He'd come up with the plan on the fly, but the more he thought about it, the more he liked it. He'd give the jubatus everything they needed to save Lilac, then he'd collect his gear from his yurt and hightail it to Bastion. The capital city had portals to every important location in FFO. It also had the Portal Keepers, the order of mages who specialized in opening doorways through time and space. If anyone in this new world knew how to get him home, it was them. First, though, he had to get away from the murderous cats.

Arbati had stepped back to whisper with Gray Fang. Their flattened ears and murderous expressions weren't encouraging, but James had them over a barrel. Sure enough, Arbati came back a few moments later, tail lashing as he forced the words he clearly did not want to say through his teeth. "Tell us."

"After you let me go."

The warrior sneered. "So you can vanish or portal or 'GTFO' or whatever it is your kind calls it? I think not. You will tell me how to save Lilac first. Once I am satisfied, I promise I will escort you to the edge of the village. After that, you're on your own."

That sounded an awful lot like Arbati was planning to shoot him in the back, but it was probably as good as James was going to get. Using the warrior's sister against him was giving James a bad taste in his mouth, anyway, so he decided to go for it.

"You've got to smash the lich's orb," he said. "There's a cave system full of undead below the gnoll village in the Red Canyon. It was a dungeon back when this was a game, and the lich who runs all of the undead's operations in the savanna was the final boss. His laboratory is at the very back of the cave. He has a big glowing orb in there that acts as his hotline...I mean his conduit to the Once King, which is where the ghostfire comes from. Smash that orb, and the curse on Lilac will be broken."

That was the quick-and-dirty version of a very long questline, but Arbati was nodding. "I will take a hundred warriors and go at once," he said, turning on his heel. "We will destroy the filthy gnolls and the undead they hide and save my sister before nightfall."

With every word he spoke, James's stomach sank. He'd meant to give the information and bolt, but now that he'd heard Arbati's plan, James realized the glaring flaw in his own. "Um, no offense, Arbati—"

"It's Ar'Bati," the warrior growled.

"You aren't going to make it," James finished, talking over him. "You're talking like this is going to be a simple smash-and-grab, but you used to be in this questline. You know how badly things end for—"

"*That was not me!*" Arbati roared. "I am free of the Nightmare's hold! I will not fall to some stupid ambush set by primitive and weak hyenas, especially since I already know where the ambush will be!"

"It's not about the ambush," James said. "Look, dude, you're a two-skull, level fifty NPC. I'm sure you can kick all kinds of asses, but that doesn't mean shit in this situation. If the original quests are still true *in any way*, then you're outnumbered ten to one. Forget a hundred. You could bring every warrior in Windy Lake, and it still wouldn't be enough. Plus, there's five, count 'em, *five* bosses in the Red Canyon dungeon. It's meant to be a challenge for a full party of players. Your warriors won't stand a chance."

Arbati sneered. "You think we are weak?"

It wasn't that, but the last half hour's train of constant abuse had taught James many things. Mainly, that some of the game's mechanics, particularly levels and damage, still seemed to be in effect. Without his gear, James estimated he had about 60,000 health. That was pathetic compared to the 350,000 he would have had with his stuff on, but it was still an incredible amount for a low level zone like this. The villagers, on the other hand, were all level 1 to 20, which mean they only hit for

200 damage tops.

Those tiny numbers were the only explanation for why James was alive right now, but they also meant that Arbati's plan would be a slaughter. The gnolls of Red Canyon were balanced to be a challenge for players levels twenty-five to thirty. They were tough, hit hard, and came in annoyingly huge packs. Being a higher-level two-skull, Arbati could probably handle a lot of them, but all the other Windy Lake NPCs would be slaughtered, and James didn't know if they could respawn.

He closed his eyes with a sigh. He didn't like where this was going, but he'd taken a gamble when he'd decided to bargain Lilac's life for his freedom. Technically, he'd held up his end. He'd told them how to save her, but what good was that information if it was impossible? Arbati was the best warrior in Windy Lake, but he was alone in his power. Any attack he mounted was bound to end in disaster. If they didn't do something, though, Lilac would turn undead, and there'd be no server reset this time.

But that wasn't the worst of it. The whole point of the Poison Patrol questline was that the gnolls and their undead masters were planning to slaughter Windy Lake. It was supposed to be up to the players to stop the plot and save the day, but what happened if there were no more players doing the quest and no arbitrary reset to put everything back? Would the invasion just keep going? What would happen to the village?

James gritted his teeth. This whole thing just got worse and worse the more he thought about it. But as eager as he was to get out of here, there were lines he couldn't cross, and running away while an entire village got slaughtered—even a village that hated him—was definitely one of those.

"Let me help."

"What?" cried Arbati.

"Why would you help us?" Gray Fang asked at the same time. "We are your enemy."

"No," James said patiently. "You *think* I'm your enemy. But I like Windy Lake. I chose to live here, remember? And I don't want to see it reduced to smoking ruins by the undead, so here's my proposal." He turned to Arbati. "I told you how to save Lilac, but there's no way you can get through the gnoll camp or the dungeon below it on your own. I, on the other hand, am a level eighty. I can solo that whole place no problem. All you have to do is give me back my gear, and I'll go kill everything and break the orb for you. Lilac will be saved, and you won't have to do a thing. How does that sound?"

"Like a lie," Arbati snarled. "Let you go alone? You'd run the minute our backs were turned."

"You were going to let me go after I gave you the information anyway," James reminded him. "Or was *that* a lie?"

The warrior looked insulted. "I am not dishonorable like your kind," he said stiffly. "But I will not trust my sister's life to a player."

"You can't do it," James said plainly, earning himself another snarl. "I'm just telling you the truth. There's no way you can save Lilac on your own, so unless you're willing to kill her yourself before she turns undead, you have to trust me. You always died before the time limit, so you've never seen how this quest event plays out if players fail to smash the orb in time."

"But you have?" Arbati spat.

James nodded. "Once Lilac's body is filled with ghostfire, she turns into a three-skull boss, slaughters your entire village, and fills the corpses of everyone you've ever loved with ghostfire. It's implied that the gnoll army arrives to claim your land after that, but the servers always reset before they got here, so I never saw if that was true. But there doesn't seem to be a server anymore, or a reset. If you let Lilac turn, that's it. No one wants that to happen, but unlike you, I can solve this problem easily. Just let me go."

Arbati's answer to that was to spit on James's foot. "If you're lucky, we will let you live in miserable servitude to pay for what you've done to us!"

"Come on!" James yelled, dancing back. "I'm trying to help you here!"

"We don't want your help, *player*," the jubatus snarled. "I've been forced to accept your *help* for eighty years! My people have served your petty vanities, suffered for your heroics, and endured your mockeries for decades. You deserve nothing but our hate!"

"That's not our fault!" James said. "Of course we didn't take things seriously. We didn't know you were real. We thought this was a game!"

"I don't care what you thought!" the warrior growled. "I care what you did! Now I will keep my promise to escort you out of the village in exchange for the information about my sister, but beyond that, I give nothing. If I catch you in the savanna again, I will slaughter you before you see me coming."

"Did you not listen to anything I just said?" James asked angrily. "You can't do this without me! I am your only—"

"No," Gray Fang said, her sharp voice cutting through the room. When James turned to look at her, the old woman's face was resolute.

"I do not want Lilac to die," she said. "Like the Ar'Bati, she is my grandchild, my own blood. I want nothing more than to see her rise from that stretcher and run into the planes as she always does, but your price is too high."

"But I'm not asking a price," James said. "All you have to do is let me go and—"

"*That* is the price," she snapped, her eyes narrowing. "I saw your lightning in the square. You have the power of the greatest Naturalists, but you are decades too young to understand it. If you were one of us, you would be our savior, but I have seen too much of the violence players do. The evil you create."

She looked back over her shoulder at the village. "Whether you imprisoned us knowingly or not, you bring out a hate in my people that we have never known before. Deeper even than our hatred for the gnolls who stole our ancestors' lands. As spiritual leader of the four clans, I would rather kill poor Lilac with my own hands than see you corrupt who we are any further."

"Grandmother!" Arbati cried, but the elder held up her hand.

"You might be the most dangerous of them all," she said, turning her eyes on James. "Trapped in this lodge, I have watched you come and go from our village for a very long time. You stopped participating in our village's quests and events ages ago, but still you stayed. I've long feared that you desired something from us beyond experience points, reputation, or items, but whatever you want from my people, we do not want you. You and your kind are as great a threat to us as the undead, and while I would much rather kill you, I will be satisfied to never see your face in our lands again."

Her pronouncement done, the wrinkled jubatus took a long puff on her pipe. James, however, couldn't say a word. He was dying to explain that he'd stayed in Windy Lake because he liked it here. He found the history and atmosphere of the jubatus village more soothing and homelike than anything in his own world. But how did you explain to someone that you used their life to escape? The language of Wind and Grass had no words for *computer*, *video game*, or *MMO FSVR RPG*. Even with all the new knowledge that had been shoved into James's head, there was still so much frame of reference missing that it was impossible to explain to the elder that while this *had* been a game, it had been so much more than that to him. FFO had been his sanctuary, his escape from the hell of his life. Now he was in it, actually *here*, but everything was all wrong, and that was horrifying.

He wanted to help, James realized with a jolt. It wasn't just a ploy. He *needed* to save this place that had been his home in game, because being told to walk away was too sad for him to bear. To do that, though, he had to convince these people he wasn't the monster they saw, and without any common reference, the only way to do that was to tell the truth.

The *actual* truth.

"You want to know who I am?" James said, ears drooping. "I'm a loser. In my world, I owe more money than I can ever pay back. I blew my life there by wasting my time in *here*, pretending to be someone I wasn't. Worse, I got my parents into debt as well. My little sister couldn't get loans for her own education because I'd already leveraged our entire family to the hilt. I don't even have a degree to show for it, no trade skills or craft. My life is shit, and it's all my fault, because I'm a loser who runs from his problems and is going to die overworked, unloved, and alone."

These were not words he'd wanted to say to a stranger. They weren't even words he'd managed to say to Tina, the person who deserved to hear them the most. They were, however, the words he'd told himself every day since he'd realized he could no longer afford his classes. Words that haunted him every time he'd had to find a second job, or a third one, just to make his payments.

"Demon? Slaver? Monster?" James shook his head. "I'm afraid all I can offer you is disappointment. In his own world, this mysterious and dreadful being from the Nightmare is just a twenty-eight-year-old college dropout, but that's not who I am here."

James looked Gray Fang straight in the eyes. "You want to know why I stayed in Windy Lake even after I didn't need the quests? Because I liked it. Even though none of you could actually talk to me, I felt like I had a village. A home. I used to help fight the monster version of Lilac when other players failed to save her in time. I didn't have to, and it didn't make a difference in the quest, but I just hated seeing Windy Lake destroyed, because it was *my* village, too. And while I know now that I had no right to think that, I still don't want to see it burn. I don't want Lilac to die or the savanna to fall to the undead. I don't want any of it, but unlike in my real life back home, I can fix this. I have the power here to change things for the better. Clearing the Red Canyon in time to save Lilac will be easy for me, so please, let me help. I know it won't atone for what I unknowingly did back when this was a game, but it will save lives *now*, which is what we both want."

By the time he finished, James felt like he'd dropped his heart on the floor and kicked it into Gray Fang's lap. He held his breath, waiting for her to speak, but the elder just stared at him, her yellow eyes never leaving his face as she puffed on her long carved pipe.

As the minutes ticked by, James began to sweat. He wouldn't wish what he'd been through today on anyone, but James was still sad that there were no other players around. A friend would be most welcome, but even a stranger would work. He just wanted someone from his own world who could understand, because standing alone in front of the furry, fanged, alien-looking old woman as she stared right through him was becoming more unnerving by the second. For all he knew, though, there were no other players. Maybe whatever this was had only happened to him. Maybe he was the only Earthling left in this entire world.

James swallowed. He didn't want to believe that was true, but if it was, then convincing Grey Fang to trust him was more important than ever. The world of FFO was full of NPC towns and factions, but James wasn't naive enough to think they'd welcome him any more than the jubatus had. If they really were all people who'd been trapped playing roles in a game for his amusement, then the entire population of this planet probably hated his guts. That was a horrible world to walk into alone, but if he could save Lilac, then maybe Gray Fang and the jubatus of Windy Lake wouldn't want to murder him quite so badly. It was a long shot, but ensuring there was at least one place that didn't see him as a monster was starting to feel like a very important thing.

He was still thinking about it when the elder set her pipe down at last. Whether it was to accept his aid or order his death, though, James could not begin to guess.

CHAPTER 5

Tina

SilentBlayde was trying to stop a murder, and it wasn't going as well as he would have liked.

"I'm going to kill him!" hissed NekoBaby, clutching SB's short cape across the ripped front of her robes.

"Please don't," SB said. "Anders wasn't in his right mind, and Roxxy stopped him before he did anything truly regrettable."

"Doesn't change the fact that he *tried* to do it," the jubatus Naturalist hissed, her yellow cat eyes narrowing to slits. "And he ripped my robes! Do you know how much grinding I had to do to get this set?" She looked down at the torn white-and-gold fabric with renewed fury. "I'm going to kill him slowly, then I'm going to rez him so I can kill him again!"

SB sighed. Tina had asked him to keep things calm, but he couldn't blame Neko for being upset, and not just because of what had happened with Anders. He had no idea what Neko looked like in real life, but her character model was a five-foot-tall cat-girl with pert little ears, swaying hips, and breasts bigger than volleyballs. The proportions were inhuman, even for a jubatus, and every dude in the raid was having a hard time keeping their eyes to themselves. It was enough to make SB feel uncomfortable too, and he wasn't even the target.

Fortunately, their position at the front of the raid meant that everyone else was stuck staring at their backs rather than Neko's exposed chest. SB had been hoping they'd get bored as the march dragged on, but he should have known better than to underestimate male gamers' interest in breasts. One of the Berserkers actually walked into a dead tree because he was trying too hard to get a peek at NekoBaby's front, earning himself a hiss from the healer as she brandished her stubby claws.

"It's so damn *annoying*," she growled, clutching the cloak tighter to her chest. "I swear, I'm gonna fry the next one. Chain lightning, right to the balls. *Bam.*"

"Maybe they think you don't mind, dude," SB said nervously. "I mean, you used to strip down to your underwear and dance on the mailbox for tips. The attention never bothered you then."

"Yeah, well, it bothers me now," she huffed. "And don't call me dude. I know English isn't your first language, but that shit's not cool."

SB blinked. "Why not? I've always called you dude."

"It was fine before, but shit's gotten real now, and I can't risk anyone finding out that I'm a guy in real life!" She lowered her voice to a hiss. "I made this character for *me* to enjoy! You know, cute name, female voice filter, shake that booty so douchebag bros give me raid spots and phat loot. Back in the game, if anyone found out the truth, I'd just threaten to tell their guild buddies they were hitting on a guy, and that was that. But this *is* my body now. These stupid ears and tail and giant hooters, they *are me*, and it fucking *sucks!*"

The karmatic irony of Neko's situation wasn't lost on SB, but pointing out how fitting a punishment this was for the Roughneck's most obnoxious homophobic troll wouldn't help the current situation. Terrible personality aside, NekoBaby was still a guildmate in trouble and an ally in a world where those were few, so SilentBlayde shelved the sharp retort he'd been writing in his head and focused on the crisis at hand.

"It'll be okay," SilentBlayde said gently. "I'm pretty sure Roxxy and I are the only ones here who know you're a guy in real life. We'll keep your secret. I promise. Just be sure to stick by us and other Roughnecks who aren't Anders. Our guild should be safe, but I'm not sure yet how many of the tryout recruits we can trust."

Neko nodded rapidly. "Thanks, SB! I really appreciate you guys having my back." She looked nervously over her shoulder. "FYI, though, I don't actually remember all the people I scammed. I wouldn't be surprised if some of them were in this raid right now, so heads up."

SB pressed a hand over his face. Leave it to NekoBaby to save the worst until *after* he'd made a promise. "I'll let Roxxy know to be on the lookout," he said tiredly.

"Thanks," she said again, reaching up to poke her twitchy cat ears. "I still can't believe I'm stuck in this porn body, but I guess it could have been worse. At least I'm not like MuffinBurgler."

"Who's MuffinBurgler?" SB asked, confused. "Is he in our raid?"

Neko laughed. "No. It'd be funny as hell if he was, though! He plays a short, fat, pug-eyed Schtumple. Dude looked like a pug balloon on legs, and that was before shit got all hyper realistic." She pressed a hand over her mouth. "Oh man, I hope he was in game when this hit! I'd kill to see him running around on those short little Schtumple legs!"

SB didn't think that MuffinBurgler would find it funny, but he forced himself to laugh along with Neko in the hopes of moving the conversation to safer topics. Hopes that did not pan out, because the moment she stopped laughing about poor, possibly ill-fated MuffinBurgler, NekoBaby went right back to fuming. After the fifth deadly glare over her shoulder, SilentBlayde sighed.

"*Please* don't kill Anders. We need him."

"Yeah, well, I probably can't, anyway," Neko said sourly, glaring at the staff in her hands. "I'm stuck as a stupid healer, which means my damage is too gimpy to kill a rabbit. But I *want* to kill him so badly." She tapped her lip, thinking. "Maybe I can poison him. I've got some herbs in my bag. I bet I could brew them into something deadly!"

"Those herbs are the only edibles we have besides the bread in Roxxy's backpack," SB chided. "Don't go wasting food on revenge."

"All right, all right," Neko grumbled, crossing her arms over her chest. "But I'm not healing him."

SB nodded. "Fair enough."

"And he should give me his robe since he ripped mine."

"You'll have to get Roxxy's okay on that one."

"What's her problem today, anyway?" Neko asked. "She's been an off-the-charts bitch since this bullshit started. Did PMS hit along with the craziness or something?"

SilentBlayde's jaw clenched. He would have been happy for any change of topic except for *this* topic. The cat-girl-guy healer wasn't the only one complaining about Roxxy's hard-line methods for keeping things together.

"Roxxy is stressed out to the max," SB said, more loudly than was necessary for only NekoBaby to hear. "She's always felt responsible for her raids, no matter who's in them. Right now, she needs us to follow orders for everyone's safety, but some people aren't taking things seriously enough, and it's causing friction."

NekoBaby snorted. "Friction, huh? I heard she damn near murdered Anders earlier. Not that I mind, of course, because certain fish-heads *deserve to be filleted!*" She shouted that last part over her shoulder, and SB winced. "Still," Neko went on, dropping her voice back to a normal level. "What she did to that Berserker earlier was some straight-up gestapo shit."

"We've already lost someone..." SB said, sending the jubatus's ears flat at the mention of the Sorcerer they'd failed to resurrect.

"Yeah well," Neko said. "According to you, it wasn't her fault he died. She needs to stop taking it out on all of us. How is all this abuse taking care of people?"

SilentBlayde fiddled nervously with one of his long ears. He didn't really have a good comeback to Neko's accusation, especially since he'd disagreed with Tina's treatment of Anders. Even so. "I don't know what the right thing to do back at the Dead Mountain was, but I know that all of us owe Roxxy our lives. I couldn't have gotten Anders to cleanse the raid on my own, and while she might have gone a little too far with the Berserker, it kept us moving and together, which is probably why we're still alive."

"Stop White Knighting her," Neko said scornfully. "You always cut Roxxy miles of slack." Her lips curled in a sneer, showing her sharp cat teeth. "I bet she's just having that time of the month and taking it out on us. Not that our Glorious Leader has ever needed an excuse to be a hard-ass."

SB scowled. "That time of the month is coming for you too now, you know."

The look of horror on NekoBaby's feline face was priceless, and SB was just angry enough to enjoy it. He was pretty sure the jubatus healer didn't actually mean it—Neko had always had a bad habit of saying whatever popped into her head—but SilentBlayde was extremely tired of listening to her bash Tina. As good as it had felt, though, that comment had been an uncomfortably low blow for him, and SB guiltily pulled his mask farther up, tugging on the cloth until it was right below his lower lashes.

They were both quiet for several minutes after that. The silence stretched on so long, SB was starting to hope the whole topic had been forgotten when Neko suddenly boiled over.

"Oh my god," she said, her voice squeaky with horror. "What if I *do* get a period? I mean, I'm a girl now, and that's something girls get, or have, or whatever. But what if there's blood? What will I do?"

"You'll live," said the curt and deep voice of Roxxy from behind them.

They both jumped. Despite being half a ton of rock-person covered in layers of magical plate armor, Roxxy had an uncanny quietness to how she moved. The dust didn't even rise around her unless she was stomping or running. Since Tina was not a quiet person by any definition, SB attributed this trait to the stonekin race itself.

"What's up?" SilentBlayde asked, angling his head to smile up at her.

She smiled back, but her copper brows stayed furrowed, and SB stiffened. He knew that look. "You have a job for me, don't you?"

"A nice one this time," Roxxy promised, reaching back to pull the raid's second tank, DarkKnight, up beside her. "Take DarkKnight and NekoBaby over to do the *Last For One* quest. It's in that forest just ahead on the left."

SB blinked in surprise. "The ghosts quest?"

She nodded.

"*Why?*"

Roxxy grinned knowingly, showing him a row of white marble teeth. "Because it has a cloth robe as a quest reward, and no one ever does it, so I'm sure that Neko can do it now." Then she leaned over, her breath brushing the inside of his long ear. "And while you're out there, teach DarkKnight how to tank."

SB had to work to keep the surprise off his face. He shot a look at DarkKnight. The other tank was looking down at the ground and shifting his feet in the dust as if he'd done something wrong.

"Got it," he said, covering up his confusion with enthusiasm. "You heard the rock," SB said as he waved for the others to follow him off the main road. "Let's roll!"

DarkKnight silently fell in behind him. NekoBaby followed more reluctantly, shooting curious glances at the second tank like she knew something was up. When they'd walked down the trail just far enough to be out of earshot of the rest of the raid, both NekoBaby and SilentBlayde stopped to turn on DarkKnight.

"Jake, man, what's going on?" SB asked. "Why is Roxxy asking *me* to teach *you* how to tank?"

DarkKnight pushed up his visor with a look of embarrassment. "Well, that's because my name ain't Jake. It's Frank."

SB jerked back. He'd thought his friend had been acting weird, but their situation had everyone acting weird. The man in front of him was definitely DarkKnight, though, or at least his character, which begged the question…

"How did you get Jake's character?"

Frank raised his hands at once. "I'm very sorry. As I already told the rock lady, I didn't know this account was stolen."

"Wait, you're playing DarkKnight's hacked account?" Neko shook her head. *"Shameful."*

"The site said it was official!"

"They always do," SB said, scrubbing a hand over his face. "But there's nothing we can do about that now. How long have you been playing his character? Jake was at the main raid this weekend, so it can't be more than a couple of days."

"Actually," Frank said nervously, "this is my first day. And my first MMO."

SB couldn't believe his long ears. "Is this also your first video game?"

"Yes sir," said Frank. "I tried playing my friend's Atari once, but it wasn't much fun. I never did get into computer games after that."

"Atari?" NekoBaby cried. "Dude, how old *are* you?"

"Eighty-six," Frank said proudly with a tip of his helmet.

SB and Neko exchanged a dumbfounded look.

"Christ," the healer muttered. "Where do we start? Do you even know what HP is?"

The Knight looked baffled. "You mean *Harry Potter?* 'Cause I haven't read that, either. Sorry, kids."

SilentBlayde shook his head. "Let's just keep moving," he said, pointing down the trail that wound through the spindly dead trees. "The quest used to be right over there, but since everything's so much bigger now, we've probably got a mile or so ahead of us, and we don't want to get too far from the raid. I'll teach you about tanking while we walk."

"Why, thank you very much," Frank said sincerely. "Though I gotta admit, I'm a little confused. I thought this game was about swords and magic and stuff. I would have tried it a lot earlier if I'd known it had tanks!"

"Not military tanks like you drive," SB corrected quickly. "Tanking is a role. In a raid—a large group of players fighting together—the heavily armored classes like you and Roxxy go out in front and get the monster's attention so they don't attack the less sturdy players like me and Neko."

Frank looked horrified. "Why would I do that? Sounds suicidal."

"'Cause you're hard to kill," NekoBaby said. "Your job is to take the beating, and while you're doing that, damage-dealing classes like LoudBlayde here are free to actually kill the monster."

"I'm an Assassin," SB said in a stage whisper.

The warrior didn't look reassured. "And what's to stop me from dying while I'm doing this?"

"Your shield, heavy armor, giant health pool, and awesome defensive abilities," SilentBlayde said, rapping his knuckles on Frank's two-inch-thick enchanted breastplate.

"And me!" said Neko. "I'm a healer. I can repair any damage you take as soon as you take it because I'm amazing and my gear is top notch." She brandished her glowing green staff, causing its eternally dancing autumn leaves to scatter in a beautiful explosion of gold and orange through the gray light of the Deadlands. "So long as you keep the monsters off me, I'll keep you alive long enough for even the weakest damage, like GossipBlayde, to finish them off."

SB rolled his eyes, but Frank still looked confused.

"But Roxxy is a tank, too, isn't she? I've already seen her lay down some damage."

"We're just telling you how it was in the game," SilentBlayde said quickly. "Roxxy is different. She has a...um...talent for violence that's come into its own in this new world."

"Her final form has been unleashed," Neko added cryptically. "Make peace with your gods."

SB was giving her another dirty look when a chill went down his spine. Insult forgotten, he scanned the spindly white trees and spotted a group of pale, shimmering figures dancing in a circle through the mist, just a dozen feet away.

"Whoa," NekoBaby whispered, eyes wide. "Those are a *lot* scarier now that this is real."

Frank gulped. "Wait, we're fighting ghosts? How do you kill a ghost? Do swords even work on them?"

Given how many ghost-based kill quests there were in FFO,

SilentBlayde couldn't help but laugh at that. "We'll be fine. We beat up ghosts all the time! Just get in there and start whacking. You'll get their attention."

"Are they dangerous?" Frank asked, pulling out his sword shakily.

"I suppose," SilentBlayde said with a shrug, drawing his swords as well. "They're level eighty-twos while we're just level eighty, but we're all so well geared that we should be able to take these one-skulls no problem. I actually soloed this quest for an achievement a few months ago."

Frank still wasn't moving, so SB waved at the monsters. "Yoo-hoo! Ghosts! Over here! You guys dance like squares!"

At the sound of his voice, all five deathly elves turned at once, their mouths distorting down to their necks as they unleashed their unearthly screeches of rage. SB waved at them one last time before ducking behind Frank.

"Protect us, tank!" he cried, giving the old man a shove before wrapping himself in a nearby patch of shadows.

From the safety of the lightless realm, SilentBlayde watched as the ghosts lost sight of him. Frank was out of the trees now, though, so they charged him instead.

"Dammit, SB!" NekoBaby yelled, backing away from their newbie Knight. "Stomp, Frank! Stomp!"

It was then that SB realized that they hadn't explained to Frank how to activate his abilities. Fortunately, Frank seemed to have been gaining in the same innate knowledge related to his class as the rest of them. No one had taught Neko how to use her magic after the transition. She'd just done it, the same as all the other healers. Likewise, SB couldn't tell anyone how he knew how to walk through shadows. Back when this was a game, he'd had a macro set up for every stealthing occasion, but when he'd seen Roxxy going down under the skeletons, he hadn't even thought about his buttons, or lack thereof. He'd just known what to do, flitting through the lightless realm to her side before he realized what was going on.

Thankfully for all of them, Frank was no different. After a moment of panic, he activated the knight's area taunt instinctively, stomping his foot and sending bright cracks of energy spreading through the dusty forest floor. The golden light laced its way up the ghosts, making their eyes flash red, then they all charged at poor Frank as though he was their ticket back to the land of the living.

For a horrible second, it looked as if their spectral fingers would pass straight through the Knight's shield. Then sparks flew as Frank lifted his shield to meet them, grunting with impact as all five specters slammed into him with real physical force. The ghosts screamed in frustration, then spread out to surround him and claw from all sides. Frank cried out in pain, turning with his shield to try to block them all at once. He was starting to panic, swinging his sword wildly without hitting anything, when the cold gray darkness of the forest was split by a vibrant cascade of green color.

Behind him, NekoBaby's staff and hands were glowing like the summer sun through trees. She waved them in a dramatic motion, and Frank was bathed in a wash of verdant energies, his whole body glowing as the healing spell surged through him.

"Whoa!" he cried, face breaking into a wondrous smile. "That feels amazing! Lemme get some more of that, please!"

Still watching from the shadows, SilentBlayde lifted an eyebrow. Pain had never been an issue in game since all unpleasant feelings had been muted in favor of fun, but now that things were real, it seemed that healing carried a measure of pain suppression as well. The ghosts were still hitting Frank as hard as ever, but he didn't seem to mind nearly as much now. He actually looked like he was having fun, whacking the transparent figures with the flat of his sword as though he was playing Whack-a-Mole.

Frank seemed to have the ghosts' full attention now, so it was time for SB to do his part. Making a mental note to tell Roxxy about the pain suppression, he emerged from the shadows right behind one of the ghosts. Silver blades flashing, he landed a half dozen lightning-fast slashes in its back in the space of a heartbeat.

Spectral miasma split beneath his glowing silver blades, and the ghost vanished in a flash of light, screaming all the while. Neko cheered when it went down, raising her hands to hit Frank with another healing spell.

"That's more like it!" she said cheerfully. "Now kill the others, and let's get my new dress! Faster, Assassin! Stab, stab!"

Grinning, SilentBlayde stepped back into the shadows, leaving Frank gleefully whacking the ghosts as he learned to manage his shield. Since this was supposed to be a training fight, SB ignored Neko's calls to hurry up and took his time, letting Frank get several more shield strikes in before popping out of the shadows to dispatch his next target.

■ ■

Back on the main road, Tina was having a far less enjoyable fight. "*Fire!*" she shouted.

A volley of colorful glowing arrows sailed over her head. From the hill on Tina's right, fireballs launched, and lightning arced. Along with the onslaught of magical attacks came a cacophony of embarrassed, half-hearted shouts.

"Poison shot!"

"Chain Lightning!"

"Fireball!"

Seconds later, the awkwardness was drowned out by a deafening series of thunder-cracks and explosions in the dirt beyond the road. Shielding her eyes from the pyrotechnics, Tina cursed the loss of her helmet as their target—an undead boar the size of a shuttle bus—vanished into the glare. It emerged a few seconds later, its singed fur leaving a burning trail behind it as it began to charge.

"And...stop fire!" Tina said, holding up her sword.

Two extra fireballs launched before she'd even finished. These were followed by a lightning bolt, an Assassin's bolo shot, and several arrows before Tina could whirl around. "*I said stop!*"

The gigantic boar was now only thirty feet away. It charged across the dead gray landscape, dust and dirt flying from its powerful hooves. Hateful blue-white fire flickered in its hollow, leaking eye sockets, making the black ichor that flew from its metal tusks glisten as it homed in on Tina.

"Wait," she said, stepping out in front of the raid with a nervous glance over her shoulder to make sure she wasn't about to get shot in the back. "Waaaaait."

When the boar was only twenty feet away, she swung her sword down. "*Now! Charge!*"

A dozen Knights and Berserkers lunged forward to attack the boar along with her. As they ran, more embarrassed cries rang out.

"Frenzied Strikes!"

"Storm of Blades!"

"Kamehameha!"

"Shield Charge!"

That last one was Tina, who winced even though calling out their abilities had been her idea. The shame would have been deeper, but she had to stay focused on the monster she was rushing.

Her shield slammed into the oncoming boar like one truck colliding with another. The screech of metal on metal echoed up the mountains that surrounded the Deadlands' gray valley. But as big as Tina was, the giant boar was easily three times larger, and as it pushed against her shield, her feet began to slide in the loose dirt.

"Steady Ground!" she yelled, drawing from the deep earth. The bedrock magic answered, causing the dust and gravel to solidify into ultra-hard rock around her feet. As it anchored her in place, the boar finally ground to a halt on her shield.

By this point, the other melee players had spread out to form a rough circle around the beast. There was much jostling and cursing and stepping on toes, but eventually, they were all in position to begin hacking away at its sides. Finally, a pair of Assassins appeared out of thin air and dropped onto the monster's back, stabbing their swords and daggers into the rotting flesh on either side of its spinal column. The rotting boar roared at the onslaught, and Tina slapped the flat of her sword against its snout to keep its attention.

"Mocking Strike!"

She wasn't sure how one mocked a rampaging undead boar, but the ability must have worked, because the monster's head swung back around to try to gore her. Spear-like tusks grated off her shield in a shower of blue sparks. A few landed on Tina's cheek, singeing the smooth stone of her face. She shook them off and smacked the boar again, hacking its rotting nose with her sword to make sure it stayed locked on her.

Despite being a three-skull monster, the boar didn't last long under attack from over a dozen players. Tina was just getting into the rhythm of step, block, strike when the monster tumbled to the ground, its hind legs hacked clean through. After that, the living corpse-pig could do nothing but thrash helplessly on the road as the remaining players turned it into fetid mincemeat.

The moment it stopped twitching, the accusations began.

"Watch out, asshole!"

"Dude, bad aim!"

"You dick! Don't use Storm of Blades while we're standing right next to you!"

Tina watched the bickering with a bleak expression as she contemplated whose butt to kick first. Since the melee team was already digging into each other, she decided to start with the ranged.

"What part of 'Only attack once' do you not understand?" she yelled, turning to glare at the spell casters she'd positioned on the hill behind them. "I saw those extra shots! How many times do I have to say this? There. Is. No. More. Friendly. Fire. It's all *un*friendly fire! If you keep attacking after melee is engaged, you risk hitting us as much as the enemy. There's no damage meters to top anymore, so just cool your junk and *wait* until I tell you to fire again."

When all the ranged classes looked suitably downcast, Tina turned to the mass of Berserkers, Knights, and Assassins standing around the dead pig. "All right, melee," she said, shifting to a more positive tone. "That was our best charge yet, but you still have to get it through your heads that you can only use single-target attacks. Also, you all have to remember your positions! I saw way too much tripping over each other, and we don't have time to waste on that shit. Once we're engaged, the ranged can't fire anymore, so we need to get in and get the job done."

A lot of victorious smiles vanished at her words, and Tina belatedly realized that some positive reinforcement might also be useful.

"Good job on the ability call-outs, though!" she said cheerfully. "I know it feels stupid to shout out activations, but we don't have the interface to tell us who's doing what anymore. We have to have some way of keeping off each other's toes and coordinating. It'll get old soon enough, so stop snickering."

She eyeballed one of her Knights. "And please call out *real* ability names from now on. I heard you over there, Mr. Kamehameha!"

The Knight shrugged unapologetically, and Tina rolled her eyes, motioning for everyone to get back into formation on the road. Grudgingly, the raid obeyed. No one said anything she could hear, but there were a lot of grumbling and dirty looks. They *were* finally obeying orders, though, so Tina let it slide, letting out a frustrated breath as she signaled for everyone to march on.

She probably should have ordered a rest. The Strength-geared classes all seemed fine, but several of the casters were starting to lean on their staffs. It was a pathetic sight, but Tina was determined to keep going. Not only did marching keep the raid busy and out of trouble, but constant movement was their only hope of making it to the safety of the Order Fortress at the other end of the Deadlands before nightfall. She couldn't feel Grel's footsteps rumbling through the ground anymore, but that didn't mean he wasn't still coming, and unlike them, skeletons didn't need rest. If they stopped, the gap she'd worked so hard to put between them and the Once King's army would close, so until they got to safety, pushing forward was their only option.

"Roxxy!"

The cheerful voice of SilentBlayde cut through the grim silence of the raid. As always, the sound made her heart leap, and Tina spun around to see the trio of questers jogging up the road behind them. SB was running as gracefully and tirelessly as the mythical creature he was supposed to be. Frank looked a bit more red-faced, huffing from the multiple-mile run in full armor with NekoBaby sitting on top of his backpack like a feline Yoda. Hitching a ride was classic NekoBaby behavior, though, so Tina didn't think much of it until the group got close enough for her to see the deep circles under the healer's eyes.

"What's wrong with you?" she asked as Frank helped the cat-girl down.

"She went MOO," Frank explained. "I'm given to understand that's bad."

"For the *last time*, it's OOM," Neko said, wavering on her feet. "As in 'Out Of Mana.'"

Tina gaped at her. "How did *you* run out of mana? Naturalists are regen machines. Was Frank that hard to heal?"

"No, he was okay," Neko said, giving up and sitting down on the ground. "But something's weird about healing now, Roxxy. It takes a lot more juice than it used to. I was fine to start, but by the time LazyBlayde there finally decided to dispatch all the ghosts, I was empty."

"I wouldn't have taken so long if you'd said something," SB said irritably. "And you *said* you'd regenerate your mana if Frank carried you."

"I thought I would," she said, mouth opening in a yawn. "But I still feel like butt." She fluttered her eyelashes at Frank. "Can you carry me a bit longer?"

"No," Roxxy said as the Knight's face turned scarlet. "His job is to tank, not taxi." She looked down at the knee-length plain white robe Neko was wearing. "But at least you got a new dress."

"But I didn't!" the Naturalist cried, yanking up the plain muslin to show Tina the ripped robes she was still wearing underneath. "This is Frank's undershirt!"

Tina blinked. "Why are you wearing Frank's undershirt? What happened to the quest? Was it not there?"

"No, we did it," SB said. "But—"

"There was *no loot!*" Neko yelled. "They cheated us! We killed all the stupid ghosts *and* put their damn remains back in their graves, and we got nothing!"

"The fog parted to reveal a chest when we were done, just like it was supposed to," SilentBlayde explained. "But there was nothing inside it. Not even gold."

Tina's face fell. "Really? Damn, dude. I'm sorry. I didn't mean to send you on a wild goose chase."

"It's okay," SB said immediately. "Honestly, it makes sense. Back when this was a game, quest rewards spawned as needed. Now, though, where would the loot even come from? It's not like ghosts would actually have a bunch of brand-new caster robes just lying around. They don't even wear clothes."

That did make a certain amount of sense, but it didn't help with their problem. "We'll make you a new set of robes as soon as we get time and materials to craft," Tina promised Neko. "Do your old robes still work even with the rip?"

"I think so," Neko said, looking down the front of her shirt-slash-dress. "I can't see my stats anymore, obvs, but taking them off makes me feel weaker, so they must be doing something. Anyway, Frank's shirt is better than SB's cape. That little thing couldn't even cover my womanly assets, if you get my drift."

She winked obnoxiously at Tina, who rolled her eyes and turned to Frank. "Will you be okay? Shirts don't have stats, but you might need it for other reasons now that our armor is real." Chest hair, she imagined, would be a real pain in plate armor without something to protect it, but Frank shook his head.

"I'll be all right," he said with a lopsided grin. "We're Knights, right? Helping damsels in distress is in the job description."

"I'd never call Neko a 'damsel,' but she is quite distressing," Tina said, grinning back. "I'm just happy you're all okay. Now hurry and get back in line. We've got a lot of ground to cover and not a lot of light left to do it in."

Neko stalked back to join the other healers, grumbling under her breath about cheap broken quests that didn't even give you cash. Roxxy sent Frank to watch the front of the raid, then she pulled SB aside to get the real story.

"So how did Neko actually run out of mana?" she whispered. "Was Frank's tank training *that* bad?"

"He actually did okay," SilentBlayde said. "Not great. I wouldn't let him solo tank anything complicated, but I don't think he'll die so long as he's got a competent healer."

"That's better than I'd hoped," Tina said, but even with his mask, she could tell SB was frowning. "What else?"

The elf looked worried. "Neko wasn't just faking to get a free ride. Healing is a lot harder now, Roxxy. A *lot* a lot. Mana recovery, too. Even with her robe ripped, Neko should have been able to heal a geared tank against five one-skulls for days, but she ran out of mana after only a few minutes. By the time I'd killed the last ghost, she could barely stand up."

That was new. Normally, being out of mana just meant not being able to cast spells, not falling over. "Since when does being OOM make you physically tired?"

"Since this happened, I guess," SB said, waving his hand at their new bodies. "My guess is that healing real wounds takes a lot more magic than just refilling numbers on a health bar. Whatever the reason, we can't count on our healers to be able to heal like they used to."

"Crap," Tina said. "Low heals. That's just what we need."

"It gets worse," he said quietly, turning to show her the empty satchel that normally held his poisons on his belt. "Remember how I threw night powder to blind that one skeleton? Normally, that ability has a two-minute reset, but my packet never came back. It looks like ability timers don't refresh if the action takes a physical material that we don't have."

"You mean you were only carrying one packet, so one packet was all you got?"

SilentBlayde nodded, and Tina turned with a curse to examine the raid marching away from them. The Clerics, Naturalists, and Sorcerers were all noticeably more tired than everyone else, but what really worried her were the Rangers' quivers. In the game, they'd always been full. Now, every one she saw was half-empty.

"Shit, shit, shit," Tina said, furious with herself. "I've been running combat drills on every monster we've come across. I didn't realize mana and ammo were no longer infinite." She'd used up half their resources on goddamn boars.

"Hey, you didn't know," SilentBlayde said gently. "But do we have any food for Neko? If the old eating and drinking mechanics still work, then she might be able to eat to recover her mana pool."

Tina shook her head. "We've all eaten it already. Twenty loaves of bread split between thirty-nine people goes fast, and there's nothing edible in this wasteland. Just bones and dust." She kicked the ashen dirt at their feet.

"What about conjured food?" SB asked, his eyes brightening. "I've always wanted to know what mana cake tasted like!"

"Good call," Tina said. "Let's see."

They jogged together back to the raid and snagged a Sorcerer named Bobinator. Five minutes of conjuring later, and everyone was holding a piping-hot mana cake. Mouths watered at the fluffy white cupcakes, which were each as big as Tina's fist and topped with whirls of pink frosting. Tina could smell the sweetness of their sugar on the air, but she didn't have mana, so she restrained herself from eating one, which might have been the hardest thing she'd ever had to do.

"How's it taste?" she asked hungrily.

"*Sooo goood,*" Neko moaned around a mouthful of frosting. "And I certainly feel better!"

"Yeah, but the Bobinator over there looks worse for it," said SB, pointing at the Sorcerer, who was lying flat on the ground, chest heaving and face pale.

Tina sighed. "Looks like we're shuffling deck chairs on the Titanic."

"Nothing else you could be doing," Frank said, walking over to join them. "No matter where you go, the law of conservation of energy still applies."

"What do you mean?" Tina asked.

"Well," Frank said, his thick Southern accent making the word sound more like *wheel.* "I don't know much about mana, but there's nowhere in the universe where you can get something for nothing. Once you take out the video-game part, it makes sense that it'd become impossible for someone to make something out of his energy that gives another person more energy than he put in."

That *did* make a depressing amount of sense. "There goes our last good idea," Tina said, kicking a rock. "I'm so stupid. I should have been prioritizing food for the healers this whole time." She shook her head angrily. "We'll just have to deal. At this point, we'll make it, or we won't. As simple as that."

None of the others looked happy about that. "We can't keep going like this," SB said quietly as Frank pulled the Bobinator back to his feet. "If we get in a serious fight, all of our healers might be OOM before we finish."

"I know," Tina snapped.

SB flinched at her harsh tone, and Tina cringed.

"Sorry," she said. "But stopping's not an option. We'll just have to make it work until we get somewhere with food. Once we get to the Order's fortress, things will be better. It can't be that much farther. We just have to push through."

"Right," SilentBlayde said, but he didn't sound convinced. Honestly, Tina wasn't, either, but there was really was nothing else to do but keep going, so she climbed on top of a rock to address the raid.

The faces that looked up when she clanged her shield for attention were tired, dusty, and miserable, and Tina was about to make it worse. Knowing that made her feel like a villain, but there was nothing for it. This was the reality, so Tina cleared her throat of gravel and started explaining the new rules of food, healing, mana recovery, and ammunition.

Many of the spell casters nodded, as though she were confirming something they'd all suspected. The Rangers, however, looked shocked, peering over their shoulders in alarm at the half-empty quivers on their backs.

"I know," Tina said when they looked at her in panic. "I wish I'd figured this out earlier, too. But it is what it is. Until we solve our mana and ammo problem, though, all casters, Rangers, and anyone else who uses mana or consumable items won't be fighting unless I specifically order you to. This includes Assassin special abilities like throwing knives and poisons. Instead, we're gonna rely on the melee fighters—

people whose abilities don't use up limited resources—to deal with any monsters we run into."

This announcement was met with a lot of cries of *"No fair!"* and *"Boring!"* and Tina's glare hardened.

"It's not about fun anymore!" she bellowed. "Maybe you haven't noticed, but shit got real! If we use up our ammo and mana on stupid crap, then we risk having *no* mana or arrows if we have to face *that*."

She pointed at the now barely visible plume of dust rising from the Once King's army, many miles behind them, and the whole raid began to grumble.

"Who cares about that thing?" someone shouted.

"Yeah! It's slow as hell!" another yelled.

"This sucks!"

Tina banged on her shield. "Stop bitching!" she yelled. "This isn't going to last forever. We just have to make it across the zone to the Order of the Golden Sun's fortress. Many of us have legendary status with the Order. We should be able to walk in, get resupplied, and kick the dust of this place from our heels as we walk through the portal to Bastion. Once we make it back to the city, you can go do whatever you want, but *right now*, we have to stay together and stay alive, and the way we do that is by getting out of the Deadlands before Grel'Darm the Colossal catches us."

"So what?" said a Berserker. It was the same asshole with the black hair and ridiculously oversize ax that had given her trouble before, and Tina glared at him murderously.

"So what what?"

"So what if Grel catches us?" the Berserker said, stepping to the front of the crowd. "You guys have him on farm status, right?"

"The Roughnecks do," Tina said. "But you're not my core raiders. With a random group like this, untrained, with limited mana and ammo, we'll be wiped out for sure."

"So what?" the Berserker said again, tilting his head back to look her in the eyes. "Wiping sucks, but the graveyard's right over there. Who knows? If we all die, maybe he'll break aggro and go back to the mountain. Even if he doesn't, fighting's better than another hour on your death march."

There was some discreet applause at this, and Tina clenched her jaw. She didn't know the Berserker's name without nameplates, but she'd seen him fight enough now to know that he was a meathead who never got his position right, ignored orders, hit the other melee with his sweep attacks, and had generally failed at everything Tina had asked of him far. But what *really* annoyed her wasn't that she was having to deal with this asshole. It was that the Berserker seemed to have a lot of support in the crowd.

All around him, tired raiders were nodding. Tina couldn't comprehend *why*. After experiencing the very real pain of this new world, why anyone would want to risk *dying* rather than running made zero sense to her. She wasn't about to let this moron's contagious idiocy get them killed, though, so she hopped down off the rock.

"Fine, asshole," she said, drawing her sword. "You want to get us all killed? You first. Prove that the graveyard works, or shut up and march."

Her opponent carefully unfastened his ax. When it was free, he grabbed it in both hands, flexing his Atlas-sized shoulders beneath his plate-and-mail armor. "Fat chance, bitch. I'm not here to give you a show. I'm just saying we should man up and go kill the bastard that we came here today to fight instead of running like little bitch cowards."

"Right," Tina said flatly. "And the chance that we might *permanently die* in the process didn't even cross your mind. We've already lost—" She froze, her shame trapping the perfect comeback in her throat. Now would have been a great time to bring up the Sorcerer she'd let die back at the Dead Mountain, but using the poor nameless player as evidence for someone as stupid as the Berserker was being felt like an insult to his memory, and it didn't help that Tina was in no hurry to admit her failures to this meathead. Even if she had been, she didn't think it would do any good. This guy's problems clearly had nothing to do with facts, nor did the ample evidence that this was not the old FFO seem to bother any of the players agreeing with him.

"I bet we pop right back up at the graveyard," he went on, propping his ax on the ground. "Lots of game stuff still works. Why not that?"

"Because a lot of other game stuff *doesn't* work," Tina snapped. "I'm not going to let you risk everyone's lives just because you're bored. It takes a special kind of asshole to gamble other people like that."

"Better an asshole than a bossy bitch," he spat back at her. "You're so busy playing commander, I bet you don't even know my name yet."

There were some corroborating *oohs* from the crowd, and Tina winced. She *didn't* know his name, mostly because she'd been too busy to find out. If she'd been less angry, this would have been a good place to grudgingly apologize and ask, but Tina's capacity for being reasonable had been thinning with every foot she'd had to shove this raid down the road. Now that she was being taunted by the asshole at the heart of it, her patience had gone from thin to nonexistent.

"I don't have a clue what your name is," she growled. "And I don't give a shit. I only bother learning the names of people I want to know. Not some stands-in-fire, hits-your-friends, bullheaded moron. You're so bad at this shit, I bet you bought that gear you're wearing."

"You really are a fucking Care Bear tank if you don't know what this is!" he cried, holding up his giant ax for her to see. "I got this shit the man's way, by kicking other players' asses!"

Just when Tina thought she couldn't get any madder, he pushed her to new heights. "You son of a bitch!" she yelled, shaking the ground in her fury. "You came to a *raid* in PVP gear? That shit's worthless unless you're dueling other players! Did you think we were just going to carry your lazy ass through the dungeon?"

The Berserker sneered. "Gear doesn't matter. It's how well I fight that counts."

"I've seen how well you fight," Tina snarled. "You're better off relying on gear."

"Oh yeah? Bring it and see." He looked her straight in the eyes. "Cunt."

CHAPTER 6
James

"**Y**ou put us in a difficult position."

James began to sweat. Across the lodge, Arbati was hunched over the still form of his sister, glaring at James as if he needed only a hint of the elder's approval before ripping James's throat out. But Gray Fang gave no such order. She just sat there, staring at James through the rising pipe smoke with yellow, considering eyes.

"I don't understand most of what you just said," she admitted. "But I know the sound of truth when I hear it."

"*Grandmother!*" Arbati hissed, but the old cheetah woman held up her hand.

"I believe you when you say you wish to help us," she went on, keeping her eyes locked on James. "But as much as I want to save Lilac, I cannot ask a player for help. You have done too much, hurt too many for too long. There is nothing that will make my people trust one of your kind after eighty years of suffering. All I want is for you to be gone from our lands before you cause any more trouble."

James slumped. Banished to the savanna, it was, then. At least he wouldn't have to fight his way out of the village now, so that was something, but it still felt like he'd failed. Even in his pretend home, they thought he was more trouble than he was worth.

He was getting good and depressed about that when Gray Fang said, "Unless."

James froze. "Unless what?"

The old woman's eyes grew sly. "Unless you were willing to change," she said, leaning forward on her pillow. "We could never accept a player's help after all your kind has done, but if you were no longer a player—if you became one of us—there would be no such trouble."

"Become one of you?" James repeated, glancing at Arbati, who looked ready to explode. "How?"

"You just said how much you respected my people," Gray Fang reminded him. "If that is true, I will allow you to petition to join the Four Clans."

"Grandmother, *no!*" Arbati said, horrified. "A player among the clans? It would be an insult!"

"If he's one of us, he won't be a player anymore," the elder pointed out, giving him a weighty look before turning back to James. "I will set you a trial by which you may prove yourself worthy. If you pass, and if you can find someone who is willing to sponsor you, then you will become one of the Four Clans the same as if you were born in our village."

James couldn't believe his ears. "I would love to join the clans," he said. "But didn't you just say you wanted me gone?"

"I would like nothing better," Gray Fang replied with stinging honesty. "But for Lilac to survive eighty years of nightmare only to die now, in the first moments of our freedom..." She shook her head. "It is too bitter. If you are even half as powerful as you claim, I cannot afford to reject your help, and this is the only way I know to make my people accept it."

"I'll do it," James said immediately. "What's my trial?"

The elder looked down at the jubatus girl on the stretcher. "Save my granddaughter. If you can smash the orb of the lich in Red Canyon before the next dawn breaks, we will welcome you as one of our own. If your power is truly what you say, then it should be an easy task. But if you have lied, and Lilac becomes undead, you will be named an enemy of the clans and hunted to the ends of the savanna. Those are the terms of the trial. Do you accept?"

She said that like a threat, but James felt a rush of relief. Joining the village of Windy Lake was a better possibility than he'd known to hope for. In one night's work, he could go from hated outsider to hero of the village. Not only would he save the place he'd come to think of as home, but he'd earn himself a haven. Somewhere he could be safe in this new, confusing world that hated him and all his kind. That sounded like a miracle after the events of this morning, and James bowed his head. "Thank you, Elder Gray Fang," he said humbly. "I accept the trial."

The elder nodded, but her hard scowl remained. "I hope you succeed for Lilac's sake, but don't think this will fix everything. Joining the clans will not erase our anger. All it will do is grant you the rights of a clanship and make it harder for any jubatus to abuse you, at least in obvious ways. In return, you will accept the responsibilities of our community and be bound by clan law. This is not a free ticket. We all help each other around here. Life on the savanna is neither easy nor peaceful."

James had quested in this zone long enough to know that much, but he had his own stipulation. "I'm okay with all of that," he said. "And I'm happy to help however I can, with Lilac or here in the village, but I still need the freedom to search for a way back home. So long as I can do that in addition to my clan duties, there's no problem."

"We can work it out," Gray Fang said. "Honestly, everyone will be much happier to see you go back to your own people rather than trying to fit in around here. But we've wasted enough time fighting each other. Come."

The old cheetah lady gestured for him to approach. Cautiously, James obeyed, walking forward and lowering himself until he was kneeling in front of her. When he was still, she reached for the mask covering his face, crumbling the already cracked clay with the barest touch of her fingers.

"There," she said, brushing the dust from his fur. "Do not make me regret this."

"I won't," James promised, blinking as his full magical sight came rushing back. "Thank you."

She nodded curtly and stood up, turning to her grandson, who'd been watching their conversation like it was a horror movie. "Cut him free."

Growling so loudly it echoed off the lodge's rafters, Arbati obeyed, cutting the leather strap that bound James's hands with a slash of his long knife. When he was free, Gray Fang led them both outside, where, to James's surprise, a large crowd was waiting in the square. Their hushed conversations dropped off as the elder emerged, then fell to dead silence when James came out behind her, unmasked and unbound.

"I cannot cure Scout Lilac," Gray Fang announced to the gathered jubatus. "Her wound is cursed by magics I cannot touch. As in the Nightmare, the Poisoned Patrol event proceeds beyond our control, but *we* are no longer bound to be helpless." She waved her hand at James standing behind her. "This player wishes to join our tribe. After judging his character, I have accepted his petition on the condition that he use his power to defeat the undead at Red Canyon and save Lilac Clawborn from undeath."

The crowd began to hiss.

"We cannot accept this!" cried an old jubatus at the front, a scarred warrior whose muscular body still looked quite capable of ripping James apart despite his graying fur. "You'd trust one of the monsters who enslaved us with saving my daughter? *And* welcome it into our village?" He spat on the dusty ground. "You know that thing is not the jubatus that it appears to be. We should kill it now, before it does something worse!"

The naked hatred in his voice made James take a step back, but Gray Fang didn't look intimidated in the least. She just leveled the same quiet, implacable gaze on Lilac's father that she'd used on James. "I feel the same as you," she said calmly. "But we cannot afford to let the hate of the past blind us to the needs of the present. If Lilac is to live, we need to send someone with a player's power. If this James wishes to prove himself by saving our child, we should give him a chance."

"A chance to betray us!" cried Lilac's father. "He is unknown, untrustworthy, and dangerous! We don't even need him." He looked proudly up at Arbati. "My son can lead our warriors to victory!"

The crowd began to nod in agreement, and Gray Fang's mouth pressed into a hard line. But though James could see her plotting how best to defend her decision, there was no time to go through all of this again. The sun was already high in the sky, and he owed the elder for taking a chance on him, so before she could say a word, James came to his own defense.

"You *do* need me, because you guys can't win this alone."

Everyone turned to glare at him, and James gulped. It was too late to bail now, though, so he plowed on. "I've done these quests dozens of times. I know every inch of the Red Canyon gnoll village, and I'm telling you, it's not something your warriors can handle. I don't know what the gnolls were like before FFO was a game, but the undead's arrival seriously upped their power level. The Once King's forces have militarized their village into a fortress, given them weapons and armor and magic. Also, with the exception of Arbati, every gnoll in Red Canyon is at least five levels higher than your best warriors. It's just not a fight you can win."

"But you can?" Lilac's father sneered.

James nodded confidently. "Of course I can. I'm a level-eighty player! This is a low-level village in a quiet part of the world, so you've never seen what max-level players can do, but me and my kind have killed dragons and giants and lichs fifty times more powerful than the one beneath Red Canyon. You guys carried me off before I could collect my gear, but I use a staff I took from one of the Once King's own lieutenants. Trust me, I can handle this."

"Ludicrous boasting," Lilac's father said, but he no longer looked so sure. His eyes were full of the same fear James had seen in the crowd when they'd turned on him before: the fear of players. Now as then, it made him feel dirty, but it was also useful, because if he was going to get his chance at saving Windy Lake and gaining his safe haven, he needed every tool he could find.

With that, James reached up to snag a tiny string of lightning magic out of the air. It wasn't enough to make a bolt, but it still filled the square with the crackling of ozone, making the crowd step back. When he was certain they believed in his power, James let the lightning go and put his hand to his chest.

"I understand that you don't trust me," he said quietly. "If I were you, I wouldn't trust me, either. But if you want to save Scout Lilac and all of Windy Lake, you *need* me. I'm not just going to Red Canyon to break a curse. I'm going to wipe out *all* the undead, including the lich who's pulling their strings. Once they're gone, the gnoll menace will be over, and the savanna will finally have peace."

He hadn't actually planned on it, but as he spoke, it dawned on James that he had the power to change an entire zone for the better. His biggest complaint back when this was a game was that questing never actually fixed any of the world's problems. Even if you worked your way through an entire story line, solving every single problem in a zone, it would all go back to how it was the next day when the servers reset. Now that things were real, though, James had the chance to actually make the world a better place! He'd have to fight his way through the gnoll village and the dungeon below it to get to the orb anyway, so why not go for broke? Once he got his gear back, it would be easy for him to do what was impossible for the villagers of Windy Lake. He was getting excited about the prospect of being an *actual* hero for once when Lilac's father sneered.

"Pah," the old cat said. "Big words and long tails. My money's on you winding up as gnoll food, but if you *can* pull it off and save my daughter, I'll sponsor you to the tribes myself."

He said that last part with incredible sarcasm and bitterness, but James started grinning like he'd just won the lottery. "Thank you, sir," he said earnestly. "I'll be happy to hold you to that when I come back."

The old jubatus turned away with a sour look, and Gray Fang sighed. "You'd better get going after all that bragging," she said quietly, motioning to her grandson. "Ar'Bati will go with you to be witness to your trial."

"And to make sure you don't run out on us," the big warrior added, eyeing James suspiciously.

"Fair enough," James said. "But would you mind waiting an hour? I'd like to get my gear back and power through the opening quests that lead to Red Canyon without worrying about being stabbed in the back."

It was meant to be a joke—well, sort of—but Gray Fang and Arbati both gasped as though he'd insulted their ancestors.

"If you wish to join our clan, you must start learning our customs," Gray Fang snapped, wagging a clawed finger at him. "Ar'Bati has not treated you well, I know, but we *do not* accuse tribesmen without proof! Now that I have accepted your petition to join, Ar'Bati will have to treat you with honor, and you likewise for him, so no more foolish words! Lilac has no time for your ignorance."

"Yes, Elder," James said, lowering his eyes. Apparently, scornful grandmother voice was universal.

The old woman nodded curtly and waved him away. "One of the warriors will escort you through town to collect your belongings. Meanwhile, Ar'Bati will prepare runners and gear for the journey to Red Canyon. You can meet him by the lake when you are ready, but *do not* leave without him. He is your witness. Your trial won't count without his say so."

"Yes, Elder," James said again, doing his best to ignore the murderous looks the head warrior kept shooting him. "I'll be right there."

The old cat-lady nodded and walked back into the lodge. Arbati followed her, tail lashing, leaving James alone with the angry-looking young warrior who'd been assigned to babysit him. Thoroughly dismissed, James headed back to his yurt to collect his gear.

As awkward as it was having a cheetah-man stalking behind him, James liked having a guard. It helped minimize the alarm his presence generated in random villagers as they walked through town.

Now that every soul in Windy Lake was no longer packed into the square, James could see how empty the village was. Of the hundreds of white hide yurts that crowded the lake's shore, most looked abandoned. Counting as he walked, James estimated this village was built to house five, maybe even ten times as many jubatus as he saw walking around. The decimated emptiness of the abandoned homes was haunting, especially since he could look inside and see the lives they'd left behind. All the common objects left sitting out, as though their owners had just set them down for a moment and never come back. Worst of all, though, were the jubatus who walked the empty rows, their faces bleak with sorrow for the missing who weren't alive or dead and thus couldn't be mourned, rescued, or buried.

Watching them pace was the saddest thing James had ever seen. He was wondering how it had happened—why these people had vanished instead of becoming town NPCs like Arbati and Gray Fang and everyone else here—when he suddenly remembered just how much bigger the world had gotten the moment it stopped being a game.

Of course. No online role-playing game used a map or population on a real, Earthlike scale. Aside from being way too much work for developers to make, a realistically sized world with a realistic population just didn't make for a fun game. No player wanted to be that insignificant or to have to run that far.

As a questing game in which every inch of the world was important, FFO had been scaled smaller than most. It took only four hours to go from one end of the world to the other on a standard flying mount. No actual planet could be that tiny and support an atmosphere. Now that everything else was real, it made sense that the distances had grown back to realistic lengths as well. Looking at the distant acacia trees shimmering in the morning heat—trees James remembered being right next to the village—he estimated the scale of the landscape had increased by an order of magnitude. A hundred, maybe even a *thousand* times larger than it had been in game. And if the world had been shrunk to fit, why not the population as well?

The implications of that made him shudder. Assuming this world had had a realistic population before the game, a lot of people would have had to be cut when it was scaled down. But while the land had returned, it seemed the people hadn't. James had no idea what happened to them—if they'd died, vanished, or been sent to some other place entirely—but if the population had shrunk on the same scale as the land, then it was possible that ninety percent of the people living here had been obliterated. Forget nightmare—that was apocalyptic, and a good reason for those who survived to hate James and every player like him.

That depressing thought stayed with him all the way back to his yurt. The tent was still empty when they reached it, which James took as proof that its owner was one of the missing. Though sad, it was convenient right now, and James hurried to the backpack he'd dropped when the sensory overload hit, eager to get out of his dirty, bloody clothes and into his lovely enchanted armor. Level advantage aside, he needed the extra power his equipment and weapon provided to make good on his boasting. He was down right now, but once he equipped some proper gear and his weapon, he'd be an unbeatable god, which sounded *very* nice after this morning's humiliation. But as he shoved his hands into his pack, his fingers found nothing.

Cold sweat bloomed over his body. Normally, when he shoved his hand into his bag, the dark space lit up with a grid of pictures showing the items inside. Now, though, no such grid appeared. The thing he'd shoved his hands into was just a sack, a sturdy but perfectly normal cloth backpack. Out of sheer hopeful denial, James waved his hand through the inventory gesture, but just as there was no health bar, mini-map, or shortcuts for his abilities, no window full of loot appeared.

Desperate, James turned his backpack upside down, dumping the sack out in the hope that it was bottomless. A magical bag of holding, or something like that. But other than a pile of carefully packed herbs and a few random coins, nothing fell out. Not his weapons, not one of the three alternate sets of armor he carried at all times. Not even one of his hundreds of carefully collected in-game toys.

James sat back on his legs in disbelief. In hindsight, it made a horrible sort of sense that a single backpack couldn't actually hold multiple full sets of armor, three staffs, one hundred iron bars, two hundred thousand gold coins, four dragon mounts, and so on. What he really couldn't believe was that he hadn't realized the truth sooner. All his boasting, his promises of power—they were worthless without the gear to back them up.

That was what he should have been most worried about, but honestly, the loss just plain *hurt*. The stuff in his backpack wasn't just powerful. It was the product of hundreds of hours of work. Some of those items had taken him months to get. His staff was a literal artifact of legend, one of the few top-tier items he'd scored from the nights Tina had managed to guilt him into raiding. And his mounts! He'd had nearly every rideable animal, machine, kite, ghost, and dragon in the game, and now they were *gone*.

The loss of so much hard work almost brought James to tears. How was he going to achieve anything now? Plan A had been "rain lightning down on gnolls from the back of a flying fire-breathing dragon." There was no Plan B. A level eighty without gear had a lot of health, but damage-wise, he was little better than an NPC. He had no idea how he was going to beat the lich like this, let alone the entire dungeon guarding the lich. Or the town full of gnolls guarding the dungeon. Or the three deadly bosses guarding the town. Or—

"Is there a problem?" the warrior accompanying him asked, poking his head through the tent flap.

"No problem," James said quickly, gulping down his panic as he swept the pile of herbs and coins back into his bag. "I'm ready. Show me to Arbati, please."

His voice shook despite his best efforts, but the warrior didn't seem to notice, or maybe he just didn't care. He just turned on his heel and marched back through the village, leaving James to hurry along behind him.

As they walked, James struggled to pull himself together. There *had* to be some way to get his stuff back. After all, the interface for his abilities was gone, too, but he could still cast spells. Maybe his backpack had a trick to it as well? Some word he could say or motion he could make to send his gear tumbling out. The very ordinary nature of the rucksack on his back didn't give him much hope, though. He couldn't see any glowing lines of magic inside it. Just normal old burlap, and the more he poked it, the more depressed he became.

As promised, Arbati was waiting at the edge of the lake. He had a pack at his waist and a large sword on his back, and he was standing beside two of the most terrifying animals James had ever seen.

Back when this was a game, the jubatus-racial mount had been a beautiful snow leopard that, granted, made absolutely no sense for a bunch of cat-people living in an arid grassland. These animals were entirely different. They looked a bit like a greyhound mixed with a horse, with long, slender bodies, short brown-and-gray mottled fur, graceful legs, and small, sharp hooves. Their necks were ridiculously long for their bodies, and their small heads were almost completely taken up by a set of razor-sharp fangs big enough to bite a jubatus in half. Arbati was fitting a set of reins between the teeth of the larger one when James walked up.

"What in the world are those?"

"Runners," Arbati replied as though he couldn't believe he was having to answer this question. "Don't tell me you can't ride."

It was on the tip of James's tongue to say of course not, but the moment he thought about it, the information came to him. He hadn't even known what the runners were a few seconds ago, but now, somehow, he knew the trick of mounting them from the front side, along with how much food, rest, and water each animal would need. He knew that they would run tirelessly for hours, and spit on you if you annoyed them. James didn't know *how* he knew all of that. It was simply there in his head, just as magic, his knowledge of herbs, and the jubatus language of Wind and Grass had been.

Given that all of those had come from his skills in game, he could only assume this had as well. After all, he'd learned the Master Riding skill years ago back when he'd first hit level fifty. If being an Herbalist in game meant he now knew which plants were poisonous, why shouldn't he know how to ride this animal?

He was about to hop on the mount closest to him when Arbati turned around. "Wait," the warrior said, grabbing his arm. "Where's your fancy armor? Players normally dress like they're going to a costume party, but you look the same."

For a frantic moment, James considered making up an excuse before he realized how stupid that was. Whatever story he told, his gear was still gone. Might as well come clean now before Arbati saw the truth of his new uselessness in the field and cut his throat for lying.

"It's gone," he said, shrugging helplessly.

Arbati went still. "What?"

"I don't have my stuff," James explained. "Everything was in my backpack when I logged out, but whatever brought me here must have destroyed the magics that stored it, because it's not here anymore."

For a several heartbeats, the warrior stared at him in disbelief. Then he threw James to the ground. "You liar!"

"I wasn't lying!" James said, scrambling back to his feet. "I really did think it was all there!"

"How are we going to save Lilac now?" Arbati yelled over him. "What do you intend to do? Talk the gnolls to death?"

"I'm still level eighty!" James yelled back. "That's a lot higher than you!"

"Gnollshit!" Arbati snapped. "You couldn't even defend yourself against the people in the square! You told us you would be an unbeatable demon, but *I* could kill you right now." He shook his head in disgust. "I should leave you here to rot."

"I can still cast spells," James said angrily. "And I'm the only one who knows the quests."

"There are no more quests, *player!*" Arbati spat at him. "The only thing you'll be good for is bait!" He growled a moment longer then reached down to grab the long knife from his belt. "Here," he said, throwing it at James. "If you must come, at least try to die while stabbing a gnoll."

James caught the dagger reflexively then stared at it in wonder. The Naturalist class wasn't supposed to be able to equip bladed weapons. In FFO, he'd been physically unable to hold a dagger, but he didn't seem to have a problem now. The short knife had no enchantments or special properties, which made it total crap by FFO standards, but it wasn't as though he had anything better. Arbati would probably take it as an insult if he tried to give it back, anyway, so James meekly tucked the dagger into his belt, lowering his head respectfully.

"Thank you, Head Warrior Arbati."

The tall warrior grunted and hopped onto his mount then slapped the reins to send the runner dashing down the road, leaving James coughing in a cloud of dust. Clearing his throat, James turned to climb onto his own animal, taking care to stay clear of the runner's sharp fangs. He was settling his new body onto the thin padded blanket that served as a saddle when it suddenly occurred to James that he could still run.

They were at the edge of the village, on the bank of the lake, where the water met the open sky and endless golden grass of the savanna. His mount was just as fast as Arbati's, and the head warrior had already started down the western road. If James made a break for the north, there was a good chance he could get away. Arbati was on a timeline, and he thought James was useless now, anyway. If he ran, the warrior might not even give chase. James wouldn't have to face the consequences of just how badly he'd screwed them all over with promises of power he could no longer deliver.

For a tantalizing second, the prospect of escape was impossibly tempting. Even with the new distances, the capital city of Bastion couldn't be more than a week's ride away. If there were other players like him trapped here, that was where they'd be. And the bank! His inventory might be gone, but the bank in Bastion would certainly still be around. He had tons of spare gear in there, including his raiding set. He could get his power back! All he had to do was get to the city.

He'd actually turned his mount toward the north road when shame washed over him like a hot tide. What was he thinking? He always did this. He *always* ran away. He could almost hear Tina's accusing voice in his ears, calling him a coward, and she was right. Gear or no gear, he was still level eighty. He might not be the all-powerful force he was used to being in these low-level zones, but he was still miles more effective than Arbati or any of his warriors, and he'd *promised* to help save Windy Lake. If he backed out now, what did that make him?

A coward, Tina's voice repeated in his head. *And a liar.*

Cursing himself, James yanked his runner back toward the western road. "Arbati!" he yelled, kicking the animal to a gallop. "Wait up!"

■ ■

An hour later, James had never been happier that he'd chosen to do the right thing.

On a ground mount, going by standard FFO mount speeds, Red Canyon should have been fifteen minutes away. But they'd been galloping for over an hour now, and they were barely past the first set of hills. The brown-and-tan savanna surrounded them like a sea, a thousand times larger than it had been in the game. If he'd tried to make a break for Bastion, he'd have been hopelessly lost by now in the endless rolling grass.

At least the ride itself was fun. Arbati refused to speak to him, and their speed meant dust was constantly blasting him in the face, forcing James to pull his shirt up over his nose to keep the grit out of his lungs. But neither the dust nor the sour company could shadow the sheer joy that was being on a runner.

Despite their long legs, the strange mounts ran much lower than a horse. The runners practically flew down the road as the ground rushed by less than a foot below his feet. He had to crouch low over the beast to stay streamlined, but the pose made him feel like he was racing a motorcycle down the highway. The sheer physical joy of riding was completely unexpected and the first nice thing that had happened to James since he'd come here. He just wished it weren't the only one.

Whenever they rode past a crossroads or a hut, James looked for other players. Every time he failed to spot one, the feeling of being utterly alone grew sharper. He told himself there was no reason to panic. The savanna had been a big zone even back when this was a game. It made sense he'd have trouble finding people now that it was even bigger. Still, James couldn't shake the feeling that if there *were* other players out here, they were probably in a lot more trouble than he was. He'd had the advantage of being alone in a nice safe yurt when the transition hit. Going through that same sensory hell out here in the wilderness where anything could attack you would be another story entirely.

He was still cycling between enjoying the ride and worrying himself sick when his nose caught the smell of smoke. Looking at the horizon, James spotted a dingy column shimmering in the hazy air. As they got closer, a sickly-sweet odor of decay joined the acrid smell of woodsmoke. The combination was enough to make his fur stand on end, especially when he spotted the vultures floating on the thermals above the smoke.

Fifteen minutes later, they were close enough for James to make out the blackened shapes of two covered wagons by the roadside. Arbati kept their speed up to make a fast approach. Or at least that was what James assumed he was doing until Arbati blew right past the wagons without a glance.

"Arbati! Stop!" James shouted, pulling up on his reins.

The warrior turned his own mount around with a fierce scowl. "Why? We have no time for this!"

"We need to see if anyone needs help," James said, hopping down. "This used to be the quest hub for the Crazy Schtumple Brothers."

"Why do you care?"

"I don't know," James snapped. "Maybe because searching for survivors is the right thing to do? The Schtumple Brothers were good people, and there might be other players here." He started poking through the charred wreckage of the first wagon. "If anyone's still alive, it's my duty to help them. I *am* a healer."

"No," Arbati said with scorn. "You *played* a healer, just like you're *playing* with my sister's life by wasting our time!"

James glared at him. "How would you feel if you were dying in the grass and the only two people who could save you just ran by because they wouldn't spare five minutes?"

"That would be the last eighty years of my life!" the warrior roared, making his runner rear. "Where was your mercy, *player*, when I was trapped in the Nightmare? Doomed to be captured, tortured, and killed every single day only to rise and do it all again every sunrise? Countless players ran by me without a care!"

"So that makes *this* okay?" James said angrily. "No one saved you, so screw everyone else?"

"You are not in charge here, player," the warrior growled. "I am. You lied to Elder Gray Fang about your powers, and now your life rests in my hands. You will do as I say if you wish to survive, and *I* say we have no time to spend looking for the corpses of stupid, lazy, greedy, cheating Schtumples who were obviously killed by gnolls."

"You can't just write them off because they're Schtumples!"

"Again, you show your ignorance," Arbati said with a sneer. "All Schtumples are conniving, selfish liars. I would kill them myself if I caught them on our lands. Thankfully, the gnolls saved me the trouble this time, so we are moving on."

James turned away in disgust, focusing on digging through the charred wreckage so he wouldn't have to look at the warrior's hateful face.

Unfortunately, it looked as though Arbati was right about that last part. Just like in the game, this place was a small merchant camp with a semi-permanent fire pit flanked by two large, colorfully painted covered wagons. There was a makeshift hitching post off to the side, but no beasts of burden were tethered to it. James found plenty of arrows stuck or broken against the blackened sides of the wagons, as well as gnoll paw prints in the dirt, but no bodies, living or otherwise. He was about to check the tall grass around the camp when he heard Arbati start to growl.

"No," James said before the warrior could hurl whatever insult he was thinking of this time. "We've already spent more time arguing about this than it's taken me to search. I just need a few more minutes, so why don't you just sit there and think of how you can be a bigger racist asshole."

A deadly silence fell over the road, and James knew he'd gone too far. He began to search more quickly, desperate to cover as much ground as possible before Arbati came over to drag him back to his mount. He was frantically pushing the waist-high grass aside when he spotted a pack of black buzzards eating something behind the first wagon.

James ran over, scattering the birds...and was almost sick on the spot. The chopped-up, half-eaten remains of the two Schtumple Brothers lay like empty sacks in the bloody grass. The first had been split open with an ax, his squashed pug-like face cracked right down the middle between his round, wide-set eyes. The other Schtumple had been shot with arrows until his round body looked like a pincushion.

Both were long dead, their bodies pecked apart by scavengers, but James began to cast his Raise Ally spell anyway. Dead didn't really mean dead in FFO. If he could bring back players who'd been dissolved in pools of acid or drowned in lava, then this was nothing. As he pulled the mana together, though, he discovered that there was nothing in the Schtumples' bodies for it to latch onto. Their corpses were inert, no more resurrectable than a door would have been. If it hadn't been for the horrible stench of death, he wouldn't have known they'd ever been alive. He was about to try to force the spell into them anyway, just so he could say he'd tried, when the iron clap of Arbati's hand landed on his shoulder.

"You do not get to speak to me like that, player," the warrior growled, whirling James around.

James glared right back. "If you don't want to be called an asshole," he said through clenched teeth, "don't *be* an asshole."

The warrior raised his arm to backhand him across the face for that, but James ducked away. "Oh, hell no," he said, ripping away from

Arbati's grip. "I'm not letting you hit me anymore."

"Like you get a choice," Arbati replied, advancing on him.

James took another step back, eyes going wide. Was the jubatus really going to fight him here? *Now?* They were on their way to the enemy's camp. There was no room in the plan for beating each other up beforehand.

But as he opened his mouth to tell Arbati he was being a moron, James realized that everything he was about to say applied to him as well. The warrior wasn't the only one turning on his allies. James had insulted him, too, and while that didn't excuse what Arbati was doing—or what he'd said—fighting him back now made James just as bad.

With that, James changed his footing, bracing his legs in the tall grass as he let Arbati close in and deck him across the face. The punch was strong enough to knock him flat back on the ground, but while his head was left spinning, his pride hurt more than anything else as he put up his hands in surrender.

"Okay, okay, I'm sorry," he said, forcing the words out. "But we don't have time to fight each other. Lilac is counting on us."

For a second, it looked as if the head warrior was going to hit him again anyway. But he must have cared more about his sister than taking out his anger on James, because a moment later, he dropped his fist.

"Let this be a warning, player," he said, stabbing his finger at James's face. "You only continue to live by my mercy alone. You would do well to remember your place."

"Understood," James said bitterly, but the word met Arbati's back as the cat-warrior stalked across the burned camp to the road. With a final look at the poor dead Schtumples, James followed, pulling himself onto his runner without a word. The moment he was mounted, Arbati took off, leaving the remains of the Crazy Schtumple Brothers' camp smoking in the hot sun behind them.

■ ■

The next five hours was a different repeating cycle of anger at Arbati and self-blame at his own poor handling of things at the camp. After all, James had been in the right. Arbati was the one being a racist rage-junkie. He should have stood up to the warrior, but there was no undoing it now. At least Arbati had kept his mouth shut, riding in angry silence as the sun sank lower and lower in the sky.

By the time it touched the tall hills in the distance, James had something new to worry about. Dark would be on them in less than an hour, and they weren't even in sight of the Red Canyon village yet. They had to be at least fifty miles from the Windy Lake by now. The road had turned from a nicely paved, if slightly overgrown, path to a wagon-rutted dirt track. They still cleared it with amazing speed, but it didn't seem to be doing any good. Every time he looked around, all James saw was grass, grass, and more grass dotted with the occasional squat grove of trees. There was no sign of the low, rocky hills that ringed Red Canyon or the smoke that would rise from a militarized town full of smithies. He didn't even hear the sounds of a village. Just the empty howl of the wind in the grass, blowing for miles in every direction.

James gripped his reins tighter. His theory that the world had returned to its original size had been well proven by this point, but as they rode deeper into the wilderness, he was beginning to worry that scale wasn't the only thing that had changed. Maybe locations had been rearranged as well when this place ceased to be an environment whose only purpose was keeping gamers entertained. The rolling grassland made it easy to miss things, too. The hills surrounding Red Canyon were high compared to the rest of the savanna, but it would only take being off by a few miles in either direction to ride right past the village without ever knowing.

James's worries became suddenly short-term, however, when a volley of arrows screamed out of the tall grass from his right. Bolts peppered his runner from head to flank, and the animal went down with a bloody scream, sending James flying head over heels off its back.

He twisted instinctively in the air, landing on all fours in the dirt road. Ahead of him, he heard the scream of Arbati's runner going down as well. He turned to see the warrior trapped beneath his dying mount. Arbati shoved the animal off with frightening strength, rolling to his feet to face the wave of gnolls that was now pouring out of the grass on either side.

Howling their battle cry from dozens of throats, the short, hairy, hyena-like creatures charged with axes raised high. Most went for Arbati, but six of the muscular dog-men split off to attack James, running at him with black eyes bright with bloodlust.

James shot to his feet. Snagging a fistful of his mana, he used it to grab the ever-present streams of magical light floating around him. Weaving air and earth together, he made a conduit between the ground and sky before unleashing it in a massive blast of lightning.

Back in the game, chain lightning had been a satisfyingly dramatic spell with shots of white lightning arcing between targets like a Jacob's ladder. Now, there was only a flash and a thunder crack followed by the stench of burning fur as four gnolls fell dead in their tracks. The remaining two fearlessly charged forward, raising their axes to attack.

James stared dumbly at the gleaming weapons. Logically, he knew this should be an easy fight for him. He had fifty levels and an entire foot on his attackers, but that didn't seem to matter to his body. Now that his one big shot of lightning was gone, every part of him understood that this was now a life-or-death situation and panicked accordingly.

Thankfully, decades of martial arts held up when his brain could not. James caught the first gnoll's ax handle before he realized his hand had moved, twisting it sideways to send its owner flying into the dirt. The second gnoll swung hard at his left, but when James reached out to grab his wrist, his arm refused to move that way. He must have landed on it wrong when he'd been thrown from the runner, he realized, but it was too late to switch up. The gnoll's ax had already bitten into his arm, sending burning pain deep into his bicep as blood went everywhere.

James screamed. Gasping from the shock, he wrenched his arm away from the gnoll's ax, using his free hand to clutch the wound, which had already soaked his sleeve in red. But as terrifying as the pain of the cut itself was, what terrified James even more was the numb chill he could feel spreading out from the wound like water through his flesh. The blade must have been poisoned, he realized, heart pounding. Maybe with the same cursed poison that had crippled Lilac.

Desperate and terrified, James fell back. Letting go of his wound, he used his good hand to grab a few lines of amber earth magic and spun them around the feet of the gnoll who'd chopped him. As soon as he released the spell, a massive hand made of rocks rose up from the road to engulf his target, leaving only a brown paw poking out from between the fingers.

Barking in anger, the remaining gnoll raised its ax over its head with both hands. James rolled to a knee, managing to catch the gnoll's paws in his hand. Since he was much taller than the creature, he surged to his feet, carrying the hyena-man right off the ground.

It yowled as he lifted it, snapping at his face with his fangs, but James barely noticed. He was too busy marveling at how he'd been able to lift what had to be a hundred fifty pounds of scraggly, beady-eyed gnoll one-handed.

In the back of his head, he realized this was likely because he was level eighty. Even though he was a caster, his base strength would still be four to five times higher than the average level-one human. Scared for his life and soaked in adrenaline, he reveled in the power. Ripping the ax from the gnoll's hands, James dropped the creature into a knee strike before throwing it to the ground. It yelped in pain as it crashed into the road, clutching its stomach where his knee had dug in. Grabbing its dropped weapon, James took advantage of its shock to bring the stolen hatchet down right in the middle of the terrified gnoll's snout.

The curved blade landed with a sickening crunch. Hot blood and bits of bone went flying as his victim screamed and went still.

One enemy down and the other trapped in a fist of rock, James turned his attention to casting a cleansing spell. It was hard to do with only one working arm, especially since this was not a condition he'd had to deal with in normal FFO. This was a spell he'd cast countless times in the game, though, and the ingrained habit carried him through. As the cooling magic landed, the terrifying numbness in his arm vanished, leaving only the normal burn of pain.

Immediate death avoided, James let out his held breath and looked around for his enemies. When he laid eyes on the gnoll he'd axed, though, his stomach churned so hard he was almost sick.

The gnoll's face was bisected down the center by the ax, but it wasn't dead. It was still twitching under the ax, whimpering with a whine that cut straight to the quick of him. Heart pounding, James grabbed the knife Arbati had given him with a shaking hand. It was technically unnecessary—the gnoll would be dead soon enough—but letting it lie there suffering was too cruel for James to bear. But when he leaned down to slit its throat, the knife fell from his shaking fingers into the bloody mud of the road.

"What am I doing?"

Normally, James loved fighting. He enjoyed good combat in normal and full-sensory VR games. He liked it in real life, too, so long as protective gear and a dojo were involved. After spending thousands of hours fighting in this game, sparring in gyms, and going to competitions, he'd never even considered that actual violence would be a problem for him if he ever found himself in a life-or-death situation. Now, though, with bodies everywhere and blood all over his hands, all James could see was what he'd done.

The gnoll whimpered at his feet, sending up bloody bubbles as it struggled to breathe through its destroyed face. Watching it try so desperately to live broke James's heart. *He'd* done that. The start of this battle had been out of control. He hadn't thought before he'd thrown his lightning, and now there were four smoking corpses on the ground. Corpses *he'd* made.

As the iron reek of gnoll blood filled his nose, the reality of what was actually happening here hit James like a sucker punch. These weren't computer-generated monsters anymore. They were real, as alive as James or the jubatus or anything else in this world. They had families, or maybe packs, but the exact terminology wasn't important. What *was* important was that someone was going to miss this gnoll when it didn't come home from its patrol. If no one found its body, this gnoll's friends and family could be left wondering about its fate for years, never knowing why it hadn't returned.

James closed his eyes with a curse. He knew he was being an idiot, but he couldn't take the possibility that he'd orphaned some gnoll pup today. Pulling bright-blue mana from himself, he wove together the vibrant-green life magics of the grasslands and laid them across the dying gnoll's body, wrapping it in a verdant cocoon as he released the spell.

Marvelous green light bathed the dusty road, and the gnoll's sundered face started to reconstruct itself. Watching it, James nearly lost his lunch. It was one thing to see this stuff in a movie, but actually being present for bones and flesh knitting back together was almost too gross for him to take.

Fighting not to barf, he heard a cracking noise as his earthen hand spell from earlier finally ran out of magic and began to crumble. Shaking off the nausea, James forced himself to pick up Arbati's knife with his good hand. To do what, though, he couldn't say. After what had just happened, killing anything else felt forever off the table.

To his left, the magical light of the healing spell finally faded, and the gnoll he'd almost killed got up. It touched its paws to its healed

121

face in wonder, then it grabbed its fallen ax and yelped at its buddy. The two gnolls barked and whined at each other for several seconds, eyeing James the entire time. They were both distracted, leaving James a prime opening to attack with his knife, but he didn't move. Instead, he stood there, staring at the gnolls until, with a final bark, they both turned tail and ran, vanishing into the tall grass as swiftly and silently as rabbits.

James could have collapsed from the relief, but he didn't have time. Up the road, Arbati was still under attack. James was about to go help him when the warrior beheaded the last gnoll, roaring like a lion as the hyena-man's head bounced across the rutted dirt road. It was still rolling when Arbati whirled on James.

"*You traitor!*" he bellowed. "I knew you couldn't be—" The warrior's rampage was cut off as he fell to the ground, his body shaking violently as white foam began to froth from his open mouth.

"Shit!" James ran to the seizing warrior's side. One look at the energies flowing through Arbati's body confirmed that the arrow still stuck in Arbati's leg was indeed poisoned. He didn't see any of the black death magic that had covered Lilac's wound, or the cinders of the ghostfire, but the poison would still kill him if James didn't act fast.

Arbati's lips were turning gray when James jammed his knife handle into the warrior's mouth to stop the jubatus's sharp teeth from puncturing his tongue. When he was sure the warrior wouldn't choke, he frantically attempted another cleansing spell. His right arm was still an aching, bleeding mess, so he had to grit his teeth and do it one-handed. Again.

He botched his first attempt due to his nervous shaking. Seedlings of grass started to sprout around them as wasted nature and water magics spilled on the ground. The second casting held together, though, flowing through Arbati like a gentle stream as James swept the poison out of his blood and into the ground.

Arbati's violent shaking stopped the moment the poison was gone, but the head warrior didn't wake up. Nervous, James checked the jubatus's breathing and pulse. Both felt fine, or at least what he assumed was fine for jubatus anatomy, and his life energy was still strong and bright despite the blood loss.

Satisfied Arbati wouldn't die in the immediate future, James slumped to the ground against the body of his dead runner. For several minutes, all he could do was stare at the four blackened corpses his lightning had made. Even with the constant wind off the savanna, the foul smell of charred flesh and burned fur hung over the road like a judgment, twisting his stomach into knots. He would have sat there forever if the terrible ache of his arm hadn't forced him back to the present.

The wave of dizziness when he looked down reminded James that he was still seriously bleeding. When he examined his bicep, though, all he found was a deep gash, which made no sense. He'd been struck head on with an ax at the end of a two-handed swing. The gnolls weren't weak. That blow should have shattered his bone and sinews, leaving his arm useless, but James could still move his fingers just fine. Other than blood loss and the pain of the cut itself, he'd taken almost no damage. Lifting his arm, he marveled at the bright, colorful energies he could see inside his body. Until he saw how those same beautiful green, gold, and blue flows were leaking out of his arm onto the ground.

"Shit," James muttered, quickly pulling together more life magic. As the green glow blossomed across his right side, he was almost blown away by the euphoria. The moment the healing magic touched him, the whole world grew brighter, smelled better, and sounded clearer. All the pain was gone, leaving only a perfect feeling of rightness and contentment. It was easily the best high he'd ever had, and James lost himself in it for the entire twelve seconds the spell lasted.

As the green magic faded, the world returned to its normal burnt-hair-and-sticky-blood smells. His arm still ached, but he wasn't bleeding anymore. Just deeply bruised. Still, James was amazed by the spell's effectiveness. Without his gear, it should barely have done anything. Of course, without his gear, James had a tiny health pool, which meant tiny spells would work on him just fine.

"A dollar is a feast for a beggar," he muttered, rubbing his arm.

Of everything left over from the game, James was most grateful for strong healing spells. Thinking back on the battle, he wondered if he was stuck in the Naturalist's healing specialization. It was impossible to tell without the interface, but being a full healer would explain why he only had one offensive lightning spell and why it took so much of his mana to use. That was fine with him, though. Having no good attack magics sucked, but James would take healing abilities over lightning any day, especially since this battle had confirmed that he could now fight with whatever weapon he could pick up.

That thought made him smile. James didn't want to go around axing people—especially not after what had happened with the gnoll—but being able to defend himself in hand-to-hand combat was a game changer. He might not be much of a spell-slinger, but James had been practicing martial arts since he was a kid. His character was much stronger than he'd been back in the real world, too, though James wasn't sure how that strength stacked up here. Arbati, for example, was clearly *much* stronger than he was. Still, it felt good to know he had options.

Thinking about Arbati made James look down at his companion. The huge cat-warrior was lying on his back in the dirt, completely out. Part of James wanted to leave him that way, but as dearly as he would have loved to ditch the hate-fueled jerk, he'd vowed to kill the lich at Red Canyon, and as a gearless healer, there was no way he was pulling that off without Arbati.

With a grimace, James started weaving more healing spells around himself and his abusive chaperon. Flourishes of green light and vibrant euphoria filled James again and again as the pain was washed away. As glorious as it all was, he was still grossed out watching arrows remove themselves and seeing bloody gashes regenerate, but at least he didn't feel the need to barf again.

Eventually, his mana ran out. He was trying to gauge if he'd managed to heal them enough when Arbati's eyes snapped open, locking on James with a look of pure, furious hate.

"You filthy traitor."

CHAPTER 7

Tina

"**B**ring it and see, cunt."

There wasn't much to say after that. Tina raised her shield and charged the Berserker, whose name she still didn't know. He lifted his ax to meet her, bracing his feet in the dusty road. They met with a crash like two trains colliding. Tina's charge was as powerful as a big rig, but Berserkers wore a lot more Strength gear than she did, and it showed. He met her charge with a swing of his ax directly into her shield, throwing her off balance with raw power.

As she struggled to keep her guard up, Tina saw the other players forming a circle around them. The nearest was only about fifteen feet to her right. She hoped they had the sense to move back. The last thing she needed was for someone's arm to get chopped off by accident, but she had no attention to spare worrying about bystanders. She had to look out for herself, ducking behind her massive shield as the Berserker swung for her head.

His excessive strength made his oversize weapon much quicker than it should have been. The seven-foot ax came at her lightning fast, and as polished as Tina's parry skills were, she still wasn't quick enough. Her shield came up a split second too late, allowing the club-sized butt of his giant ax to slip over its edge and slam into the side of her head.

Tina's skull rang as her vision went blurry. By pure luck and years of battle instinct, she turned her shield to the right in time to block the next strike, but the Berserker was roaring now, his eyes flashing red as he began hammering on her with his weapon like he was trying to pound her into the dirt.

The ring of steel was constant and deafening. Tina took most of the hits on her giant shield, but his ax nailed her across the shoulder at least twice, leaving two huge gouges in her three-inch-thick shoulder plates. It was a terrifying reminder that players did a lot more damage than normal monsters, but his constant attacks meant she had no chance to strike back without risking her defense.

But taking damage was what Tina did. She'd never bothered with PVP back when FFO was a game, which meant she had zero experience fighting other players, but the habits and instincts she'd honed over years of tanking came to her rescue. As soon as the damage started leaking through, Tina drew strength from the stones at her feet and put it into her body just as she'd done against the skeletons. The stonekin's Earthen Fortitude ability hardened her whole being with the toughness of the Bedrock Kings, turning her normally glowing magical armor and bright-copper hair as gray as the stone at her feet.

This didn't stop the Berserker's ax from falling. At least the blows only dinged her now instead of gouging, but even though he was doing no damage, he kept the onslaught up. Even after his red-glowing eyes returned to normal, he just kept hacking away at her as though he was trying to hew down a tree.

"GG, Care Bear!" he taunted, slamming his ax down on her stone head. "You blew that ability way too early! We're just getting started!"

Inside her shell of rock, Tina huffed. He was right. Earthen Fortitude's long cooldown meant it couldn't be used in rapid succession, and it only lasted for six seconds. It was also as obvious as hell, which meant the moment it started to fade, her opponent knew. The Berserker's eyes gleamed in delight as the last of the dull bedrock color faded from her armor, and he swung his ax high over his head for a downward chop. Watching it fall, Tina cursed silently. The bastard clearly knew about the half second when Earthen Fortitude ended but she still couldn't fully move. What he didn't know, though, was that full movement wasn't necessary. Since Tina had frozen with her shield up, all she had to do was lift her arm a few inches higher to catch his big attack square in the center of her bulwark.

The impact vibrated all the way down to her feet, but her shield was a rare drop from Grel'Darm the Colossal's bonus chest, which only became available during certain achievements. It was the best in the game, and the Berserker's giant ax bounced off it like a pinball. Cursing, he tried a hooking strike at her right side next. Tina turned to meet it with her sword, but the attack was a feint. The moment she moved, he spun the ax in his hands like it didn't weigh a hundred damn pounds, reversing the strike to smack her hand with the butt of the weapon.

The blow stung like hell. If Tina hadn't had metal for bones, it would have crushed her hand, gauntlet or no. But while her fingers weren't broken, the attack still made her hand go numb, causing her sword to slip from weakened fingers.

The blade landed on the road at her feet with a ringing clatter, the red runes on its edge shining angrily through the dust. Her first instinct was to dive down to pick it up again, but Tina knew better than to take her eyes off her opponent. She backed up instead, circling to avoid backing into the cheering players behind her.

The moment she started to retreat, the Berserker roared again, his eyes flashing red. Tina had never played a Berserker, so she couldn't remember exactly what that ability did, but it had been bad news the last time he'd used it, and she didn't have Earthen Fortitude this time. Desperate and weaponless, she braced both hands behind her shield and rushed him for a shield slam. She was just hoping to knock him off balance and waste his cooldown, so she was surprised when the impact knocked the six-foot-six human right off his feet, sending him flying several yards across the road before landing on his back.

Tina blinked in amazement. Shield Slam had never done anything like that in the game. Now that real physics was involved, though, it made sense. Humans—even giant muscle-bound idiots like this one— were hundreds of pounds lighter than a stonekin. Add in her armor and door-sized shield, and Roxxy was a freight train. No wonder the guy had been sent flying. He wouldn't stay down for long, though.

Across the road, the Berserker was already rolling back to his feet. Cursing herself for getting distracted, Tina took what was left of the opening she'd made to dive for her sword. She grabbed it just as her opponent stood up, and they started circling each other. Tina was sure he was just buying time for his stun and disarm abilities to refresh so he could do all of that to her again, but she had no idea how to stop him. Everything she had—her abilities, her gear, even her weapon— was designed to let her take damage, not dish it out. She had to figure something out quickly, though. Even she couldn't defend forever, and if she didn't figure out how to turn this fight around soon, she wouldn't be able to at all.

■ ■

SilentBlayde was having a hard time watching Roxxy get her

ass kicked. He shifted anxiously from foot to foot, his hands white-knuckled on the hilts of his blades, but he couldn't do anything. This was Tina's duel. If he tried to help, he'd do more harm than good.

It was a shame, too, because he could have ended this in seconds. As was appropriate for a highly geared and good-looking Assassin such as himself, SB had done a *lot* of player-versus-player. Tina, however, had not. It was the only part of FFO that she hated, so he'd never pushed. Watching her get chewed up now, though, SB deeply regretted all those times he'd let her turn down his invitations to fight in the arenas.

The Berserker—a player SB knew was named Killbox, though he didn't remember much else—was actually pretty good. He'd opened with a stun, then he'd used his most damaging ability, Frenzied Strikes, while she couldn't defend properly. Finally, just when Roxxy had been about to recover her defense, Killbox had disarmed her. It was a textbook player-versus-player takedown, and Tina was falling for it like a newbie.

"She's gonna die," NekoBaby said beside him, biting her lip with her sharp cat teeth. When Killbox's ax took another chunk out of Roxxy's armor, the Naturalist squeaked. "That's it. I'm healing her."

"Don't," SB said sharply, grabbing her staff.

"Why not?" Neko hissed.

"Because if you heal Roxxy, it's going to undermine her whole point here. Worse, if you heal Roxxy, then someone sympathetic to Killbox will heal him."

NekoBaby bristled. "You think I can't out-heal Anders or David? Just 'cause my robe is busted doesn't mean I'm gimped. Can't loot skillz!"

"That's not it," SB said, nodding at the circle of players watching the fight, a good number of whom were cheering for Killbox, not Roxxy. "If you heal her, and someone else heals him, what's to stop others from taking sides as well? This whole thing could dissolve into a brawl if people start jumping in."

"Like him?" the jubatus healer asked, flicking her ears toward the other side of the circle.

SB looked where Neko's ears were pointing. Sure enough, on the opposite side of the fight, one of their clerics, a Roughneck named David, was quietly gathering golden light in his hands.

"Yeah, like him," SilentBlayde said quietly. "Be right back."

With that, he stepped down into the shadows at their feet. It was a strange feeling. The dark was cold and slick, like jumping into a pool of crude oil. He wasn't entirely comfortable with it. The Assassin class's ability to move through the Lightless Realm had always been questionable. He often heard things whispering as he walked on the opposite side of the light. Back when this was a game, SB had always assumed they were just ambient sound effects to make sneaking through shadows feel more dangerous and mysterious. But things were real now, and the whispers were still there, making him distinctly on edge as he walked through the shadowy reflection of the world.

The fight was below his feet now, the duelists' movements moving below him like reflections in dark water. Time was distorted on this side, letting him watch Roxxy block a hit from Killbox's ax in slow motion. He breathed a sigh a relief as the blade slid off her shield before turning back to his goal.

His target was a short, blue-scaled ichthyian fish-man. David was a friend under other circumstances, and a long-time raider in their guild. But while SB usually enjoyed playing with him, the Cleric was famous for being a first-rate troll. He was at it again now, his bulging fish eyes locked on Killbox's wide back as he gathered golden magic for his healing spell. SB wasn't sure if David was planning to heal the Berserker out of legitimate sympathy or just to screw with Roxxy, but either way, he couldn't allow this to continue.

David's spell was almost complete when SB stepped out of the shadows behind him and pressed his sword against the Cleric's back, the blade sliding discreetly under the fish-man's white-and-gold cloak to rest between his shoulder blades. Blue scales shimmered as his target jumped in surprise, but SB's other hand had already grabbed his arm, pinning him in place.

"You're casting that healing spell for the blisters on your feet right?" he whispered in David's ear hole. "Because I know you aren't thinking of doing something so unfair as to heal Killbox."

David lowered his glowing hands with a sigh. "When did you become Roxxy's dog, 'Blayde?" he asked, glancing over his shoulder. "This is sad, even for you."

"I'm not anyone's dog," SB replied calmly. "I just don't want to die. Are you not also a fan of this survival thing? Because getting in on this fight is a fast way to get us all killed."

"Come on, man," David whined. "Roxxy's always been bossy, but these last few hours have been ridiculous."

"She's trying to keep us alive," SilentBlayde snapped. "That's kind of hard to do when the rest of you aren't taking this seriously."

"She's the one who needs to be taken down a notch," the Cleric snorted. "She's a guild leader, not the president."

"Just let the magic go, dude," SB said, pressing his blade a little harder into the fish-man's back. "Don't make me use my interrupt. You're not gonna like it."

David gave him a dirty look. "Threats? Really? You two are out of control, trying to ride herd on everyone. This drill sergeant shit would never fly normally."

SB flinched. That remark hit too close for comfort. Maybe it was the undead army nipping at their heels, but SB had been feeling increasingly desperate ever since they'd gotten here, and increasingly impatient with people who didn't understand the reality of their new situation. He was actually feeling surprisingly willing to stab David to teach him a lesson about screwing around. A very alarming urge since, although he played an Assassin, SB didn't think of himself as a violent or demanding person.

"I know we've been hard," he said. "But it's for your own good. I could sneak my way out of this zone no problem, but I'm not going to because I want us *all* to get out alive. Why do you think I've been sticking around for all this?"

He'd meant to imply that he was staying to help his friends and fellow players, but David started to chuckle. "I know why," he said in a sleazy voice. "You can't run because you've got a crush on Roxxy. You've always had the hots for her, and now that we all have bodies with working bits and pieces, you're hoping you can finally score."

By the time he finished, SilentBlayde's face was burning. Thankfully, his mask hid most of it, and he covered up the rest by stabbing a little harder into David's back. "Nice try, but what I really want is to ride into Bastion like a boss so I've got a better chance at landing some of those amazing elf chicks. Being at the head of a raid like this is a good start."

"Bullshit," David said, grinning like there wasn't a sword poking into his vertebrae. "Don't even try, man. Everyone in the guild knows you've had it bad for Roxxy for years. You never even look at other girls. You've passed on every single blind-date dungeon group I ever invited you to!"

"That's because you can't know how many of those 'girls' aren't guys."

"First, they were vetted to be real, and you knew it," David said testily. "Second, the same could be said about all those supposed 'elf chicks' in Bastion, except now we have no way of figuring out which hoes are bros and which bros are hoes. Even if we *could* tell, you'd never do more than look. You're caught on Roxxy hook, line, and sinker. I've seen the videos you guys make together, the ones where you show people how to beat bosses and shit. You must put twenty hours a week into those things for her. No one does that much work for free. I know she doesn't pay you because she's always broke, so there has to be something else."

He finished with a suggestive wiggle of his eye-ridges, and SB looked away with a wince. This was his least favorite topic. David knew it, too, which meant he'd never let it go. Once he had your weakness, he held onto it like a pit bull. As annoying as that was, though, it also gave SB an idea. It would mean putting a target on his own back, but the golden healing magic was still floating around David's hands. If he wanted to distract the Cleric from messing with Roxxy, he had to give him someone better to troll.

"Fine," he said, heaving a huge sigh that was only partially for show. "You got me, dude. I like Roxxy, and I've finally got my chance, so would you *please* stop messing it up for me?"

The fish-man's face transformed into the devil's own piranha smile. "No worries, man," he said, letting the magic go at last. "It was totally worth it to get you to finally admit that you like her. Just don't be getting too high and mighty on your quest to get laid, Mr. Right-Hand-Man. Oh, and you owe me one for making you look good."

"Sure," SB said, sheathing his sword. "Just don't tell anyone else, okay?"

"Of course," David said, running his webbed fingers over his robes as he crossed his heart.

From the way the fish-man's round eyes were sparkling, SB was certain the whole raid would know his secret within the hour. Just thinking about that made him want to crawl under a rock and die, but Tina was still fighting, so he slipped back into the shadows instead, moving through the crowd in case anyone else decided to be a dick.

The fight had gone on for way too long.

Tina and the Berserker circled each other on the broken road. She'd managed to avoid taking serious damage, but her head still throbbed from the stun attack earlier, and her chest plate had some new ventilation. Beneath the metal, her front was drenched with silvery blood from all the smaller cuts he'd landed. The only reason it wasn't worse was because the Berserker kept striking at her heavily armored torso for some reason.

Watching his feet for the attack she knew was coming, Tina couldn't help but wonder why he hadn't gone for an easier target. Given the size of his ax, he could have taken an arm off. That was what she would have done. She might not be a PVPer, but *hit your enemy where it hurts* was Fighting 101. But the only cheap shot he'd tried so far was the blow to her head.

It had to be a holdover from the game. In FFO, players could hit an enemy anywhere, but it all did the same damage. Because of this, most people just whaled on whatever part was easiest to hit, which on Roxxy meant the torso. He also kept giving her breaks, using his abilities then backing off to let their timers reset even though it gave her, the wounded enemy, time to recover. In short, the Berserker was still fighting as if this were the game. Like they were just having a duel outside of town instead of trying to kill each other on a road in the middle of nowhere, and that was where Tina found her advantage.

The next time he charged her, Tina didn't brace behind her shield. She knew his pattern now, and she was going to use it against him. Very unfairly. It was time to make this idiot appreciate the new reality they were in, and to convince all the other players who were watching just how real this shit had gotten.

As always, the Berserker came at her hard, swinging his ax with the torque of his entire body. The crescent blade caught the edge of her shield, tearing open her guard. This time, however, Roxxy let it go, allowing the ax's momentum to tear the heavy slab of enchanted metal right off her arm and into the surrounding players, who dove out of the way.

In a normal fight, this would have meant Roxxy was dead. Without her shield, she was just a big lady with a low-damage sword. But the Berserker had been swinging at what he'd thought was the iron wall of her defense. When her shield had just given way, the momentum of his attack had carried him far and high. *So* high, the heavy ax almost flew out of his hands. And as the Berserker struggled to keep hold of his giant weapon, Tina took her chance.

Dropping her sword, she rushed him like a linebacker. There'd been no grappling in old FFO, so he was completely unprepared as she wrapped her tree-trunk-like arms around his waist and lifted him right off his feet, turned him sideways, then slammed him into the road with all the force her eight-hundred-pound stonekin body could bring.

He gasped as he hit, the breath knocked from his body, but despite the crater he'd made in the road, the bastard was still kicking. He was about to kick his way out of her grasp when Tina grabbed his leg.

Roaring with pent-up fury, she heaved the Berserker over her shoulder, swinging his entire body high over her head. He screeched as he flew, face white with panic. When she'd worked up a good momentum, Tina let go, flinging him face-first into the boulder she'd stood on for her speech earlier.

The jeering crowd went quiet as the bolder split with a thunderous *crack*. The Berserker's armor crumpled on impact, and Tina braced herself for the blood, but there was surprisingly little. She was even more amazed when her opponent peeled himself out of the broken rock and started getting back to his feet.

Like hell if she was going to give him the chance. With a snarl, Tina leaped on top of the Berserker. Driving both her feet into his back, she grabbed his face and smashed it down into the granite once more. Then she used her Ground Stomp ability, the one she normally taunted monsters with, to hammer him down again.

Tina hadn't forgotten how Ground Stomp had turned the road to gravel when she fought the skeletons. Furious with bloodlust, she brought the full force of it down on her opponent's back, hammering the Berserker through what was left of the rock and into the ground. Shards of rubble went flying as her enemy roared in pain, but Tina didn't stop. Unlike her defensive abilities, Ground Stomp had no reset time, so she just stomped again. Then again. Then again and again and again.

She stomped him until he stopped screaming. Until the boulder was dust under his body and the ground was cratered beneath. Only when his armor was so mangled she could barely make out how the pieces fit together did she finally stop, lifting her boot to let him lie still.

He was breathing, but blood oozed from every crack in his armor. Satisfied, Tina hopped off and calmly walked over to retrieve her sword and shield. Around her, the rest of the players were dead silent. Some had expressions of horror, others scorn. At whom, Tina couldn't guess, and she didn't care.

Placing her boot on the Berserker one last time, Tina reached down to undo his helmet straps. She stripped the battered covering off his head and tossed it on the ground with an ominous thud. When his bare face came into view, she grabbed a handful of his thick black hair and wrenched his head back, forcing him to look at her.

"Do you yield?"

"Screw you, bitch!" he yelled, drops of bloody spittle flying from his broken teeth. "This isn't over!"

"You were cool with sending other people to their deaths for your fun and ego earlier," she reminded him, pressing her sword against his exposed neck. "You ready to man up and be the first to find out how death works?"

"You can't threaten me!" he cried, wiggling in her grip. "I've got way too much health for your weak-ass damage to kill me!"

"Oh yeah?" Tina said, pressing her blade down until a trickle of blood welled up from his neck. "Are you completely sure that if I *slice open this artery*, you aren't going to permanently die?"

The man began to stammer, his eyes rolling down to try to catch a glimpse of the sword biting into his throat. He started to shake next, and Tina froze, worried this was some new ability he was activating to throw her off and reset the fight again.

Then she realized that he was crying.

"Please don't kill me!" he sobbed. "I don't want to die!"

Tina had to bite her cheek to keep from grinning in triumph. "That depends on you," she said cockily. "Do you yield?"

"Yes! Yes! You win!"

"All right," she said, removing her sword from his neck. "Fight's over."

She grabbed him by what was left of his armor and peeled him out of the crater, setting him back on his feet. When she was sure he wouldn't fall over, Tina handed him his dropped ax. "What's your name, dude?"

The Berserker put his helmet back on to hide the tear streaks running down his bloody face. "Killbox."

"You want us to call you that?" she asked gently. "This here is real life for now. You can use your real name if you want."

Killbox blushed, mashing his helmet tighter. "Killbox is fine."

"Then Killbox, it is," Tina said, offering him her hand. "We cool now?"

"Yes, ma'am," he said. Loudly, so the rest of the raid could hear. "To be honest, this whole thing didn't feel real to me until you put that sword to my throat."

"Awesome," Tina said, slapping him on the shoulder. "We're both cool, then."

That statement earned her a genuine smile of relief, then Killbox punched her in the arm. "You fight pretty well for a Care Bear. Gotta work on your counters, though. You know you can out-range Frenzied Strikes just by backing up, right? I can't move while I'm doing it, which is why I always drop the stun first."

"We'll have to work on my dueling sometime," she said, rubbing her arm. Dude punched like a truck. They exchanged fist-bumps for a good fight, but when Tina turned back to the raid, everyone was *still* staring at them.

"Show's over," she said loudly, pulling herself to her full height. "We've wasted enough time. Let's march!"

Even as she gave the order, it felt too soon. The whole raid looked rattled, their eyes begging her to say something that could explain the horrific violence she'd just unleashed. But while Tina knew she should do something leader-y here to ease their fears and address their complaints, she was too pissed that so many people had been cheering for Killbox to trust her voice. If she opened her mouth now, no good words would come out, and the wrong ones might rupture the rift she'd just bled to keep shut, so Tina said nothing, just pointed imperiously down the road.

The raid went, shuffling with their heads down and every eye avoiding hers.

"Okay, NekoBaby," said the ever-cheerful SilentBlayde from the back. "*Now* you can heal them."

Hours later, even Tina had to admit that marching through the Deadlands was misery incarnate.

It was freezing cold, which wasn't too bad until the howling wind picked up, blowing the stale air straight through the fragile warmth of armor and cloaks. Worse, it was dusty. Tina had never considered dust a problem before now, but the gray road was more grit than stone. Even when the raid walked carefully, their footsteps raised a cloud of ashy dust that choked them and made it hard to see monsters before they attacked.

Several times, they bumbled straight into dangerous enemies. A rare Grim Reaper miniboss had jumped out from behind a boulder and nearly killed three people before they'd nuked it down with their overwhelming firepower. With no rest or food, though, that was running out as well. Each mile marched and monster killed took a bit out of the raid, and Tina wasn't sure how much more they had to give.

"Night is going to be a problem," she muttered, squinting at the fading light in the gray sky.

"Why's that?" asked NekoBaby, who'd been hovering nearby ever since the fight with Killbox. "It's not like this place changes at night."

"Not before," Tina said. "But we didn't have to deal with the cold in game, and we're gonna lose our light."

"Is dark a problem?" the healer asked, tapping her magical staff. "We're all covered in so much glowing bullshit, we're like walking neon signs. Plus, I can totally see in the dark now. Meow!"

She made a cat-paw motion at Tina, who had to smile. "Good for you, but seeing's not the problem." She lowered her voice. "Look around. We're running on empty. I'd really hoped we'd be at the Order's fortress by now, but things must have gotten even bigger than I thought, because I haven't even seen the sign for it yet."

"So much walking," Neko groaned, leaning on her staff. "I'd kill for even the crappiest mount right now."

"You and me both. Even that gross riding slug thing from Forever-Con III would be awesome."

Neko wrinkled her nose. "Is there a reason we can't just stop? You know, make camp for the night or something?"

Tina arched a metal eyebrow. "Uh... Grel'Darm the Colossal, remember?"

"But we haven't seen him or his army for *hours*," Neko whined, gesturing at the empty dust bowl behind them. "We're way outside their area now. They probably broke aggro long ago and went back to have cookies with the Once King or something."

Tina looked over her shoulder. Sure enough, there was nothing but gray wasteland and dead trees for as far down the valley as she could see. No cloud from a chasing army, no footsteps rumbling through the ground. Nothing.

"I found a copse of trees we can camp in," said a suddenly present SilentBlayde. Tina's hand made it to her sword hilt in surprise before she caught herself. Despite being dusty, a little sliced up, and tired looking, SB still had a sparkle in his blue eyes. She was getting a little annoyed at his disappearing-reappearing act, though. Proof positive that she was more tired than she realized. She normally enjoyed SB's antics.

Tina looked back at the raid. Everyone was staring at the ground, their attention focused on putting one foot in front of the other. Once-beautiful suits of armor were caked with gray dust. Even the magical stitching on the Sorcerer's robes was too coated in filth to glow. Like her, all the Knights and Berserkers had grit in their armor, which caused a grinding noise every time they moved. It was truly pathetic, and Tina's shoulders slumped.

"All right," she said, her voice defeated. "I give up. There's no way we're making it to the Order fortress tonight, so we might as well choose where we stop."

"I've got a good place," SB promised. "Follow me."

Tina called for a halt, and the whole raid turned to follow the Assassin off the road and up a steep hill to the crown of leafless trees at its peak. The copse was small but dense, a tight circle of dead hardwoods just big enough to fit them all. The ground was rocky and sharp, but Tina approved of the cover and visibility the hill gave them. From this high up, she could see miles down the rambling, shoddy road behind them, where not even the tiniest cloud of dust rose to mark the approach of an undead army or anything else.

"This is good," she said, setting her pack down. "We'll spend the night here."

The moment she gave the okay, the rest of the raid fell over.

They didn't even bother with beds or fires. Everyone just picked a comfy-looking rock or tree and retreated into their cloaks. Cowls and visors were pulled down as players tried to hide from the glow of their enchanted gear to get some sleep.

Tina picked a withered log for herself and sat down with a sigh of relief. She had a lot of Endurance on her gear, which clearly helped with the marching, but she was also wearing a massive suit of armor, which did not. She debated taking her armor off, an action unheard of in game, but thought better of it. This hill was only "safe" in that nothing was actively attacking them, but that could change at any moment, and she needed to be ready.

As she got comfy, SB settled down beside her. They stayed like that for a while, too tired to plan, joke, or even speak. Even the wind seemed exhausted by the day, finally dying down to leave only the lifeless silence of the Deadlands and the dusty coughing of the raid.

She must have fallen asleep sitting up, because when Tina became aware again, she was in her bed back in her room. It felt incredibly real, but this wasn't a lucid dream like the ones she'd had about FFO, just a normal one.

A *lovely* one. Tina luxuriated in the warmth of her lumpy mattress, basking in the beauty of not having to run for her life. The worn sheets and heavy blankets made her feel soft and small again. Human. She was reveling in the sensation when a faceless friend walked in and asked how she'd done on her test.

Tina leaped from the bed in a panic. She'd forgotten all about her public librarianship final! Still in her pajamas, she charged out the door into a blizzard, the blinding sort they never had in Seattle. It was bitingly cold as she frantically tried to find her classroom, but nothing on campus made sense. All she could do was keep running, begging faceless strangers for directions as it got colder and colder.

At some point, SilentBlayde joined her. Or at least, there was a tall guy who looked like he was part elf, part Japanese. All these years playing together, and she *still* didn't know what SB looked like in real life. Her dream self firmly believed this guy was him, though, especially when dream SB wrapped his arm around her shoulders and promised to help her find her class. She was hugging him back in relief when a tremor went through the ground. Tina looked down in alarm, wondering if it was an earthquake, when another, even stronger tremor hit, knocking her over. The lovely warmth of Dream SB vanished as she fell to the ground. She was struggling to get back up when—

"*Roxxy!*"

She woke with a start to SilentBlayde, the real one, yelling in her face. The elf was standing between her legs with his hands on the collar of her breastplate, using his whole body to try to shake her awake. Tina stared at him groggily, wondering why he was so upset, when a huge tree fell over right behind them.

The crash snapped her completely awake. All around the little forest, players were staggering up from their sleeping positions. Tina surged to her feet as well, cracking the sheen of frost that had formed on her armor while she'd slept. When she looked around for the threat, though, she couldn't see a thing. Night had fallen, and the world was as black as pitch around them. The only light was the rainbow glow from the raid's gear, but that only lit the icy ground at their feet, making everything else even darker.

Another tree crashed somewhere in the forest to her right. As the cracking boom faded, Tina heard scratching, clanging noises moving through the woods on all sides. The other players were up now, drawing their weapons, but when they looked at Tina for orders, she didn't know what to do.

They could run again, but between the dark and the noises, she had no idea which direction to run to. She wasn't even sure where the road was anymore, and anyway, she was tired of running. The hill was a good position, and the raid had had a lot of practice. If they killed Grel'Darm here, then this death march would finally stop. It couldn't be any riskier than charging through a forest into unknown numbers of enemies in the dark, and now that her raid was finally following orders, they had a chance.

"Roxxy?" SilentBlayde asked, his voice trembling. "What are we doing?"

"Sshh," she said, trying to listen for the enemy. How they fought would depend entirely on where Grel was and how many enemies he'd brought with him. If they were lucky, this was only a forward patrol. If Grel himself was still somewhere down the hill, they could take out this group quickly and engage him alone on their terms. But as Tina opened her mouth to order the raid to form up behind her, the whole forest went silent.

The tremors stopped. The scraping sounds stopped. Everything was still except for the players' frantic breaths puffing in the ice-cold air, then...

"*It's here!*" screamed a jubatus Ranger.

Before anyone could react, the feline archer loosed a fire arrow into the forest. Tina watched in silent horror as the flaming orange arrow sailed up, and up, and *up*. Then when it was just a tiny spark sailing over the tops of the looming trees, the arrow hit something huge in the blackness, and its fire winked out.

For a second, there was only darkness again, then a pair of ghostfire eyes the size of funeral pyres opened in the empty black above the forest. More eyes followed in the woods below, countless smaller flickers of blue-white fire igniting like waves down the hill behind their master.

That was the moment Tina knew they should run. Before, Grel had been little more than a pair of boots to her. He was so big, that was all she could see while she was tanking him. Even when she'd seen him walking around inside in his room at the beginning of the Once King's fortress, he'd just been another oversize art asset. A big, annoying obstacle on their way to better bosses.

All that was different now.

This time, when Grel'Darm the Colossal stepped out of the forest, fear came with him. This was no art asset, no in-game mob. This was a *giant*, an armored skeleton the size of an eight-story building. He emerged from the darkness like a cargo ship, his enormous boots crushing the trees as he stepped forward, breaking the hardwoods like dry grass. That one step carried him all the way through the forest into their clearing, and as his foot crashed down, everything went to hell.

The undead army howled, but their thousands of voices were drowned when Grel'Darm roared. The deep, primal bellow echoed across the whole Deadlands, declaring the Once King's endless hatred for all the living. His hatred for *her*.

Tina's body began to shake. She had to move. They *all* had to move, right now, or they would die.

"*Run!*" she yelled, waving her sword at the cluster of players cowering at the middle of the clearing. "*Retreat down the hill! That way!*"

No one moved. She didn't even know if they'd heard her through their fear. The only reason Tina wasn't frozen, too, was because this was her second time experiencing the new mortal terror of the undead. The giant was much, *much* bigger, but the ice that formed on her bones when he raised his massive club was the same as she'd felt yesterday when the Dead Mountain patrol had nearly executed her. But despite their skirmishes with random monsters on the road, this was the first time the others had faced a true servant of the Once King, and the shock of it left them still. Even SilentBlayde wasn't moving. So since words weren't working on her people, Tina decided to try Grel instead, yelling out her taunt to focus the raid boss on her.

She wasn't fast enough. The giant's head swiveled toward her, but its huge club was already falling. She and SilentBlayde were lucky—they were on the edge of the clearing. The healers were not.

Because they were the most fragile, Tina had positioned the Naturalists and Clerics in the middle of the makeshift camp. Unfortunately, that was exactly where Grel's club landed. Some, like Anders, managed to snap out of their terror and dive out of the way. Others, like NekoBaby and David, did not.

The jubatus healer was on the edge of danger, but David was right below the strike. Tina caught a glimpse of the terror in his fish eyes as the mountain of iron-banded wood filled his vision, and she knew that David knew he was hosed. The Cleric didn't even try to run as the club came down, cratering the rocky ground where he'd been standing.

There was a flash of white light right as the club hit the dirt, then the impact of Grel'Darm's attack blasted them all backward. Tina scrambled back to her feet just in time to see the giant's club lift, revealing a bloody crater with a tatter of white robes and a shattered staff. A second later, SB appeared like magic beside her, carrying an unconscious NekoBaby.

"I'm sorry, Roxxy," he said frantically. "I couldn't get close enough to save David. He must have used his knock-back ability to blast Neko out of the way."

A lump of ice formed in Tina's throat. It had happened again— she'd hesitated, made a mistake, and now someone was dead. A friend, this time. Her eyes locked on Grel'Darm's club as it lifted off the ground, but there was nothing left of David in the crater. Just blood and broken bits.

Her vision blurred after that, forcing her to look away. David had been a troll and a dick for as long as she'd known him, but if there'd been any body left to gather, she would have run in to grab it. She would have run after the healers herself and held Grel off with her bare hands while they cast the rez, but there was nothing to bring back. David's body had been obliterated, and like the sorcerer, she couldn't bring him back.

Something awful happened in her stomach at that thought, but there was no time for further remorse. As if that opening strike had been their cue, hundreds of undead monsters charged out of the woods, their ghostfire eyes flaming bright white. Above them, Grel roared and hefted his club again, searching for the next target.

Cursing under her breath, Tina was looking frantically for some way to stop what was coming when she spotted Killbox standing by a huge tree. The guy was hurling rocks the size of beach balls at the oncoming army of zombies and skeletons. The boulders smashed and crashed through their ranks, sending the lightweight undead flying, which gave her an idea.

"Killbox!" she yelled. "Hulk out on that tree! Get us some space!" She made some swinging motions to make sure he got the idea, and Killbox gave her a thumbs-up. Plan in motion, Tina and SB ran to the dead center of the clearing.

The raid was falling to chaos. Spells and arrows flew randomly through the trees at the incoming army, but the attacks were spread out and did no good. Grel'Darm roared again as his forces rushed ahead to attack the scattered players. A defensive line could have stopped them, but between the raid's fire and the incoming army, the melee players couldn't attack, so they just stood in confusion, unsure whether to charge or defend.

"*Form up on me!*" Tina yelled, banging her shield.

The others jumped then ran to her instinctively. As she got the raid into position, Tina waved her sword at Killbox. The crazy-strong Berserker had done exactly as she'd asked. At her signal, he used his ludicrously oversize ax to finish felling the tree he'd already weakened, sending the massive trunk crashing into the clearing in front of her to form a six-foot-tall wall of wood between the players and the incoming undead.

As she'd hoped, the charging army slammed into the tree like a speeding car. Skeletons bounced off the wood, falling to pieces on the icy ground, but Tina wasn't done. She motioned to Frank and Killbox, and the two huge humans teamed up to lift the entire tree by one end. Once they had it, they started swinging, sweeping the giant trunk back and forth across the undead army like a baseball bat.

It worked even better than expected. Most of the undead were skeletons and zombies—things that had lots of magical health but little actual mass. The ancient tree swept them off their feet easily, completely fouling the remainder of the enemy's formation as entire squads were flung off the hill. Satisfied they wouldn't die in the next five seconds, Tina grabbed the Ranger next to her—a dark-skinned elf whose uniquely curly, bright-green hair stood out even in the dark.

"Zen!" she shouted, relieved she'd *finally* recognized someone without the aid of nameplates. "Flare Arrow that way! *Now!*"

To her credit, Zen didn't ask questions. She just calmly nocked an arrow and yelled, "Flare Arrow!" before firing over the trees behind them. The arrow sailed high into the night and exploded, blossoming into brilliant-yellow light that illuminated the forest to their left.

With a nod of thanks, Tina banged on her shield and bellowed over the din. "*Everyone,* follow the flare! Retreat! *Retreat!*"

Puffing from the effort, Killbox and Frank continued to wave the giant log around while backing up, buying the others time to race down the hill. They were almost out when Grel'Darm reached down to grab the top of the felled tree. With one hand, the colossus ripped the improvised weapon from the players' hands, then he rocked back and threw it with hurricane force at the fleeing raid behind them.

Tina's eyes widened. She could already see what was coming. The giant hardwood was going to flatten everyone. They'd all be crippled or killed, then the army would finish off what was left. It was doom any way she looked at it, so Tina did the only thing she could think of. She stopped running and whirled around, raising her shield as she charged to intercept the incoming tree.

As the massive oak filled her vision, Tina realized this was probably not the smartest idea she'd ever had, but it was too late for second thoughts. The tree was going to hit her no matter what she did at this point. She twisted her feet and called out her anti-knockdown ability.

"*Steady Ground!*"

The dust beneath her feet turned to stone, anchoring her to the ground. Ducking behind her shield, Tina gritted her teeth for impact.

There was a terrifying empty second as she waited, then a tree with a six-foot-wide trunk, traveling at a hundred miles per hour, slammed straight into her.

The impact blasted through her. The boar had been nothing compared to the strength of Grel'Darm's throw. Tina's shield flared with magic as its enchantments struggled to hold it together. If she hadn't had metal for bones and stone for skin, the force would have turned her to paste inside her armor. But she wasn't a squishy human anymore. She was an elemental monster, and she held together, standing her ground as the trunk splintered and cracked in half across her shield, the two pieces flying off to her left and right.

Hardened in place, Tina couldn't look to see where they landed, but she didn't hear any cries of anguish. That was a relief, but while it seemed she'd saved her raid from death by log roll, the defense had come at a brutal cost. Even hardened in stone, Tina's body ached from toes to scalp, and her head felt as if there were rocks rattling around inside it. When the bedrock's blessing finally faded, she swayed on her feet, falling forward to lean on her shield for balance. She was still trying to get the world to stop spinning when a shadow engulfed her, and Tina looked up to see the bottom of Grel'Darm's iron-clad boot.

"Oh shit."

■ ■

SilentBlayde shoved the unconscious NekoBaby at Frank. The Knight blushed and stammered as the cat-girl was dumped into his arms, but SB didn't have time for his modesty. Friend secured, he turned around to go make sure the rear of the raid was getting its move on, which meant he was just in time to see Tina vanish beneath Grel'Darm's dump-truck-sized foot.

"ROXXY!"

The blast of wind from the giant's stomp knocked him off his feet. He was back up again in an instant, unable to breathe as he raced through the woods toward her. In the back of his mind, a calm voice reminded him that Roxxy had the most health and armor of any of them, and she'd tanked Grel'Darm countless times before. But the reality and unstoppable force of the giant threw all of those experiences out the window, leaving only overwhelming fear and the desperation to do something, *anything*, to get her out.

"*Frank!*" he shouted. "Get aggro! We have to help Roxxy!"

Dimly, SB was aware that he shouldn't have said that. Frank didn't know enough about tanking to handle Grel'Darm in a proper raid yet, let alone solo. The guy might die trying, but in that moment, SilentBlayde didn't care. Saving Roxxy was all that mattered, and suddenly, no cost was too high.

Behind him, he heard Frank hand NekoBaby off and charge back into the undead army. SB raced through the dust ahead of him, dancing around the skeletons that were already regrouping.

"Hey, big guy!" Frank yelled at Grel'Darm, banging his sword against his shield. "Your mom's so basic, she denatured my enzymes!"

High overhead, the giant's massive head turned.

"Yeah, you heard me!" Frank shouted, banging louder. "Why don't you come over here and—"

The rest of his taunt was drowned out by the monster's roar. Like a barge, Grel'Darm turned toward the taunting knight, finally lifting his foot out of the crater where Roxxy had been. The moment the giant boot was out of the way, SB dove in, sliding nimbly down the embankment of the monster's giant footprint. When he got to the bottom, though, he didn't see Roxxy anywhere.

Heart pounding, SilentBlayde ran around the crater, frantically kicking at the packed ground. When his foot clanged painfully on something hard and metal, he dove to his knees and began to dig. Thankfully, all the undead were zeroed in on Frank now, leaving him free to dig until he finally unearthed Roxxy's head from the ground.

"*Tina!*"

Roxxy's copper metal hair was wet with her silver blood, and her eyes were closed. SB could feel her breath when he held his fingers under her nostrils, but it was so weak it made his stomach sink. "Hang on," he said, prying his fingers under her glowing armor. "I'll get you out."

He braced his feet and yanked, pulling as hard as he could, but it was no good. As a level eighty, SilentBlayde had about a hundred base strength naturally. That made him four times stronger than the average human but still way too many average humans shy of the strength needed to lift a heavily armored stonekin out of the ground.

Releasing her with a curse, SB looked around for something,

anything, he could use to pry her out. What he really needed was help, but Frank was already vanishing under a pile of undead, and Grel'Darm was almost to him. "We need help over here!" SB yelled, hoping that someone in the retreating raid was still close enough to hear.

Unfortunately, the nearby undead answered him first.

The yell had barely left his mouth when a dozen armored zombies came lurching into the crater at him. Desperate to keep them off Roxxy, SilentBlayde leaped forward, landing with his feet on a zombie's chest as he stabbed the creature through the head with both swords. The zombie staggered, and for a horrible moment, SB worried that these were two-skull monsters, too tough for one player to manage. But the zombie must have just been too stupid to die immediately, because it fell to the ground a moment later, collapsing into dust with a soft *urrr*.

With the utmost elven grace, SB flipped off the falling zombie and landed next to Roxxy to block the rest of the pack. Silver blades met rusty ones as SB deflected hit after hit, bouncing the decaying axes and swords back into their owners' faces. A brush of wind on his back made him spin, avoiding a decrepit-spear thrust by millimeters. He sliced the head off its owner as his spin finished, coming back around with his blades up for the next one.

While he was fighting, SB kept yelling. "Roxxy's unconscious! We need a heal! Anders! *Someone!*"

But no one came. Only undead. A centuries-dead elven woman slipped behind him and grabbed Roxxy by the head, opening her mouth to bite the stonekin's face. SB kicked the zombie he'd been fighting away then back-flipped and landed with both feet on the woman's head. The zombie elf's face was driven into the ground by his weight as he slashed off her arms with a silver swipe of his blades. For good measure, SilentBlayde kicked the rest of her into her friends and fell back, guarding Roxxy as more undead poured into the crater.

Somewhere above him, Grel'Darm's step boomed very close, and he realized with a chill that the giant had probably reached Frank's position. SB looked down at Roxxy in despair. He was going to have to cut her armor straps to get her out alive. It would be painful to sacrifice a legendary set of end-game tanking gear. Irreplaceable, really, but he wasn't going let her die. She could be mad at him later, if they lived through this.

He cut down two more zombies and dropped to the ground,

digging into the dirt on Roxxy's side to see if he could find the fastenings for her chest plate. After a few frenzied seconds, he realized the armor wasn't strapped on at all. It was held together by ancient elven binding scripts, each one glowing with a unique golden light of its own.

The moment he saw the scripts, SilentBlayde knew exactly what they said. He had no idea how he could read the elven words, but they told him exactly what to do to disengage the armor's locks, and that was good enough for him. Immediately, he started to dance his fingers along the sequence, following the glowing lines with shaking fingers. He was nearly done when he sensed something huge above his head.

He'd taken his eyes off the enemy for too long. Letting go of Roxxy's armor with a curse, SB raised his swords to block the massive weapon swinging toward his head, but the huge ax wasn't aiming for him. Instead, it bit into the zombies behind him, cutting all three in half with a single stroke. The armored corpses gurgled as torsos flew and legs toppled, then a gruff voice spoke in the dark.

"Yo, 'Blayde boy."

SilentBlayde looked up to see the towering shape of Killbox standing over him with a cocky grin on his blood-splattered face. "I got this," Killbox said, pushing SilentBlayde out of the way like he weighed nothing. When the elf was clear, the hulking Berserker used his ax's spike to hook Roxxy's armor and pry her out of the ground, dumping her in the dirt at SB's feet.

If Killbox hadn't been there, he would have cried in relief. It was still a near thing as he reached down to check Roxxy's breath. The weak brush of air against his fingers made his heart skip several beats, and he lowered his head. "Thank you," he whispered.

The Berserker nodded and reached down to grab Roxxy, hoisting the giant stonekin into a fireman's carry across his ridiculous shoulders. "Cover me!" he yelled as he stood up. "We're getting the hell out of here!"

With that, the guy started to jog away, vanishing over the edge of the crater as suddenly as he'd appeared. His feet sank several inches into the ground with every step, the only indicator of the true weight he was carrying. SilentBlayde watched in silence before he remembered to close his mouth. Just how much Strength gear was Killbox wearing?

As the Berserker carried Roxxy out, SB became uncomfortably aware of the greater situation. Off to his left, he could still hear Frank

147

yelling, "That's right! You kick like my grandma! That big boot of yours ain't so bad! These ankle-biters hurt more than you do, I bet!"

SilentBlayde's blood ran cold. Frank was yelling at Grel'Darm to keep the giant's attention. It was same tanking technique SB had taught him, but in this situation, it was a suicidal move. Grel's stomp had knocked out *Roxxy* in one hit. It would turn Frank into paste.

Desperate, SB leaped to the top of the hole made by Grel's boot print. He didn't even see Frank when he first came up, then he spotted the Knight a dozen feet away, buried under a mass of biting, clawing undead. He couldn't tell if the zombie swarm was trying to eat him or just hold him in place for their colossal master. Either way, it was a deadly situation and one that was entirely his fault. Frank was in over his head because he'd been doing exactly what SB had asked him to, to a degree that bordered on blind faith.

Guilt stabbed into him like a knife in the back. He needed to get to Frank somehow and kill all those undead so the newbie tank could run. Before he could take a single step, though, he was forced to duck as Grel'Darm pulled back his leg for a kick.

As the knight's doom wound up for delivery, Frank brandished his shield in front of him. "That's right!" the old man yelled. "Let's see what you've got!"

"No, Frank!" SB shouted frantically. "Defensive! Use a *defensive* ability!"

But the knight didn't seem to hear him. He just stood there watching the incoming foot from behind his shield. Cursing, 'Blayde started to run toward him but had to drop to the ground again as Grel'Darm's foot passed overhead like a low-flying jumbo jet, landing on the knight's shield with a deafening *clang*.

SB squeezed his eyes shut. There was no way a sound like that didn't end in a blood explosion. When he forced himself to look a second later, though, there was no blood. There was no Frank, either. DarkKnight's gear must have been better than he'd realized, because instead of killing him instantly, Grel's kick had sent Frank rocketing backward out of the pile of undead, through several trees, and down the hill before finally smacking into a rock. SB was still gaping in astonishment when the knight sat up and waved at him, grinning through his visor.

"Did you see that?"

SilentBlayde grinned so hard it hurt. He was about to yell back when a rusty sword stabbed into the soil inches from his face. Twisting to avoid it, SB suddenly realized that he was alone and surrounded. The rest of the raid was long gone, retreating as they'd been ordered, which meant it was now just him and the undead army on the hill. High overhead, Grel'Darm looked down with white beacon fires for eyes, his black mouth opening in a hollow laugh.

SB smiled back. "See ya, suckers," he whispered, crossing his swords for the Blade Flash blinding move. He'd been saving his wide-area blind for a special occasion, and now definitely counted. But when he scraped his swords together, the flash didn't happen.

He stared at his swords in horror, cursing in his newfound elven. He knew all of his abilities' descriptions by heart, and the text of Blinding Flash was very clear—his swords bounced sunlight to blind all enemies in a glaring explosion. It had *never* failed before, but as he struggled to understand what had just happened, SB realized how dark it was around him.

That made him curse again, at himself this time. Of course. In game, abilities worked whenever they weren't on cooldown, but now that things were real, Blade Flash must need *actual* sunlight to function. In the dust, at night, in the Deadlands, there was nothing bright enough to trigger the explosion. The only light here was the cold glow of the ghostfire shining from thousands of eye sockets around the clearing, all of which were looking at him.

Sheathing his blades again, SilentBlayde crouched down, glad no one was around to see what he was about to do. He'd had a theory for a while now, something the other assassins hadn't figured out yet. If a hundred Strength made him four times stronger than an average human, what did over a thousand Agility do?

He'd assumed "as fast as all hell" was the answer. Now, though, cornered by a raid boss and surrounded by an entire army of undead, SB was desperately hoping it was more like "become the Flash." There was no time like the present to find out, so SB dug his boots into the ground and put on the speed. Not the usual speed he used in raids when he was trying to show off or get to a monster first so he could do max damage. His *real* speed, kicking off the dirt as fast as he could go.

The moment he started to move, the air turned to syrup. The world of screeching undead slowed to a crawl around him, leaving him free to kick the zombies over as he flew between them. Laughing with sudden delight, SilentBlayde danced across the seemingly immobile undead, plucking their arrows from the air as he raced out of the deathly forest and down the hill. Finally, a hundred yards and less than a second of real time later, he slid to a halt at Frank's side, throwing up a wave of dust.

"Whoa!" Frank said, surprised. "Where did you come from?"

Gasping for breath, SB pointed at his face. "Assassin, remember?" He looked at the Knight's armor, which was badly dented but mercifully bloodless. "You okay?"

"Don't you worry about me," Frank drawled, shoving himself to his feet. "Big-and-Ugly just dented my monkey suit is all."

"I thought you were gonna die," SilentBlayde admitted, trying to keep the shaking from his voice. He was *really* glad he hadn't actually gotten Frank killed. Now that Roxxy was safe, the guilt of what he'd done was eating him alive, but Frank just laughed.

"Pshaw! I had a plan," the old knight said cheerfully. "Turns out, they take insults to heart, and with physics being kinda wonky around here, I figured I'd line up my own firing line." He pointed at all the trees he'd crashed through on his way out here. "I'm just glad that Big-and-Stompy didn't miss the field goals I set up for him. If those trees hadn't broken my momentum, I'd have splatted on this rock for sure."

"Frank, you're awesome," SB said with a grin, still trying to catch his breath. "Now let's get moving before we get caught."

They both glanced up the hill at the undead, who seemed reluctant to leave their giant—but very slow—leader, then started jogging in the other direction. Thanks to his dented armor, Frank was moving more slowly than usual, but SB was still finding it hard to keep up, which made no sense. Even when he was exhausted, SB was normally faster than everyone. No matter how hard he pushed now, though, he kept falling behind.

This wouldn't do for the world's fastest elf, so SB put everything he had left into picking up the pace. But a few minutes later, he was no closer to Frank, and his breath was coming in ragged gulps. Even when he stopped completely to focus on gasping in air, it didn't seem to help. No matter how hard he breathed, it wasn't enough. His whole body was screaming for air as if he were suffocating from the inside. Falling to his knees, SilentBlayde tried to call for Frank only to find he didn't have the air left to form the words.

Frank! he mouthed silently as the Knight's back as it vanished into the darkness ahead of him. *Fraaank!*

But Frank was already gone, leaving SB gasping on the ground as the night grew darker and darker.

CHAPTER *8*

James

"Y ou filthy traitor."

James sighed, tossing away the poisoned arrows his magic had pushed out of Arbati's flesh. "You're welcome for me saving your life."

"If you can heal, then healing is your job," the warrior snarled back. "Is that not how players work? Do you expect the tanks to owe you their lives for every spell you cast on them?"

James's eyebrows shot up. He hadn't realized Arbati understood how player parties operated. He supposed it made sense given how much player chatter the cat-man had had to listen to as a quest giver, but this new knowledge gave him an idea.

"Well, then," he said, smiling smugly. "You can't say I didn't do my job. I healed you back from nearly dead."

"Except you shouldn't have let me get that bad in the first place! Why didn't you cleanse immediately? And where were my mid-fight heals?"

"I had gnolls on me!" James cried. "If you're the tank, then you screwed up by making me deal with them for so long."

"You had plenty of time to *heal the enemy*," Arbati growled back.

James winced. "I don't suppose having a crisis of conscience means anything to you?"

"Sounds like a crisis of loyalties to me."

"It wasn't," James said. "I just..." He looked down at the ground. "I didn't want to kill them. It's not their fault they're being used by the undead. They have lives and families, too."

"You killed those four easily enough," Arbati said, pointing at the charred corpses of the gnolls James had hit with his lightning. "Kill these gnolls, don't kill those gnolls—make up your mind! What about your promise to end the Red Canyon threat? Will you pick and choose there, too?" He looked away with a sneer. "I was right not to trust you. You are now as you were in the Nightmare, saying and doing whatever pleases you at the time. *Playing* at being a hero."

James clenched his fists. "I'll keep my promise to help save your sister," he said angrily. "But I never said I'd commit genocide! I'll kill the undead, but the gnolls are as much victims of this as Lilac."

"The gnolls are putrid scavengers," Arbati snapped. "And you bragged you'd 'slaughter the camp.' Your words, player."

James bit his tongue. He had said that, hadn't he? But that was before he'd known. Before he'd...

He looked at the charred corpses again, stomach twisting at the stench of burned fur. "I promised to end the threat," he said quietly. "And I will. But I'm not going to kill again. Not if I can help it."

"A worm-worded excuse," Arbati said, turning up his nose. "Why bother going on a raid if you're not going to kill? Not that it matters now. You've already shown yourself to be a traitor and a coward, which means this trial is already a failure."

James shook his head. "No. It's not over until Lilac's dead or I am."

"That last one can be arranged," Arbati growled, rising to his feet. "I still need what little help you can offer to save my sister, but I'm watching my back for your dagger, coward. The moment you show your true colors, my blade is ready to take off your head."

"Thanks for the second chance," James muttered, standing up as well only to stop again when he spotted the arrow-riddled corpses of their mounts. "I guess we're walking to Red Canyon now."

Arbati shot him a look of utter scorn. "Of course a fake jubatus like you wouldn't know," he said, stalking over to yank the pack off his dead runner. "We go like this."

With that, Arbati fell to all fours and took off down the road, his long legs and arms propelling him over the rutted track only slightly more slowly than their runners had moved. James watched in awe. The sight of the cat-warrior racing through the savanna on all fours was the most alien thing he'd seen yet. There was nothing human or even Earthlike about the scene in front of him. He was still trying to wrap his brain around it when Arbati stopped, glaring over his shoulder with an impatient hiss.

Not knowing what else to do, James dropped down to his hands in the dirt road. To his surprise, the position felt natural to his body, but his mind was completely out of its element. His first attempt at running on all fours ended up with him tripping over his own feet.

When he tried again, he ended up with his face in the dirt. Spitting the grit out of his mouth, James decided he was overthinking things and resolved to let his body decide how to move on its own.

After that, running got a lot easier. It was still awkward at first, but once he matched Arbati's long, bounding gait, his body found its rhythm, and running started to be fun. Jubatus weren't as fast as the beasts they'd ridden here, but he seemed to be able to sustain speeds an Olympic sprinter would have been proud to hit. Racing down the road at a pace he never could have dreamed of in his human body put a smile on his face until a bug smacked into his teeth. After that, James learned to keep his mouth shut, pumping his body even faster to keep up with Arbati as they ran through the evening light.

They raced across the savanna for the next several hours. It was dry, dusty traveling, but James was quickly discovering that jubatus were amazingly well adapted for running through the hot grasslands. The tough skin on his hands didn't get scraped by the rocks, and his short claws were excellent for getting a grip at those times when the road was sandy. His short fur protected him from the sun and the abrasive wind, yet it wasn't so long that it trapped sweat. Everything evaporated as it should, keeping him cool.

While he was lost in the rhythm of long-distance running, the sunset snuck past him. He didn't even realize how dark it had gotten until he noticed stars glittering on the horizon. He skidded to a stop at once, terrified of breaking a leg in the dark, but to his surprise, the landscape looked just as bright as it had when they'd started running. Despite FFO's complete lack of a moon, everything was still sharp and clear though strangely lacking in color. James was wondering how that was possible when the truth suddenly hit him.

Jubatus can see in the dark!

A giddy smile spread across his face. Back when FFO had been a game, nowhere was truly dark. Even in the dead of night, light filters had been applied to make sure night-owl players wouldn't be at a disadvantage. Now, though, the empty savanna was pitch-black save for the faint light of the stars, not that it seemed to matter to James. He could still see everything perfectly, including Arbati's scowl when the warrior looked back to see why he'd stopped.

Dutifully, James started running again, but that didn't stop him from craning his neck in every direction as he tested out his newfound ability. When he looked directly up, he almost fell over. He'd heard the term "the dome of the heavens" before, but he'd never realized how accurate that was until he saw the pure, unpolluted sky filled with a curved sea of stars and pastel-colored nebulae. The sheer beauty of it brought tears to his eyes. He could have stared at it for hours, but the road took priority. Regaining his footing, James promised himself a better look when they stopped.

Assuming they *did* stop. The last sunlight had been completely gone for hours, but Arbati still showed no sign of slowing. He kept a grueling pace, pushing them relentlessly down the road for what felt like forever. Finally, panting, sweaty, and hungry, they stopped for a break.

James drank all the water in his pouch the moment he stopped moving. Digging into his bag of supplies, he found some delicious-smelling jerky and shoved that into his mouth as well. As he was tearing at the tough meat with his teeth, he noticed Arbati frowning at the scrubby grassland.

"What's wrong?"

Arbati's fierce eyebrows drew closer together. "The Red Canyon is not where it should be."

"Things have changed a lot," James reminded him. "Maybe—"

"I grew up in these plains," the warrior snarled. "I know where things are supposed to be! To get to the gnolls' village, we only have to take the trade road past the twin hills. There are some time-walker ruins by the road that mark where the old ghost creek is. We used to follow it the rest of the way when we went on raids, but the ruins aren't here, and I haven't heard the ghost creek yet."

Arbati's face turned stricken. "The Nightmare ruined everything! Even when we are free, the world itself is twisted beyond repair. The Red Canyon is not where it was in the game or before, and I don't know how to find it."

James winced at the implied "it's all your fault," but he wasn't sure what to do. His mental map of the savanna had stopped making sense shortly after they'd left the village. He looked up at the beautiful stars for a clue, but unaided stellar navigation wasn't a skill he'd had back home, let alone in a world with all-new stars. But just as he was getting caught up again in the beauty of the sparkling sky, he noticed something on the horizon. The stars to the south were harder to see due to a faint orange-tinted haze. His first thought was another nebula, but the sickly orange didn't match the other streaks of color in the sky. It looked more like...

Light pollution! James didn't have a map of the savanna zone anymore, but light pollution could only mean a large settlement. There were only two of those in this entire zone, and one was nearly a hundred miles behind them.

"Arbati!"

The warrior turned around, his eyes narrowing at James for the sin of reminding him that he existed. James ignored it, pointing at the glow on the horizon instead. Arbati's gaze followed his finger, and the warrior nodded with a grunt. They finished their jerky, then they both took off through the tall grass in that direction.

As they moved silently through the grass like lions in the night, it struck James that he was honest-to-god *prowling*. The wildness thrilled him, but the best were the magics of the earth and life that curled up to meet his hands from the ground. The power of an entire world lay beneath him, making James feel alive in a way he never had before. He'd also never been so aware of the fact that he had claws and fangs. A small bird chirped as he slid by, and his ears twitched. *Prey.*

The word was still moving through his mind when he was seized by a sudden urge to pounce. He wanted to snatch the bird from its perch in the grass so he could eat it hot, raw, and twitching. He was imagining how delicious it would be when the James part of his mind came back, and the thought of eating a bloody, *living* bird went from awesome to disgusting in a heartbeat. All the feelings of animal power and natural connection fled with it, leaving him self-conscious as he looked down at his claws.

They weren't nearly as large as those on a predator of his size should have been since jubatus were humanoid tool users, not actual giant cats, but the small, dark points still felt alien. Everything did. Now that he was thinking again instead of losing himself in the physical joy of prowling through the night, his whole body felt unknown, like it belonged to someone else. For the first time since he'd woken up here, the thought *I'm not human* crossed his mind.

James took a bitter breath. It was *so* unfair. If someone back home had asked him, "Hey, wanna become a magical cat-person with amazing powers?" he would have been all over it. He could have made a human

Naturalist, after all. He'd chosen this body because he'd loved the idea of being a jubatus, but he was finding the reality to be less on the exciting end of the spectrum and much more into disturbing territory. He'd already seen how his new instincts could take over his rational mind. Even now, the idea of eating a raw bird didn't sound *that* bad, and that terrified him. Was he in danger of losing his humanity like this?

His existential crisis was interrupted by an impatient snarl, and James's head shot up to see Arbati waiting impatiently for him beside a scrubby tree. The warrior motioned for him to come over, and James obediently slunk through the grass. He wasn't sure why Arbati had stopped until the warrior hauled himself up into the tree. When James followed, using his claws to scale the stout trunk all the way to the topmost branches, he understood.

Red Canyon was directly in front of them. He hadn't been able to see it until now because of the high grass and the gentle hill they'd been climbing. Now that they'd cleared the crest, though, the canyon's deep scar in the ground and the brightly lit gnoll village beside it were clearly visible just half a mile away. But while there was no question this was their destination, the village was not what James remembered.

Back in the old vanilla FFO days, this place had been the worst of all the leveling grinds. Since the Red Canyon quests were necessary to complete the savanna zone story, the developers had purposefully lowered the monster density to discourage farming and drag out the time it took to level up. The result had been a mostly empty village populated exclusively by soldiers and their bosses, but the settlement in front of him now was nothing like that at all.

The city—for this was no village—was *enormous*, sprawling across multiple hills and sticking far out into the grassland. It was bordered on one side by the deep gash of the Red Canyon, which split the earth like a cleft. The remaining three sides were guarded by a twenty-foot-high wall made from the canyon's namesake crimson sandstone and topped with wide wooden battlements. Burning braziers lit up the border wall every fifty feet, highlighting the multiple patrols walking its ramparts, and even a few light catapults.

That was all *definitely* new, but the walls and the soldiers weren't the only change. From his vantage point in the tree on the hill, James could see over the barricade into the fortress itself, which was no longer a shabby collection of mud huts. Instead, the gnoll city was a grid of stone buildings laid out with military precision. Packs of patrols marched through the well-lit dirt streets, and ember-dotted smoke rose from numerous forges, their windows glowing brightly from the huge bellows fires inside.

That last one made James's blood run cold. The zone plot for the savanna had always involved the undead raising an army of gnolls to conquer Windy Lake, but the result had always looked like more of a rabid pack of hyenas than an actual fighting force. This, though—this was a true *army*, complete with what appeared to be a functional military base. Huge packs of gnolls were moving supplies into warehouses and bringing up wagons of mysteriously marked crates from the canyon below, where the lich and his officers lurked.

All of that was very troubling, but what really worried James for their immediate mission was how much tighter security was in this new version of the gnoll town. In addition to the patrols and the bonfires at every intersection, there were multiple checkpoints with guard stations. What really set his fur on end, though, were the long rivers of nature magic covering the city's walls. Magic he could feel throbbing all the way out here.

"Crap," he whispered, crouching low on his branch. "That's a raid-level ward."

"Is that a problem for you?" Arbati whispered back.

James gave him a shocked look. "Dude, raids take fifty players! It's not something I can handle solo."

If this were still a game, a barrier like that would have taken an entire questline to bring down. A very long one, involving multiple group-quests. Since this ward was a new development, James had no idea if the old standards still applied, but he was certain they didn't have time for them. He wasn't certain how long they'd been running through the dark, but it had to be close to midnight by now. Lilac had been poisoned at dawn, which James believed meant that they had until the next dawn to save her. That timeline didn't allow for surprise giant questlines, but other than catapulting themselves over the wall into the patrols, there didn't seem to be a way around.

"This is going to be harder than I thought."

Arbati sneered at him. "Oh, so you *aren't* just going to walk in there and kill everything, then?"

"You know I lost my gear," James snapped. "Even with my

legendary equipment, though, I don't think this would be solo-able. There's thousands of gnolls down there, and that ward will cook us if we try to sneak over."

"Then we won't go over," Arbati said, pointing at the Red Canyon on the other side of the fortress. "That side has no walls, and the lich we need resides at the bottom, correct?"

"Yeah," James said, impressed the warrior had remembered. "But it's not as simple as just climbing down the canyon. Remember what I said about there being a questline to access the dungeon?"

Arbati nodded. "The one you said you were going to handle."

"Yeah, well, the gnolls used to have three leaders, kind of like chieftains. When the undead arrived, those three guys sold the rest of the gnolls out in exchange for immortality and power. The catch was that, in exchange for all that power, each one of those traitor chieftains had to give up a shard of their life essence to help maintain an anti-living barrier over the dungeon's entrance. If we climb down there while that barrier is still in place, we'll be trapped like rats between the gnolls at the top and the undead at the bottom."

"So we kill the chieftains and remove the barrier," Arbati said with a shrug. "Easy enough. I kill gnolls all the time."

"Not like these," James cautioned. "Don't forget. This place was balanced for *player* parties. Those undead chieftains are all three-skull bosses. They're built to challenge at least five same-level players, which for this area means level thirty. By the way, you're level fifty and two-skull rated, or at least you were in the game. That should give you the advantage, but don't expect any easy fights. This place was one of the first dungeon questlines put into FFO. It's famously brutal, *especially* the third boss, Gore Maul, the Chief of Chiefs. He's probably the most dangerous thing out here other than the lich himself."

Arbati snorted with disdain. "I do not fear a gnoll."

"Dude, I'm serious," James said. "Gore Maul is some three-and-a-half-skull bullshit from back when the game devs didn't know how to balance bosses properly. He's the reason most veteran players skip this zone. Dude does colossal damage, has ludicrous armor, attacks fast, and has a massive health pool. I've seen him wipe entire parties, and that's when the players knew what they were doing. He's so feared, there's even a special Halloween event where he—"

"So how do we beat him?" Arbati said impatiently. "I know players didn't quest through here in large groups all the time. How did they kill him?"

"By following the quests," James said. "All the gnoll bosses have special quests you can do to reduce them from three-skull status to two. That means they'll still take two players to beat, but we're both over-level, so we shouldn't have any trouble."

He went on to detail each of the three questlines that could be used to weaken the bosses of the village. It was classic FFO stuff like getting bodyguards drunk, stealing a special poison, and finding a locket to remind one of its long-lost love. Unfortunately, each boss's storyline required four to five quests' worth of effort. As he explained this, James became more and more aware of just how impossible their task was given the time frame, not to mention doing it all inside a highly secure military camp without being discovered.

This must have occurred to Arbati as well, because the head warrior was uncharacteristically silent during his explanation. By the time James finished, Arbati was just staring down at the village, his long tail twitching as he thought.

The uncharacteristic silence went on for so long, James finally asked, "Are you okay?"

"Lilac is my little sister," the warrior said from his perch in the tree beside James.

"I know, dude," James said gently. "I'm worried about my little sister, too. But we can do this. We just figure out a way in, then—"

James cut off as he heard yip-yipping from below. Clutching the branch he was crouching on, he peered down through the leaves to see a patrol of six gnolls coming through the grass. Waiting with absolute stillness, James held his breath as the pack walked up to their tree and sat down beneath it, snickering at each other casually. When he realized the patrol was just taking a break, James let his breath out silently. He was about to signal to Arbati that everything was okay when he felt something land between his shoulder blades.

It was a boot. Arbati had leaned down from his branch to plant his *boot* in James's back. When he looked up in horror, the warrior's cat eyes flashed in the dark.

"You will be of use to me one way or the other, James," he whispered. Then with that menacing statement, the jubatus kicked him out of the tree.

In the silence of the night, the breaking of branches and the yowling sound James made as he fell were astonishingly loud. The patrol of gnolls began barking as James hurtled down. Half-way to the ground, some jubatus instinct took over, and James twisted to land on his feet, but the beautiful recovery was ruined as he landed right on top of a gnoll.

The hyena-men scattered and drew their weapons. Grossly outnumbered, James hopped off the wiggling gnoll and put his hands up in what he hoped was a universal sign of surrender. Thankfully, the gnolls didn't attack. They just kept their weapons on him, yipping at each other in discussion.

As they talked, James was sorely tempted to drag Arbati into this. The damn cat had just thrown him to the hyenas. He'd deserve it if James outed him, especially since the patrol he'd "accidentally" fallen into were now making suggestive chopping motions with their paws. But as hot as James's resentment at being thrown to the gnolls burned, he was starting to see the plan. If the gnolls took him prisoner, they'd have to open the gates to take him in. That meant opening the ward, which would be their chance to get inside.

James locked his fangs in outrage. He hated it, but assuming the gnolls didn't kill him here, it wasn't actually a bad plan. So instead of revealing his frenemy in the tree, James swallowed his pride and kept his hands up, doing his best to look nonthreatening as the gnolls debated his fate.

"Um," James said as their deliberations dragged on. "I surrender."

Whether it was coincidence or them actually understanding him, the gnolls' chopping motions stopped, and two gnolls stepped forward to mash James down to the ground. Once he was down, the rest of the patrol jumped in to help tie him up. Finally, he was hoisted onto their shoulders and hauled off toward the town.

As the gnolls marched him down the hill and along the red stone walls to the gates, James took his chance to get a better look at the ward. As he'd noted from the tree, it was entirely nature magic, glowing green and smelling of the wilds. He was squinting at the giant patterns, trying to work out exactly what they did, when the gnolls reached the giant doors that opened into the fortress. When they arrived, the glowing green magic snuffed out, and the wooden gate cracked open just wide enough for his captors to wiggle through.

As the gates swung shut again, James saw a shadow flit through behind them at the last second, followed by a faint breeze that smelled of jubatus. Then they passed the gate guards, and the familiar scent was overpowered by the reek of rotten flesh. Twisting to see what could make such a stench, James saw that the guards were not living gnolls but decaying zombie ones with rotting fur and flesh hanging from their exposed bones.

His captors dropped their eyes when they passed the undead and made double time into the Red Canyon city. As they entered the militarized town, James saw many more zombie gnolls standing at guard posts like unblinking statues. The undead didn't talk to the living gnolls at all, but their burning white ghostfire eyes watched everything.

From the way their hackles went up, James got the impression that the undead scared his gnoll captors, but things really got interesting when a tiny tremor rattled the gravel in the street. That little shake must have been significant, because the patrol stopped in its tracks, the gnolls quivering in terror as the distant booming sounded again.

Within seconds, every living gnoll on the street except for the ones carrying James scattered. Trembling, James's escort hauled him into a nearby hut, closing the wooden door as the booms grew louder. Their fear was infectious, and James found himself breaking into a cold sweat as the crashes stopped in the street just outside their hut.

The firelight coming through the gaps in the wooden door vanished, and a rotten stench began to seep in, making James's eyes water. In the dark, he could see ribbons of death magic floating through the air like hunting snakes. There was a loud snort outside, then the reeking shadow moved on, thumping away down the terrified street.

It took several minutes for his escort to gather the courage to carry James outside again. When they finally left the hut, James craned his head back to see what monster had caused this. What he saw made him wish he hadn't.

Far down the empty main street behind them was a truck-sized gnoll covered in heavy iron plates. His burning eyes marked him as undead and explained the smell, but it was his size that squeezed the breath from James's lungs. He was easily ten feet tall, much taller than James, which was a problem. Undead or otherwise, there was only one gnoll in all of Red Canyon who was taller than a jubatus, and that was the Chieftain of Chieftains, final boss of this area.

Gore Maul.

Sweat trickled through James's fur as he realized how close he'd just come to death. If Mr. Three-Point-Five-Skulls had caught him tied up like this, that would have been the end. Even if he'd been free, James wasn't sure he could have taken him. The fifty-level difference didn't mean much against a monster like that when he was gearless and alone.

Thankfully, Gore Maul wasn't looking in his direction. The giant undead gnoll had stopped at one of the town's many smithies to talk with the blacksmith inside. He must not have liked what the smith had to say, because a few seconds later, there was a roar of displeasure, and James watched in horror as Gore Maul picked up the anvil with one hand and smashed it down on the screaming smith who'd been using it, flattening the gnoll instantly.

James's captors started to run after that, charging through the town at breakneck speed. As they went, James arched his neck left and right, searching for some sign that this was more than just a military installation. Women, children, anything to show there were gnolls here who weren't soldiers, but he saw nothing. Every brown-furred hyena-man he saw was armed, armored, and doing martial work of some kind. The forges in town rang constantly, and the stone huts were black with ash from the round-the-clock fires. As they passed a yard full of completed catapults, James had to wonder just how far off the full-scale assault was.

His captors slowed down when they arrived at a place that smelled of blood and fresh mud. Held backward on their shoulders, James couldn't see what was making the stench, but there was no way he could miss the trails of death magic flying over his head. The black streams blocked the light from normal magic whenever they overlapped in his vision, making the whole world flicker. Snickering wickedly, his escort set him down, turning James around to show where they'd brought him.

He was standing at the edge of a muddy pit. Larger than a football field, it was wide and deep with steep sides reinforced in places by large wooden timbers. The shape plus the high ring of packed-down dirt that surrounded the pit reminded James of a sunken arena, but no gladiators could have fought here, because the floor was filled with a forest of gory wooden spikes.

Spikes covered in *bodies.* James staggered back into the paws of his snickering captors. No wonder this place was full of death magic. There were dozens of corpses impaled on the spikes at the bottom of the pit, their faces frozen in the terror of their final moments. Worse, one glance was enough to see that they were all players. Without the interface, he couldn't see their nameplates anymore, but there was no other explanation for why there would be bodies from five different races here, all wearing the classic mismatched armor of low-level questers.

As he stared at their lifeless eyes, a cold dread began to spread through James's chest. Up until this point, he'd only pondered what would happen if he died. Not being able to resurrect the Schtumple Brothers hadn't really told him anything. They were non-player characters, and they'd clearly been dead for hours before James had found them. No matter what state their bodies were in, though, players who died always came back to life with their gear at the nearest shrine, time-lost ruins, or graveyard. When that happened, their old bodies disappeared, but these player bodies were still lying where they'd fallen. From the flies and the smell, he knew that some of them had been staked out here all day.

Struggling not to be sick, James forced himself to look harder, searching the corpses for any sign that he was wrong. Maybe these weren't players after all? Then his eyes caught sight of a shiny bar of dark metal in the hands of a dead Cleric, and his hopes fell.

If he needed more proof, that was it. The Eclipsed Steel Staff was a random drop from Dead Mountain Fortress. The only way to get your hands on one was to be a raider or buy the weapon from a guild. There was no way the NPCs here could have done either of those things, which meant those were dead players down there for certain, and they definitely hadn't respawned.

James's breath quickened as the implications of that landed. He *could* die here, and die for good. He was still working through the shock of that when the gnolls started pushing him toward the edge of the pit.

He fought back, body-slamming the shorter hyenas as he struggled against the ropes, but the dog men just snickered and pulled their weapons, poking at him with their swords and axes until his feet were at the edge of the pit.

They were about to push him over onto the bloody spikes below when a nasally, almost mechanical voice cried, "*Stop!*"

James's would-be executioners froze. Balanced on the edge of the pit, James didn't dare look to see who had saved him, but he caught a glimpse of a staff covered in crystals and feathers out of the corner of his eye.

"Me want this one," said the strange voice, the metallic words speaking over what sounded like yipping and clicking of teeth. "You give!"

As close as he was to death, James was sorely tempted to look anyway, because for the life of him, he couldn't figure out *what* was speaking. The yipping was definitely gnoll, but the mechanical voice sounded like a bad sci-fi robot. Hearing both together felt like being in a badly dubbed movie, starring gnolls. He was still trying to work it out when his captors barked back, growling low in their throats.

"No!" cried the strange auto-tuned voice. "You kill all players so far. Your hate has been fed enough blood. Me claim this one!"

Magic followed the words, followed by the familiar smell of lightning. James's captors backed off after that, snatching him away from the pit and dumping him into the mud face-first. He was spitting dirt out of his mouth when a hand grabbed the rope that bound his feet and started dragging him, face-down, back down the street.

James strained to arch his back so that his face didn't drag in the mud, but his shirt pulled up and stuck around his neck, piling up dirt and probably gnoll droppings. It got worse from there as his rescuer-slash-captor left the dirt to pull him across paving stones, a rough, splintery bridge, and finally, up a flight of stairs. By the end of it, James was feeling battered and grosser than he'd ever been. He was still struggling to get his shirt down from around his head when a door creaked, and he was pulled into a surprisingly clean, floral-smelling hut.

Wiggling, James finally got his tangled shirt down from his face to find himself lying on a floor of mill-cut boards—very expensive by savanna standards—covered in green-and-gold rugs. Even more interesting, though, was the nature magic that hummed through the whole place. Every crystal, feather, and painted hide hanging from the hut's walls and ceiling had the hum of magic in them. There was something powerful coming from the back of the house as well, but James was only able to get a slight impression of it before his captor let him go.

Taking advantage of his new freedom, James rolled himself over to finally see the face of the gnoll who'd taken custody of him. It was an old hyena-man with a broken fang and a scar closing one eye. Just like the hut, his clothes were covered in gems, crystals, feathers, and claws that were all glowing with tightly woven magics, though thankfully no deathly-black ones. The streams of color that rose from the old gnoll were all blues, whites, greens, and browns, and James sighed in relief.

Until he saw the collar.

A large, deathly-black obsidian collar was locked around the old gnoll's neck. It was throbbing with magic, but a type James couldn't see very well. Since he'd had no problem seeing every sort of Naturalist magic, his best guess was that the collar was sorcery or necromancy or maybe both. The sense of dread that emanated from the black metal certainly made James think necromancy was involved. Just looking at it made him want to cringe. He couldn't imagine what it must be like to wear the damn thing.

The old gnoll cleared his throat, making James jump. Embarrassed to have been caught staring, he pushed himself into a sitting position with his bound hands and tried to make a better first impression.

"Hello," he said tentatively.

The gnoll stared at him, his one black, beady eye examining James's tattered clothing.

"You can speak the Language of Wind and Grass," James went on. "That surprised me. I didn't think your kind had the throat for it."

In response, the gnoll pulled his knife. James tried to scoot away, but the old hyena was surprisingly quick, his hand darting down to cut the ropes that bound James's feet. Relieved but confused, James turned to let the old gnoll cut his arms and hands free as well. Released at last, he fixed his filthy shirt as best he could, trying to knock the mud clods out of his fur without making too much of a mess of the pin-neat house.

When he'd finished, the gnoll spoke at last, opening its mouth to yip and yelp. As it barked, the collar pulsed darkly, and the mechanical voice issued forth. "Did you kill four hunters with lightning on the trade road?"

James jerked back. He'd known something weird was going on, but he'd never have guessed the horrible collar was a translator. But while this gnoll's barking sounded just as animal-like as the others', the mechanical voice was clearly speaking his words. It even carried a bit of his inflection. Accusation, in this case.

James sighed. There was no point hiding the truth. If the old gnoll wanted revenge, he'd have let the others toss James into the pit. Since he hadn't, James decided to take a risk.

"Yes."

"You are player, then?" the gnoll said, looking him up and down. "No one else so young and so powerful."

James started to squirm. Every time someone asked him if he was a player, it had ended badly. But he was in it now, so he answered truthfully again. "Yes."

"Are you 'level-eighty Naturalist'?"

James blinked. "Um, yeah. I'm *a* level-eighty Naturalist."

The old gnoll nodded as if that was exactly what he'd wanted to hear and put up his knife. "Me called Thunder Paw. You, Player, come with Me."

With that, the old gnoll turned on his paw and trotted over to the door that led to the back room of the hut. Curious, James stood up to follow, bending over slightly to avoid hitting his head on the gnoll-height ceiling.

The moment the old gnoll cracked the door, the smell of fresh water poured out. Thunder Paw opened it only enough to slide his body through, motioning for James to follow. Wincing at the tight squeeze, James obeyed, contorting his body to wiggle through the tiny opening. When he came out on the other side, what he saw made him gasp.

They were standing in a room that must have once been a sleeping chamber. Now, though, its floor was painted wall-to-wall with a bright-turquoise seal. In the middle of the magical markings, a globe of pristine blue water nearly as tall as James hovered in midair, and floating at its center, curled into a ball, was a gnoll pup.

"Whoa," James said, leaning in to examine the water ball. He'd been able to see magic for less than a day, but even he could tell how flawlessly the spell had been constructed. Every flow of power fed neatly into the others, leaving nothing to waste.

"You really know your stuff, Thunder Paw," he said in awe.

The gnoll waved the compliment away. "Me Naturalist long time," he said. "Now your turn." Thunder Paw turned to James, clunking his feather-covered staff on the floor. "Me save you life. Now, Player, heal him."

"*Me?*" James squeaked, pointing at the flawless spell. "Dude, you're a *way* better Naturalist than I am! What can I fix that you can't?" He glanced at the little pup sleeping inside the water. "What's wrong with him, anyway?"

Instead of answering his question, Thunder Paw leaned down to place his paw on the seal that covered the floor. The blue markings pulsed when he touched them, and some of the water inside the sphere pulled away from the pup's arm. Immediately, there was a hiss as blue-white ghostfire ignited, devouring the pup's fine fur. Thunder Paw took his hand away again at once, and the watery seal closed back in, smothering the ghostfire.

"I see," James said gravely.

Thunder Paw's lone eye showed his heartbreak. "Me not strong enough to put it out. Need strongest Naturalist. You level eighty. You strongest."

"Right," James said, pushing up his muddy sleeves. "Stand back, then."

He had no plan, but he didn't need an angle to save a gnoll puppy from becoming undead, and this was a problem he might actually be able to help with. Ghostfire was a status effect that came part-and-parcel with any undead dungeon. Gray Fang's cleansing hadn't worked on Lilac because she'd been afflicted with death magic, not actual ghostfire yet, but James had cleansed the Once King's cursed fire off of other players loads of times. Of course, those conflagrations were normally on the surface since the ghostfire was usually applied externally via ghostfire weapons. When he peered at the life energies inside the boy gnoll, though, James was alarmed to see the fire simmering inside his major energy veins.

That didn't look good. He didn't have the game's interface telling him if the status effect could or could not be cleansed anymore, though, so he wouldn't know until he tried. Fingers crossed, James started weaving the Cleanse spell. As he put it together, plucking magic from the air, he made sure to add more water than usual. Water was a very effective cure for most ghostfire-related problems, and he had a feeling this one was going to take a *lot* to extinguish. The damn stuff was magical napalm.

He gathered the magic until he could hold no more. Then when his arms were coiled with huge ropes of turquoise magic, James shoved his hands, and the spell, into the bubble of water, pushing magic into the pup hard. Maybe *too* hard, because the boy cried out in pain, but James didn't dare stop. If this was going to work, he needed to completely overwhelm the ghostfire, flushing it out once and for all.

It looked like it was working. The life magic in his spell hooked onto the pup's vital energy, creating a channel for all the water James had gathered to pour inside him. The ghostfire hissed and spat as it came in contact with the bright-turquoise magic. Encouraged, James kept up the pressure, chasing the fire as it shifted and slid, but every time he put it out in one place, it would reignite in another. Minutes ticked by. James's whole body ached from the effort of channeling for so long, but he couldn't stop. He was so close to stamping it out. So *close*. But then, just when he felt he was finally gaining the upper hand, the water magic he'd gathered ran out. His mana faded, and the spell fell apart.

The moment his hands dropped, Thunder Paw rushed forward to undo the seal. James grabbed the gnoll by a hairy shoulder to stop him.

"Don't," he said. "I failed."

Despite all the water he'd poured into the pup, he could still see spots of ghostfire flickering like embers deep inside his thick life energies. The flames spread as he watched, racing to reclaim their previous positions. If not for the crushing weight of Thunder Paw's seal, the cursed fire would have consumed the boy completely.

"I'm sorry," James said quietly, turning to the grief-stricken old gnoll. "I've cleansed ghostfire before, but never this deep." His shoulders slumped. "I'm just not enough."

It wasn't his fault, but James felt terrible all the same. FFO had always been the one thing he was really good at. Beating the toughest quests, getting the rarest items, finding areas of the game no one else had—he'd always been able to do what most players could not. For years, this world had been the one place where he wasn't a failure. Now it was real, and he *still* couldn't do what mattered.

The bitter defeat that followed that thought was a depressingly familiar sensation. But no matter how bad James felt, nothing compared to the look of utter despair on Thunder Paw's face. "Who is he?" James asked gently.

"Son of Me son," the Naturalist said in a small voice. "Last of line. Rest of family undead. He all Me have left." Thunder Paw's one eye swiveled to look at him. "You level eighty, the strongest. You last chance to heal him."

The gnoll shook as he finished. Tail down, legs shivering, the snaggletoothed, one-eyed hyena-man started whining softly as he clung to his staff. It was a pitiful, heartbreaking sound, and as it went on and on, something inside James snapped.

"Don't give up yet," he said fiercely, grabbing the old gnoll by the shoulders. "I almost did it! I just didn't have enough water magic in the spell. If I can get more, I can save him."

The gnoll shook his head. "You strongest. There is not more."

"But I'm *not* the strongest," James said. "I had power, but I lost it. You need a real healer, and I'm afraid you got me instead. But this isn't over yet." He leaned down, looking the gnoll in the eye. "How far are you willing to go to save him?"

"Anywhere," the gnoll said instantly.

"Would you fight monsters?" James pressed. "Travel to the end of the world? Make a deal with the gods?"

The gnoll nodded rapidly, and James nodded back. "Good," he said. "Because that's what we might have to do. Just don't give up just because the first player you tried is a loser. I might not be able to heal this, but there are stronger cures for ghostfire than the Cleanse spell. Pan-elixirs, Unfallen Water potions, things like that. And if we can't get one of those, I have a friend who's a top-of-the-world Cleric. No lie, he wears robes sewn from the high clouds blessed by the Sun itself. Surely *he* can heal your grandson. We'll find him if we have to, but you can't quit when you still have a chance."

James didn't know if those were the right words. He wasn't even sure he could keep those promises, but he had to say something. He couldn't leave this loving old grandfather in a pile of broken hopes on the floor. He just couldn't. Thunder Paw's struggle was a world different from his, but James knew all too well the hopelessness of facing an overwhelming problem by yourself. He knew what it was like to try your hardest and still fail, so he said to Thunder Paw what he wished his parents, his sister, or *anyone* had said to him.

"We can do it. I'll help you until it's done. You don't have to do this alone."

When he finished, the gnoll's legs had stopped shivering. "You sure?"

"I'm sure," James said, giving Thunder Paw a big smile. "We may not even have to go far."

His sudden change in attitude made the old gnoll blink, but James was rolling. He'd been so caught up in pulling the Red Canyon questline off, he'd hadn't bothered to think about how it ended until this moment. Now, though, he remembered, leaving him vibrating in excitement. "We don't have to go far at all," he said, grabbing the short gnoll by the shoulders. "There are four pan-elixirs right here in Red Canyon!"

The Naturalist tilted his head. "We have such things?"

"The gnolls don't," James said. "But the lich does. It's been so long, I'd forgotten, but listing the ghostfire remedies just now made me remember that the lich of Red Canyon has four pan elixirs in his loot cache! They're in the chest at the back of his boss room. We just have get in and take them."

The gnoll's ears fell. "Then it impossible. Lich control Grand Pack. Is very, very strong."

"Not as strong as you think," James replied. "I actually came here tonight to take him out."

"You can defeat lich?" said Thunder Paw, awestruck.

"Yup," James said proudly. "He should be way easier to beat than this bitchy ghostfire infection. The main problem is—no offense—you gnolls. Back when this was a game, Red Canyon was just a militarized village. Now you're an army, and I can't handle that."

Thunder Paw stamped his staff in renewed determination. "You save Grand Pack? Then Me, Thunder Paw, Speaker of Storms, will help you! What you need?"

"I need you to take me to the lake on the north side of the village," James said immediately. "There's a locket hidden underwater there. Once we get it, I can use it to take down Gore Maul. My friend in the city should be handling the other two chieftains as we speak. Once they're all down, we can sneak into the lich's lab."

"Then we have big problem," Thunder Paw said flatly. "There is no more lake."

"What do you mean?" James asked. He hadn't seen the village's reservoir earlier when he'd been looking from the tree, but things were bigger now, so he'd figured it had moved. Surely an entire lake couldn't just vanish.

"Lich ordered lake gone," Thunder Paw explained. "Said it useless waste of space. Need more land for war. You were almost thrown into it earlier."

So *that* was where the giant spike pit had come from. It was the drained lake bed. James closed his eyes with a curse. If the lake was gone, that meant the locket quest was, too, which meant he was going to have to face a full-strength Gore Maul. He didn't even know if that was possible without his gear. When he explained the situation to Thunder Paw, though, the old gnoll scoffed.

"Me can fix that," Thunder Paw said proudly. The one-eyed gnoll got up to retrieve a coil of rope out of a basket. "You missing weapon and armor? Me get you those. Tons of dead players not using gear anymore. You take, then you kill undead and give Me pan-elixir."

James frowned. Horrors of looting the dead aside, that would have been a good idea save for one critical problem: the game's equipment-binding system. In FFO, magical gear bound itself to you the moment you equipped it. After that, it became forever unusable for anyone else. When he opened his mouth to explain this to Thunder Paw, though, James remembered the Eclipsed Steel staff he'd seen in the dead Cleric's hand. In the game, dead players always respawned with their equipment. Now that death seemed permanent, though, maybe that broke the binding system as well. After all, the lore explanation was that magical items were bound to your soul, but if your soul was no longer there, that was another story.

"Okay," James said. "Let's give it a shot."

Thunder Paw nodded. But when he advanced with the rope, James put up his hands. "Whoa. What's that for?"

"Me tie you up," the gnoll explained. "Take you as prisoner to player weapons."

James didn't want to be tied up yet again. He'd *just* gotten free. He didn't want to go back to being helpless while someone else decided his fate, but the gnoll Naturalist was having none of it.

"This only way," he snapped, the black collar turning his angry yips into stern words. "I take you to weapons, you get power, you kill undead. Easy plan. Good plan."

"Can't I just prowl after you?" James pleaded. "I'm pretty sneaky."

"No," said Thunder Paw. "You say many good things, make good promises, but other gnolls tell Me players kill my people lots during Nightmare. Something called 'farming.' You not friend of gnolls."

"Wait," James said, confused. "You were only *told* about the Nightmare?"

Thunder Paw ignored his question, brandishing the coil of rope in James's face like a stern grandfather. "We have saying. 'Do not follow he who never follows. Do not trust he who never trusts.' Me not trust you with player power if you not trust me with rope. You must follow Me first."

James sighed, filing his burning curiosity away for later. It was probably a long discussion, anyway, one they didn't have the time for right now. He still didn't want to be tied up, but he couldn't back out after all he'd said, so fur flat in distress, he stuck out his hands.

"All right," he muttered, trying not to look as the gnoll wrapped the rope around his wrists. "I trust you. And the name is James, by the way."

CHAPTER 9
Tina

Tina woke up with an ax in her back. After a second of freaking out, she realized the curved blade was merely hooked into her armor rather than into *her*.

"Welcome back, boss," said the gruff, tired voice of Killbox.

"Thanks," Tina said, amazed she was here to say that at all. "How'd you save me?"

The Berserker lowered her gently off his giant shoulders. "I had the easy part. GabbyBlade and Frank the Tank did all the hard stuff."

That was a relief to hear, until Tina realized that she didn't see SB or Frank standing with the rest of the raid on the dark road. "Where are they?"

Killbox shrugged. "Not sure."

Fear tightened Tina's throat. "Then we have to look for them," she said angrily. "If we've got MIA, we gotta send a rescue."

"What about David?" someone asked from the back of the group. "He got stomped. If we're going back, we gotta raise him."

Tina shuddered as she remembered the shredded robes and red splotch that was all that remained of the healer when Grel's foot had come up. "I don't think there's much left to raise," she said quietly. "And I'm not sending anyone back up on that hill. I won't follow one death with more."

A grim silence spread through the group, but no one argued. Looking around, Tina could see why. Even in the pitch black of the road, the raid looked terrible. The Knight closest to her had a bloody gash across his forehead no one had healed yet, and he wasn't alone. Everyone in the raid had an injury of some kind, and no wonder. The healers were wrecked. With David gone, there were only five of them now, and every one was being supported by another player to keep from falling over.

The Sorcerers didn't look much better, but it was the nonphysical damage that bothered Tina the most. Several of her veteran raiders looked crushed in a way that had nothing to do with tiredness or injury. Watching them sink to the ground, Tina was awkwardly aware that she should have felt the same. David was an original Roughneck, someone she'd known for years. His death should hurt like a knife in her side, but nothing could pierce the wall of anxiety she felt over SilentBlayde or the anger she felt at herself.

She'd blown it. *Again.* The battle on the hill had been a complete rout, and it was all her fault. Why the hell had she let everyone fall asleep at the same time? Even teenagers playing D&D knew to set watches. Grel was a skeleton the size of a building, leading an army of rattling, clattering undead. If she'd been smart enough to put *anyone* on watch, they would have heard the danger coming from miles away and given them all a chance to run. Now David was dead, and SB and Frank were missing, possibly dead as well, and it was all her fault.

The only silver lining in this disaster was that at least the others were *finally* taking this seriously. For the first time since they'd woken up in front of the Once King's mountain, no one was complaining or goofing off. They were all just looking at her, quietly and expectantly, waiting for her to tell them what to do.

For most people, being stared at by a crowd like that would be terrifying, but Tina was different. This was her raid. They needed her to lead them, and as always, that gave her strength. It was the reason she played FFO so relentlessly. When she was here, she wasn't the fluffy-haired library sciences undergrad no one ever listened to. Here, she was Roxxy, guild leader and world-class tank.

No one at home ever looked at Tina the way raiders looked at Roxxy. No one in the real world ever asked, "What now, Tina?" In FFO, though, she could always see it. The same question that had been in their eyes in the game was there now, asking her, "What now? How will we make it out of this?"

Given how much she'd screwed up, Tina wasn't sure she had the right to answer that, but it didn't matter. She had to step up, because no one else was going to do it. There was no room for doubts or weakness when nearly forty people were depending on you. Meeting their eyes, Tina clenched her shield's grip and straightened to her full height so she could look down at them. Not as Tina, but as Roxxy, guild leader of the Roughneck Raiders, one of the best damn guilds in the game.

It didn't even matter that there was no game anymore. They'd earned their place at the top, and Tina would be damned if she wasn't going to live up to that now.

With that, she launched into roll call. Since fighting Killbox, she'd been working on learning the raider's names. She still slipped up a few times, but after several corrections, she'd determined everyone had made it down the hill except for the ones she already knew.

"Okay," she said when she'd finished. "Looks like we're only missing three people: David, Frank, and SilentBlayde."

Her voice shook when she said SB's name, but she covered it up with bluster. She turned to the raid's two remaining Assassins, who were standing together at the rear of the crowd. "ZeroDarkness, KuroKawaii, go south to the graveyard and see if David has come back to life there." They hadn't had a chance to check the graveyard by the Dead Mountain to see if the Sorcerer she'd let die had raised there, so Tina felt there was still a small chance that David wasn't gone. A very small chance, but she refused to let go of the hope.

"Right-o," said KuroKawaii as both Assassins vanished into the shadows.

Next, Tina turned to Zen, the dark-skinned, bright-green-haired elven Ranger whom she'd asked to shoot the Flare Arrow back on the hill. Zen wasn't a Roughneck, but she was one of Tina's most reliable fill-ins on pickup raid nights. She was also a nurse in real life, which might prove very useful in their current situation.

"Your boots are still enchanted with the speed-bonus, right?"

When the elf nodded, Tina jerked her thumb back toward the hill. "Go see if Frank or SB is coming up from the rear. Don't take any chances, though. The enemy is still right behind us. First sign of trouble, you come back."

Zen gave her the thumbs-up and took off, long ears bobbing as each step carried her half again as far as it should. Tina watched her race away with a sigh. She wished they all had that enchantment now. She also wished she could be the one to go look for SilentBlayde and Frank.

Tina shoved that desire down. Zen would make much better time, and Tina was the only one who could keep this mess together. Speaking of mess, the rest of the raid was still waiting for orders, so Tina raised her stonekin's booming voice again, belting out the words until they rang in the dark.

"We're not dead yet!" she cried. "The plan is still the same: get to the Order of the Golden Sun's fortress before the enemy gets to us. We outpaced Grel'Darm once. We can do it again. Undead don't rest, and neither will we until we reach that fort. Now let's march!"

Everyone winced at the word march, but once again, no one complained. They just nodded and started shuffling down the broken old road. Watching them go, Tina felt as if she should say something comforting like "we're almost there," or "it'll be okay." But those lines lacked credibility even in her head, so Tina just let them walk, watching from the back to make sure no one lagged behind. She'd just gotten them to a slow but steady pace when something caught her eye.

"*Anders!*" she snarled, stomping through the crowd. "Why the hell are *you* carrying NekoBaby?!"

The fish-man Cleric turned his head, scales glinting dully in the light of his magical staff as he stammered in fear. "I-It's not my fault! Frank threw her at me and told me to carry her. I haven't done anything!"

It was good for all of them that Tina was too tired to be as angry as she should have been. "Give her to me," she said, exasperated. "We don't need any more complications, and you don't look like you can go much farther on your own power, anyway, let alone hauling double."

The statement brought actual tears of relief to Anders's huge fish eyes. Tina had never seen an exhausted ichthyian before, but his scales had a papery look to them that couldn't be good. He was handing the sleeping Naturalist to Tina with a murmur of thanks when NekoBaby's eyes popped open.

"Aw," she said, sliding off Anders's back with a pout of disappointment. "Ride's over."

"*What?*" said Anders and Tina at the same time.

NekoBaby gave Anders a cruel fanged grin. "I was just letting you carry me so I could shove my boobs into your back," she said, poking the Cleric in the ribs. "By the way, I'm actually a guy. How's it feel to get a boner from carrying a dude, huh? Ready for all the 'Anders is gay' jokes?"

Anders stared at her in disbelief, and Tina smacked her forehead with her palm to keep from strangling the cat-girl right then and there.

"Anders," she said in a cold voice, "go rejoin the others. I'll talk to you in a bit."

Clutching his arms around himself, Anders nodded and shuffled back toward the main line of players. Once he was far enough away, Tina turned angrily on NekoBaby.

"What the hell is wrong with you?"

"Uh-oh," the Naturalist said. "Mom's mad."

"Fucking right I'm mad," Tina yelled. "This group of ours isn't some caveman collective like *DrunkChicksCantSayNo*, so I highly doubt Anders is afraid of being called gay. You've been scamming too many manly-men if you believe that's even an insult anymore."

Neko's ears went back at that, and Tina rubbed her stone temples. "I know you want revenge for earlier," she said, more quietly this time. "But this isn't the time. We're down a healer after what happened to David, and I need Anders functional. Can you please wait until we're not hauling ass two steps ahead of our deaths before you resume your campaign of attempting to make his life miserable?"

"Maybe," NekoBaby grumbled. "I'll think about it. I still have my damaged armor to get back at him for."

"Has it occurred to you that we've got more important shit to deal with right now than your revenge?" Tina snapped. "You took your joy ride on his back at the worst possible time. Do we look like we can afford to have half the raid carrying the other half?"

"Why are *you* defending him?" Neko demanded. "He ripped off my clothing, Roxxy! He was going to *rape* me! You're a girl in real life. How can you excuse that shit even for a second? The creep deserves whatever I do to him and then some!" She crossed her arms angrily over Frank's undershirt, which she was still wearing over her ruined robe. "If you aren't going to punish him, I will."

Tina didn't know what to say. She'd felt the exact same way back at the Dead Mountain, and she hadn't even been the victim. Neko had every right to feel the way she did, but they didn't have time to deal with it right now. Still, Tina didn't want to tell Neko to just store it 'till the crisis was over...

She bit her lip, trying to think of what her brother would say in this situation. For all his other faults, James had always been the politic member of the family. Unfortunately, channeling James came about as naturally to Tina as bike riding did to a fish. No matter what angle she tried, nothing felt right, so Tina just sucked it up and told Neko the truth.

"There's no question that what Anders did was horrible," she said firmly, "but I can't kick him out of the raid. That would be a death sentence for him, and maybe the rest of us, too. We only have five healers now. I can't punish all of them for something he did."

The jubatus's fur puffed in anger. "So I get the short stick, huh? No consequences for trying to rape an unconscious girl?"

"Maybe not the ones you wanted, but there *have* been consequences," Tina said. "You've been staying away from Anders, so you haven't seen the hell he's reaped, but I've been in the back this whole time. I've done nothing but watch the raid march, and while we're all pissed as hell about having to do this, Anders is the only one who cries."

"Oh, boo-hoo," Neko sneered. "Fish-boy has a case of man-guilt."

"That's not it. At least, that's not all of it. Everyone in the raid knows what he tried to do to you. I hear the bad names they whisper at his back, just loud enough for him to pick up. The whole group hates him. No one will let him walk close, and people trip or spit on him when he does. Hell, I'm pretty sure one of the Assassins knifed him just because they could."

"Wish they'd finished the job," Neko grumbled.

"We're all lucky they didn't," Tina said sternly. "Like I said, we need his heals, but all that stuff adds up. The raid's all we have out here, and Anders is a pariah. That's gotta hurt deep, so how much punishment is enough? You just sexually harassed him a lot. When's the buck gonna stop?"

Neko huffed and gave Tina an annoyed look. Tina glared right back. "Also," she went on, "I thought we were supposed to be keeping your real gender a secret. How the hell am I supposed to protect you when you're blurting out the truth after *riding on the back of your assailant?*"

The cat-girl's ears went flat. "I didn't think about that."

"Well, you need to," Tina said sharply. "Because no matter who you are inside, you've chosen to be a girl in this world, and that means shit like this has consequences. I've seen plenty of girls try to use their bodies as weapons against dudes who hurt them, and it never ends well. What Anders did to you would mess anyone up, but this sort of revenge only makes things worse. I don't know if anything can ever make it totally better again, but I bet some counseling would help. Zen's a nurse. Why don't you try talking to her?"

"Okay, okay, Roxxy, *gah!*" NekoBaby cried, her face scarlet beneath her short fur. "I'll chill, all right? Just stop talking! But I'm still mad at Anders, and I *don't* trust him. Don't you dare put us on any teams together."

"Works for me," Tina said. "Thanks, Neko."

NekoBaby huffed and stalked off, tail still bristling. Unfortunately, Tina wasn't done with awkward conversations. Now that NekoBaby was mostly sort of taken care of, it was time to talk to Anders.

She found him alone, as always, dragging his feet dejectedly a good ten feet off to the side of the raid. Now that she had time to look, Tina noticed the ichthyian was far dirtier than anyone else. His robe was stained with ash from all the times he'd been knocked down or tripped, and there was a bloody stain over his ribs that none of their legitimate fights could account for. The rest of the raid watched out of the corners of their eyes as she walked over, but Tina didn't want an audience, so she guided Anders back to the rear of the raid. The distance wouldn't stop any really determined eavesdroppers, but at least it would force them to be obvious about it.

"How are you doing?" she asked quietly, doing her best to keep her voice neutral. "I worry that Neko took her revenge too far."

The Cleric leaned heavily on his glowing staff. "To be honest, it doesn't bother me. I got what I deserved."

She arched a copper eyebrow. "Really? 'Cause it looks like it's bothering the hell outta you."

"*I'm* bothering the hell out of me," Anders said, shoulders drooping. "I acted like a monster, and now I'm a literal one."

He held up a webbed hand with spines on the ends of his fingers, and Tina sighed. "We're all different now, dude. I'm an eight-foot-tall lady made of rocks. And it's not like you're the only ichthyian."

"It's not that," Anders started then stopped, turning to look up at her. "Do you know what having Leylia's is like?"

Tina shook her head, and the fish-man's hinged jaw clenched. "It's hell. I never know what's real and what isn't. My parents can't afford to have me institutionalized, so they hide me in the attic and tell our family I'm a vegetable. No one visits me except my mother, and she only comes up to bring me food. She doesn't talk to me or stay longer than she has to. She's never pulled it, but I know she keeps a Taser in her pocket. You know, just in case I confuse her for a monster."

His eyes dropped as he finished, but Tina didn't know what to say. The reality of Leylia's was horrifying.

"I didn't know Neko was real," Anders continued, putting a webbed hand over his face. "There was no interface. That's new for you guys, but for me, it's every day. I had no reason to question what I was seeing or to think I was hurting a real person. I knew it was gross, but my life is so miserable... I just wanted to be happy for a bit, even if I hated myself later. As despicable as that is, though, it's not even the worst part. The *worst* part of this is that I've ruined my own salvation."

Tina frowned, confused. "Salvation?"

Anders cupped his hands in praise of the Divine Sun, just as the game's actual priests always did. "I haven't had an episode since I got stuck here," he said quietly. "I used to have them every few hours, but once I woke up here, all I've seen is what's real." He flashed her a sad smile. "That's a *miracle*, Roxxy, and I've ruined it by letting my leftover delusions run away with me. I got a second chance at life, and I started it as a would-be rapist."

Tina patted Anders awkwardly on the shoulder. She wasn't sure where she was on the spectrum of pity or disgust with the Cleric, but she knew her duty as the raid leader. "It's not over yet," she said, forcing cheer into her voice. "I'm not gonna punish you any more for what you did, and Neko's promised to knock it off at least until we reach the fortress. Just stay alive, and I bet you can find atonement."

"Doesn't matter," Anders said, his voice defeated. "I'm still a monster."

"You're only a monster if you act like one."

"No, I mean I'm *literally* a monster," he said, waving his webbed hand at her again. "I was saved, but this existence is already warping who I am. Who *everyone* here is."

"What are you talking about?" Tina asked, exasperated. "Yeah, we don't look human anymore, but we're still us."

"Are we?" Anders turned and pointed up the road at one of the elven Rangers walking in front of them. "What's that guy look like to you?"

Tina squinted at the archer. "Like an elf. Blond, pointy ears, maxed height sliders, default face and hair settings. Honestly, they all look kinda the same." She winced. "Crap. That's racist now, isn't it?"

Anders chuckled. "Yes, it is, rock girl. But that's not what I meant." His tone became salacious. "You don't have *anything* else to say about him?"

Tina didn't like the way he said that one bit. After everything else he'd said, though, she didn't think Anders was being sleazy, so she dutifully stared at the elf again. Unfortunately, she didn't see anything new.

"I give up," she said at last. "What should I be noticing?"

"Do you think he's cute?"

"No more than any other elf," she said, getting frustrated. "I'm not in shape to deal with this, Anders. Just spell it out."

"So you're saying the six-foot-tall male elf with a Photoshop-perfect face and the body of a god wearing formfitting leather armor doesn't do *anything* for you? Nothing at all?" He shrugged. "Can't spell it out any more than that."

Tina's head whipped back to the elf Ranger, but Anders was right. He *was* insanely handsome to the point of being beautiful in a masculine way. Even worn out, tired, and limping from the long walk, he moved with a grace professional dancers would kill for. The human men were just as remarkable—tall and broad shouldered with the muscles and rugged good looks normally reserved for A-list action movie stars. But while a distant part of her brain recognized that as smoking hot, her body felt nothing.

"Okay," she said slowly. "It is a little weird that I never noticed how many amazingly hot dudes we have, but I've been kind of busy. Why are *you* noticing?"

"Because the same thing's happening to me," Anders said. "We've been here for less than a day, but NekoBaby isn't attractive to me anymore. None of them are. I'm surrounded by women who are fourteen out of ten on the beauty scale with bodies crafted by 3-D modelers to be better than the human ideal. I *loved* that back when this was a game, but now they're all just too...mammalian."

Tina recoiled at Anders's confession. His sanity had been kind of questionable from the start, but now she was seriously concerned he was going off a whole new deep end.

"Now, MarziPain over there?" the fish-man continued. "The ichthyian Sorceress? She's *amazing*. To the point of being really distracting, actually. She has beautiful crest ridges, and her *gills...*"

He made a gurgling noise in his throat, and Tina cringed.

"Okay, I get it," she said. "You're finding fish-girls attractive instead of humans now. I can see why that would freak you out."

"But it's not just me," Anders said earnestly. "That's what I'm trying to tell you. The fact that you didn't even notice you're surrounded by hot elf guys proves that it's happening to you, too. And if it's happening to both of us, then it's probably happening to everyone."

"Shut up," Tina said. "Just because I don't find some random elf sexy doesn't mean anything. We're running for our lives! How can you even think about sex right now?"

Anders arched a scaly eye ridge at her. "We're all superhuman, in perfect health, with young, physically ideal bodies. Most of us have been secretly lusting after the FFO character models for years. Now we're in real *fully* functioning versions of those bodies. Oh, and we're all away from home and in the sort of danger that makes you want to celebrate being alive. If there's anything weird here, Roxxy, it's how are you *not* obsessing about sex?"

"Because I'm busy keeping everyone alive," she growled. "And you're being ridiculous."

"Am I?" He nodded at the raid in front of them. "Haven't you noticed how many people are walking in pairs?"

She hadn't, though now that Anders had pointed it out, it was painfully obvious how many hands, tails, and fins were being held between the raiders. "Fine," Tina admitted. "You're right. It's senior prom night up there, but so what? I still don't see how this applies to me."

Anders stopped and turned to look at her with his huge, double-lidded fish eyes. He held her gaze for several seconds, long enough for Tina to watch his gills flex and facial scales shift. "Stonekin don't have sex, Roxxy," he said in a pitying voice. "Your kind are birthed from magic in the realm of bedrock deep underground. I don't know what sort of partners you preferred before we changed, but I find your lack of interest in sex now to be *very* appropriate to your new race. You sound just like that stonekin quest-giver from the Valentine's Day event. You know, the one who can't understand why everyone else is making such a fuss. Look at all those pairings and think about that."

With that, Anders turned and walked back toward the raid. Dumbfounded, Tina stayed put, staring at the group in front of her with new eyes. Now that she'd seen them, she couldn't unsee the number of people who were walking shoulder to shoulder, leaning into each other in suspiciously race-compatible combinations. All except for GneissGuy, the only other stonekin in the raid. He was just plodding along, steady and alone.

■ ■

Tina spent the next mile in miserable, lonely silence.

She'd always loved playing Roxxy. The stonekin was powerful and invincible, not to mention tall. She was the exact opposite of Tina's real life, and though things since they'd come here had been painful and terrifying, they'd also been exhilarating. She'd gotten to *be* Roxxy in a way the game could never deliver, to live that power.

Now, though, she was feeling the weight of her armor and her shield like never before. In her pack, she still had her ration of bread. Everyone else had long since wolfed theirs down, but every time she tried to eat, the bread was unappetizing. She wasn't hungry, anyway, despite marching for a full day and most of a night, which only now struck her as alarming.

Scowling, Tina reached up to scrape some of the dried silver blood off her temple. Anders had been right on a lot of levels. Being Superwoman was cool, but now that the reality of not being human had set in, it was unsettling. She'd never paid attention to the game's lore beyond what she needed to run dungeons and beat bosses. She'd chosen a stonekin because they made good tanks, but beyond that, she knew nothing about her race. For all she knew, she didn't need to eat at all.

That was a scary thought. If she didn't eat, was she even alive? Perhaps she was some kind of weird elemental robot now, and if so, how was she different from the undead behind them?

Nervous, Tina glanced down at her reflection through the dust that caked the inside of her shield. Her granite skin was painfully close to the pervasive grayness of the Deadlands, and her copper metal hair looked like it had been welded, not grown, but it was the eyes that unnerved her the most. Roxxy didn't have green eyes. Normal people had green eyes. She had living magical emeralds. Hard, sharply faceted jewels that focused and unfocused like camera apertures. Meeting their inhuman gaze in her reflection made Tina feel more like a monster than anything else had so far, and the fact that Frank and SB *still* weren't back wasn't helping.

Lowering her shield, she glanced over her shoulder for the millionth time. As always, though, there was nothing to see. Just the dark, empty road running off behind her. She was scowling at it when NekoBaby appeared beside her.

"Hey, Rocky Road!"

Tina arched an eyebrow at the overly enthusiastic greeting. "I thought you were upset."

"Pfft, that was, like, twenty minutes ago," the Naturalist said. "I'm cool now, especially since you pointed out how miserable Anders is." She glanced over her shoulder at the empty road behind them. "So why the long face? You aren't worried about TalkyBlayde, are you?"

"Of course I'm worried," Tina snapped. "He and Frank are still missing."

"They're fine," the cat-girl said flippantly. "Frank's a tank, and SB's a machine. He's farmed the Deadlands so much, I bet he knows this zone better than the developers. You know, before I joined the Roughnecks, I used to think he was a bot." A mischievous light gleamed in her eyes. "Say, Roxxy, you know 'Blayde in real life, right? You guys make all those tanking videos together, so you must talk outside the game."

"We talk," Tina said, which was the understatement of the century. She and SB texted all the time when she wasn't online. She'd nearly gotten her phone confiscated over it back in high school. "Why?"

Neko pounced on her. "What's his deal? He's *always* online."

"So?" Tina said defensively. "We're on all the time, too."

"Not *that* much," Neko said. "I've checked his log on the guild screen. Dude plays FFO sixteen hours a day, *every* day. That's not normal." She clapped her hands together. "I bet he's a NEET! You know, one of those Japanese kids who turn their backs on life and hole up in their parents' houses to play video games all day. Either that, or he's a creepy forty-year-old Japanese salaryman playing FFO from the office so he can hit on teenage girls."

"Okay," Tina said. "First, there's no job in the world that would let you play a full-immersion VR MMO on the clock. That's just stupid. Second, SB's *not* middle-aged. He's only a year older than I am."

"How do you know that?" Neko prodded. "Have you ever seen him IRL?"

Tina clenched her jaw. She and SB were as close as two friends could be. They'd been playing FFO together for seven years now, but in all that time, she'd never actually seen his face. Not a picture, not on webcam, nothing. It felt crazy considering they'd been running an FFO video channel together since before she'd gone to college, but though SB provided tons of in-game footage, she was the only one who recorded her actual face. She'd tried to get a photo out of him several times, even tried to trick him into it once, but SilentBlayde was as slippery in real life as his Assassin was in game. No matter what she did or how pointedly she asked, he always found a way to change the subject and slip away.

If he hadn't been such a stand-up guy in literally every other area, Tina would have called bullshit years ago. By the time it had become an issue, though, he'd already become a pillar of her life, and she'd never been willing to risk that over something as trivial as a photo. Neko was poking her in the ribs, though, so Tina gave the only answer she knew.

"It doesn't matter," she said, slapping the cat-girl's hand away. "SB's always there for us, and that's what counts. Why do you care, anyway? It's not like any of our IRL stuff matters so long as we're stuck here."

"I was only curious," Neko said grumpily. "He's such a social guy. I swear the dude knows everyone in the game, and he's a legend on the forums. I just can't imagine someone that outgoing living in his mom's closet, you know?"

Tina had never been able to, either. Before she could say so, though, a distant voice shouted behind them.

"*Help!* We need help over here!"

Tina whirled around and squinted through the dark and the dust until she spotted Frank running up the road after them. She almost didn't recognize him because, for some reason, he'd taken off all his armor, leaving him wearing nothing but the human-racial starter leather breeches as he staggered to a stop in front of her.

"Break time, everyone!" Tina yelled, banging on her shield before reaching out to steady Frank. "What happened?"

Frank shook his head. Poor guy was panting so hard he looked as if he was going to throw up. Tina was about to ask if anyone had some water left for him when he grabbed her arm. "Roxxy!" He gasped. "SB needs a healer! He's dying! Zen's barely keeping him alive!"

186

Tina felt like her stomach had just been kicked down to her feet. For a moment, she just stood there, frozen in panic, then she whirled around. "*Killbox!*" she bellowed, running down the road in the direction Frank had come from. "*Neko!* Come with me! Everyone else, break for ten minutes. After that, get marching whether we're back or not."

Leaving the raid leaderless was a bad idea. But while the rational part of Tina knew that pointing a headless mob of players down the road was asking for disaster, the rest of her didn't care. Saving SilentBlayde was all that mattered.

She was about to yell for Killbox again when he suddenly appeared beside her, running down the road with NekoBaby perched on his back like a feline Yoda. They both cringed when they saw her, and Tina realized belatedly what her face must look like. She didn't bother fixing it, though. If any situation deserved a death glare, it was this one.

"Where am I going?" she yelled over her shoulder at Frank.

"Straight down the road," Frank yelled back. "Can't miss them. And save my armor, please!"

Tina gave him a thumbs-up over her shoulder and started running faster, kicking herself all the while for sending one Ranger instead of a full party. Retrieval should have been her top priority, but she'd left them back here without even sending a healer for support. If SilentBlayde died because of her bad decisions, she'd never forgive herself.

"Stupid, stupid, stupid," she muttered, pushing herself even faster until Killbox was struggling to keep up. They were both panting by the time they finally spotted the two small figures in the dust ahead. One was lying on his back. The other was bent over his body, giving him what appeared to be CPR.

The sight of the emergency measures spurred Tina even faster. She sprinted the final distance, sending her own mini dust storm rolling over Zen and SilentBlayde as she skidded to a halt.

"*How is he?*"

The Assassin's face was a horrible ash-gray color that no living being's should be. He was so still, Tina almost couldn't look at him. Still, she held on to hope, dropping down beside Zen with a crash that shook the road.

"Well?"

Zen looked up from her CPR, her dusty face streaked with tears.

"I'm sorry, Roxxy," she said, her voice hoarse. "He died of hypoxia right after Frank left."

"Hypoxia?" Tina repeated, her voice terrifyingly flat even to her ears.

"Lack of oxygen to the cells," Zen clarified, staring down at SB's still body. "I've been an ER nurse for ten years, but I've never seen a case this severe. It's as if all the oxygen in his body was used up all at once. If we'd been in the hospital, I could have administered some O2 to get his blood oxygen up, but there's nothing like that out here. I've been giving him CPR for the last twenty minutes on the off chance, because you never know what people can come back from, but now..." She shook her head. "I'm sorry. I did all I could."

"You did your best, Zen. Thank you."

Tina's response was automatic, just words that fell from her mouth. She wasn't actually sure where they came from, because everything else—her concerns about the guild, the march, mana and ammo, food, even the army behind them—had vanished, leaving nothing but emptiness behind.

After almost half a minute of silence, Killbox said what Tina couldn't. "We're outside the six-minute window for the Raise Ally spell. If the graveyards and shrines don't work, that's—"

Tina cut him off with a jerk of her hand. She didn't want to hear it, because she didn't want it to be true. She refused to accept that SilentBlayde was really dead, especially when he didn't even look injured. "SB," she whispered, leaning over his still body. "Haruto, please, don't leave me. I can't do this without you."

The emptiness in her chest stabbed with every breath. It couldn't end like this. SilentBlayde had been her first real online friend. She'd met him back when she was fourteen and he was fifteen. Since then, they'd played FFO together almost every day for seven years, but it was so much more than that. *He* was so much more. Of all the stupid, annoying, boat-anchor people that filled Tina's life, he was the one who'd been different.

She wouldn't have gotten into college without him. When James had screwed her over for getting a loan and she'd needed money for tuition, she'd gone to SB with the idea of filming their guild's raids and turning the footage into how-to videos that showed other gamers how to do the fights. He'd volunteered to help right away, recording footage, editing, even doing solo runs for achievements so they'd have more content. Some of their videos had racked up over a million views, paying her way to college and then some. When she'd offered SB his split of the advertising income, he'd refused to take a penny. He'd said he didn't need it since his family paid for everything, but he knew she did, so he'd given it all to her.

At first, his generosity had made her feel like a moocher, especially since SB put so many hours into their channel. Eventually, though, she'd come to accept that that was just who he was. In game and out, he was the only person in her life who'd always been there for her. Who'd always helped. And now she'd failed to help him.

"You deserved better than this," she whispered, resting her heavy head on his chest. So much better than to die here, in this gray shithole of the Deadlands where she couldn't even bury him properly. She hadn't even gotten to say goodbye.

Tina wasn't sure how long she knelt there, but the other players were shifting nervously, watching the road.

"Tina," Zen said at last, pointing at the first of the undead army turning the bend, several miles away. "We have to go."

Tina didn't know if she could. Fighting that army to the death over SilentBlayde's body sounded more appealing than trudging alone back to the recalcitrant raid that hated her. But as her hand fell to her sword, NekoBaby plopped down beside her.

"I don't think all of that CPR was for nothing," the Naturalist said, prying open SB's closed eyes. "There's still something in here!"

Tina's heart jerked so hard it nearly stopped. "*What?*"

NekoBaby leaned over him, poking various points on SB's body as if she was exploring pressure points. "There's still a spark of something in him, but it's fading fast." She shot back to her feet. "I'm going to try the Raise Ally spell."

She grabbed her staff and began hastily weaving together the magics that only casters could see. Tina stood up as well, barely daring to breathe. Then disappointment crashed down again as Neko's hands dropped. "I don't have enough mana!" she cried in despair. "I'm so sorry, Roxxy! I just don't have the juice. It recovers so slowly without food and sleep. I've been nearly dry since we went on that stupid ghost quest, and Raise Ally takes too much!"

Neko's words hit her like punches, but now that Tina knew

189

there was a chance, the emptiness inside her had been replaced with determination.

"Zen!" she cried. "More CPR! See if you can buy us some time!"

Zen immediately started cycling breath and chest compression into SilentBlayde once more. While she worked, Tina tore off her backpack, going so fast, she ripped the stitching on the top as she flung it open. Bread. She needed to find her ration of bread. It was the only food they had.

At last, her searching fingers closed around the stale half loaf, and she thrust it at NekoBaby's face. The jubatus grabbed it and dropped to the ground, gagging in the effort to eat as fast as possible.

"Gah!" She choked. "How'd we ever eat like this in game?"

"*Eat*," Tina ordered, looming over her.

Eyes wide, Neko kept shoving the dry bread down her throat.

When the last bite was gone, Tina yanked the Naturalist back to her feet. "*Please* tell me that's gonna be enough."

"Only one way to find out," Neko said, raising her hands again.

Tina held her breath as the jubatus began weaving the magics. Back in the game, Raise Ally was a ten-second cast. Many more than ten seconds later, though, Neko was still at it. Sweat poured through her fur as she cast and cast, her clawed hands weaving in increasingly wild motions. Tina couldn't see magic herself, but she could feel the immense power building in the Naturalist's hands, and a look of fear crept onto Neko's face. Then just when it felt like it was all about to spiral out of control, the jubatus suddenly leaped up on her tiptoes, throwing her hands into the air in what Tina recognized as the final motion of the spell.

For a second, nothing happened, then bright-green-and-golden light exploded from underneath SilentBlayde's body. Flowers, grass, and other glowing plants filled the broken road to form a verdant bed around him. As their light blossomed, the horrible ashen color retreated from SB's face. Zen stopped compressing his chest a few seconds later, sitting up just in time as SB coughed and drew in a ragged breath.

It was the most beautiful sound Tina had ever heard. NekoBaby immediately began to strut, dancing down the empty road as she crowed, "Boo yah! I did it! Who's the greatest healer *ever?*" Zen, who normally looked on such antics with disdain, grinned from ear to ear, giving Neko a high five before leaning down to help SB sit up. Even

Killbox looked overwhelmed, though he was doing his best to hide it behind manly posturing as he bent over to slap SB on the back.

Tina was the only one who didn't move at all.

She wanted to. She wanted to rush in with the others and hug SB until every bit of her was convinced he was really alive. But her feet stayed rooted in place, because she didn't trust this body yet. Raise Ally only brought people back with twenty percent health. If she hugged SilentBlayde as she wanted to, she might kill him again by accident with her strength. That would be a sorry way to end a miracle, so Tina forced herself be still, smiling down at him instead until her whole face ached.

"Whoa," SilentBlayde said shakily, looking around in confusion. "Was I dead?"

"As close as a living person can get," Zen said, the brilliant smile slipping off her face. "But what the hell happened to you? How did your blood-oxygen levels get so low?"

SB shrugged. "I have no idea. All I know was that after I put on the speed to get away from the army, I had trouble breathing. No matter how much I panted, I just couldn't seem to get enough air. Then I passed out."

Zen frowned, her lovely elven face scrunched into a stern scowl. "Not enough air after running," she muttered. Then her eyebrows shot up. "Wait, you said you 'put on the speed.' Just how fast were you running?"

"*Really* fast," SilentBlayde said with a smug smile. "Do you know how much Agility gear I'm wearing? I'm practically the Flash now." He winked at Tina. "World's Fastest Elf."

Tina smiled weakly back, but Zen punched SB in the arm. "There's your problem! You must have used up all the oxygen in your body when you moved faster than anything organic should."

"Wait," Tina said, staring at her. "You're saying he *literally* ran his body out of oxygen?"

The green-haired Ranger nodded. "His gear gives him godly speed, but that doesn't mean his body can take it. He probably burned everything he had in that burst, and his lungs just couldn't work hard enough to replenish his O2 levels." She glared sternly at SB, who was rubbing his arm. "Don't you *ever* do that again! You're lucky you didn't give yourself a heart attack."

"Yes, Sensei," SB said, crestfallen. "But this sucks. I just found out

I have super speed, and you're tell me not to use it. I was outrunning arrows!"

"Better slow than dead," Tina said angrily.

"You can still go fast," Zen said assured him. "I'll admit, I ran faster than I probably should have, coming to find you. The speed boost from Agility gear is heady stuff, but you have to be careful. It's easy to lose track, and I might not be there to give you CPR next time you decide to go faster than a speeding bullet."

SilentBlayde nodded, pulling his mask back up over his face. "Thank you, Zen."

The Ranger nodded and rose to her feet. SB was moving to stand as well when Tina stepped forward and offered him her hand, the most she could risk. "Come on," she said gently. "Let's get back to the others."

SB nodded and grabbed hold, letting her pull him to his feet. When she released him, though, his legs gave out immediately, dumping him back into the gray dirt. He was struggling to stand again when Tina leaned over and picked him up.

He looked comically shocked as she lifted him into her arms. "No fair, Roxxy," he said as a blush crept up past his mask. "I wanted to be the prince."

"I'm a little harder to carry than you are," she said. Then in a softer voice, she added, "I'm happy you're okay."

"I'm happy to *be* okay," he replied, his blue eyes warm. "Thank you for coming to save me."

Tina was glad that stone cheeks couldn't blush, because mentally, she was fire-engine red. "I actually did the least," she said brusquely, looking away before she started stuttering like a teenager on her first date. "Zen, Neko, and Frank were the real heroes. They're the ones who—"

A piercing howl cut her off. Down the road, they'd been spotted by one of the packs of rotten hounds that scouted ahead of Grel'Darm's army. The undead mastiffs were still far enough away that they didn't seem willing to charge, but they were still much closer than Tina was comfortable with.

"Time to go," she said, nodding for Killbox to grab Frank's gear, which was still lying in a pile on the roadside. Once the Berserker had shoved all the armor into his pack, they took off, sprinting up the road back toward the raid.

■ ■

It was a dreadfully upset raid that greeted their return. When they ran up, everyone was standing in the road with their shoulders slumped and their heads down. When Tina looked around to see why, she noticed that the two Assassins she'd sent to check the graveyard were back and were back alone.

Tina's stomach sank. "Let me guess," she said, turning to set SB down gently on a nearby rock. "David wasn't at the graveyard."

The jubatus Assassin, ZeroDarkness, shook his head. "There was nothing," he said angrily, cat ears lying flat against his head. "No gear. No body. Nothing."

The words hit Tina like a punch. That was it. The sliver of hope she'd been holding onto ever since the Dead Mountain had just turned into the final nail in the coffin. The Sorcerer really was dead. So was David, and that made her chest ache even more than she'd expected it to.

She was still processing that when she realized the rest of the raid was staring at her. "Looks like there's no more respawn," she said, keeping her voice calm. "Good thing we've been playing it safe."

She'd meant that to be reassuring, but the other Assassin, KuroKawaii, jerked as though she'd said something unforgivable.

"Don't you care that David is dead?"

"Of course I care!" Tina yelled at her. "David and I leveled together. He was my friend! It hurts like hell!"

KuroKawaii's elven eyes narrowed to slits. "Whatever. I bet you're happy he's gone because it means you were right. Death is permanent. Satisfied now?"

The hate in her voice made Tina take a step back. "You think I give a shit about being right?" she said, suddenly furious. "I'd pay to be wrong right now, because perma-death sucks! The only thing I'm glad about is that we've made it this far with so many of us still alive. It could have been way worse."

KuroKawaii turned away, but Tina still heard the elf mutter, "It's your fault he's dead."

With one giant step, Tina lurched forward to grab the Assassin. Her stone hand completely engulfed the short elf's petite shoulder, and the thought of how easy it would be to break such a squishy, fragile creature flashed through her mind. Instead, she turned KuroKawaii around to look at her.

"Say that again," she ordered. "To my face, this time."

KuroKawaii bared her teeth. "You want to hear the truth?" she growled. "Fine! It's your fault David died! You wouldn't let us fight Grel when we were fresh! You made us, veteran players, *practice fighting* like we were noobs! You wasted all our mana on bullshit, then when it actually counted, we had to run because of you! If we'd been prepared on that hill, David wouldn't have died. You didn't even try to rez him, though that clearly wasn't because you had problems with the spell." Her gleaming eyes flicked to SilentBlayde, who looked like he was focusing everything on not passing out. "Why did you have to carry him back? And why does he look like that?"

Tina bared her own teeth. "That has nothing to do with—"

"The hell it does!" Kuro shouted, her fists clenching as she tried to wrench herself out of Tina's hold. "I saw the Raise Ally light go off in your direction! He died, didn't he?"

Tina let her go after that. Not voluntarily, but because she was shaking too hard to hold on.

"Why'd you save SB and not David?" Kuro continued, standing on her tiptoes in an effort to get in Tina's face. "Is it because David didn't jump to follow your orders like Silent—"

"*Enough!*" Tina roared, turning to face the rest of the raid, who were all watching the argument very carefully. "Yes, SB died, and we got lucky as hell that Raise Ally worked on him. But he died on the road, where we could reach his body. David, on the other hand, died *under Grel's boot*! He was reduced to a bloodstain! What were we supposed to do? Keep the whole raid back fighting Grel—who crushed me in one hit, by the way—while our healers scraped up what was left of David and tried to raise it? We didn't even know the Raise spell would work! It barely worked on SB, and his body was still intact. David was *obliterated*, and we might all have been obliterated, too, if we'd stayed there, trying to raise him in the middle of Grel and his army."

Kuro lifted her chin defiantly, and Tina gritted her teeth.

"Hindsight is real twenty-twenty. It's easy to look back and say we should have done this or we should have done that. I admit I've made some mistakes, but I'm doing my damnedest to keep us all alive." She pointed at her battered armor. "I've nearly died twice saving your hides. Don't forget."

"How could we forget?" Kuro asked sarcastically. "You're always reminding us. But the fact remains that if we'd fought Grel back at the beginning like we should have, none of this would have happened."

"Fought Grel?" Tina said, her voice turning nasty as well. "Are you stupid? Have you been paying attention at *all* for the last day? This is no longer a tank-and-spank raid encounter in a nice clean boss room. We're stupidly outnumbered, and the only reason you've stayed ahead of the ax this long is because *I've made you!*"

That last part was going too far, but Tina couldn't help it. She was madder than she could ever remember being. Mad at herself for not being smarter, mad about what had almost happened to SB, and especially mad at Kuro for not understanding how hard she'd worked to get them this far. It was all so unfair she wanted to punch something, preferably the Assassin. She was fighting to keep her fists at her side when the bright gleam in KuroKawaii's perfect elven eyes turned into full-blown wetness as the Assassin burst into tears in front of her.

"You're sick. You know that?" Kuro shouted. "You don't care about David or any of us! You just want us to fall in line and fight on command like this is still a game. Well, screw you! I'm not doing this anymore! I quit!"

Tina froze, uncomprehending. "What do you mean you 'quit'?"

"I'm leaving the raid," Kuro said, wiping her eyes. "I don't want to be your stupid little soldier anymore."

"You can't—" Tina cut herself off before she shoved her boot any farther into her mouth. "I can't make you stay," she said more calmly now. "But seriously, where are you going to go? The Deadlands are a valley. It's not like there's more than one way out."

"I don't know," Kuro said. "But I'm not sticking around so you can get me killed, too."

Tina closed her eyes with a silent curse. She needed to say something, something nice, but she had no idea how to convince this idiot not to go off and die.

Instead, she pointed to the east. "Grel's army is that way." Then Tina pointed west. "The Order fortress and the portal to Bastion are that way. Every other direction is impassible mountains, which means this road might as well be a railroad track. We all have to travel in the same direction, so if you want to leave, all I ask is that you don't go so far away that we can't help you if there's trouble. Because no matter what you think, I *do* want to get everyone out of here safely. You can be pissed at me all you want, but don't make everyone else here worry about you on top of everything else."

"Like you really care," KuroKawaii said, turning away.

"I do," Tina replied. "Which is why I'm going to tell you one more thing. Something that you in particular, as an Assassin, need to know."

"What?" Kuro said, not looking back.

"Don't go too fast," Tina said, struggling not to look at SB behind her. "Everyone with Agility gear needs to listen up. You're now capable of amazing speed, but you gotta keep the brakes on."

"Why?" yelled a Ranger from the crowd.

"Because your bodies can't handle it," Tina said. "If you go too fast for too long, it'll kill you. That's how SB died." She turned back to KuroKawaii. "You're a pretty geared Assassin, so watch your speed. We won't be close by to heal or rez you if you don't."

"Like I'd trust you save me," Kuro snapped, then she vanished into the shadows.

Tina gripped her shield so tight, the metal groaned. She should have handled that better. It didn't matter how angry she got or how unfair Kuro was being. They needed to stick together. This whole raid was already an out-of-control train. If they started losing pieces, the whole thing could easily fly apart. Especially right now, with emotions running so high. A player leaving was already the worst thing Tina could imagine, but it turned out she was wrong. Things could go even farther downhill, because after Kuro vanished, ZeroDarkness stepped out of the crowd as well.

"I'm leaving, too," the jubatus Assassin said, turning away from Tina to nod at the rest of the raid. "Good luck."

Then he vanished as well, leaving Tina cursing the empty air.

The moment the Assassins were gone, the entire raid began to buzz. Tina held her breath, listening to the nervous whispers. It seemed she was wrong again. *This* was the worst outcome. Was the raid going to split on her? And if it did, would any of them stand a chance? The Deadlands weren't just a max-level zone. This was a place designed to challenge max-geared players who'd run out of content. The fights out here were harder than anywhere else in the game, and there was no more dying and starting over if things went wrong. Every mistake they made was now permanent, which meant they needed to stick together more than ever.

She knew she needed to say something to reassure them, to keep the raid together, but Tina had no idea what. She'd kept everyone in line up to now with force and the bleak reality of their situation. That was clearly no longer enough, but she didn't know what else would work. How did you convince people to save their own lives? Should she shame them? Threaten? Beg? She was still trying to decide when Killbox stepped out of the crowd.

Tina's stone body went cold. This was it, she realized. The Berserker had been pretty even-keeled since their duel, but she'd humiliated him twice now, and he and David had been friends. Thinking back, Tina dimly remembered David asking during invites if he could bring his PVP buddy to the raid. If she was right, and that was Killbox, then the Berserker owed far more to David than he did to her. When he opened his mouth, she braced for the worst.

"I'm staying with Roxxy," Killbox said, glaring at the raid. "So she hasn't been perfect. So what? Shit happens. But you people need to get your feels out of the way of the reals if you want to survive. Roxxy's the one who understands that, so I'm staying with her."

He gave her a quick salute as he finished, but Tina could only stare at him in shock. Then Frank, having finally finished getting back into his armor, stepped forward as well. "I'm staying, too," he drawled. "Seems to me that when there's an army on your tail, staying together is the thing to do."

"I'm staying as well," chimed in SilentBlayde from his rock.

"Me too," said Zen, raising her hand.

The show of support was almost enough to make Tina cry, but then an awkward silence settled in as no one else stepped forward. For a horrible moment, that seemed like it, then Anders shuffled to the front.

The ichthyian Cleric raised his staff above his head, making it flash with golden light. When he had everyone's attention, he announced, "I'm staying."

This was met with gasps of surprise, but the healer shook his head. "I know a lot of you think Roxxy shouldn't have treated me so rough back at the Dead Mountain, but that situation was entirely my fault.

Even if it hadn't been, though, you're all forgetting that *we would be dead right now* if not for her. Worse than dead, because we're up against the armies of the Once King. Now that things are real, I'm betting ghostfire isn't just a status effect we can cleanse anymore. An eternity of slavery to undeath might very well await us if we don't keep our shit together, stick together, and stay alive."

Everyone, including Tina, gasped as Anders finished. She hadn't thought about it before, but his words made sense. All the zombies in the undead army chasing them had come from the Once King's defeated enemies. Now that they were no longer infinitely respawning immortals, that might be their fate as well. The possibility was enough to chill even Tina's stone skin, and she wasn't alone. Anders's threat had clearly hit a lot of people hard, because once he finished, more players started to step forward. They came in ones and twos, shuffling up the road until, to Tina's amazement, they were all standing together, looking at her.

Watching it happen brought an unfamiliar thickness to Tina's throat. Up till now, she'd told herself that it didn't matter what they thought of her so long as she kept everyone alive. She'd thought she was fine with everyone hating her, fine with being the villain, but she hadn't realized how much she'd hated her role until everything had started to fall apart. Now, though, the raid was united. They might not approve of everything she did, but for the moment, at least, they were trusting her to save them, and Tina was determined to make that trust count.

"Thanks, guys," she said when her voice worked again. "I think we've all had enough shocks for now." She pointed west down the road. "Y'all know the drill. Grel's getting closer, so let's get farther." She paused there, holding her breath. When no one objected, she gave the order. "Roll out!"

With only a slightly put-out sigh, the raid obeyed, resuming their march through the ashy wasteland.

■ ■

For the next hour, Tina carried SilentBlayde on her back. He tried to protest, but he wasn't up for moving on his own yet, and she didn't trust anyone else to carry him. Practicality aside, though, Tina was doing this as much for herself as his safety. After nearly losing him and the narrowly avoided mutiny, she wanted her dearest friend and best ally as close to her as possible.

"Wow, it's quiet back here," NekoBaby said, falling back to walk beside them. "What gives? SB normally talks up all the oxygen."

"Raise Ally only gives back twenty percent health," Tina said sharply, turning to put her body between the jubatus and SB. "If we were back home, he'd be in a hospital right now. Don't bother him."

"Okay, okay. Cool your tits," the cat-girl said. "I'm just super curious. I mean, we *rezzed* someone! You know, cheated death! Brought him back from the Great Beyond!" She darted around Tina to peer into SB's face. "What was it like?"

"Neko," Tina growled. "You know that saying about curiosity and cats? You're testing it."

"It's okay," SB said, lifting his head from her shoulder. "It's an important question."

"See?" Neko said smugly. "SB's cool. Don't be such a grouch."

Tina sighed. "Fine. One question, but then he has to rest."

She didn't want Neko bothering SilentBlayde while he was still so pale, but Tina would be lying if she'd said she wasn't curious, too. So much of this didn't make sense. Why had the Raise Ally spell worked when shrines and graveyards didn't? How had he come back, and what was it like?

"So what happened?" Neko said, wiggling her clawed finger through a gap in the Assassin's red-and-black leather armor to poke him in the side. "Did you see a light at the end of the tunnel? Life flash before your eyes?"

"Nothing so nice," SB replied, ignoring her poking. "It's more like..." He trailed off, struggling to find the words. "I've never really been worried about death," he said at last. "I've gotten close to it several times in my life, but it never got to me before. Here, though? In this place?" He shuddered. "Let's just say I'm afraid to die now."

The haunted way he said that sent shivers up Tina's spine. "So what happened? Did you go to hell or something?"

His mask brushed the back of her neck as he shook his head. "I'm not sure. All I know is that there's something desperate at the core of this world. It was frantic to drag me down. Zen was the only reason I didn't fall. Her efforts let me cling to the edge, but I was about to slip anyway when the Raise Ally spell grabbed me. It pulled even harder than the thing below. I felt like I was being ripped in half. It was even more terrifying than wherever I was being dragged down to."

"Damn, dude," Neko said, ears flat. "That's heavy."

"It's important," SB said sternly. "Death isn't cheap anymore. I got out whole this time, but if I have to go through that again, all you might get back is a torn-up soul."

"Then make sure you don't die," Tina snapped. It came out sharper than she wanted, but the idea of SB dying for real did something awful to her insides.

Neko sighed. "We have to get out of this screwed-up world."

"Damn straight," said Tina. "As soon as we're not running for our lives, we're doing everything we can to find a way back home. Right, 'Blayde?"

SilentBlayde dropped his head back to her shoulder, not saying a word.

CHAPTER *10*

James

James was being dragged through the gnoll village again. This time, though, he was cool with it. He would have preferred not to be facedown in the mud, of course, but that was an important part of the plan. A plan that, so far, was working perfectly.

Dragging the tied-up James behind him, Thunder Paw stumped his way right past the guards—living and undead—back toward the pit of spikes. A few gnolls snickered as they went by, but most of the hyena-men were too busy preparing for war to pay attention to the old Naturalist and his captive. Tied up and backward, James smelled the pit before he saw it. The fetid mix of old lake bottom and rotten flesh hit his new, sensitive jubatus nose hard, making him gag as Thunder Paw jerked him up to his feet and barked at him to move to the edge of the pit.

The drained-lake-turned-murder-spike-pit was near the center of the new Red Canyon village, and the only dark spot in the place. The rest of the camp was daylight bright thanks to the countless braziers, forge fires, and endless patrols carrying torches, but the pit had nothing. James supposed this was because you didn't need light to hurl players to their deaths, but the darkness made the forest of stained wooden spikes look more even ominous.

He'd hoped the lack of light would also hide the bodies, but he'd forgotten about his new ability to see in the dark. Even without the torches, James's jubatus eyes picked out every corpse. Their terrified faces burned themselves into his mind. Some were still frozen in their final scream, the black curls of death magic rising from their open mouths like dancing snakes.

Shuddering, James tore his eyes away from the gory spectacle and forced himself to focus on what was really important: finding a safe place to land. Thunder Paw was already nudging him to the edge. Once the old Naturalist shoved him over, James would have only a few moments to find something suitable among the dead players' equipment. A good landing was critical, but as he scoured the bloody mud at the pit's bottom for a likely spot—preferably near a choice weapon—a huge shadow fell over them.

"What you got there, Thunder Paw?"

The booming voice had the same odd, unnatural overtones as Thunder Paw's, but it was much, *much* bigger. Trembling, James turned to find himself staring at the iron-plated feet of the biggest gnoll he'd ever seen. The same one who'd killed the smith with his own anvil earlier.

Gore Maul, Chief of Chiefs, the undead warrior boss of Red Canyon.

James shrank back. He'd played FFO for a long, long time. He'd been toe to toe with uncountable nightmare creatures, most of which were much larger than him. But all of those monsters had been in the game, safe behind the wall of virtual reality. But the ten-foot-tall undead gnoll in front of him now was *real*, and James felt the terror of that all the way to his bones.

Just like in the game, Gore Maul was covered from head to toe in crudely pounded armor made from inch-thick iron plates. Only his eyes were visible, two ghostfire torches flickering in the dark of his helmet. At his neck, he wore a black collar like Thunder Paw's but far larger and reeking with death magic. *Everything* about him reeked. The stench of rot rolling off the undead gnoll was strong enough to overpower even the smell of the pit, but even more terrifying were the plumes of cold, oily black magic that rose from his body like smoke, curling on a wind that only the dead could feel.

"What you got?" Gore Maul asked again, his giant collar translating the growl into a booming demand that made James's ears ache.

Thunder Paw cowered with a high-pitched whine that his own collar seemed unable to translate. "Me done with this one," he said meekly after several seconds of shaking. "Killing him now like the others. See?"

He pointed at the bloody pit, and Gore Maul's white-fire eyes narrowed. "What you use him for?"

"He very good with lightning," Thunder Paw lied. "Me wanted to learn secrets. But him have nothing to teach, so he die."

Gore Maul grinned, showing a wall of dark-yellow, pointed teeth through the jaw-hinge of his giant helmet. "Good, good! But you old. You not throw proper." He reached out, grabbing James in a huge metal-gloved paw. "As chief, Me get pleasure of throwing this one."

Thunder Paw leaped to stop him, but it was far too late. The giant gnoll was already rearing back like a pitcher, taking aim at the very middle of the pit before he lurched forward, lobbing the still-tied-up James as high as he could into the air.

James couldn't help but yowl as he sailed over the spike pit. In midair, he got himself together and grabbed his right thumb to dislocate it. It would hurt like hell, but he only needed one hand to slip through the ropes so he could catch himself with a Stone Grasp spell. No matter how hard he pressed, though, his thumb stayed stubbornly in its joint. It seemed the same health system that had kept him from dying from all the random choppings and beatings was also now preventing him from the one minor act of self-maiming necessary to escape. Too bad that wasn't going to save him when his chest landed on a spike.

Cursing his luck, James pushed on the ropes with all his strength, twisting and struggling in the air while Gore Maul laughed. Then when he was close enough to see the spiky death rushing toward him, instinct took over, twisting his body just right to orient himself facedown on all fours. James was resigning himself to the fact that "jubatus always land on their feet" would be his last thought when, suddenly, a huge earthen hand smashed its way out of the pit.

Wooden spikes exploded as the giant hand reached up and snatched him out of the air. It was the same spell James had used on the gnoll who'd attacked him on the road—the Stone Grasp spell—but he wasn't the one who'd cast it.

His poor shaken brain was trying to figure out who had when Gore Maul's booming voice bellowed, "*Traitor!*"

James wiggled his head out of the giant stone fingers just in time to see Gore Maul backhand Thunder Paw with the force of a truck. The blow sent the poor old gnoll flying, and he landed with a crunch at the far edge of the pit. When he raised his head, his flat, hyena-like jaw was crumpled, and his arm was turned in the complete wrong direction from his body. He grabbed it with a whine of pain, struggling to pop the mangled limb back into its joint as Gore Maul stomped over.

"Me knew me smelled a traitor!" the giant gnoll roared, towering over Thunder Paw as he raised his iron-encased foot. "Everyone know what traitors get!"

"*No!*" James cried, fighting against the hand that held him, but it was no use. The stone fist had him from neck to knees. Worse, his hands were still tied behind his back, leaving him no way to cast, no way to do *anything* as the thousand-pound undead warrior brought his giant foot down on Thunder Paw's broken body.

The horrible crunching noise that followed was a sound James knew he'd remember for the rest of his life. With a gleeful cackle, Gore Maul twisted his boot, grinding Thunder Paw's body into the rocky dirt, and the stone hand holding James crumbled to sand.

If the spikes below had still been intact, James would have fallen to his death then. As it was, he dropped harmlessly into the pile of splinters the stone hand had created when it burst through. Dropped and stayed, because his brain was too shocked to function. When he'd made his promise to help, he'd had no idea that Thunder Paw was willing to *die* to ensure James could finish the mission. It was too much. James wasn't worthy of such sacrifice, but then, Thunder Paw hadn't done it for him. He'd done it for his grandson, the pup in the water, slowly being burned to death by ghostfire. He'd sacrificed his life to give his family a chance. Now it was up to James to make sure the old gnoll hadn't died in vain.

Up on the edge of the pit, Gore Maul finished crushing what was left of Thunder Paw and turned around, sniffing loudly through the gaps in his metal helmet. When he saw James, his ghostfire eyes flash brightly with glee.

"It lives!" he cried, reaching back to pull two massive, wickedly curved axes off his back. "Yes, Master! We will kill it!" With an excited howl, the monster jumped eight feet down to land on the muddy floor of the pit, shattering the smaller spikes at the edge into kindling.

Swearing loudly, James began wiggling his body frantically between the bloody spikes, eyes searching for something—*anything*—he could use to defend himself. There was a low-level jubatus Berserker impaled just a few feet away. His ax was broken in half, but at least James could use the shattered edge to finally cut the rope binding his hands. That was a good start, but it was nowhere near enough. Gore Maul was now smashing his way toward him, swinging his ax like a machete as he cut his way through the forest of stakes.

James whirled around and ran as fast as he could in the other direction, his bare feet squelching in the disgusting mud. Choking on the smell, James looked around frantically, but it was so dark down in the spikes that even his cat eyes were having trouble. He knew if he kept going, he'd eventually reach the edge of the drained lake, but James wasn't looking for an escape. He was still searching for what he'd come down here to get in the first place. He was pretty sure he remembered where it was, too, so even though he could hear Gore Maul crashing toward him like an avalanche, James turned around and headed back toward the middle of the spike pit, straining his eyes as hard as he could until, at last, he spotted something gleaming blackly in the dark.

James's heart skipped. Directly in front of him, dangling from the gray hand of a long-dead human Cleric, was the Eclipsed Steel Staff. The Dead Mountain raid weapon lay halfway between him and Gore Maul. To reach it, he'd have to charge the rampaging gnoll boss, which was suicide, especially since he wouldn't actually be able to use it yet. As powerful as the staff was, he'd need to bind it to himself before he could use its stats. Until then, the top-level weapon was just a beautifully wrought, remarkably hard metal stick.

A stick wouldn't do much good against a monster like Gore Maul. He'd do much better to double back and find something that would actually be useful as a weapon, like a sword or a pike. But as James started to turn, he remembered Arbati accusing him of just playing a hero. Of making idle promises and never following through.

Given what had just happened to Thunder Paw, the memory stung even deeper than usual. Worse, it called up another. One he tried never to think about but would never go away.

"You asshole!" Tina cried, punching him in the chest with her tiny fist. "You said you'd be good if you got more money! Just two more years, you said!"

"I'm sorry," James pleaded. "I tried, but I couldn't get my grades up in time. It was drop out or flunk."

"At least flunking would have been something!" Tina spat, her brown eyes so resentful they stung. "You said the loans would be no problem because the job you'd get when you graduated would let you help pay for me! Now my college fund is spent, too, while you have no degree and no job!"

"I can still get a job. I can—"

Tina put her hand in his face. "Save it. You promise and you promise, but you never keep a damn one, because the moment things get difficult, you quit. You run away because you're a coward who's never given a shit about the *people who count on you!"*

James stumbled back. There was no way she could have known how much those particular words would hurt him. But Tina had always had an instinct for weakness, and she homed in on his now.

"You don't care about anyone but yourself," she growled. "But I don't need you anymore. I'll find a way to pay for college on my own."

"You don't have to do it alone," he said, desperate to fix what he had broken. "I'll help you however I—"

"You want to help?" she said coldly. "Stay out of my way."

Then she slammed the door in his face.

As it closed, James felt other things closing as well—their childhood, their closeness, their team against the world. Everything he thought of as home vanished with his sister behind the scuffed wooden door of her childhood bedroom. And it was all his fault.

A roar kicked him out of the sudden memory. Gore Maul was less than twenty feet away, sending spikes and bodies flying as he smashed his way to James. On the rim above them, squeals filled the air as gnolls stopped work and ran over to watch the show. In another few moments, the crowd would surround the pit on all sides, which meant this was James's last chance to run. If he didn't make it to the edge before the gnolls cut him off, the crowd would just throw him back to Gore Maul. But though his heart was pounding so hard it was making his vision jump, James's feet stayed put.

Staying meant death. He couldn't beat Gore Maul, not as he was now, but fleeing would spell doom for Lilac and for Thunder Paw's son. It would be a rank betrayal of the old Naturalist who'd just died to save him, but the truth of what kept him rooted was far more selfish. James couldn't run, because if he did, he'd be everything Arbati and Tina had accused him of being. He'd be a coward, a screwup, a liar, someone who couldn't be trusted. In one move, he'd prove all of his greatest fears about himself true, and that scared him more than Gore Maul ever could.

The moment he realized that, James stopped shaking. He turned to face the monster cutting its way toward him then charged toward the Eclipsed Steel Staff between them. He picked up speed with every step, using his claws to dig into the wooden spikes as he hurled himself between them. Ahead of him, Gore Maul laughed and started smashing faster, sending shards of wood flying at James like spears. One almost went through James's head before he ducked, his arm flying out to grab the staff at last.

The moment he touched the black etched metal, magic hummed up his arm. He'd never felt anything like it, but as powerful as the staff clearly was, something was wrong. The magic had an incomplete feel to it, like he was grabbing an empty bottle. The binding, he realized. The staff wasn't bound to him.

Tightening his fist around the metal, James probed the weapon with his magic, desperately searching for the trick, the hook, whatever it took to connect. He was still trying when the towering shadow of Gore Maul fell over him, and James knew he was out of time.

The giant gnoll roared, spraying foul-smelling spittle everywhere as he swung for James's head. Stuck right in front of him, James had no choice but to use his new staff. Incomplete or not, the Eclipsed Steel Staff was still a max-level weapon made from very magical materials. He was reasonably sure it wouldn't break. Whether he could hold on to it, though, was another matter entirely.

But the ax was already flying at his face, so James planted his feet and put his staff in its way. The moment the weapons clashed, he tilted his hands to slide the force of the ax down the staff's body and into the ground. Sparks flew as metal scraped on metal, but it worked. With the angle changed, all the power of Gore Maul's blow went into the mud rather than into James. There was no time to feel smug, though. James barely managed to yank the staff back and brace it over his head before Gore Maul's second ax landed in his shoulder.

Again, sparks flew, and again, James tilted his staff, sliding the blow safely away from himself. But even with most of it deflected, the force of the blow was still enough to sink him into the mud to his ankles. He yanked his feet out as fast as he could, swinging his staff around to catch the next strike before it lopped off his arm.

The attacks were relentless. Gore Maul swung back and forth with alternating strikes from his twin axes. The only reason James was able to keep his footing, his weapon, and his head was years of practice and the fact that the Eclipsed Steel Staff really did seem to be as unbreakable as he'd hoped. But while his weapon was solid, defending still took every scrap of his attention. Thanks to Gore Maul's strength, any hard parry would immediately crush his arms, so James focused on redirecting the oncoming attacks instead, sliding the axes off over and over into the mud.

No defense could last forever, though. After a dozen successful parries, the mud at James's feet was a minefield of holes and pits. One wrong step was all it took to send him staggering left when he should have leaned right, ruining his tilt and forcing him to catch Gore Maul's next blow head on before it cut his torso in half.

With nothing to deflect it, Gore Maul's attack struck the staff like a bus. James braced, waiting for the pain of his arms being crushed, but it didn't come. Instead, the staff rang like a bell, sucking the blow's power into the shadows that fluttered inside the eclipsed steel. For a moment, a deep, grave-like silence fell over the pit, then Gore Maul swung again, smashing James's staff out of his hands and sending him flying into the air.

Tumbling uncontrollably, James barely managed to flip over in time to grab a spike before he was impaled on it. His staff landed in the mud below, and James lunged for it, diving for the ground seconds before Gore Maul's ax splintered the wood he'd been clinging to. Weapon back in hand, James staggered to his feet and whirled to face his enemy again, but while he was impressed with his recovery, the hit hadn't been without consequence. His whole body was pulsing in pain, and his right arm hurt so badly, he could barely hold his staff up.

Dread began to curl in James's stomach. He couldn't keep this up. If he was going to have a chance of surviving, he needed to hit back, not just defend. But where? Gore Maul was two tons of muscle wrapped in armor as thick as a car door. What could anyone do against that?

He was still scrambling for an answer when Gore Maul finished hacking down the last few spikes between them. The giant hyena-man snickered behind his helmet at the naked fear on James's face. On the rim of the pit, hundreds of gnolls were now watching the fight—or more accurately, the execution—but there was something odd about the crowd. No one jeered or cheered for Gore Maul. They weren't even throwing things. They all just stood there with their ears down and their tails quivering, watching in fear as the Chief of Chiefs closed the final distance to James.

Sweating through his filthy fur, James tucked the now-useless staff under his injured arm and started casting Chain Lightning. He wasn't sure if Gore Maul would even feel it, but with his arm down, he couldn't pull the misdirection trick anymore. But while he was no good at hitting, he *was* still a level-eighty Naturalist, and he still had some mana left. Praying it was enough, James pulled on the magic inside him, grabbing the glowing white threads from the air to form the lightning strike with his good hand.

When the magic was brimming in his fingers, James let loose, and the dark night flashed with a deafening *boom*. The thunder-crack was so loud he felt it in his chest, but not half as hard as Gore Maul did. The moment the flash went off, mud, iron, and a good bit of rotten gnoll flesh exploded. James had to duck to avoid being impaled by the flying shards of bloody metal, but a grin spread over his face when he heard Gore Maul roar in pain.

The spell had blown a smoldering crater the size of a cannon ball in the monster's chest. James could actually see exposed ribs sticking out through the wound. He was looking to see if that was enough when the dizziness hit.

As the thrill of the spell faded, the loss of the mana he'd spent to cast opened a yawning emptiness inside him. Weak and shaking, he plunged his staff into the mud, leaning on it as he fought to keep from passing out. He was focusing on his breathing when Gore Maul straightened back up.

With a sickening crunch of bone and metal, the giant gnoll pushed himself up out of the mud where the spell had blasted him back. He rolled his massive shoulders then reached down with one giant paw and casually folded the blasted metal of his chest plate back into place. When the wound in his chest was more or less covered, he picked up his dropped axes and turned back to James, the white ghostfire in his empty eyes sparking with glee.

There was no thinking about it this time. After that one look, James broke and ran. *Really* ran. The low-mana weakness vanished beneath a wave of adrenalin as he booked it to the opposite edge of the pit, once the deepest part of the drained lake and now the tallest side. Fear was his only thought as he hurtled between spikes and past dead players, brain scrambling to find some scenario in which he wasn't screwed.

He had, at most, one more lightning spell in him. Casting it would leave him completely dry, though, and even if he did, it wouldn't be enough. Without proper stat-boosting caster gear, he just didn't have the power to down a monster like Gore Maul. If this had been the game, he would have just died and come back with a better plan. But while respawning was clearly out, dirty tricks were still in, and as he spotted the wooden boards that marked the far edge of the spike pit, James had an idea.

When this had been a lake, the shores on this side had been steeply sloped. The gnolls must have dug things out when they'd made it into a murder pit, though, because the dirt shore was now held back by a wooden retaining wall. A rickety, hastily constructed wooden retaining wall.

Back when this had been a game and all the environments were static, the terrifyingly hasty construction would have just been color, but it was finally starting to hit James that *everything* here was real now, which meant *everything* was on the table. There was no more invisible rule set forcing him to fight monsters in a particular way. It was just him and physics, so as Gore Maul bulldozed his way through the last remaining spikes toward him, James turned around to pull the oldest trick in the book.

Brandishing his staff, he put his back to the wall and waited, holding his ground as the charging, truck-sized monster got closer and closer. Finally, right when the snickering Gore Maul was picking up speed to trample him under his boots, James dove low and to the left, protecting his injured arm with his good one as he flung himself gracelessly into the mud.

Gore Maul's ax sliced inches over his head as the freight train of undeath rampaged past at top speed. But when Gore Maul tried to turn to go after him, his feet lost traction on the slippery mud, sending him sliding face-first straight into the wall.

The whole pit shook. Gore Maul had hit the wall like a speeding cement truck, but though the wooden boards cracked and flew apart, the dirt behind them didn't collapse and bury him.

Something better happened.

Wiping mud out of his eyes, James sat up in amazement as the gigantic Gore Maul pushed himself off the broken wall. The impact had flattened him cartoonishly, crushing his muzzle into his face. James didn't understand how that was possible until he saw the stones poking out of the mud behind the broken wood.

That was why the wall hadn't collapsed, he realized. There was an old fieldstone drainage tunnel buried behind the wood. It looked normal enough, but the crushed-faced Gore Maul was staring at the unearthed stones like they held the secrets of the universe, and suddenly, James knew why.

This was the deepest part of the former lake, which meant *that* was the drainage tunnel from the locket quest. *Gore Maul's* locket quest, the one that had been put in to weaken him so normal players would have a chance. Now that he knew what he was looking at, James could actually see the metal grate the locket was caught in. All he had to do was grab it, and the quest would be complete.

Launching off the ground, James threw himself between the still-stunned boss and the wall he was staring at. The sudden movement broke the spell, and Gore Maul roared in fury. Ignoring him, James dropped to his knees and shoved his good arm deep inside the metal grate, grasping with his fingers for what had to be there.

He was still digging when a giant paw seized his leg with bone-crushing force. As it pulled him back, James felt his claws snag something metallic. He managed to take the thing with him as Gore Maul hauled him into the air, dangling him upside down in front of his hideously smashed face. He was about to shove James's entire body into what was left of his broken mouth when James flung out his filthy hand.

"Hunter of the Endless Grass!" he cried. "Remember who you are! Do not let undeath steal your honor!"

Gore Maul stopped, and James looked frantically at his outstretched hand. His fingers were so dirty, he had no idea if he was holding the locket or just some old gnoll trash. Either way, though, it was working, so he pressed on, reciting the words from the old quest as best he could remember.

"You were loved once. A leader who protected his tribe at all costs. Don't let them take that from you!"

Slowly, tentatively, the giant monster reached up to pluck the dirty object from James's hand. When his armored fingers brushed away the muck, James saw it was indeed a small locket made of bone and red stone, just the size a female gnoll would wear.

"Loved once," the giant gnoll muttered, the words shockingly gentle even with the harsh resonance of the translation collar. "She loved, yes, but gone now." He closed his ghostfire eyes. "Not want to see me like this."

James let out a huge breath of relief. He had no idea if the quest had actually weakened Gore Maul or not. The giant certainly didn't look any less scary, but though he still had his axes, the gnoll looked as if he'd rather cry than fight. He'd already dropped James in the mud so he could cradle the locket in both paws, keening pitifully through his broken teeth. He was curling himself into a ball around the trinket when an arctic chill fell over the pit.

Every hair on James's body stood on end as eerie blue light flickered above the undead warrior. Moments later, a ghostly image of the canyon's lich boss appeared in the air. The undead sorcerer had once been an elf. One of the true ancient elves from the Age of Skies. Even ravaged by undeath, he had slender, achingly beautiful features and a grace that made the current elves look like bumbling children, but there was nothing beautiful about the cutting malice that shone in his ghostfire eyes as he glared down at his battered champion.

"*Get up.*"

The giant gnoll whined pitifully, and the lich bared his black teeth. "*You will obey!*"

Clutching the lost locket, Gore Maul roared in defiance, spluttering blood and teeth through the lich's ghostly projection.

"*Obey!*" the lich's image shouted again, thrusting out his hand to launch a plume of ghostfire down the warrior's open mouth.

The gnoll choked as the white flames poured into him. Scrambling away from the giant's kicking feet, James hid his face from the glare as terrible white light began to pour from Gore Maul's eyes. This wasn't part of the quest that he remembered, but the lich was clearly trying to get Gore Maul back under control. If that happened, James's advantage from the locket would be lost, and he'd be dead. He needed to shut this down fast, so he pushed himself back to his feet and used his staff as a cane as he hobbled in front of the spasming Gore Maul and picked up the locket the giant gnoll had dropped when he'd fallen.

"Hunter!" he cried, holding the trinket out. "Remember your name! Resist!"

It hurt to say such cheesy lines, but Gore Maul was listening intently. Even with the lich pouring ghostfire down his throat, the gnoll's burning eyes were locked on the necklace in James's hand. Unfortunately, James had now reached the end of what he remembered from the quest text. Racking his brain for something else to say, he looked up at the gnolls for inspiration only to see that the crowd had changed.

When he'd glanced at the rim of the pit before, it had been nothing but warriors. Now, though, the edge of the drained lake was packed with all sorts of fearful hyena people. For the first time, James was able to spot women and children, stupidly adorable pups with little floppy ears. But though some of them were clearly very young, not a single one made a sound. The whole pack was watching Gore Maul and the lich as if their lives hung in the balance. Then as if a signal only they could hear had been given, they all began to howl.

It was a haunting sound of loss. Closing his ghostfire eyes, Gore Maul answered in kind, lifting his broken face to the starry night sky in an earsplitting, heartbreaking cry as he grabbed his ax out of the mud. James jumped back instinctively, but the weapon wasn't pointed at him. Instead, Gore Maul turned the blade on himself, plunging the giant metal spike deep into the hole James's lightning had made in his chest.

There was a squeal of metal on metal as the monster gnoll punctured his repaired chest plate. This was followed by a sucking noise as the ax broke through, its curved blade digging deep into his chest cavity. Black blood began to pour from the wound as the monster dropped his weapon and shoved his hand inside instead, moving his fingers around as though he were searching for something. Then with a sickening *snap*, the monster gnoll pried loose something that was lodged inside.

A gory lump fell out of the giant gnoll's chest. When it hit the mud, James saw it was an amulet. A beautiful, curving black metal knot that pulsed with necromantic magic like a heartbeat. The moment the amulet came free of Gore Maul's flesh, the image of the lich vanished, and the Chief of Chiefs fell over into the mud.

James clutched his staff, unsure of what to do. He was about to try sneaking quietly away when Gore Maul opened his eyes. His *dark* eyes. The white ghostfire was gone, leaving two dark-brown eyes staring at James through a grayish film of death.

The poor gnoll looked so tormented that James's heart went out to him. He stepped closer, crouching down in the mud beside the broken chief. "Do you want me to kill you?" he asked quietly.

The giant gnoll nodded, his sad eyes closing in pain.

James nodded back. "I'll send you on, then, Hunter of the Endless Grass."

He rose to his feet and began to gather the lightning, dragging out the casting time as long as possible to give a bit of ritual to the mercy killing he was about to perform. But lightning didn't like to wait. In a few moments, his hands were crackling ferociously, forcing James to unleash the full torrent onto the former gnoll chieftain.

Once again, the night was split by a flash of white brilliance. Thunder echoed across the village, leaving a heavy silence in its wake as the undead giant slumped into the mud, blackened almost beyond recognition. As he died, remnants of the ghostfire flickered from his fur like a pyre, the blue-white flames dwindling smaller and smaller until no more remained.

When the last of the fire died, James looked around nervously to see what the rest of the village was going to do. There had to be a thousand gnolls surrounding him at this point, but no one looked ready to make a move. They all just watched him fearfully, noses and ears quivering.

When it became clear no one was going to come at him, James decided to make another stab at escape. Hurrying toward the pit's broken wall, he tossed the staff up to the ledge then pulled himself up, cursing as the move put pressure on his injured arm. The gnolls at the top made room for him, shuffling warily. It wasn't until James had pulled himself all the way out of the pit, though, that he realized he'd come up right next to Thunder Paw.

Bile and pity rose in his throat. Gore Maul's stomp had split the old gnoll's head wide open. The rest of his body had been crushed into the ground, his limbs turned at horrifying angles. It was a cruel, pointless death that no one deserved. Especially Thunder Paw, who'd only been trying to save his grandson and free his people. But when James turned to apologize to the gnolls for getting their Naturalist killed—assuming such a thing *could* be apologized for—what he saw stopped him cold.

All through the crowd, furry paws were passing green magic back and forth between them, weaving the glowing strands of earth and water like a rope. It was so beautiful, James didn't recognize it as the Raise Ally spell until it went off, lighting up the night sky with a golden flash even brighter than his lightning. When the golden light faded, Thunder Paw's body was back together like nothing had happened. He'd just sat up, blinking his one good eye, when the whole pack rushed him, yipping and barking in excitement while James stared in bewilderment.

Of course, he realized, too dumbfounded to notice the Naturalists who were now pouring healing magic into his wounded arm. Why wouldn't NPCs be able to resurrect? Raise Ally was just another spell, the same as lightning, and they cast plenty of that. They also weren't NPCs anymore. They were alive, just like him. Why wouldn't they want to bring their friends and loved ones back from the dead? If James had been thinking or had the mana left, he would have cast it himself. The fight with Gore Maul might have felt like forever, but it couldn't have actually been more than a few minutes, well within Raise Ally's six-minute window.

Still, this opened up a world of possibilities. He already knew the graveyard respawn system was gone, but if Raise Ally worked, that was a whole new ball game. He was going through all the implications when he heard a polite growl.

James looked up to see Thunder Paw standing in front of him, the same as ever. *Better* than ever, because the old gnoll was grinning, showing James all of his small, sharp teeth as he raised his hands.

"James defeated Gore Maul!" he declared loudly, his translation collar's words barely audible over the loud bark that had actually come out of his mouth. "All hail James, Chief of Chiefs!"

The crowd exploded in ecstatic barking. The gnolls rushed James, paws up to offer him semiprecious gems, crystals, herbs, feathers, and all sorts of other valuables until he could hold no more.

They were piling it up at his feet by the time he managed to get free enough to ask, "What is going on?"

"Grand Pack have three chieftains," Thunder Paw explained, his face smug. "But need big chief, too. Gore Maul, real name Hunter of Endless Grass, was Chief of Chiefs. You kill him, so now you big chief."

James stared down at the gnoll pups clutching his legs. "If you're all so happy about this, why didn't anyone help me fight Gore Maul? Or you? Why didn't they rez you earlier so you could lightning Gore Maul in the back?"

There was a bunch of yipping and barking from the nearby Naturalists at this question, which Thunder Paw translated. "Chief of Chiefs killed Me. They cannot defy. Same for helping you. To defy big chief is death, even if he bad for everyone. But you killed big chief, so now we all help you."

James stared at him openmouthed as all the implications of that

215

statement finally clicked together. "Waaaiiit, you mean *I'm* the new Chief of Chiefs? But I'm not even a gnoll!"

Thunder Paw shrugged. "Not-gnoll outsider not supposed to be big chief. But we happy you kill Gore Maul, so we make exception. We follow you for a while."

There was lots of happy yipping in agreement to this statement, and James ran his hands through his fur in bafflement. "So what does that mean, exactly? Like, can I ask the Grand Pack for help? Because I really need to get down into the canyon where the lich—"

He was cut off by a chorus of whining and growling. His first thought was that they didn't like his question, but then he realized the gnolls weren't growling at *him*. They were growling at the new figure who'd just appeared from between the storage buildings behind them.

Standing a few dozen feet away, up the hill by the buildings where the undead kept their weapons stockpiles, was Arbati. He was blood-splattered and dirty, and his tail was comically puffed up, but there was nothing funny about the lit torch in his clenched hands or the large barrel under his boot labeled *Wind-Fire Powder*.

James sucked in a breath. Wind-fire powder was the FFO equivalent of magical fuel-air explosives, and it was crazy dangerous. Typically, the stuff appeared only in highly unethical quests to raze enemy bases, usually with a follow-up quest in which players would have to face the horrible consequences of using weapons of mass destruction. This, however, was not a quest, and from the deadly look in his eyes, Arbati was not playing around.

Swallowing, James looked down at the gnolls, who were perfectly packed in around him. Behind them, the lake bottom was muddy, but every other bit of the village was as dry as kindling. Add in the winds from the savanna, and even one barrel of wind-fire powder would be enough to turn this entire fortress into a fiery tornado.

"All right, dog-faces!" Arbati yelled, lowering his torch. "Time for two hundred years of payback!"

"Arbati, *no!*" James cried, waving his arms frantically. "I'm okay! Don't light it! We won, man!"

The tall warrior scowled in confusion, and James ran toward him, pushing his way through the gnolls. Fortunately, being Chief of Chiefs apparently meant he was now head butt-kicker, and the crowd parted immediately, practically shoving him to the front before forming up behind him in a massive, menacing pack.

The sight made Arbati sneer. "I see you've betrayed us and sided with the Red Canyon." He spat on the ground. "I knew you'd show your true colors eventually. I will take pleasure in watching you die!"

"God dammit, Arbati, that's not how it is!" James yelled. "They just made me their leader, which means we don't have to fight them anymore. They can help us save your sister!"

James didn't expect his words to get through Arbati's wall of hatred, but to his surprise, the warrior pulled his torch away from the barrel. "What did you say?"

"I said, 'They can help us save your sister,'" James repeated with a relieved breath.

Arbati shook his head. "Not that. The other part. How did *you* become leader of gnolls?"

"Oh," James said. "It's a combat thing, apparently. Gore Maul was Chief of Chiefs, so when I beat him, the title passed to me." His face split into a smile. "But this is great! We don't have to kill each other anymore! We can fight the lich together instead!"

To his enormous relief, Arbati dropped the torch into a nearby brazier and set the barrel of wind-fire powder on its end so it wouldn't roll down the hill into the waiting gnolls. James was about to thank Arbati for being so understanding when the cat-warrior stomped down and got right in his face.

"I challenge you to a duel."

"What?" James said, stumbling away. "*Why?*"

"You insulted me on the plains earlier," Arbati replied with a lift of his chin. "You, an outsider, slighted the honor of the head of warriors for the Four Clans. I have not yet had my redress, so I challenge you here and now to a duel to the death."

He drew the two-handed sword from his back as he finished, but James was too busy trying to figure out if the cat-man had gone crazy to be afraid.

"We don't have time for this!" he cried, keeping his eyes on the five feet of perfectly straight, very sharp steel between them. "We're supposed to be saving Lilac!"

"I am saving her," Arbati growled. "Without you."

With those words, James finally understood what was going on. "You asshole," he whispered, clutching his fists. "You want to beat me so *you* can be chief."

Arbati's smile turned cruel. "And you're out of magic, Naturalist. It's time for your reckoning. I will kill you for all that your kind has done to us, then I will command these gnolls to fight the undead while I sneak into the lich's chamber and smash his orb to save Lilac. This way, my enemies will kill each other, cleansing the entire savanna. The only thing left in my way is you."

By the time he finished, James was angrier than he could ever remember being. Behind him, the gnolls began to growl as well, but James waved them back. "What about the barrier?" he asked.

"Already taken care of," Arbati said proudly. "I killed the other two chieftains myself while you were off playing with gnolls. Ambushing them from behind was far easier than your stupid quests. You're the only chief left. Once I kill you, there's nothing keeping me from walking into the lich's stronghold with a disposable army at my back."

"The gnolls won't follow you," James said firmly. "They only follow me because I killed Gore Maul. If you kill me, you won't be their leader. You'll just be dead."

Arbati sneered at that, and James growled in frustration.

"We've already got this in the bag, dude. We could be on our way to save Lilac *right now*, and you are *messing it up*."

"You players were the ones who messed everything up!" Arbati yelled. "You players ruined my home worse than the gnolls ever did, and they've been raiding us for two centuries! You all deserve to die, and I'm proud to be the one who does it."

James's mouth tightened to a hard line. He should have known reason wouldn't work with Arbati. He was every bit as stubborn, angry, and hotheaded in real life as he had been in the game. If he fought James and won, it wouldn't just be their mission that failed. He'd be screwing the gnolls over, too. With Gore Maul gone, this might be their only chance to take on the lich and win their freedom. They had to push *now*, before the lich recovered and took back the town, but they couldn't, because Arbati was being a colossal *dick*.

"These gnolls deserve better than you," James said coldly, wiping the mud from his hands. "You want a duel? Fine. Let's do this. Thunder Paw can start us off."

With that, they turned their backs, and each walked to the edge of the circle the gnolls had formed around them. As Thunder Paw carefully stepped into the middle, James gave the one-eyed gnoll a determined nod.

The old Naturalist nodded back and grabbed a pebble from the ground. "When it falls, you fight," he said, holding the little rock where they could see. "Ready?"

When James and Arbati nodded, Thunder Paw dropped the pebble and dove for the sidelines.

The split second the little rock touched the dusty ground, Arbati leaped at him, swinging his monstrous two-hander high over his head to chop James in half. Even knowing how strong the cat-warrior was, the speed and ease with which he moved the giant sword still caught James by surprise, leaving him no time to dodge out of the way. He was tired of dodging, in any case, so James gripped his black metal staff and swung. Not to deflect as he'd done with Gore Maul, but a straight, hard strike that slammed his staff directly into the sharp edge of the oncoming blade.

James's new Eclipsed Steel Staff was a relic of the Once King's fortress, a treasure forged of corrupted sun metal by processes no mortal could understand. It smashed into the sword with a thunderous ring, but unlike Gore Maul's enchanted axes, Arbati's blade had no magic protecting it. For all the warrior's strength, the mundane metal stood no chance. One strike was all it took to explode the sword into a thousand pieces.

The watching gnolls shrieked and ducked as shards of metal flew over their heads. Arbati stumbled forward, looking in horror at the broken nubbin of blade that remained in his hands. Then he tossed it aside with a snarl, putting up his clawed hands instead.

Looking him straight in the eye, James calmly handing his staff to Thunder Paw.

"What are you doing?" Arbati demanded.

James cracked his knuckles. "Keeping the fight fair. You aren't going to be able to say shit about my honor when this is over."

"Overconfident fool!" the warrior hissed, baring his claws as he charged.

Taking a tight stance, James clenched his fists and waited. He knew for a fact that the game's hit point system lingered, but after his fight with Gore Maul, James had come to suspect that normal biology and physics also played a huge role in which attacks were effective and which weren't. Back in FFO, all you had to do was hit the target to do your damage. That was how Tina kept a giant boss's attention even if the only part of him she could reach was his foot. Now, though, the rules were different. Where and how you hit mattered, or at least that was James's theory. If he was right, he had options. If he was wrong... James clenched his fists and hoped he wasn't wrong.

Arbati ducked low, coming in for a tackle. James waited until the cat-warrior was almost on top of him before stepping to the side, snapping two sharp jabs into Arbati's face as he rushed by. They were perhaps the most perfect form punches he'd ever delivered. He wished the guys back at the dojo could have seen them.

Arbati's charge turned into a stagger as James's hits caught him by surprise. Too soon, though, he shook it off, whirling around to grab James in a crushing hold. The taller warrior was about to lift him into the air for a throw when James drove a chopping right into the side of Arbati's head. The warrior's eyes crossed as the hit connected, and his grip released as he staggered backward, freeing James to trip him sideways into the dirt.

Now it was James's turn for a wicked grin. It looked like he *was* right. For all his strength and speed, Arbati was now subject to the same laws of biology and physics as the rest of them. Unlike the half-ton, metal-covered mountain that had been Gore Maul, Arbati lacked the size and armor needed to ignore direct attacks to vulnerable areas like the head, nor did he have the mass needed to swing a similarly sized opponent around.

That was all the edge James needed. Dancing back, he waited intently for his opponent to get back on his feet. He was tempted to jump on the dazed warrior and end the fight with a hold since he was certain Arbati had zero grappling skills, but he didn't want a quick choke-out win. If he was going to avoid having to do this again, he didn't just need to win. He needed to beat the bullshit out of Arbati so undeniably, it never came back. With that goal in mind, James held his ground, watching closely as his dazed opponent pulled himself together.

It was a painful show. He'd seen Arbati in a few fights now, and while he seemed to be effective enough against gnolls and tied-up players, it was clear the head warrior had a serious lack of formal training. When he'd shaken his head clear, Arbati confirmed this by charging James again, swiping his claws rapidly and thoughtlessly.

James dodged easily, feet barely touching the ground as he danced back. Then he darted in again to land three more lightning-fast lefts into Arbati's face.

The warrior yowled in pain and rage, raising his arms to protect his head. But while the guard might have done something if they'd been in a boxing match, James wasn't feeling *that* generous. The moment his hands went up, James shifted to deliver a brutal kick to the side of the warrior's knee, sending him to the ground again.

But not all the way. Arbati threw down an arm at the last second, catching himself before he hit the dirt. Smiling, James stepped in again, throwing his hips into the blow this time as he swung his left fist in a hook through the gap made by Arbati's dropped hand.

The punch hit Arbati's head so hard there was a cracking noise. His opponent spun sideways from the impact but stayed up, lifting his hands to guard his head but leaving his body exposed. Grinning now, James kept up the pressure, delivering a storm of compact one-two punches to Arbati's abdomen and sides that the warrior's leather armor did nothing to stop. Frantic and pushed back, the jubatus threw a sad, poorly aimed swipe that James dodged easily. He feigned a left hook next. When the poor bastard stiffened up in defense, James drove a powerful right directly into Arbati's unguarded gut.

He was rewarded with a highly satisfying gagging noise. The lack of tightness in his opponent's abs told James that the warrior had not prepped for a body blow, and he jumped back to avoid the resulting barf. Again, James waited patiently until the head warrior was finished before retaking his fighting stance.

On and on it went. When Arbati covered his head, James delivered liver and body blows. If the warrior tried to hunch to protect both body and skull, James attacked his knees and feet. When that made Arbati's guard drop, James drove relentless left-right combos to his opponent's unprotected head. Whenever the warrior tried to punch or kick him back, he'd dodge the strike and deliver a brutal counterpunch or cross kick.

If this had been an MMA match, it would have been over multiple times, but while targeted hits were definitely a thing now, Arbati was still a level-fifty two-skull. He had a health pool like an ocean, which meant beating him would be a war of attrition. So James focused on keeping his breathing steady and his endurance up, working his opponent over systematically like a jubatus-shaped punching bag.

After twenty brutal minutes, though, James was starting to wonder if an unarmed support character like him *could* do enough damage to win. He was a lot stronger than a normal human thanks to being level eighty, but though Arbati had yet to land a single hit, he wasn't going down, and James was starting to wear out. His legs were so tired that he hadn't dared lift them beyond basic footwork for the last five minutes, and his breathing was ragged no matter how hard he tried to keep it in check. The gnoll Naturalists had healed his arm, but the rest of the damage he'd taken from Gore Maul was still with him, not to mention the bruising his knuckles were taking from constantly pounding a hard, muscular cat body. Then just as he was settling into a new rhythm, James made a dumb mistake, and Arbati's claws suddenly raked down his cheek and neck.

Swaying away, James risked a look down to check his neck. Blood was running hotly down his chest, making his head swim, but the cut didn't feel deep. He still had his artery, it seemed, but the hit had shaken his confidence. He was giving Arbati the beating of both their lifetimes, and the guy just kept coming. One real hit from him, though, and James felt like he was going to fall down. Years of martial arts practice gave him miles of advantage in a fight like this, but it was all for nothing if he couldn't take Arbati out before exhaustion did the same to him.

But just as he was getting spooked, he remembered what the coaches said. What *he'd* said to fighters a hundred times as a ringside assistant when a fight had gone too long and everyone was bloody.

"You never know how much the other guy is hurting."

It was a boxing platitude, one of those sayings like "it's not over till you're out" or "when you see the desperation in their eyes, that's when you've got them" that every fighter hears a million times. But the reason coaches said those things over and over was because they were *true*. Just because Arbati wasn't panting as he was didn't mean James hadn't done damage. In any event, giving up wasn't an option, nor was winning dishonorably. The only way James could keep his promises and pass his trial was with an unquestionable, straight-up victory. So switching to a wide stance, James decided it was time to put his own advice to the test.

The next time Arbati closed in, James didn't back up. Instead, he braced his shaky knees and swung back, letting the head warrior's iron fist clock him in the jaw just as he delivered a powerful right straight into Arbati's face.

Given Arbati's super strength, the punch should have knocked James off his feet. But while the blow made him see stars, he stayed standing. Arbati, however, was swaying.

James gave him a bloody smile. It looked as if the old wisdom held out. He'd hidden it well, but the warrior *was* tired, and he *was* weakened. Unfortunately, so was James. *Too* tired to keep dancing around, so he gritted his teeth for a slugfest, holding position as the warrior came back in for more.

As soon as Arbati was in range, James snapped a left hook into his head, but the warrior managed to rake James's right shoulder. In return, James landed two hard body blows to Arbati's ribs, but the head warrior slashed his left arm.

Gritting his teeth at the stinging gashes, James realized he could use his claws as well. But scratching Arbati felt too much like bringing a knife to a fistfight, so James kept his hands curled tight, delivering solid punches even though Arbati's strikes were covering him in cuts. Finally, James landed a smash to the warrior's stomach that made Arbati double over. As his opponent's head came down, James slammed him with an uppercut to the chin. When the warrior's head popped up from the blow, he hit with a hook that opened a cut above Arbati's eye.

The warrior was staggering back when James finally saw what he'd been waiting for: desperation. Face half-covered in blood, Arbati looked like a demon, but James could now see the fear beneath the anger, and he sucked a big gulp of air to try for the finish.

In a final burst of defiance, the tall warrior roared and tried to power past James's guard for another tackle. When he got close, James slapped the warrior's hands straight down, grabbed his hair, and pulled Arbati's face into a knee strike. There was a bloody crunch as his hard joint connected with the warrior's nose, then James felt the jubatus sag.

That was his signal. Letting go of his head, James grabbed Arbati's left arm and kicked the warrior's feet out from under him. Betting that the head warrior was almost out of hit points, he locked Arbati's wrist and twisted as the warrior landed, using his opponent's momentum to pull the joint out of place. There was a slurping, popping noise as Arbati's shoulder dislocated, then James let the screaming jubatus drop into the bloody dirt.

Drenched in sweat and gasping for air, James staggered back to look down at his mangled foe. The warrior was clutching his shoulder in agony and writhing on the ground, clenching his teeth to keep from screaming. When it was clear he wasn't going to get up again, James raised his voice so everyone could hear.

"It's over, Arbati. I win."

"Never!" Arbati snarled, his voice ragged with pain. "I'll *never* surrender to a player!"

That was to be expected, so James limped over to retrieve his staff from Thunder Paw. When the old gnoll gave it to him, James turned and walked back to Arbati and stepped on the warrior's dislocated shoulder to hold him down as he placed the butt of his staff against the jubatus's throat.

"You can still live," James said patiently, "*if* you yield."

"Go ahead and kill me," Arbati snarled. "That doesn't mean you win! You have a player's power. No one will accept your victory! It is honorless for you to beat me!"

"*Honorless?*" Despite his best efforts to not be a sore winner, James's outrage took over.

"You challenge me to a duel to the death on the thinnest pretense ever, and you have the gall to call *me* honorless? You're bigger than me! You're stronger than me! You have armor, and I don't! I gave up my weapon when you lost yours! I let you get up without attacking every. Single. Damned. *Time.*"

He hunched down to grab Arbati's bleeding face. "I am a *healer!*" he yelled. "My character gives me no fighting skills other than magic! Magic that you so 'honorably' waited until I couldn't use to challenge me! Now I've won and am giving you a chance to live when you would have killed me! So you tell me, cat-man, who's the honorless one here?"

Arbati lowered his eyes, and James released his grip on the jubatus's head in disgust.

"I didn't beat you because I was a player. I beat you because I, *James Anderson*, know how to fight! I won because I've been training at this since I was *eight years old!* Hell, even when I was sunk deep into FFO, the one other thing I did with my life was work as an assistant trainer at a MMA gym. I take punches from professional fighters sixty hours a week for minimum goddamn wage to pay a debt I can't afford for a career I'll never have!"

He was shouting inches from Arbati's face now and perhaps not making the most sense, but James didn't care. "You *lost* because you fight like you've never trained for a single damned day! All of *your* power and ability comes from being a level fifty in a level-thirty zone, and it shows! You don't own your strength because you never earned it. I've worked for twenty years on being a good fighter, and I've spent tens of *thousands* of hours working on this character, and you have the nerve to say I won just because I'm a *player?*" He bared his teeth. "Don't you *dare* act like you're somehow more deserving."

With that, James straightened back up and limped over to Thunder Paw. It gratified him to see that even the gnolls were also looking at the head warrior in contempt.

"I've won," James said with forced civility. "Accept it and yield, or I'm going to have the gnolls throw you into the plains to walk home. On the way, you can figure out how to explain this to Gray Fang in a way that doesn't make you look like total scum."

James would have said more. He was still shaking after his second brutal fight of the night, and the urge to keep pounding Arbati until the idiot accepted his victory was burning in his skull. The only reason he didn't was because Thunder Paw had mashed a waterskin into his hands. Blinking out of his angry, jittery haze, James got the hint to shut up, taking a long drink instead.

The water and the silence helped cool his outrage as the battered jubatus dragged himself to his feet. Now that the battle rush was fading, James was ashamed of how badly he'd mauled Arbati in the end. In any other world, one without healing magic, the guy would need to be taken to the hospital.

Left arm dangling uselessly, the head warrior of Windy Lake shambled over to James. Clutching the waterskin, James readied himself to dodge whatever final stupidity Arbati was about to try, but the warrior didn't swing at him. Instead, Arbati lowered his head.

"Kill me."

James blinked in surprise. "Excuse me?"

The warrior sagged to one knee. "You're right." He panted. "I didn't earn my power. Any of it. I was made head warrior when I was seventeen because the previous head warrior died and my father bought me his position. I was supposed to lead our warriors, but they wouldn't follow me. They wouldn't even train me. I'm actually lucky the Nightmare hit when it did, because I never had to face a serious battle. Then it broke, leaving me with all the power I needed to finally *be* my position, but now..."

He looked down at his useless arm. "With all this, I still lost, because you're right. The power the Nightmare gave me is nothing against real skill. You held back our whole fight. Never used your claws even though I used mine. You've laid my dishonor bare for all the world to see, and I deserve it, because I have treated you with nothing but misplaced disrespect. I blamed you for the Nightmare without proof. I have bullied and hazed and beaten you, though you had done nothing to me. You've risked your life to save others, where I've only used mine to try to take what you earned."

Arbati bowed his head lower. "I have heaped more shame upon myself than I can ever erase. You are the winner of the duel, so please, kill me that I might regain some small measure of my honor."

"Denied," James said immediately.

Arbati growled. "But—"

"I forgive you instead."

The warrior's head shot up, his one good eye wide in disbelief.

"All your shame is how you treated me, right?" James said, holding out his hand. "So I forgive you. There. It's all gone."

"You cannot get rid of dishonor so easily!" Arbati said angrily. "A good death is my only—"

"Death is the coward's way out," James snarled. "So you messed up, and it sucks. So what? Are you going to quit life over it, just because you're ashamed? Were you only playing at being the head warrior then?"

Arbati flinched, and James knew he'd struck true. "You accused me of playing the hero," he said gently this time. "And maybe that was true, but it's wrong now. Look around. We've got so many lives riding on us. Lilac needs us. Thunder Paw's grandson needs us. Hell, if we can kill the lich and destroy his hold on this place, the fate of the whole damn savanna could be up for grabs. We don't have time for self-pity, so no more playing around for either of us. All I want from you now is what I've always wanted. I want you to *help* me."

"Help you?" Arbati arched an eyebrow. "But you *won*."

James laughed and gestured at the remains of his clothing, which was so shredded and filthy it bordered on public indecency. "You're crazy if you think winning means I don't need help. Dude, I'm homeless, penniless, practically *naked*, and I'm stuck in this world with no family or friends. I could *really* use someone on my side, so please. Help me."

The warrior sighed. Then at last, he reached up to grab James's offered hand in his shaking one. "You are right," he whispered. "I am sorry. I will help you." That last word came with a pained smile, but it was a smile nonetheless, and it banished the last of James's lingering anger.

"Apology accepted," James said, pulling Arbati to his feet.

"Just one request," the warrior said, straightening with a wince. "Stop calling me 'dude.' I don't know what it means, but it's insulting."

James smiled. "Sure thing, Arbati. But you'll have to start calling me James and not 'player.'"

"Deal," the jubatus said, rubbing his dislocated shoulder with a wince. "Now, James, can you please heal my arm?"

CHAPTER *11*

Tina

For one glorious hour after the raid had rallied around her, Tina finally achieved her goal pace of "bats out of hell." Then everyone remembered how tired, hungry, and thirsty they were, and things began to slow. By the time the first hint of the false dawn began to light up the gray-clouded sky, she was grateful for any distance at all. Even with her taking point to set the pace, the entire raid was dead on their feet. The only reason they hadn't fallen over yet was because then they'd be *actually* dead.

Fittingly, the Endurance- and Strength-based characters were handling the march the best. When it became clear the casters couldn't keep even this slow pace, Tina and SB—who'd insisted on walking under his own power again—organized a piggyback rotation. Tina volunteered to take NekoBaby since the Naturalist had wiped herself out bringing SB back to life. The jubatus was curled up on top of her backpack like a giant pet cat, which would have been cute if it hadn't meant Tina had to carry her shield on her arm instead of her back, making her entire right side ache as the miles wore on and on.

At least no one was complaining anymore. Ever since the Assassins had left, no one had issued a peep of disobedience. They'd had a few more fights with random monsters, but the packs of shambling zombies and undead hounds were easier than the ones they'd fought yesterday. Tina took that as a sign they'd finally crossed into the western half of the Deadlands. Everything got easier as they got farther away from the Once King's mountain.

But even though the fights weren't as deadly, the fear that they'd come around a bend and find KuroKawaii's or ZeroDarkness's corpses— or worse, their *reanimated* corpses—didn't go away. She'd even sent Zen ahead once to scout for them, but the elf had returned empty-handed.

"Are we there yet?" Killbox asked wearily, dragging his giant boots.

"Five more miles, I think," NekoBaby said from atop Tina's

backpack.

"How do you know that?" Tina asked. She'd spent forty hours a week grinding quests in the Deadlands when the place first opened, and she *still* couldn't wrap her head around the new distances.

The Naturalist shrugged. "Intelligence gear."

"Nice," Tina said. "Does that mean all the casters are super smart now?"

"I wish," NekoBaby said with a snort. "It mostly seems to augment memory and analytical skills. Ask me to name the first one thousand prime numbers sometime."

"That's still pretty cool," Tina said.

"And hella useful," Neko said. "That's how I know how far away from the Order of the Golden Sun's fortress we are. I can remember the old game map's grid system perfectly now, so I've been using familiar landmarks to build an updated version in my head."

Several impressed "oohs" went up from the surrounding players, and Neko preened.

"So how much bigger is the world now?" Tina asked.

"Hard to say," Neko replied. "Most stuff seems to be a thousand times bigger than it was in the old FFO, but not everything fits that measurement. For example, the destroyed caravan we passed should have had two thousand feet between burned-out carts, but it had the usual two-foot gaps. Trees are likewise not a thousand times taller, and so on."

"So everything's bigger but not consistently so," Tina said with a sigh. "Great. But how did you know the Order Fort was five miles away if we're not there yet?"

"Because I can smell the forges on the wind," Neko said, tapping her nose. "I'm regular old smart, too, you know."

Tina was too excited about the possible end of walking to even shake her head at that. "We're almost there, folks!" she called back to the others. "Just keep putting one foot in front of the other!"

A smattering of weak cheers was her only answer, though she did see SilentBlayde wave at her from the back, where he was bringing up the rear. Despite him insisting he was fine to walk now, Tina couldn't miss how exhausted he still looked. Seeing it made her feel like a failure all over again, but just as she was about to start beating herself up again for the fiasco on the hill, she spotted a figure walking out of the darkness on the road ahead.

Her first thought was KuroKawaii or ZeroDarkness, but the person was wearing a robe, not leather armor, and leaning on a staff. A player then, but not one of hers, which was exciting. Up until now, the only other players they'd seen had been dead bodies.

"Hey!" the new player called, waving his arms as he hobbled faster.

"Hey to you, too!" Tina called back. "I'm Roxxy, and this is the Roughneck Raiders guild. Who are you?"

"I'm KatanaFatale, Sorcerer amaze!" replied the new player proudly, making guns at her with his fingers.

Tina fought the urge to roll her eyes.

"So," KatanaFatale continued, dropping his hand back to his staff, which seemed to be the only thing keeping him up. "You guys coming back from a raid at the Dead Mountain?"

"Yes and no," Tina said. "We were going into the dungeon, but then this shit happened. Now we're kiting the first boss toward the Order's fort so we can get out of here."

"Right, right," Katana said, nodding way too much. "Just raiders doing raidery things. Gotcha. But um, can I tell you something kinda crazy?"

Considering how insane everything was, that made Tina smile. "Go for it, dude. Gimme your best crazy."

The Sorcerer lowered his voice to a whisper. "I think I'm trapped in the game."

Tina blinked. "Uh..."

"I know!" KatanaFatale said, his face panicked. "It's nuts. But I can't log out, and there's no UI, and everything hurts for real now. If you're still logged in, I need you to put in a ticket for me or something, because I can't—"

He didn't make it any farther than that before the entire front of the raid started laughing. NekoBaby almost rolled off Tina's back, she was cackling so hard. Tina was just as bad, clutching her side as her aching muscles protested. She knew it was terrible, but she couldn't seem to stop. The stress was definitely getting to her, she decided, and judging by the other players' reactions, she wasn't alone.

KatanaFatale's face turned bright red. "I didn't expect you to believe me," he said over their laughter. "But it's really happening! I'm stuck as my character!" He pulled up his robe to show them the ugly, bloody gash on his leg. "I'm in real trouble here!"

The wound shut Tina up instantly. "Sorry, man," she said. "You didn't deserve that. We do believe you. That's why we were laughing. We're *all* trapped in here."

The Sorcerer's jaw dropped. "You mean it's not just me?"

Tina shook her head. "On the up side, you're not trapped here alone. On the down, none of us have any idea how to get back, and we're stuck out here with no mounts and no teleports. That's why we're running for the Order fort. We're going to use their portal to Bastion to GTFO. You're welcome to join us if you want. We can always use more damage dealers."

"Thank you so much," Katana said in a rush, grabbing Tina's shield arm. "You have no idea what I've been through! This place is really dangerous alone. But if you're headed for the Order, you might want to go another way. I've already been to the fortress, and it's not pretty."

"What do you mean 'not pretty'?" Tina asked sharply. "Is it already overrun with undead or something?"

"No, the fortress is fine," Katana said, tugging on his long black hair. "That's actually the problem. Let's just say they're not in a welcoming mood."

He pointed at his wounded leg, and Tina did a double take. "The *Order* did that to you?"

The Sorcerer nodded. "I was questing at the hub in front of the fort when the game...um...you know..." He waved his hands around his head in a spinning motion, and Tina nodded impatiently for him to get on with it. "Anyway, when I came to, I was alone. All the NPCs had retreated inside the fortress, and there were monsters everywhere. When I ran to the doors to get them to let me in as well, they opened fire."

He turned his leg to show her the back of his calf, where the tip of an arrowhead could just be seen poking through his pale skin. "I'm lucky this is the only one they landed. They were shooting to kill, but their aim is awful. I ran away after that, but I didn't want to go through the Never Swamp, and I figured there'd be players raiding Dead Mountain, so I started walking east, hoping I'd meet someone. You're the first players I've seen."

"Shit," Tina muttered, looking back at the rest of her raid, who were still too busy laughing at the Sorcerer to have heard the rest of his story. Their rudeness was her salvation, though. She wasn't sure what she was going to do yet, but if the others found out the safety they'd been marching hell-for-leather toward wasn't actually safe, things could get ugly again. She needed time to think, so she put a hand on Katana's shoulder and dropped her voice to a rumble only he could hear. "I'll handle things from here. There's an elf Assassin in the back named SilentBlayde. He's my second. He'll fill you in on what we know and the rules of the raid and get someone to heal your leg. Just do what he says, and you'll do fine." She smiled. "Welcome to the Roughnecks, KatanaFatale."

By the time she finished, the Sorcerer looked like he was going to cry. "Just Katana is fine," he said, rubbing his eyes. "Thank you, Roxxy. I can't say how nice it is not to be alone out here anymore."

Tina smiled and let him go, watching the Sorcerer hobble to the rear of the group, where SB immediately scooped him up to start explaining all the important new facts of life. When he was safely under 'Blayde's wing, Tina raised her hand and got the raid moving again.

"Oh em gee," Neko said, hopping back up to her perch on Tina's back. "That poor guy! I thought I was going to bust a gut."

Tina nodded impatiently, her emerald eyes locked on the road ahead where it vanished around a curve, possibly the last curve before the Order's fortress came into view. "Neko, you ran into some non-player characters for your quest, right? What were they like?"

"Huh?" Neko said, confused. "Uh, like normal, I guess? They said their canned bit after we freed them just like most of FFO's 'put the dead to rest' quests. They were legit ghosts, though. Just lost spirits with no brains."

"Damn," Tina said. "So utterly not helpful, I take it?"

"Nope. Sorry, boss," Neko said, yawning. "If you'll excuse me, I'm gonna sleep on your back some more. You're like a warm rock. It's really nice."

Tina snorted. "Enjoy it while you can, because I'm not doing this again."

But NekoBaby was already asleep, her carefree smile fading as the very real exhaustion set in. When she was quiet, Tina let the smile slip off her face as well, glaring down the road as she struggled to figure out how she was going to handle the promised safe haven that might now be a fortress against *them*.

■ ■

The main road of the Deadlands ran east and west between the knifelike peaks of the mountains. The eastern side dead-ended at the Once King's fortress, but the western end of the zone followed the land down through the foothills and into the gloriously wet, soft, green Verdancy, the previous highest-level questing area before the Deadlands were introduced, and one of the prettiest zones in FFO. It was still pretty now with its giant glowing trees shining like green-and-gold beacons through the predawn dark. The vibrant color was a shock after the relentless gray of the Deadlands, but Tina could only see it in glimpses thanks to the enormous stone building blocking the way.

The Order of the Golden Sun's fortress had been built in the very last narrowing of the mountains before they shrank into the rolling foothills of the Verdancy. Perched high on an artificial hill, the square fort stretched across the entire pass, creating an impassible wall between the Deadlands and the brilliant forest of the Verdancy beyond. The only way around was an old goat-trail through the mountains to the south that led down into the Never Swamp, a level-seventy-five zone full of mud, giant spiders, giant crocodiles, and giant lizard-men.

Standing on her tiptoes, Tina could just spot the Never Swamp's gloomy trees between the mountains. Though more colorful than the Deadlands, their green was sickly and cold compared to the shining Verdancy, and that wasn't even counting the noxious brown haze they gave off. Grimacing, Tina turned away from the swamp to focus on the fortress's sixty-foot-tall white stone walls.

As the world's wall against the armies of the Once King, the Order's fortress had always been well defended, but she'd never seen anything like the force that filled it now. There had to be half a thousand armored soldiers wearing the white-and-gold tabard of the Order of the Rising Sun crowding the battlements. Worse, the weapons in their hands weren't the worthless mundane swords they'd had in the game, but the glowing golden hammers that Tina recognized as the reward item from the faction's reputation vendor. Many of the soldiers carried bows as well, some already nocked with arrows ready to fire.

"Great," Tina muttered, glancing at her newest raid member. "And you say they shot you on sight?"

"Pretty much," KatanaFatale replied, leaning on his staff to take pressure off his bandaged leg. They hadn't had the mana to spare for healing a non-life-threatening wound, but a few cloth bandages plus Zen's real-life experience as an ER nurse had been enough to make do. "I knocked on the gates and yelled hello, and they yelled back with a lot of arrows, so I hit my cooldown and ran. They hosed my illusionary double with pretty extreme prejudice, by the way."

"What's your factional status with them?" Tina asked. "Any reason for them to hate you?" The Order was normally friendly to players by default, but she was hoping that maybe Katana had done something stupid in game that would explain this.

"Ally ranked, last I checked."

Tina gritted her stone teeth. So much for that. If they were shooting allies on sight, she didn't think her Legendary rank was going to count for much. But hostile or not, that fortress was the only way on this continent to get to Bastion. If they wanted to get to safety, they had to get inside. Fortunately, Tina had a plan. It wasn't going to be a popular plan, but it was the best of bad choices. So, with a bitter sigh, she left the overturned cart she and Katana had been hiding behind and walked back into the dead copse of trees she'd told the others to wait inside, out of sight.

They looked up hopefully when she approached, and Tina sighed. "I've got good news and bad news," she said grimly. "The good news is that we've made it to the Order's fort well ahead of Grel'Darm. Good job on marching your asses off, everyone!"

There was a smattering of applause before the raid fell silent.

"And the bad news?" someone yelled from the back.

"The bad news is they might be hostile, or at least not as welcoming as we'd hoped," Tina said matter-of-factly. "I don't know what to expect, to be honest, but here's what I want from us. We're an army. A max-level, awesomely geared raid." She held up her god-forged shield for emphasis. "We are the most dangerous, deadly group of anything in this world, even if we don't look or feel like it right now."

"No shit!" someone shouted.

"I know you're all exhausted," Tina went on. "We're hungry, thirsty, and out of everything from mana to food to ammo. But when we walk up to those gates, I need you all to pretend we're not. Looking too dangerous to ignore or attack is our best protection and our only negotiating leverage here. We have to look like we can kick that fortress's ass if they piss us off, so gimme your last energy here, people!"

"But we're not *actually* going to attack, right?" asked one of the Clerics.

Tina shook her head. "No. I know we can't take that fort. We just have to *look* like we can so they'll be too scared to shoot."

"Or we could go around," Zen said, pushing her way to the front of the group and pointing her bow at the side path that led to the Never Swamp. "If we go that way, we won't even have to get the fort's attention."

"The swamp is full of diseases, poisons, and xenophobic lizard-men who ride goddamned dinosaurs," Tina snapped. "We'd have to cross the whole zone to get to the one town by the ocean, and Grel'Darm would be behind us the whole way."

"We don't know that," Zen said stubbornly. "He could still break aggro at the zone border."

"He hasn't broken aggro for anything yet. Why the hell would he care about zone borders now?"

"Even if he does stay on us, it's still better than bashing ourselves against a fortress," Zen said stubbornly. "Everything in the Never Swamp is level seventy to seventy-five, and the pirate city on the other side is only lightly guarded. We could blast our way through no problem, steal a ship, and sail to Bastion."

"Do you know how to sail a ship?" Tina asked. "'Cause I don't." She pointed at the bend that hid them from the Order fort. "There's a perfectly fine portal to Bastion not half a mile away! All we have to do is get to it, and this shit will finally be over."

"Or we'll be over," Zen said, crossing her slender arms over her chest. "If your bluff fails and that army opens fire, we'll be dead. The Never Swamp might be a longer trip, but it has water, living trees, and animals. There's eight of us Rangers in the raid. Wilderness survival is literally our thing. We can keep everyone fed and alive no problem. Also, I used to grind faction points for The Great Mercantile in the swamp. I know all the safe paths through the disease clouds and the ambushes. I can get us through safely. There's no reason to throw ourselves at this fortress."

She said that like it was going to be a walk in the park, but Tina knew better. Even with the Rangers' skills, crossing the entire Never

Swamp could take days, maybe even weeks with the new distances. There was no way the raid could make that. So far, the Strength-based players had been willingly carrying the casters when the weaker classes couldn't go farther, but the Knights and Berserkers were all tired now too. How much longer would that good-will between strangers last? When would it eventually become "carry yourself"?

If Grel kept chasing them, Tina's money was on not long at all. A day if they were lucky, hours if they weren't, and then it would fall on her. She was the raid leader. If push came to shove, she'd be the one forced to decide who got left behind, and she just...

She couldn't do it.

It felt like cowardice, but after the unnamed Sorcerer and David, Tina didn't have it in her to lead this raid as they perished one by one on a hundreds-of-miles-long slog through a deadly swamp. Not when salvation was just on the other side of a damn stone wall.

That decided it for her. The Order Fortress was huge, hostile, and deadly, but they were still people. People she could bluff, bully, or bargain with. If they chose the swamp, it would only be a matter of time before someone died, but if she could just get them through those gates and into the portal to Bastion, everyone would survive and this horrible ordeal would finally be over. That was a prize Tina was willing to risk everything for, and she didn't care how much of a monster she had to be to get it.

With that, Tina pulled herself to her full towering height, glaring down on the smaller Ranger like the magical stone demi-god she was as she said, "No swamp."

Zen scowled. "But—"

"No swamp," Tina repeated, her voice as firm as bedrock. "That's final, Zen."

The Ranger's eyes narrowed dangerously. "So we're just going to beat ourselves bloody on the fort?"

"No one's going to beat themselves on anything," Tina snapped. "What part of *bluff* do you not understand?"

"The part where *you're* the one doing it!" the dark-skinned elf yelled, frustrated. "Do you expect us to believe you won't make us attack? You can't even keep from attacking your own players! The first arrow they fire, you're going to send us all to our deaths because you're too stubborn to consider anyone's ideas but your own!"

"That's not true," SilentBlayde said, appearing seemingly out of nowhere to stand beside Tina. "Roxxy listens to her raiders all the time."

"But we're not her raiders, are we?" Zen said, turning her glare on him. "You, Neko, and a few of the others are, but the rest of us pick-ups might as well be toy soldiers for all that she listens to us." Her eyes snapped back to Tina. "I've done the Dead Mountain with the Roughnecks several times now. I've seen how 'Queen Tina' runs her raids. The ruthless dictator act was great for getting us through the dungeon fast, but our *real* lives are on the line here, and I don't trust her not to throw mine away."

"I'm not going to throw anyone's life away!" Tina roared. "I've been busting my ass trying to do the *opposite*, in case you haven't noticed!" She turned back to the raid. "No one is going to die, okay? All we're doing is marching up there and putting on a good enough show to get inside. That's *it*. No fighting. I swear it. The moment things start to look actually dangerous, we'll leave."

"And go where?" Neko asked.

"Doesn't matter," Tina snapped to hide the fact that she didn't have an acceptable plan B. "Because it's going to work."

Zen rolled her eyes, and Tina tensed. To her relief, though, the Ranger didn't keep arguing, and she didn't walk out as the Assassins had, but she clearly wasn't happy. A lot of people weren't. The whole raid looked nervous and resentful, but there was nothing Tina could do about that. The decision had been made, so she bellowed at everyone to get into fighting formation.

It was a sad, shuffling show as the raid lined up. Tina and Frank took the front, flanked by a spread of formidable-looking Knights and Berserkers. Behind them were the Rangers, Sorcerers, and the healers. As the only Assassin left, SB should have been between the two groups, but he had yet to leave her side, and Tina didn't have the heart to make him.

Once they were in formation, Tina had everyone with damaged armor moved to the center to hide their injuries. The Rangers, she sent into the copse of dead trees beside the road to find long sticks to fill their quivers with so they wouldn't look so obviously empty. She was banging on her armor with her fist to try to make it look slightly less dented when Anders shuffled up to her.

"Here," he said, taking off his guild tabard and handing it to her.

"Use this."

"What for?" Tina asked, holding up the red cloth stitched with the white bull of the Roughneck Raiders guild.

"A standard," Anders said with a fishy smile. "Every proper army needs a banner to wave."

Tina smiled back. "Thanks, dude. That's good thinking."

Together, the two of them found a suitable tree limb to use as a flagpole. When she'd tied it tight, Tina hoisted her "banner" high and turned to look over her troops. They still looked sad with their dirty armor and bloody patches, but it was as good as things were likely to get, so she gave the signal to march out of the woods toward the Order's fortress.

As soon as they reached the hill leading up to the fort, Tina knew they were in trouble. The guards on the walls had gone into a frenzy the moment the raid had come out of the trees, banging alarm gongs and shouting warnings to their fellows inside the fortress.

"The players are here! To the walls!"

Tina's ears pricked at the word "players," but there was no time to hesitate. If this was going to work, they had to show that fortress they weren't worried about anything, so Tina ignored the smell of hot oil drifting toward her on the wind and held the banner of the Roughnecks high, walking straight up the road toward the sealed door with huge strides of her stone legs.

It seemed to be working. Now that she was closer, Tina could see the individual soldiers' faces in the bright torchlight on top of the walls. Some were focused and disciplined, but most looked confused and scared, struggling to hold on to their new glowing weapons. One man even had an empty bow drawn, his arrow-less string pointed at Tina's head. That should have made her feel better, but for every scared soldier, there was another who watched the approaching raid with naked hatred burning in his eyes.

"I don't like this," Tina muttered as the scared soldiers scrambled to follow the angry ones' orders. "Fear and hate are not a good mix."

"They sure don't look real happy to see us," Frank whispered back. "I thought we were on the same side as these guys."

"We were in the game," Tina said. "But a lot's changed." She nodded at the arrow-riddled road. "I'm worried that other players started some shit."

"You thinking there's bad blood here?"

"I wouldn't be surprised," Tina said. "Look at all the problems we had with people back at the Dead Mountain thinking this is a dream. This fortress is the entrance to the Deadlands and the place where everyone hung out. There were probably tons of players inside when whatever it was went down and trapped us here." She scowled. "I bet someone did something stupid."

And now her raid was paying for it. The fortress's brightly lit battlements were getting more crowded by the second, and Tina's confidence in their ability to bluff their way inside was dropping with every new soldier that came up. But there was no turning back now. Whatever Zen said, Tina had no illusions about their ability to make it through the Never Swamp. Getting to that portal was their only hope of getting out of here with everyone alive, so she stuck to the plan, walking calmly forward with her chin up.

She'd just stepped onto the wide circle of light thrown off by the bonfires that burned on either side of the fortress's front gate when a single guard yelled, "Death to the monsters!" and loosed his arrow.

The raid froze. The fortress went stock still as well as the arrow whistled through the air. Tina forced herself to appear relaxed as she watched it fall, but her shield-hand was fisted so hard it hurt as the arrow sank into the road in front of her, ten feet shy of its target.

Her.

"I said *hold*, you morons!" an officer shouted, cuffing the soldier over the head. "Don't fire without orders!"

Cowed, all the soldiers nodded, and Tina saw her chance. Putting up a hand to make her raid stay put, she walked forward alone until she was standing only a few dozen feet away from the fortress's enormous barbican. When she was in position, she planted the guild's banner in the dusty gray ground with a *thunk* and took a deep breath, filling her giant lungs with air to shout up at the guards on the battlements above.

"Why do you fire upon us?" she cried, careful to keep her language to the "ye olde" style all the NPCs had used in game. "I am Roxxy, leader of the Roughneck Raiders guild. We have fought many undead in your name and brought you countless trophies of their defeat. Explain this treachery!"

Tina had thought long and hard about what to say on the walk up here, and she was pretty pleased with what she'd come up with. It was important to remind these people that, whatever might have happened before her raid got here, they were all ultimately on the same side. If she could make them feel like they were the ones in the wrong, maybe fear would turn into apology. But while she was happy with her opening attack, the soldiers didn't seem to know what to make of it. They talked back and forth across the walls in low voices, some shaking their heads, others making angry gestures. When she tried to move a little closer, one of the officers pointed his bow at her chest.

"Stop!" he cried, voice shaking. "Don't move! We will treat any advance as hostile!"

Tina scowled but stayed put, tapping a finger impatiently against her shield, fighting the urge to glance nervously over her shoulder at her raid. She hadn't heard movement, so she was reasonably sure they were all still in position, but her people weren't going to be able to keep looking like capable hard-asses for much longer. The predawn dark was doing a lot to hide their true shabbiness, but if the soldiers had too much time to study their empty quivers and slumping shoulders, the whole charade would fall apart. Then just as Tina was opening her mouth to ask what the hold-up was, an extremely tall, dark-mustached man wearing glittering gold-and-white plate armor appeared on the wall.

Tina recognized him at once. It was Commander Garrond, Paladin of the Order and the main quest giver for the fortress. More importantly right now, he was also a level-eighty-one four-skull. That made him the biggest badass in the Deadlands who didn't work for the Once King, and from the way he was looking down his nose at Tina, he knew it.

"I am Paladin-Commander Garrond of the Order of the Golden Sun," he said, his voice booming across the empty battlefield. "You players are no longer welcome in our fortress. Leave now, or face our wrath."

"What the hell, fucker?" Tina shouted back, abandoning her attempt at quest-text-style dialog. "We've fought the undead for you assholes for a year, and now you're sending us away? What happed to the honor of the Order?"

Given all the quests she'd had to do involving the Order's honor, Tina thought that angle would be a shoo-in. To her surprise, though, the commander and his soldiers looked angrier than ever.

"What do you know of honor?" Garrond roared, his pale face turning scarlet. "You players imprisoned us to serve as slaves for your glory for years! You plundered our wealth and magic as 'rewards' for fighting *our* enemies, and yet you achieved *nothing*! The Once King's armies are larger and stronger than they've ever been! Worse, now that we are free, we've seen your true colors emerge. You are all *evil*! Demons and madmen in cursed bodies! Once the Order of the Golden Sun has destroyed the undead menace, we will purge your kind from this world as well!"

A huge cheer went up from the guards as he finished, but Tina could only stare in shock.

"Wait," she said at last. "You mean you guys were real this entire time?"

"Of course we are real," Garrond said, insulted.

"But you were NPCs!" Tina cried. "Programmed characters! This was all just a game until two days ago!"

If the soldiers of the Order had been mad before, then her words brought a veritable storm to the battlements now.

"Our years of unending torment were *not* a *game!*" Garrond thundered, almost too angry to get the words out. "We existed long before your Forever Fantasy Online ruined our world! But we may not last much longer thanks to what you've done."

In the back of her mind, Tina knew she should be amazed at the implications of alternate worlds going on here, but she didn't have the time. She could already feel the raid wilting behind her, and with it, the rapidly closing final window they had for survival.

"That shit's not our fault!" she boomed back in her own parade-ground voice. "We don't know anything about slavery or ruining worlds, but we sure as hell fought a mountain of undead for you ungrateful assholes, which means you owe us. We don't want your crap loot anymore, anyway! All we need is your portal to Bastion. Let us use that, and you never have to see us again. Now open up before me and my friends decide to give you a real problem to worry about."

"*Never!*" Garrond shouted, pounding an armored fist on the battlement wall so hard, a chip flew off the stone. "Do you have any idea what it was like to be stuck in place, watching you play soldier? We were trapped! Compelled to sing praises for all your petty, meaningless achievements like you were actual heroes of legend! For years, we have cried as we've been forced to hand over our highest honors and artifacts for your childish endeavors, but no more! *Nothing* you say will convince me to let such immoral, dangerous, selfish creatures into my fortress ever again. You should be grateful I haven't ordered my men to kill you where you stand!"

Several people in the raid behind her groaned in dismay, and Tina's grip on her shield tightened. She'd really hoped she could just talk her way in and to not create a situation, but it seemed that push had now come to shove, which meant it was time to play her card.

"We're not going away," she snarled up at him. "I didn't come here for trouble, but you're facing an army capable of taking on the Once King himself, so if you don't want something unfortunate to happen to your pretty white fortress, you'd be wise to open those gates and let us through."

The commander laughed in her face. "You bluff, player! I can see the condition of your 'army.' Do you think I can be fooled by sticks for arrows and half-dead healers held up by their fellows?" He shook his head. "I am being merciful far beyond what your kind deserves. Now leave before my patience runs out and I decide to deliver the justice of this world upon you."

Tina's scowl stayed firmly in place, but inside, she was cursing up a storm. This was falling apart in the worst way, but what could she do? They couldn't go forward, they couldn't go around, and they couldn't turn back. The idea of dying in front of the Order's gates—literally a hundred feet from safety—was intolerable. Marching through the swamp and watching everyone die one at a time was also intolerable. That left only one option. Tina just hoped she lived to regret it.

"All right, asshole!" she shouted. "You think you know so much? I'm gonna tell you how it *really* is." She drew her sword and stabbed it at the road behind her. "The Dead Mountain is on the move! There's a goddamn army of them coming, and Grel'Darm the Colossal is leading the way. They aren't that far behind us, and that train is running straight at this place."

Gasps of alarm rose up from the Order's soldiers. Even Commander Garrond's thick black eyebrows rose in surprise, and Tina smirked. She'd found her lever at last, and she was going to use it to pry this place open.

"You want us gone?" she went on. "Well, *too bad*! We couldn't leave if we wanted to. We're stuck between Grel and you assholes, but that's your bad luck, because dying in battle here is a lot better than being filled with the ghostfire!" She swung her sword back around to point at the fortress's double doors. "We've got enough shit-kicking left in us to bust this gate and stomp you all. Especially you, you weak-ass four-skull. You might kill us thanks to sheer numbers in the end, but we'll sure as shit wreck the hell out of this place before we go. So you tell me, Mr. Paladin Commander, how's your oath to defend the world against the undead going to hold up when Grel'Darm turns that corner and all you've got left is a smoking ruin?"

Dead silence waited when she finished, and Tina knew she'd hit a nerve. She just hoped it was enough. Her raid wasn't as big a threat to the fortress as she claimed, but Grel was. If she could convince Garrond that she was more trouble to fight than to overlook, they might make it to that portal yet. But while Tina had painted the most horrible picture she could think of, the commander still wasn't ordering his soldiers to stand down.

Clearly, a stronger point needed to be made.

"Naturalists forward!" Tina commanded, holding her ground. "Focus lightning on the front gates. Let's bring 'em down!"

The order echoed off the silent walls, but nothing happened. Growling, Tina looked over her shoulder to see Neko staring back with her ears down.

"You said we were only bluffing!" the Naturalist hissed. "Lightning isn't bluffing!"

"Yeah, well, you heard the man," Tina said, her voice cold. "Bluffing has failed, so now we're punching."

Neko's ears pressed even flatter against her head. "But you said—"

"I know what I said!" Tina roared. Now was not the time for arguments. With every second that lightning wasn't frying soldiers, her ability to force Garrond to let them through shrank. Another few moments, and it would vanish altogether, but Neko wasn't moving. She just stood there, clutching her staff with her tail between her legs, until Tina looked away in disgust.

"*Sorcerers forward!*" she cried instead, turning back to the wall. There was some shuffling, then KatanaFatale limped up beside her. "Finally," Tina snapped, pointing at the gates. "Start casting Rising Inferno. I want those things in splinters. The moment they're down,

243

we run for the portal."

As pale as the dust at his feet, KatanaFatale nodded and began the long casting ritual for the high-damage Rising Inferno spell. Satisfied that much was going to plan at least, Tina used the mirrored inside of her shield to check the rest of the raid behind her.

It wasn't pretty. Everyone looked terrified and betrayed, which was no surprise since Tina had just done exactly what she'd sworn she wouldn't. If Garrond hadn't been right there listening, she would've explained that they only needed this one attack. Once the doors were down, all they had to do was run for the portal and they'd be safe. There was no way to tell them that without giving her game away, though, so Tina resolved to say she was sorry later. As soon as she made sure there *was* a later.

"Be ready to charge on my command," she ordered, bracing her feet as Katana's cast neared completion.

"Are you mad?" Garrond cried, leaning over the battlements. "You would destroy us, the holy Order of the Golden Sun, out of *spite*?"

"You put us in this position!" Tina yelled back. "Don't like it, then let us in!"

"You truly are monsters," the commander said scornfully. "We are the first and best line of defense against the ghostfire! If this fortress falls, the whole continent will be put at risk!"

"That's not my fault!" Tina cried. "You're the one trying to throw us to the undead! *Of course* I'm going to fight back!" She pointed over her shoulder at the raid. "I would do anything, kick *anyone's* ass, to keep my people alive another day! I will climb up there and feed you to Grel'Darm piece by piece if that's what it takes to save the Roughnecks! I'm all in on this, asshole, and if you don't want to find out how bad I can get, you will shut your face and *open the damn gate*!"

Commander Garrond stepped back in alarm, and Tina risked a glance at the Sorcerer. "How many more seconds, Katana?"

"Not sure," he replied, sweat dripping down his face as he struggled to control the massive wave of fire forming in his hands. "But if this really is a bluff, he'd better fall for it soon, 'cause I don't know if I can hold this much longer."

"You ignorant, *arrogant*—" Garrond cut off mid-insult, squinting over her head toward the eastern horizon as though he'd just spotted something behind them. From the way his red face turned pale, Tina

244

could guess what it was.

"Fine," the commander said, his voice as bitter as ash as he changed his tune. "Unlike you, I work for the greater good. Call off your fire, put down your weapons, and you may enter our fortress."

Tina let out a huge breath of relief and motioned for Katana to stop casting. The Sorcerer dropped his hands with a gasp, and the stone of her skin flashed hot as the fiery magic fell away. Ahead of them, the fortress's enormous wooden gates swung open with a grinding sound to reveal the outer gate yard: a boxed-in stone corridor that ran between the protruding front gatekeep Garrond was standing on top of and the square body of the main fortress.

The space between the outer gatekeep and inner defenses was roughly a hundred feet, or as long as two tractor-trailer trucks parked nose to bumper. It was half again as wide, but the heavy stone walls made the large space feel narrow. At the end was another, even more heavily reinforced inner gate that led into the keep itself, but it was currently closed. To reach it, Tina and her raiders would have to walk through the front gates, under the giant stone gatekeep with its massive towers and hundreds of archers, and between the walls that connected the keep to its front gate. Huge, thick, stone walls whose battlements were also bristling with soldiers.

The whole thing reeked of a trap. Once they were inside, all Garrond would have to do was close the front gate, and they'd be cornered, stuck like rats in a stone box while archers rained fire down on them from all sides. There was no other way into the fortress, though, so Tina crushed her fears and marched forward, striding proudly through the fort's giant front doors as she waved for the rest to follow her.

The raid obeyed faster than it had all day, practically running through the front gate into the inner yard. As they piled inside, the back of Tina's neck began to prickle. Now that she was right below them, she couldn't help but notice just how *many* soldiers had packed themselves onto the walls. She'd been questing out of this fortress for a year now. It never had more than a few dozen guards, even during special events. She'd thought it was strange seeing so many soldiers on top of the gatekeep, but now that she was *in* the fortress with walls on all sides, there had to be close to a thousand people looking down at the raid from the surrounding battlements, making her wonder if distance wasn't the only thing that had expanded when FFO had changed.

When they were all inside, Garrond gave the command to close the outer gates and vanished down the stairs. Tina assumed this was so he could go open the inner gates for them, but when the commander appeared again, he was standing on one of the yard's interior battlements, leering down at her from the front of the biggest archer gallery Tina had ever seen.

"I have let you into our fortress, as agreed," he said coldly. "If you wish to proceed, however, you must disarm." He waved his hand, and the soldiers beside him began lowering wooden supply crates into the yard on ropes. "Place your weapons in the boxes, and we'll discuss opening the inner gates."

The words weren't out of his mouth before the raid exploded in protest.

"*No way!*"

"It took me a year to get this bow!"

"He's gonna kill us!"

"Screw this! Let's try the swamp!"

"*Shut up!*" Tina roared, her huge voice bouncing off the stone. When the raid fell silent, she glared up at Garrond. "It's not an unreasonable request. We're an invading army, after all. But we're not giving up our weapons forever. When will we get them back?"

The paladin's lips curled into a smile beneath his black mustache. "When you leave."

Tina didn't like the way he said that, but she didn't have much of a choice. If she showed hesitation or confusion here, it could mean their deaths. If Garrond needed to hold their weapons for security to make himself feel safe while they were passing through, Tina could handle that, and if he screwed them over, all they had to do was rush the portal and get to Bastion. It would suck to lose their best weapons, but everyone had spares in the bank. More importantly, they'd be out of the Deadlands, which meant they'd finally be safe.

That was a prize Tina was willing to risk anything for, so she drew her sword and walked over to one of the boxes the guards had lowered down. As she reached out to place it inside, though, something in her chest clenched. Her red-glowing sword was from Sanguilar, the Once King's Blood General. It was the best tanking sword in the game, *and* she'd gotten a rare roll that had maxed out its stats. It was a priceless treasure that had taken months of weekly raiding to get, and even though this whole thing had been her idea, setting it down in the chest, future fate unknown, was harder than she'd expected.

"Your shield as well," Garrond said when Tina stepped back.

Tina shot him an angry look, and the commander's face hardened. "I know how tanks work," he growled. "Your shield as well, stonekin, or no one gets in."

Cursing under her breath, Tina stripped off her shield and wedged it into the box. Letting it go felt like giving up an arm, but she'd made this bed of nails. She would lie in it just like everyone else.

"There," she said, holding up her empty hands. "Satisfied?" When Garrond nodded, Tina looked back at her raiders. "Weapons in the boxes, everyone. This is how we get to Bastion."

Her order bounced off the tall walls, but SilentBlayde was the only one who moved. He strode over and made a good show of placing his beloved silver swords into the chest, but though his movements said "chipper," his eyes were more worried than Tina had ever seen.

Anders went next, then Neko. Killbox, however, clutched his ax. "I don't know about this, Roxxy," he whispered when she glared at him. "This shit stinks."

"Same," Zen said angrily. "I'm not giving up my bow. We'll be defenseless."

Above them, Tina heard Garrond clear his throat, and suddenly, the air was full of the creak of bowstrings as the archers on the walls took aim. Zen was reaching for an arrow of her own when Tina grabbed her hand. "I'm keeping my word," she growled, baring her marble teeth. "I said I'd get everyone to Bastion alive. This is how that happens. I've already paid the price. Now put your weapons in the damn box so we can get out of here."

Zen stumbled when she let go, clutching her bow until the enchanted wood creaked. The look in her eyes had Tina bracing to take an arrow, but Zen didn't attack. Shooting Tina a glare that said this would never be forgotten or forgiven, she walked over to the box and knelt down, laying her bow down beside SB's swords as gently as a mother putting down her baby.

When she was done, Killbox stepped up. Like Tina's shield, his giant ax didn't really fit, and he didn't bother trying to make it. He just dropped it in the pile and stepped back, making way for the next player.

One by one, the raid shuffled forward and placed their weapons in the boxes. No one would meet Tina's eyes, but in a way, that was a relief, because it meant she didn't have to face any of them, either. When it was finally over, she turned back to Garrond. "It's done," she said bitterly. "Now let us in."

Garrond's lips curled in a thin smile beneath his bushy mustache as the chests full of top-tier weapons were hauled up and out of sight. When they were safely stowed on top of the walls, the fortress's inner doors swung open to reveal the parade yard of the main base, which was much bigger than Tina remembered.

Back in the game, the Order's fort had been suitably large for its importance, but it was still only a quest hub. This new fortress, though, was enormous. Other than the front gatekeep, which stuck off the fortress's eastern wall like a gooseneck, it was a perfect square of sixty-foot-tall white stone walls. Inside the walls' protection, the base itself was a miniature city of heavy stone buildings. Back in the game, these had been mostly shacks for quest givers and profession huts. Now there were multiple barracks, storage houses, smithies, workshops, a full temple to the Sun, and several other structures Tina had no idea about. Everything looked as though it had been built to withstand orbital bombardment rather than to be lived in, but what *really* gave her pause was the legit army of Order soldiers waiting for them in the giant, well-lit, smooth paved yard at the fortress's center.

That made her stop cold. She'd known the Order was bigger, but this was ridiculous. Forget the thousand she'd seen crammed onto the walls. There had to be at least *two* thousand soldiers standing in formation in front of them now. The giant yard was so packed, the players barely had room to cram themselves inside before the massive inner gates swung shut, sealing the raid inside the fort with an echoing *clang.*

Heart pounding, Tina forced herself to ignore all the new enemies and find their target. Thankfully, despite all the other changes, the marble shrine that held the Bastion portal was still where it had always been just off the main yard to their left. She was sucking in a breath to give the order to rush it when she noticed something was wrong.

The room inside the shrine's entranceway was empty. Empty and *dark.* Usually, the multicolored light from the portal reflected off the shrine's white walls, making the whole place glow like the inside of a rave. Now, though, Tina didn't see so much as a torch inside. But it wasn't until Commander Garrond came down from the battlements with that hateful smile on his face that the truth finally hit her. There was no portal to Bastion. Only the blank space where one had once been.

A sword to the stomach would have been less painful. Tina shook in her armor, fighting to keep control as the commander stepped in front of her in all his towering white-and-gold glory. Like most boss-level NPCs, he was incredibly tall for a human. Not as tall as her stonekin, of course, but with her whole body sagging in despair at the missing portal, he felt miles bigger. A true monster, and she'd played right into his hands.

"Still going to fight us out of spite?" he asked with a superior sneer.

"Hey!" yelled someone behind her. "Where's the portal to Bastion?"

"That?" Garrond said, glancing around Tina at the raid. "With the world in chaos, we couldn't very well leave a back door to Bastion open on the Once King's doorstep. We closed it down yesterday, and it won't be reopened until we're safe again."

No one said a word. They didn't have to. Tina could feel the news crushing them just as it had crushed her. Several people actually collapsed where they stood, their legs giving out as their last hopes vanished, making Garrond's smile even wider.

"You may camp here in the courtyard while we fight," he said dismissively. "When the undead threat is defeated, we'll discuss your surrender. I sent all the players who woke up here to Bastion in chains to face the King's justice. Your fate will be the same. Try *anything*, and we will slaughter you where you stand."

Tina had no witty comeback this time as Garrond turned and walked off. Part of her wanted to blame the commander for being an unreasonable bastard, but she'd never been good at lying, even to herself, and she knew who really was at fault. It was her. It was *all* her. She'd fucked up *again*.

Her eyes squeezed shut. Zen was right. The warning signs had been all over the walls, but she'd been so focused on getting everyone through that damn portal that she'd ignored what was in front of her eyes. Even the swamp would have been better than the trap she'd just walked them into.

How could she have been so blind? Even if Grel hadn't given up, the Rangers could have scavenged them food that didn't need cooking. There was also a Schtumple trading post in the middle of the zone that always had mounts for sale. Possible irrational hatred of players aside, Schtumples could always be trusted to choose trade over murder. Why hadn't she thought of that? They couldn't sail a boat, but she probably could have bought passage with some of the precious herbs or items still in their backpacks.

Tina shook her head in disgust. There were so many things she should have considered, so much more she should have thought through, and now it was too late. They were locked in, weaponless, *helpless*, and it was all her fault.

With that truth hammering in her head, Tina took a deep breath and turned to face the raid she'd failed. As expected given how hard she'd pushed them, everyone was on the ground. They looked up when she turned around, staring at her with a mixture of desperation, betrayal, and despair. On a normal day, Tina might have been able to take that. Now, with her own exhaustion and guilt pulling on her like boat anchors, she couldn't even keep her head up.

They deserved to know, she realized with a pang. They'd trusted her, and she'd failed them. There was no way she could make that up, but she could at least tell them why. It wouldn't be kind to her ego, but that pain was the least of what she deserved for letting them down, so Tina forced herself to lift her head one last time to finally tell the truth.

"I have a confession to make," she said, prying the words out of her tightening throat. "Back at the Dead Mountain, before the rest of you recovered, I got someone killed. I don't know if any of you noticed the headless Sorcerer lying by the roadside in our rush to get out, but if you did, well, that body was on me."

A tense stillness descended upon the raid, and Tina forced herself to keep going. "I have no excuses," she said. "I was up, I was armed, I saw the monster coming. I should have picked it up, that's the tank's job, but I screwed up. I let the monster walk right past me, and he died."

Saying it out loud hurt even more than she'd expected. In front of her, the raid was as silent as the dead she'd left. She couldn't read their faces, as she didn't want to. It wasn't finished, though, so though it felt like pulling out barbed arrows, Tina forced herself to keep going.

"That's why I've been riding you all so hard," she explained. "I knew what was at stake back then. I knew death was real, and I was desperate to get us all away from the Dead Mountain before anyone else got killed. I thought I was doing what was necessary to save everyone, but then David died too, and I..."

She stopped, blinking hard. "I messed up," she went on at last. "My friend died because I was a lousy leader who made too many mistakes. I'm so sorry I treated you all so badly. I don't think you're idiots, and I shouldn't have treated you like I did. I should have yelled less and listened more. I know that now. I knew it before, it was just...every time you balked, I saw that Sorcerer's head rolling on the ground, or David vanishing beneath Grel's club. I couldn't let that happen again, so I kept pushing, and now I've pushed us off the cliff."

It wasn't until the words were out of her mouth that Tina realized how true they were. The shock of it was enough to send her to her knees. Her armor rang like a gong when she hit the stone, but Tina barely heard it. Her eyes were on the raid, on the people who'd given her trust after trust only to watch her break it over and over. Every time she'd played the monster, she'd told herself that the end would make up for it. Now the end was here, and she had nothing to give them except regrets.

"I'm sorry," she said, her stone voice cracking. "This is all my fault. I lost our gear. I almost got us all killed, again, and there's not even a portal. We would have been safer if we'd stayed on the road, but I..." She swallowed. "I'm sorry."

She held her breath, waiting for the accusations, but no one said a thing. Several people just turned away and wrapped themselves up in their cloaks. Tina didn't know if it was out of disgust or just fatigue, but the silence stung worse than any words could. Zen was the only one who didn't turn her back. She stood up and marched to the front of the raid, her perfect elven features stark with fury as she hauled back and slapped Tina hard across the face.

"That's for breaking your promise," she said, clutching her hand. Then she turned on her heel and walked back to the other Rangers, dropping down against the wall with her knees up and her face pressed into them.

Tina raised a hand to her cheek. A slap from an unarmed Ranger shouldn't have hurt, but she'd felt it all the way through her skull. It still stung, and she had a feeling it would for a long, long time. She was trying to get used to the pain when SilentBlayde rose to his feet.

A shudder went through her and Tina shrank into the floor. *No, she thought. Not him.* Please *not him.*

As silent as his name, the Assassin walked through the crowd, his expression damnably hidden behind his ninja mask. As he leaned down, Tina closed her eyes so she wouldn't have to see his anger, the hatred on his familiar face as he struck her, too.

But he didn't. Instead, SilentBlayde leaned down and pressed a delicate kiss to her forehead just below her copper hair. Even through his mask, Tina swore she could feel his warm lips as soft as a feather on her cool stone skin.

"That's for saying you'd do anything for us," he said softly.

Tina's eyes popped open to find him staring at her, his eyes gentle and sad above his mask. And it was that—not the slap, not the resentment—that finally pushed her over the edge. She curled into herself, crying as silently as possible because she couldn't do anything else. SilentBlayde dropped down beside her, putting his arm around her huge, shaking shoulders as she quietly fell to pieces.

CHAPTER *12*

James

The gnoll Naturalists were good enough to heal James and Arbati. The rush of magic felt incredible, as always, but after his wounds closed, James still felt hollow and tired. Looking down at himself, he realized he could see where the new life magics were reinforcing—but not yet absorbed by—his own natural lines. It would probably take time and actual, legit rest before the two magics fully integrated and he felt whole again. Until then, he'd just have to be gentle with himself. Fortunately, he was—at least temporarily—the Chief of Chiefs, which meant he could delegate.

As soon as the healing was done, James ordered Thunder Paw to purge the city of any remaining undead. Looking joyously bloodthirsty, the old Naturalist agreed right away. He trotted off with a few hundred of the town's warriors, and soon the quiet night was punctuated by the sound of bloody crunches.

Meanwhile, a pack of elderly gnoll grandmothers arrived with food and water. James and Arbati dug in greedily, chugging waterskins and tearing into piles of jerky with their fangs. It was James's first real meal since yesterday, and the super-spicy dried meat tasted amazing, even if it did make his eyes water.

As he ate, James asked the gnolls if there were any other players left in the city, but all he got was a lot of shaking heads. The remaining gnolls couldn't speak English or the language of Wind and Grass, but every time James said the word "player," they would point at the bloody pit.

Choking down the last of his food, James walked back down into the drained lake. As his bare feet landed in the gory mud, he wished he'd done this the other way around, searching *before* eating. Fighting to keep his dinner down, he checked the bodies but didn't find anything he didn't already know. All the players in the pit were hours past the six-minute resurrection window. Dead for real, in other words.

But while there was nothing James could do for them now, there was still something they could do for him. The gnolls had only low-level equipment and nothing in his size, but other than the wounds that had killed them, the players' bodies were untouched. James, on the other hand, was filthy and practically naked. It felt wrong, but if he was going to finish what he'd started tonight, James needed gear. So holding his nose, he started searching the bodies for something he could wear.

His first target was a jubatus Naturalist who'd died with a spike through his head, leaving his armor undamaged. James was pulling the body off the spike to claim the robe when he stopped.

He did not want to wear robes. As appropriate as they were for his class and magic, there was no way he could run or fight properly in such a long, heavy garment. He was much more drawn to the dead elven Assassin's leather armor. Back in the game, jubatus and elves had had the same base body models, which meant it would probably fit. It looked nice, too. Much more fitting to the work he would actually be doing than the stuffy caster robes.

Smiling, James pulled the elf down to claim his armor, but as the corpse slid off the spike, his eager grin faded. Looting kills was such a normal action in FFO, he'd never thought much of it. Reality, however, was proving very different. There was no loot window or neat list of items. James had to *strip* the clammy, bloody leather off the elf's reeking corpse. Even after he managed to get it free, he wasn't sure he could bring himself to put the armor on. The congealed blood coating the inside smelled like death to his sensitive jubatus nose.

Promising himself he'd clean it thoroughly, James tossed his "new" armor up onto the side of the pit and resumed rummaging through the bodies. Five minutes later, he'd acquired two healer rings and an amulet. But while these were far less disgusting than the armor, touching them gave James the same incomplete feeling that the staff did. He could feel the magic woven tightly within the items, though, which gave him hope. If items were still magical, then there had to be a way to properly equip them.

He was heading out to test his theory when he spied another dead Naturalist. He'd ignored her before because she was too low level for his needs, but she was the same level as the gnolls. More importantly, she was clutching a sapphire staff topped with a floating collection of twinkling crystals that James recognized, and that gave him an idea.

Prying the lovely weapon from her stiff hands, James apologized for his theft and quickly left the pit. Arbati and Thunder Paw were waiting when he climbed out, staring at the bloody armor he'd collected with matching expressions of horror.

"I know," James said before they could say a word. "But we need these more than they do right now."

He waved over a helper then, piled all the armor and jewelry into a basket and handed it off to a group of gnolls with orders to wash everything in boiling water and lye. While Thunder Paw translated, James picked up the blue staff.

"I have a gift for you," he said to Thunder Paw when the other gnolls had scurried off. "This is the Azure Starlight Staff."

The moment he held up the sparkling staff, all of Thunder Paw's horror at grave robbing vanished. The old Naturalist's one eye was as wide as an egg as James laid the elegant golden rod crowned with floating blue crystals in his paws.

"Me cannot use something this mighty, Chief James," Thunder Paw whispered, his awe clear even through his collar's auto-tuned voice. "There is too much power here to control."

"It looks that way," James said, holding up a finger. "But there's a trick to this. I know you're at least level thirty because you're using the same armor and staff as all the other gnoll Naturalists. This item *looks* higher level because it's a rare drop, but it's actually for your level." He pushed the staff into Thunder Paw's hands. "Just give it a try. I bet you'll find its potency easier to control than you think."

Thunder Paw swallowed nervously and took the weapon over to a nearby bench. He was examining it when Arbati grabbed James by the shoulder.

"Why are you arming the gnolls with better weapons?" he hissed in James's ear. "Have you forgotten that they will be our enemies when this is over?"

"I'm hoping that if we keep being friends, we won't have to go back to being enemies." James whispered back, picking up his own staff from where he'd leaned it against a log. "Just give me a minute to watch Thunder Paw. He's about to show me something very important. Why don't you go look for a new weapon of your own?"

He'd expected Arbati to balk at that, but to his surprise, the warrior nodded and jogged off. Suddenly alone, James turned and resumed studying the gnoll Naturalist.

Sitting on his bench, Thunder Paw laid the staff across his legs and began staring at it intently. James walked over and sat down beside him in the same position with his Eclipsed Steel Staff and waited. After several minutes of picking at the Azure Starlight staff, Thunder Paw grabbed a string of his own mana and started weaving through the middle of the staff.

James winced. Aside from the glowing magic, it looked disturbingly like the Naturalist was tying the weapon to himself using his own guts. It was working, though. The Azure Starlight Staff was binding itself to Thunder Paw as he watched, its power merging with his as he made it part of his magic. That seemed to be the trick, so James plucked a bit of his own magic and started trying to poke it into his own weapon.

It wasn't pleasant. Being a cursed metal, eclipsed steel was uncomfortable to touch magically. It contained no actual death magic that he could feel, but the magics inside were twisted in strange ways. Unlike the Azure Starlight, whose floating crystals chimed musically whenever you moved it, James heard whispered, malicious words whenever he focused on the black staff in his lap. But he could also feel its power, so he kept searching, poking the staff's magic for whatever Thunder Paw had used to start the binding.

Finally, after several minutes, James found an opening. In the center of the staff, right where you'd place your hand, loose threads of magic were dangling like ripped-out wires, probably from the death of its previous owner. Smiling, James started feeding his own magic into it. He was making good progress when something growled.

"You should not do that, Chief James."

James jumped, losing his hold on the magic. He hadn't heard the gnoll stand up, but Thunder Paw was suddenly right in front of him, his scarred face fearful. "That weapon is cursed," the Naturalist said, pointing at the black staff in James's lap. "It talks to itself. We should bury it, not keep it."

James shook his head. "I need it. I don't know how it ended up here, but this is the only high-level weapon around that I can use. Hell, it's better than the staff I lost. I can't pass this up."

The old naturalist sniffed in distaste. "It is cursed," he said again. "You should not let such magic into yourself."

"Duly noted," James said, smiling at the gnoll. "Also, no offense, but I notice you're suddenly speaking more eloquently."

"It is because of this," Thunder Paw said, holding up his new azure staff. "Me have never held such smooth power. It makes words leap to my mind and improves my memory. Me finds that Me can harmonize with the translation collar much more quickly now." He looked at the beautiful staff in awe. "It is amazing."

"As to be expected of an artifact crafted by Celestial Elves during the Age of Skies," James said with a grin. "Now, if you'll pardon me for a minute, I've got to finish my own upgrade."

He was about to pick up the staff again when a paw settled on his shoulder. "Please don't," Thunder Paw whined. "That metal is a sin against the gods. Even the wind dislikes it."

"It'll be fine. Trust me," James said confidently. "Believe it or not, this staff is a pretty common drop from the Dead Mountain trash mobs. There's probably a hundred raiders out there right now with this exact same staff, but I might never get a chance at another weapon of this caliber again. Even if my spare gear is still safe in the bank at Bastion, who knows when I'll be able to get to it. We need this power *tonight*. I can't take on the lich without it."

That earned him a sad nod. "Be it your will, then. Me will find our remaining officers and ready an attack force."

"Thanks, Thunder Paw."

The Naturalist shuffled away, and James resumed the binding ritual. He plucked a fresh thread of mana from his chest and painstakingly wove it into the frayed magic hanging from the staff. With each knot tied between him and the weapon, the incomplete feeling faded a fraction. Halfway through, he started to feel the weapon itself. Not just touching it, but as if the staff were part of him, like a limb. Then when he tied the final knot, the empty space in the magics was filled completely, and the staff settled into his hands like a joint snapping into place.

"Life is suffering. Death is salvation. All must die to be free."

James's head snapped up. He'd heard the words clearly, but there was no one there. Just gnolls preparing for battle, and none of them had a collar like Thunder Paw. Hands shaking, James looked at the weapon in his lap. Then feeling slightly foolish, he whispered, "Excuse me?"

But no more words came back.

■ ■

"We have no remaining officers," was the report from Thunder Paw half an hour later.

James looked up from the freshly cleaned leather armor he was fastening around his chest. Now that he knew the trick, he'd bound the level-thirty Assassin's armor as well as the two healer rings and the healer amulet. It was a hodgepodge mix of stats, but James loved the feeling of being stronger and more magical too much to care that his build wasn't optimal.

Having started the day effectively naked of stat-boosting gear, James had been amazed at the difference the level-eighty staff made. Creepy start aside, the Eclipsed Steel Staff was everything he could have wanted. Using his mana was a breeze now, increasing the amount of magic he could safely control fivefold. The boosts from his new rings and amulet had been less impressive but still so noticeable that James couldn't help but wonder what Tina and her raiders must be like. He had *one* item from the Dead Mountain, but most of the Roughnecks were fully decked out in the stuff. It must feel like being a demigod.

"How are there no officers?" James asked Thunder Paw as he fastened the final buckle. "I thought the undead were training the gnolls into a formal army. Shouldn't there be a full chain of command with units and so on?"

The one-eyed Naturalist shook his head. "All of our army's leaders were made undead so the lich could control us. Any officers Me didn't kill in the purge were recalled to the lich's lair at the bottom of the Red Canyon."

"Damn," James muttered, glancing out of the hut he'd been using to change at the armed gnolls waiting for them in the street. "We have plenty of trained fighters, but they're just a mob without officers."

"But we fight for the Grand Pack!" Thunder Paw insisted, stamping his new staff. "Everyone here is ready to die to take back our home!"

The army of gnolls outside barked and yipped in agreement, and James nodded.

"Good," he said, grabbing his new staff. "Because there's no way to make this not ugly."

James paused to do some mental math, converting the Red

Canyon dungeon he remembered to the new size scale then rapidly estimating how many gnolls could fight shoulder to shoulder in the corridors. Once he had that number, he ran damage-to-health ratios to try to pre-calculate casualties to see how many soldiers they'd need to win without bringing in so many that they got piled up.

The whole thing only took him a few minutes, but what really shocked James was the fact that he'd been able to do it at all. Thunder Paw had already shown him what adding Intelligence could do, but James hadn't realized just how big a jump was possible until he'd bound a staff with over three hundred Intelligence. The resulting jump made him question what intelligence really was. According to how he felt, it was sharper senses, amazing math skills, fantastic spatial reasoning, and a wickedly improved memory. He would've killed to have this power back in school. Now, though, all he could do was spin his new brainpower as fast as possible to come up with a plan that wouldn't get them all killed.

"Stop overthinking things," growled Arbati, stalking into the hut. The warrior had a new sword—a green-glowing, two-handed blade he'd claimed from one of the dead Berserkers in the pit—and from the way he was gripping the handle, he was itching to use it. "We don't have time for complicated schemes. There's only a few hours left before dawn breaks. If we don't smash the lich's orb before then, my sister will be worse than dead. You command the gnolls. Send them down, and let's go!"

"We can't just rush in," James said calmly. "The path down the canyon is narrow and heavily guarded. Superior numbers don't matter if you're all channeled into one tiny space. If we charge down blindly, our whole army will die before we reach the dungeon's entrance."

He tapped his claws against his staff, thinking the problem through. Without officers, there wasn't much he could do in terms of fancy formations. All of his orders would have to be the sort that fit in one shout, but that actually gave James an idea. He'd already seen people in massively multiplayer war games tackle this kind of problem. Why wouldn't it work with gnolls?

"Time to channel Roxxy," he muttered, giving himself a shake before stepping out into the street where the masses of armed gnolls were assembled.

"*Listen up!*"

All the hyena-people jumped and turned to face him.

"We don't have a lot of time, so we're going to keep this simple," James said, doing his best impression of his sister's raid-leader voice. "If you use an ax, sword, or spear, group up on Arbati. If you have a bow, you're following me. If you use magic, you're with Thunder Paw. If you have no weapon *or* magic, but you still want to fight, go grab something you can use as a shield. Benches, doors, actual shields, whatever. You have five minutes. *Go!*"

The square erupted into a frenzy of rushing gnolls. They ran all over the place, trading weapons with one another and ripping wooden doors from nearby houses. As the time ticked down in his head, James knew that most of the gnolls would not make it back in the allotted time, but that was part of the plan. By setting a hard limit, he ensured he was only getting the ones who obeyed orders the best and quickest.

When time ran out, James divided the gnolls who'd made the cut into squads by weapon. Then he split the ones who'd arrived with "shields" evenly amongst the three groups so that everyone had cover. When all the gnolls were where he wanted them, James raised his voice again.

"Everyone has to do two things!" he called, holding up two fingers. "First, stay by your group's leader at all times. Second, do not fight alone! If they catch you alone, you will die. Stay together, follow orders, and we can do this!"

The gnolls howled in response, lifting their weapons and makeshift shields. James raised his own staff in reply, pointing the way down the road toward the canyon rim.

■ ■

The Red Canyon was a narrow rent in the savanna. No more than a hundred feet across at its widest point, it formed a chasm that was at least a thousand feet deep, cutting into the ground like a stab wound. A comparison that was only made more grisly by the deep-red stone that formed its walls.

According to the game's lore, the canyon's unique color was the result of a primordial Bird that had died here at the beginning of the world. Its anger was supposed to still linger in the shadows, which was why the undead had chosen this place to set up shop. Peering over the edge into the heavy dark his torch could barely penetrate, James believed it. The deep cleft in the ground definitely looked like a place where dreadful things had happened.

Though built right beside it, the gnoll village stopped a dozen feet from the canyon's edge. Beyond that point, there was nothing—no fences, no railings, nothing to protect someone from toppling right over the sheer drop. Assuming the lich would be forted up in his laboratory, James marched everyone right to the canyon's lip where the switchback trail started. But the moment the first gnoll stuck his snout over the edge, a volley of white fire arrows screamed up from the darkness below.

The attack came like lightning. Gnolls fell screaming as the stench of burned flesh and blood filled the air. One unlucky warrior was shot in the leg and pitched right over the edge. James tried to grab him, but all he caught was a wisp of fur as the gnoll plunged into the dark, landing far below with a distant echoing *crunch.*

The gnoll army bayed their war cry in answer. They were about to surge forward when James realized he was going to have to give orders fast before this "army" dissolved back into a mob.

"Stay in your groups!" he bellowed, pointing with his staff. "Archers to the rim! Return fire! Arbati's group, you push down the path. Those with shields go first and give them cover, and don't run! Everyone needs to stay together! Thunder Paw, you and your group get wherever you need to be on the edge of the canyon to protect and heal the warriors below. Everyone *go, go, go!*"

At his command, James's archers ran back to the edge of the canyon. The shield group placed their benches and doors along the lip while the archers lined up behind the makeshift cover. Ghostfire arrows were still streaking up at them from below, striking the heavy wood. One punched straight through a thatch door to hit a gnoll hunter in the shoulder. The ghostfire on the arrow caught the moment it touched flesh, engulfing the hunter's entire arm. Then blue light blossomed as two of Thunder Paw's Naturalists jumped into action, dousing the hunter in magical water to put out the ghostfire before it could spread to the rest of the hunter's body. When it was over, the gnoll collapsed in a whimpering heap, burned but alive and untainted by ghostfire.

James grinned. "That's it!" he yelled excitedly. "Return fire!"

The gnolls howled and started pouring their own arrows down

into the canyon. Just looking at how many bolts were going down compared to those coming up, James could see that it was obvious they greatly outnumbered the undead positioned below. He just hoped that quantity would be enough to make up for the power difference. It was impossible to say for sure now that the interface was gone, but he was reasonably certain his gnoll military was level twenty-five to thirty on average, all one-skulls. The Red Canyon dungeon monsters were level thirty to thirty-five, and all two-skulls, which meant that each one was worth about ten gnolls in combat. If his earlier math was right, they should still have enough to win, but James couldn't help taking a peek, just to see.

Careful to not get shot himself, James leaned out over one of the upturned benches that served as a shield to watch a volley go down. Far below, deep in the shadows of the canyon, the nests of skeleton archers were visible only by their white ghostfire eyes. There were little sparks as the gnolls' arrows bounced off their bones, scraping off pieces and sending poofs of white dust into the air. It didn't look effective to him, but then a lucky arrow struck an archer's collarbone just right, and the whole thing shattered, taking the enemy's entire top half off. Its legs kept kicking, but the skeletal archer was out of commission, and James jumped back with a whoop.

"It's working!" he cried, running over to check on Arbati's group. "Keep firing!"

The warriors were already a third of the way down the switchback. Arbati led the charge in a lopsided formation, keeping the shield gnolls on the outside to protect the rest from shots from below. Just watching them run gave James vertigo. The canyon's tiny switchback would have been terrifying under normal conditions. On the warriors' left was a sheer rock wall. On their right, a thirty-foot drop down to the next part of the switch. To make things even worse, the steep path was already slick in places with blood where a few arrows had gotten through, but Arbati didn't let his group slow down. He kept them running as fast as they could without breaking formation, clearing the top of the switchback faster than James had thought possible to charge the archer nests at the canyon's halfway point.

Now that the enemy was right in front of them, the undead archers turned to start shooting at the advancing warriors. Several gnolls were immediately struck and sent flying off into the edge, but stone hands from the Naturalists above caught them before they could plummet the rest of the way to their deaths. They had cover fire as well. With no need to duck and cover anymore, the gnoll archers became much more effective. As they leaned over their makeshift barricades to rain arrows down on the undead, the skeletal archers began to falter. The undead didn't feel pain or fear, so it took far longer than it would have with mortal enemies, but eventually the onslaught of arrows and warriors hacked them to splinters, leaving their bones twitching on the ground.

At the very bottom of the canyon, the remaining skeletons emitted ghastly screeches and redoubled their attack, pelting the warriors—who were on the move again down the switchback to the canyon's base—with wave after wave of arrows. Fortunately, James and the Naturalists were up on the rim, watching them. More stone hands burst forth to provide safety and cover, while healing spells fell like rain on injured gnolls until they popped back up again. When a shield bearer stumbled, dropping his arrow-riddled door, James threw out a stone hand to fill the gap, leaving the undead's ghostfire arrows to crack and splinter on the elemental fist.

Soon, though, the warriors began to move out of range of the Naturalists' support.

As the healing spells and stone hands stopped, James yelled to Thunder Paw, "Move onto the switchback! We're right behind you!"

Thunder Paw's unit picked up their makeshift shields and started making their way down the narrow, blood-slicked cliff path. When they'd cleared the first switch, James led his unit onto the trail was well. Even with the unorthodox formation, everyone held together, and James smiled. He hated that it had happened, but the undead had drilled the gnolls into a truly fearsome, if irregular, military. They took orders well, stayed together, and fought without hesitation. The lich had made a terrifying weapon here in Red Canyon, and James was all too pleased to see it turned against him.

James had to prowl on all fours to keep his body below the gnoll-sized cover. He and his archer group were almost to the canyon's halfway point when he heard Arbati roar. Risking a peek over the edge, he saw that the warriors had reached the bottom and were now storming up the narrow trail to take on the last of the defenders' cliffside positions. Arbati himself was scaling his way to the higher ones using his claws, grabbing his enemies by their exposed ribs and hurling them down to the gnoll warriors below for dismemberment.

By the time Thunder Paw and James made it to the bottom, all the undead archers in the canyon had been reduced to twitching piles of bones. James was pleased with how well everything had gone until he noticed how many wounded and dead gnolls there were.

The bottom of the canyon was littered with small, furry, arrow-riddled bodies. Each of the skeleton archers had more dead gnolls scattered around their feet as well, some with fur still burning from the ghostfire. As he looked at the dead, the regret James had felt fighting the patrol on the road came back with a vengeance. He tried to remind himself that this was different, that these gnolls were volunteers fighting for their freedom, not indentured servants of the undead, but they weren't even inside the dungeon yet, and he'd already gotten so many killed. He was horribly aware that he didn't know what he was doing. Playing war games was good for tactics, but it was very different from actual war. Games had never made him think about how many orphans and widows he was creating, and he didn't even want to contemplate what would happen if they lost.

James shook his head to clear the doubt, then marched past the dead to join Thunder Paw at the dungeon's entrance, a horrifying hole in the canyon's red wall ringed with necromantic symbols and gnoll skulls. The old gnoll looked as tired and horrified as James felt, but the Naturalist's one good eye burned with determination, reminding James how much the old gnoll was fighting for. His grandson's life depended on their victory. So did Lilac's and through her, all of Windy Lake. The whole savanna needed them to win tonight. He'd just have to find a way to make it work.

"Archers, gather arrows," James ordered. "Arbati, Thunder Paw, let's talk about what's next."

The gnolls around him immediately scattered and started picking up any unbroken arrows they could find from the rocky canyon floor to fill their empty quivers. Arbati watched them irritably, brushing at the new burn patches on his fur as he turned to James.

"We don't have time for this," he growled. "The enemy is moving, and arrows are not useful in caves."

"Arrows are always useful," James replied quietly. "Right now, they're *especially* useful for keeping our troops occupied while we talk about how we're going to deal with the dungeon's five bosses."

"Who cares about them?" Arbati said. "We're just here for the lich."

"Who's at the very back," James reminded him. "This is—*was*—a dungeon. Before we can fight the main boss, we have to go through his underlings. There's one boss for each of the death-mixed elemental experiments the undead are running down here: fire, water, wind, and air. Each one has a strong AOE—"

"A-O-E?" Thunder Paw repeated, his auto-tuned collar mangling the strange English letters.

"Area of effect. Sorry," James said. "Massive damage over a large space that can inflict major casualties on troops. Arbati, that means you and I will probably have to do most of the fighting against them. I also doubt the bosses will be polite enough to wait patiently in their rooms anymore. Our best chance is to catch them by surprise. The moment we spot one, you and I will draw it off alone and kill it as fast as we can, okay?"

"We will make short work of these abominations," Arbati said with a fanged grin.

"Good," James said. "Then let's go."

"Warriors, on me!" Arbati shouted, lifting his sword high. "Shields up!"

"Archers!" James called. "Finish collecting arrows, then meet me in the cave. You have five minutes! Thunder Paw, your group follows the warriors! Keep up the heals on them!"

Arbati led his gnolls in first. They marched through the wide dungeon entrance in formation, forming a shield wall with their doors, pot lids, benches, and planks. Leaving his archers to pillage the battlefield for ammo, James picked up a bench of his own so he wouldn't have to crouch and ran after them, hopping over the empty space where the dungeon's swirling portal used to be. He didn't want to leave the archers leaderless, but he needed to be near the front when they ran into one—or more—of the dungeon's bosses.

Unlike the rest of FFO, the Red Canyon dungeon was exactly as he remembered. Just like in the game, the entry cave quickly widened into a stone bridge over a forest of needle-sharp stalagmites. But while the wide approach had been mostly for show back in the game, there was now a line of skeleton archers formed up behind a short wall at the other end of the bridge, blocking the double iron doors that were the only way in.

Ghostfire arrows started flying the moment they got in range, lighting up the cave with their haunting white light. The wide bridge offered no cover, and the air was filled with pained yelps and the stink of burning gnoll fur once again as the warriors charged the firing line. Baying in defiance, they hunkered down behind their makeshift shields and ran full tilt at the enemy. For a soaring second, James thought they were going to trample the skeletons under their feet, then he noticed that the front row of undead wasn't firing. He squinted at them as a flaming arrow screamed past his head, then he cursed.

The skeletons in the front weren't like the others they'd fought. Those had been nothing but bones with bows. These were covered in plate armor and shields they'd locked in front of them to form the wall the archers were firing over.

The gnolls' charge was quickly losing steam. The haphazard shields that had served them so well going down the canyon were nearly useless now that the much taller archers could just fire down at them, and with so much damage flying around, the healers simply couldn't keep up. One by one, the Naturalists stopped casting as they ran low on mana, and the hyena-like warriors in Arbati's pack started to fall, staggering under the arrow rain and not getting back up. If James didn't do something fast, they'd have nothing left by the time they got to the end of the bridge, but he didn't know what. He was starting to panic when he heard barking at the cave entrance, and he looked back to see his archers marching in.

"*All units down!*" he yelled as loudly as he could, dropping to his belly and throwing his bench-turned-shield over his head. Ahead of him, he saw Arbati and his gnolls doing the same. When they were all down, James lifted his head just enough to see the wall of warrior skeletons.

"Hold fire!" he yelled, balling his hands together around his staff as he started the Chain Lightning spell. He'd been trying to avoid using his own magic. Mana recovery wasn't going to be an option in this battle, and he needed to get to the lich with as much juice as possible. But there was no way his archers could shoot past that shield line, and the other Naturalists were out. That left him, so James wove the magic as fast as he dared, throwing the lightning low over his warrior's ducked heads and straight into the shields of the skeleton knights.

The spell went off with a blinding flash and an even louder *boom*.

Even James was surprised by the lightning's effectiveness. He hadn't realized how much stronger his magic was until it blew the skeletons' shields apart. Four warrior skeletons were scorched to ash inside their armor, collapsing into heaps as the flash of light faded. By the time the thunderclap echoed away, the undead shield line was broken, leaving the archers defenseless.

"*Now!*" James screamed, ducking his head beneath the heavy bench. "*Loose arrows!*"

The archer group let fly with a volley that shrieked inches over the warriors' heads. Feathered gnoll arrows peppered the enemy archers, breaking bones and shattering bows, leaving the undead pack at the end of the bridge in a jumbled mess. As they struggled to pull themselves back together, James leaped to his feet.

"*Charge!*"

Arbati and the gnoll warriors abandoned their shields to race across the last of the bridge and crash into the still-reeling undead. Ax-wielding gnolls swarmed the archers who were still up, severing joints and biting off vertebrae. The skeleton knights James hadn't fried swung their huge swords in response, but then Arbati charged in with his new sword, cutting through the undead monsters' armor and bones in a single blow.

After that, the warriors made short work of what was left of the defenders. While they hacked at the remaining animated bones, James turned to Thunder Paw. "Have everyone eat for mana then join us."

Thunder Paw nodded and started barking orders. The Naturalists sat down in relief, huddling behind their doors and benches as they shoved food into their muzzles. Satisfied, James picked up his own bench and waved for his archers to follow him down the bridge. They'd just about secured the entire thing when James saw the enormous doors at the end of the bridge creak to life.

"Arbati!" he shouted. "The doors!"

The doors to the main laboratory were each made of two-foot-thick slabs of metal. James had never seen them move, let alone close. He'd never thought of them as anything more than ambiance, art assets to make the dungeon more atmospheric. But apparently they were real enough, because they were closing in front of his eyes, being shoved into place by a squad of six enormous skeletal undead.

James swore. If those doors closed, that was the end. They'd never cut through that much steel between now and sunrise. But while he was still too far away to do anything, Arbati was already at the end of the bridge. The warrior leaped through the closing doors with a roar, landing sword first in the rib cage of the closest undead. He shattered its pelvis with a savage kick, then he leaped on the next one, knocking over the two-skull undead like bowling pins.

The disruption stopped the left-hand door in its tracks, buying James enough time to bolt through. He swung his Eclipsed Steel Staff hard as he went, breaking the femur of the knight on his left. The skeleton turned and swung back with a sword that was as big as James was. He blocked it on his staff just before it took his head off, more grateful than ever he'd decided to wear armor with some Strength and Agility on it.

While they fought fang and claw to keep the doors open, more monsters swarmed up from the caves below. The new undead dog-piled onto James and Arbati, forcing them to go on the defensive. But just as they were starting to be pushed back, the gnolls on the bridge surged inside to help. The wave of bloody, battle-crazed gnolls fell howling on the undead reinforcements, picking them apart bone by bone. Better still, unlike the bridge, the area on the other side of the doors was nice and wide. With nothing to constrain them, the gnolls' superior numbers quickly filled the room, overwhelming the lich's forces and pushing them back. As they solidified their position inside of the half-closed doors, the hordes of monsters coming up from the dungeon below suddenly stopped, turned, and began to run away.

"Ha!" Arbati shouted at their backs. "Victory!"

James wasn't so sure about that. This dungeon didn't have a back way out, and in his experience, undead didn't run. The lich must be pulling his forces back to a more favorable choke point deeper in. They didn't have much time left, though. James waved everyone forward to give chase.

The battle was sporadic as they moved through the dungeon. They were able to pick off the slow, plate-covered warriors, but the faster undead quickly left them behind. Soon, they were alone in the grim tunnels, walking nervously past skull-decorated doorways and rooms with iron grates and terrifying stains on the floor. In the prison area, James saw the bodies of several players swinging from cages, their surgical scars and fresh amputations testaments to how they'd died.

He sensed no life or ghostfire in them, though, so the army moved past without comment, marching in nervous silence until they reached the Jacob's-ladder-framed door that marked the beginning of the Laboratory of the Four Elements.

"What is this place?" Arbati asked, wrinkling his nose. "It smells even worse than the rest of this pit."

"It smells wrong," Thunder Paw agreed, looking down the four matching hallways, each lit with a different-color light.

"This is where the lich experimented with death-infused elements," James explained, pointing down the red-tinged hallway toward a room filled with brightly burning braziers that, in the game, at least, had been fueled by corpses. Going by the smell, James was pretty sure that was still the case.

"Ghostfire is powerful stuff, but it's difficult to work with if you want to make something more complicated than a zombie. Deathly fire is much easier to harvest. All you have to do is burn the dead. When the fire and death magics mix, necromancers can catch the tangled weaves and make whatever they want."

"I thought ghostfire *was* necromancy," Arbati growled, giving him a dirty look. "And how do you know so much about death magic, anyway?"

"It's all in the FFO Wiki," James explained. "There's also a whole paragraph about it in the mission text for this dungeon. This is stuff most players will know if they've bothered to read the quests, but what's really interesting, Arbati, is that you're right. Ghostfire and deathly fire are *both* necromancy. The difference is potency. According to the lore, the Once King stole fire from the Sun itself and took it deep underground. He and his followers made many sacrifices, merging the deaths of celestial elves with the holy Sun's fire to create the ghostfire. It's a direct perversion of the divine, which is why it's so damn powerful."

"If he had fire from the Sun already, why bother corrupting it?" Arbati said stubbornly. "You already have the power of a god. How can you hope to improve on that?"

"Not improve," James said. "*Steal.* You see, death doesn't spread. A corpse doesn't make you dead because you stand next to it. Life, on the other hand, is always expanding and growing." James swirled a bit of life magic around his hand to show how the green glow blossomed. "Even if you try to stop it, life will spread to every corner of the world, given enough time. Fire is the same, which is why ghostfire is so terrifying. It's death that *can* spread."

James waved at the four multicolored hallways. "The lich running this lab was trying to expand on that idea by corrupting other elements. Deathly water, deathly air, and so on. He's had some successes, and we're about to fight them, so watch out."

When the others nodded, James led them down the red-glowing corridor toward the first boss's room. James spotted more burning pits and harvesting cages filled with players and gnolls, but no undead. Not even a single ambush.

At last, they reached a giant circular room lit by dozens of braziers filled with burning corpses. Overhead, huge glass spheres hung on thin chains from the ceiling, and inside each one was a black flame the size of a bonfire.

"There's the deathly fire," James said, pointing at spheres. "But where's Rot Flame?"

"He's the first boss, right?" Arbati said, looking around. "And this is his room?" When James nodded, the warrior scowled. "If he did not rush out to meet us, where did he go?"

James had no idea. He'd assumed the giant fire gnoll would come out to fight them as soon as possible, but he hadn't caught so much as a whiff of his sulfurous, burning-fur stench, and that worried him.

"We need to pick up the pace," he said, jogging through the empty room. "The lich is preparing something, and I don't want to give him time to finish."

Keeping the army moving, they passed into the deathly-earth wing next. Here, the stone floors of the cave had been replaced with loose dirt, and every room was filled with fresh shallow graves, some still wet with blood. Again, though, the boss's room was empty. Or at least empty of the boss.

"Everyone stay single file, and don't touch *anything*," James ordered, keeping his hands pressed tight to his sides. The floor here was filled with tunnels packed with dormant zombies. In the normal dungeon, zombies would constantly pop out of the ground until the boss was dead. Now that things were real, though, James had no idea how deep the tunnels actually went or how many zombies were stored inside them, and he didn't want to find out.

"Walk very carefully," he said, making sure to step only on the dirt that looked firmly packed. "And stay to the middle."

The gnolls obeyed, creeping through the giant room on tiptoe. They were even quieter than James could have hoped, but that didn't stop him from sweating bullets as they crept past the lumps of the sleeping zombies James could now see buried just beneath the loose soil.

"Why aren't we fighting those?" Arbati whispered.

"Because we don't have to," James whispered back.

"Not that," Arbati said, frowning at the inactive zombies. "I meant why isn't the lich using them to attack us? We'd be outnumbered, and he would win."

That was a good question. "Maybe he fears his bosses more than us?" James said with a shrug. "The lich controls his own necromantic creations, but the Once King controls all the undead. Maybe the lich doesn't have clearance for these? I don't know. Just be glad we don't have to fight them."

The wing of deathly water was likewise devoid of undead, unless one counted undead fish. The lab of deathly air was even quieter, though James was very surprised the canisters of poisonous gas hadn't been ruptured. A room full of killer gas would have stopped them cold.

"This is so weird," he said, scowling as they marched through yet another empty boss room. "It's like the lich *wants* us to corner him."

"It definitely reeks of trap," Arbati agreed. "I don't like it."

"Neither do I," James said, but there was nothing to be done. Even with nothing in their way, it had taken a long time to walk through the dungeon. Time they didn't have. If they wanted to break that orb and save Lilac before dawn, they had no choice but to keep moving forward, so James waved his army on, filing out of the deathly-air wing and down the long stairway that led to the lich's private lab.

When they emerged into the last, long hallway that led to the orb room, James and company screeched to a halt. As the approach to the final boss, this hallway was bigger and grander than the others. It was almost as big as the natural cave they'd crossed using the bridge on the way in, and just like that bridge, the far end of this corridor was packed with another wall of armored undead hunkered down behind heavy shields.

"Damn," James muttered, looking over the skeletons' heads at the stairway behind them. That was the final ascent to the lich's chamber.

He could almost see the doors from here, but he didn't dare engage the skeletons this close to the lich himself. If the ancient necromancer joined the fight, he might start animating dead gnolls, quickly turning their numbers advantage against them.

"We don't have the time for this," Arbati said, gripping his sword. "We must charge and take down the enemy!"

"Just give me a second," James said, leaning over in an attempt to see into the lich's room, but his view was blocked by the short stair that acted as a mini-gatekeep, complete with portcullis. Thankfully, the latter was still drawn up as it always was, but after the lab doors, James wasn't taking any art asset for granted. He was wondering how the portcullis was controlled when the gnolls in the back started yipping in panic.

James whirled around and froze, heart in his throat. Standing at the top of the stairs behind them was the hulking, smoking figure of Rot Flame. The aura of black fire coming off his feet was hot enough to scorch the stone as he moved down the steps to make way for another monster behind him, the huge purple-and-green serpent boss who lurked in the corrupted water wing, Death Fang. Behind the snake were the corpse-amalgam boss of earth *and* the crackling white of the lightning-based air boss. And if that wasn't enough, behind *them* stood the countless skeleton knights and archers that made up the rest of the dungeon's patrols, standing in formation behind the bosses like clay soldiers waiting to fall down the steps on top of them.

"How did they get behind us?" Arbati cried, his voice tinged with panic.

"The teleport stone," James said, shaking. "They must have used the damn teleport stone! Every linear dungeon has a stone at the end that teleports players back to the beginning. The lich must have ordered them to use it! He let us come down here on purpose so that his troops could teleport back to the beginning and cut us off! He knows we can't rush him with all these gnolls. Now we're pincered!"

"So what do we do?" Arbati asked frantically.

James had no idea. The gnoll army was yipping in fear around them, pressing down the hallway that led to the lich's chamber. Pushing that way was death, James was certain, but they couldn't possibly fight *all* of the dungeon's monsters plus the first four bosses at once. Especially not here, where the hallway kept the gnolls packed together, allowing the bosses' AOE damage auras to hit all of them at once. If they were going to survive, they had to get to a better position, and on that count at least, James had an idea.

"Thunder Paw," he said, grabbing the gnoll. "Are you still following me?"

"Yes, James," Thunder Paw said gravely. "Me have not regretted following you yet. What are your orders?"

James pointed up the stairs behind them at the flat stone ceiling above the advancing bosses. "When I give the word, have your Naturalists cast lightning at the roof. Bring the whole thing down if you have to."

The old gnoll's one eye widened as he realized James's plan, and he nodded rapidly. "We will bring it down," he promised. "But what of the lich?"

"Arbati and I will handle him," James said. "You just focus on giving that undead army a bad day. Once the ceiling comes down, you'll still be trapped in this tunnel with the remaining undead, but you outnumber them by a lot. Use that advantage to stay alive, and I promise we'll come back to rescue you all once we've dealt with the lich."

Thunder Paw gave him a broken-fanged grin. "Do not worry about us, Chieftain. We will win."

James smiled back. "Then let's go."

The old gnoll barked commands, and all the Naturalists started winding up their lightning spells.

As the magic built, Arbati grabbed James by the arm. "How are we going to get to the lich alone?" he asked, jerking his head down the hallway at the wall of armored undead that barred the stair leading to the final boss room. "We are good, but that is too many even for us. If we fight them, we might get to the lich too broken to do any good."

"Don't worry about the skeleton doormen," James said, gripping his staff as the gnolls' lightning magic neared its peak. "I've got a plan. When the lightning goes off, we use the confusion to charge the undead line. Then when I say jump, I need you to jump like you want to hit the ceiling."

Arbati gave him a funny look, but James was already pulling a storm of air magic into his hands. When the spell was ready, he yelled at Thunder Paw.

"*Now!*"

The explosion of lightning bolts was earsplitting. Gnolls and undead alike were thrown to the ground as the raw fury of nature blasted the ceiling above the approaching bosses' heads. Instantly superheated by the electricity, the stone exploded, flinging shards of red-hot rock in all directions, then there was a deep rumble as the tunnel began to cave in.

Rot Flame was the first to go down, his smoldering body crushed beneath the avalanche of jagged stone. Bigger rocks followed after as the upper levels of the dungeon collapsed into the lower. It wasn't enough to crush all the undead, but the rockfall quickly created a wall separating the other bosses and their minions from the gnoll army in the hallway.

It was a damn beautiful thing, but James barely had time to watch any of it. He was already sprinting down the long hall with Arbati, using the explosion of dust kicked up by the cave-in for cover as they closed the distance to the undead shield wall. When they got close, the skeletons brandished their swords and readied their spiked shields to impale the two jubatus.

But then just before they got into stabbing range, James yelled, "*Jump!*"

They both launched upward as hard as they could. Before this moment, James hadn't tested the limits of his jubatus ability to jump. Going by some of the leaps he'd pulled off against Gore Fang, he was guessing it was pretty impressive, but the height he managed now surpassed even his wildest expectations. He and Arbati flew straight up, going so high, their heads brushed the hallway's vaulted ceiling. But even as they soared through the air, James knew that it wasn't going to be enough.

For all that they'd jumped an impressive ten feet straight into the air, they weren't going to clear the thirty or more feet they needed to leap over the mass of undead soldiers. So as the arc of their jump peaked, James released the storm of wind magic he'd built in his hands, unloading his Gust spell.

Gust was the Naturalist's big PVP ability. It did no damage, but the blast of air it created knocked opponents around like ping-pong balls, and sometimes off cliffs if you were good. But while James did blow over several undead, the skeletons weren't his target. He'd blasted the floor beneath them, using the spell's power to launch himself and

Arbati forward at hurricane-force speed over the heads and blades of the armored undead and onto the stone steps behind them.

As the stairs rushed forward to greet them at might-actually-break-neck speed, James began to worry he'd taken the whole "jubatus always land on their feet" thing a little too far this time. His fears were short-lived, however, as he and Arbati both twisted on instinct, landing hard on all fours at the bottom of the staircase that led to the lich's chamber. James was still boggling that he'd actually pulled it off when the wall of undead they'd just rocketed over turned on them.

"Arbati!" he cried, scrambling up the steps. "The chain! Cut the chain on the portcullis!"

Arbati jumped up at once and swung his massive two-hander like a bat to slice straight through the inch-thick chains that held up the protective portcullis James had noticed earlier. Severed from its counterweight, the heavy iron grate fell with a deafening crash, slamming down hard across the base of the stairwell.

The charging undead crashed into it a split second later. The armored skeletons hit the grate like hungry lions then grabbed the iron portcullis and started to lift it back up again through sheer brute strength. They managed to raise it almost a foot before Arbati grabbed the chain he'd just sliced through and wedged it into the portcullis's control mechanism, jamming the gears and locking the gate in place.

"Nice work," James said.

"How much time do we have left before sunrise?" Arbati asked, sheathing his sword as the undead started to hack at the iron portcullis.

James checked his new highly accurate, Intelligence-fueled internal clock. "Five minutes."

The warrior nodded and charged up the stairs toward the final room. James followed right on his heels, clutching his staff as they entered the lich's chamber.

CHAPTER *13*

Tina

If Tina had thought the raid couldn't be more miserable than they'd been during the forced march through the Deadlands, she was wrong. Sitting there, defeated, surrounded by hostile soldiers, waiting for the end to come—*that* was the most miserable.

She sat at the far edge of the group. The betrayed looks had finally stopped, but no one was talking to her, so she didn't know what anyone felt for real. Since she wasn't ready to ask yet, she and SilentBlayde passed the time by staring up at the still-dark morning sky, wondering what to do next.

"We could challenge Commander Garrond to a duel," SB suggested.

Tina shook her head. "Why would he take it? He's already got us in the corner. Even if he did accept, he's a four-skull, built for a ten-man party. Going one-on-one with him is suicide."

"How about blackmail? I could steal something juicy from his desk."

"Who would we report it to? Garrond's the big cheese out here." She rolled her eyes. "Besides, he's such a paragon, I doubt there's anything to use."

SB didn't give up. "A hostage, then. I bet I could bag his second-in-command."

"I bet you could," Tina said with a smile. "But it wouldn't do much good." She nodded at the Order priests casting protections on the massive formations of troops rallying in the yard. "So far, it looks like the NPC healers can do everything ours can, which probably includes the Raise Ally spell. Hard to be threatening if they can just kill us and raise the hostage when they're done." She slumped over with a sigh. "Face it, dude. We're out of options."

"We aren't dead yet," he said stubbornly.

"We might as well be," she said. "Even if I had a plan, no one's going to follow it. It's over."

SB looked down at his feet. "So what are we going to do?"

Tina nodded at the storehouse full of mundane weapons across the yard. "When Grel attacks and everyone goes out to fight, I say we make a play for the armory. The Order's crap is nowhere near as good as our stuff, but we can still rearm ourselves and make a run for it. I'll tank whatever Garrond sends to catch us while the rest of you go out the back door and flee into the Verdancy."

SB's mask hid his frown, but his perfect golden eyebrows were furrowed in a deep, worried crease. "That's not a plan, Roxxy. What about you?"

"I'll figure it out," she said stubbornly. "It's my fault we're in this mess. I don't mind taking a risk to get us out."

"Staying behind wouldn't be a risk. It'd be suicide," SilentBlayde argued. "There has to be something we haven't thought of yet. An angle we can use."

"He's got a huge Grel'Darm problem!" said a shrill female voice from nowhere.

Tina and SB both scrambled to their feet as ZeroDarkness and KuroKawaii stepped out of the shadows behind Tina's massive back. The elven Assassin and her jubatus companion both looked tired, but they were overall in much better shape than anyone else in the raid.

"Whoa! Hey, guys!" SilentBlayde said, hugging both Assassins. Other players perked up as well, raising their heads to see what the fuss was.

"Good to see you're both okay," Tina said, and she meant it. Despite Kuro's open hatred of her, she'd never stopped worrying. Seeing them both looking so good now made her smile. "So what was that about Grel'Darm?"

The catlike ZeroDarkness gave her a fanged grin. "Commander Dude knows he can't win a fight against Grel. He's surprisingly knowledgeable about the raid mechanics, and he's already figured out that Grel'Darm can't be taken down by the one-skull troops he's got here no matter how many he throws at him."

"How do you know that?" Tina asked.

"We might have been spying on him," KuroKawaii said, eyes glimmering with mischief. "He was just bitching about Grel'Darm's Chain Fire ability and how it had 'no known limit on targets.' If Grel uses that in this crowded base, one chain would be enough to kill every soldier here. Right now, his strat is to fight Grel alone out front and hope his siege crews and archers can kill the rest of the army before it kills him. It's a crap plan, though. He's totally screwed and knows it."

Tina looked at SilentBlayde, and they shared a nod. As happy as she was to hear this new information, though, there was one part she still didn't understand.

"Why are you telling us this?" Tina asked the Assassins. "No offense, but I thought you'd both had enough of me."

ZeroDarkness smiled at her. "Seeing you apologize was great! That's all I wante—*oof!*"

He cut off with a wheeze as KuroKawaii elbowed him.

While he recovered, Kuro picked up the story. "What he means is we're stuck here, too. The portal's gone, and like hell are we sneaking through that gross swamp." She made a face then shrugged at Tina. "You're the only show left in town, but don't think that means we're taking orders like the rest of your lackeys. I still don't trust you."

Tina sighed at the hostility in her voice. So much for making up. "I'm just happy you two are still alive. I'm not going to tell you what to do, but why don't you stick around a bit and see if you want to be in on our plan. Deal?"

The Assassins looked at each other. When Kuro nodded, ZeroDarkness did as well. Tina nodded back, and the two went off to catch up with the other raid members.

"What do you think?" SilentBlayde asked as they watched the exchange of hugs and fist bumps.

"Not much to think about," Tina replied. "Garrond and his army can't take Grel. We can. That's our leverage."

Even as she said it, though, Tina wasn't sure it was true. The return of the Assassins had perked people up, but the raid still looked broken. The Rangers had used the fake stick arrows from their quivers to make a small fire, and most of the casters were still sleeping, their faces pale and haggard. They certainly didn't look like an army that could take down a giant, and that was all her fault.

"I'm such an idiot," she muttered, dropping her head to her hands. "The others were right. I bet we *could* have taken Grel before, but we've got nothing left. No energy, no ammo, no trust. I used it all up. Even with this new information, we might still be screwed."

"We're not screwed," SB said sharply. "And you're not an idiot, Tina."

Tina's head shot up at the unexpected use of her real name to find him staring at her, his blue eyes deadly serious above his mask.

"We're on our last legs," he said quietly. "But we're not out yet. Have some faith in us."

"I do," she said. "I've actually got some new ideas for taking down Grel if he's alone, but I just don't see how we can fight like *this*." She waved her hand at the deflated raid sitting in the courtyard like prisoners of war. "I used everyone up. If I push again, we're gonna crumple."

"I disagree," SilentBlayde said. "Check this out."

He scooted a little closer to her, then he pulled off his helmet and mask in one smooth motion, sending his long, golden, salon-perfect hair tumbling down around his shoulders. The sunshine-colored mass fell perfectly around his face, framing his bright-blue eyes and handsome features so flawlessly it was uncanny, like watching a scene from a movie play out in real life. Even with Anders's warnings about her shifting physical attractions, Tina was floored. He just looked so... beautiful. Like an honest-to-god elven prince.

"Uh...umm...okay," Tina stammered, unsure where to put her eyes. "Did you just feel like having a shampoo-commercial moment, or is there a point I'm missing?"

"This *is* the point," SB said, flashing her a dazzling smile. "Look at us, Roxxy! I look amazing! Plus I'm strong, tough, and fast like a superhero. And *you*! You're incredible, a literal mountain of invincible, unstoppable power! Don't you think that's awesome?"

Tina's stone face couldn't show it, but mentally she was blushing lobster red. SilentBlayde was closer than ever now, his hair glimmering like golden sunlight despite the smoky light of the guttering torches. It would have been incredible if not for the fact that his nearness was making her feel like her old awkward self again. The pathetic, *weak* self she played FFO to escape.

"I-I guess it's pretty cool," she said at last, heart pounding. "But I'm still not following. What does this have to do with fighting?"

It might have been her imagination, but she would have sworn SB sighed in disappointment. If he had, though, it was over in a flash as he pointed over her shoulder. "Look at Frank and Killbox."

Glad for the distraction, Tina turned to see Frank and Killbox sitting on their packs with their armor off. They were face to face, taking turns flexing their ridiculous canned-ham muscles at each other and grinning like idiots. Then the two of them dropped to the ground and started doing one-armed push-ups, jeering at each other to see who could do more.

"They're wasting energy," Tina grumbled.

"They're having *fun*," SB replied. "Look at Neko."

Growing annoyed, Tina turned again to find NekoBaby sitting with the raid's other jubatus Naturalist. They were both making tiny gestures in the air that caused little flowers or grass blades to pop up between the flagstones, their tails twitching in unison as they intently explored their nature magic. A few seconds later, both the healers were distracted as Zen used a crystal from her pocket to run a spot of light on the ground between them. The catlike casters stared at it in absolute fascination for several seconds before Zen pocketed the crystal with a smug grin. They both glared at her, but then everyone started to laugh at the absurdity of it all.

"Do you see?" SilentBlayde asked.

"I'm sorry, dude, but I don't," Tina said, shaking her head as she turned back to him. "It looks like we're losing our marbles to me."

"I'm trying to show you that we're not all drowning in dangers and horrors," he said patiently. "Some of us actually like it here, Roxxy. Sure, it's been dangerous, but *some* of us think this whole trapped-in-the-game thing is really great despite the mud and the blood."

He lowered his voice, clearly not wanting others in the raid to hear him. "For example, I've been talking to Frank. He's eighty-six in real life. Back home, he lives trapped in a chair, hooked up to both oxygen and insulin while his family argues over who has to care for him. Now he's got a new young body that's stronger and better than his old one ever was. To him, that's a *miracle*, and I can't say he's wrong. My former 'real' life wasn't that great, either, but all that's changed now. Whatever happened gave us a new start, so I don't care how much I have to fight. I'm gonna live in this new world as the amazing, incredible SilentBlayde! Complete with that damn *Y* in my name."

SB reached out to place his gloved hand on her larger, gauntleted one. "I can't speak for everyone, but we're not all as beaten as we look," he said with a dazzling smile. "Yes, some people are mad at you, but mostly we're just hungry, tired, and hurt. But that doesn't mean we can't fight. We're *players!* We're here because we like a challenge, so if anyone can do this, we can. Just don't give up on us."

Tina stared at him in wonder. Whenever she looked at the raid, all she saw was defeat, but maybe that was her fault. She was sitting here wilted just like them. But SB was right. No one who got into raiding was the sort to give up easily. The Assassins' tip about Garrond had given them a fighting chance, but it was all for nothing unless someone stood up and grabbed it, and that someone had to be her.

She took a deep, satisfied breath. This was the reason she'd rolled a tank. Not because she liked taking damage, but because when tanks stepped up and said "we're doing this," the rest of the party followed. Her whole life, people had always told Tina she couldn't do it, with "it" being everything from earning money off a game video channel to getting into college to making a living as a library sciences major. No one ever thought that *Tina*—short, scrawny, awkward, game-obsessed Tina—could do anything, sometimes not even herself.

But Roxxy was different. From the moment her level-one stonekin Knight had said, "Let's go that way!" people had followed. She'd said it when she'd made her guild, and people had joined. She'd said it when they'd started raiding, and bosses had started dying. Seven FFO expansions later, her Roughnecks had followed her into the Dead Mountain, the dungeon everyone said no one could beat. But Roxxy had led them in, stomping stubbornly forward through wipe after wipe until they'd scored a world-first kill. That was *her* pride, *her* accomplishment, and it had only happened because she'd made it.

This was no different. No one else here was going to stand up and say, "Let's do this," but she could. So long as she was Roxxy, Tina could lead the charge anywhere.

"Thanks, SB," she said, rising to her feet. "Hold down the fort. I'm gonna go see if I can't get us a fighting chance."

"Always," he replied, hiding his bright smile behind his mask once again.

■ ■

Twenty minutes and several traumatized guards later, Tina scored an audience with Commander Garrond.

He looked up from his huge desk as she marched into his office, surrounded by a ten-squad of soldiers, many of whom were now sporting fresh black eyes. "If you intend to keep giving me trouble," he said darkly, "I'm going to tie you to the front door as extra armor."

"I needed to talk to you," Tina said with a shrug. "*Before* hell and high water arrived. People around here didn't get that, so I explained it in terms they understood."

She cracked her stone knuckles, and Commander Garrond sighed.

"I don't have time for player arrogance. If you have something to say, spit it out."

"Easy enough," Tina replied, leaning her weight on his desk until the wood creaked. "You have a giant-sized problem, and I'm the only one with the solution."

Garrond's hands clenched into fists. Then without warning, he shot to his feet and dismissed the guards. When the retreating men closed the door behind them, the commander walked out from behind his desk to stand face-to-face with her.

"Explain."

"Grel'Darm," she said. "You're a four-skull badass, but the rest of the Order are all level-eighty one-skulls. You can't change that no matter how much gear you give them, so now you've got a problem. You've got the armor and hit points to tank Grel by yourself, but once you get him down to half health, he's gonna cast Chain Fire. It'll hit you first, then the damage will jump to the nearest two targets. From there, it'll split to the next four, then eight, and so on. There's no limit to how many times Chain Fire can jump. Players can take the hit and get healed up after, but your scrubby little one-skull soldiers are gonna get insta-killed, then it's bye-bye Order of the Golden Sun."

"You underestimate us," the commander growled. "I know more than you think about the mechanics of your game. I was frozen in that courtyard for a very long time, learning English by listening to you players talk on 'spatial chat' about your raids and cats and tacos and 420 and so much other nonsense. I've seen your own Roughneck Raiders die, rise at my shrine, and run back to battle countless times, so you'll understand if I'm skeptical about your effectiveness."

Tina had to scramble to hide her surprise. She'd already accepted that the game world had been real to the NPCs, but she hadn't considered that Garrond would have known her guild personally. The implications of that were crazy, but she didn't have time to get into them. She was on a mission here, so Tina stowed her questions for later and got back to the point.

"You're the one underestimating Grel'Darm," she said. "You might have heard about raid bosses, but you've never tanked one before."

"You don't know anything about me," Garrond snapped.

"Don't I?" Tina snapped back. "You're not the only one who's had to stand around in this stupid fortress. I've wasted hours here, getting raids together to go into the Dead Mountain. I've seen players kite plenty of monsters into your fortress, and the guards always take them down before anything can get to you. You might have the stats for it, but I'd bet the rest of my gear that you've never tanked anything real in your life, let alone a boss as technical as Grel."

Garrond snorted. "And you can?"

"Can and have," Tina said proudly. "You saw my guild running back from wipes, but you've never seen us on all the nights we *won*. Grel is the first and weakest of the Dead Mountain bosses. I know his mechanics inside and out. You think Chain Fire is bad? That's just one of his abilities. There's also Howling Strike, which does double damage to anything it hits. You got any big defensive abilities to suck that up with, Mr. NPC? What about his Big Boot attack where he randomly kicks the tank? If you don't block it just right, he'll launch you into orbit. Oh, *and* he'll lose aggro if you get kicked more than fifty yards away. If you don't have a second tank ready to pick him up when that happens, guess who he'll attack? Your healers."

Tina shook her head. "Seriously, dude, this boss was made to be a challenge for veteran raiders with good gear. If you try to take him yourself, every one of your Order is going to die. Your only chance of survival is to have an elite force kill Grel somewhere his Chain Fire can't reach your men."

"And that would be you, I take it?" Garrond said flatly.

"Damn straight," Tina said. "He's death for you, but I've killed Grel more times than I can count. I could tank the big bastard in my sleep. He'll be a cakewalk for us."

"Then why were you running from him when you came to my gate?" Garrond asked, his eyes sharp. "If you're so good, why was your 'raid' fleeing for your lives?"

"Because Grel doesn't normally have an *army* with him," Tina said. "We're good, but even we can't fight Grel and every trash mob from Once King's mountain at the same time."

"Then it seems you are still useless," Garrond said with a sneer. "Because his army is still there."

Tina rolled her eyes. "You know, for a supposedly smart commander, you sure are acting stupid. I'm not saying we can handle everything by ourselves. I'm offering to fight Grel'Darm *with* you."

That was her big drop, but even as she said it, she saw his eyes flash with the same murderous hate she'd seen in all the soldiers since they'd arrived. "*Never,*" he snarled. "I will never permit a group of over-powered *children* fight on my battlefield! The Nightmare forced us to treat you like heroes, but I've seen who you really are! You're fools and drunks, braggarts and cowards. You play at being soldiers, but you give up and 'rage quit' at the first sign of *real* difficulty. I know what you are, player, and I will *never* trust the lives of my soldiers or the safety of this world to careless monsters like *you.*"

He turned away as he finished, signaling that the conversation was over, but Tina caught his arm.

"Maybe we were like that before," she said when he glared over his shoulder. "But things are different now. This isn't a game for us anymore, either. Grel'Darm isn't going to care who's a player and who's not when he busts in your door. This is a do-or-die situation for us, too. You can't ask for more commitment than that."

"To yourselves," he sneered. "But I've seen the way you treat us *NPCs.* You used to feed my soldiers to monsters for fun! The only reason you're willing to lift a finger for us now is because you can die, too."

"Exactly," Tina said, ignoring the hostility in his voice. "We're all in the same boat. But before you go slandering our character, you should know that I'm not offering to save you for free."

The commander did a double take at that, and Tina mentally crossed her fingers. She'd known from the moment the hate had flared in his eyes that he would never willingly work with players, but if she could get him to see them differently, maybe they could compromise. It was all she had left, in any case, so Tina gave him her best marble-toothed smile and went for the kill.

"We're an elite group of top fighters with the best gear in the world," she said cockily, clanging her fist on her runed breastplate. "Every soldier I have is armed with the literal stuff of legends. We've fought dragons, gods, demons, and worse, and we don't come cheap."

Garrond looked stunned. "Are you *insane?*" he cried, whirling around. "What game are you playing?"

"It's no game," Tina said, looking down at him. "Surely you've hired mercenaries before. Well, we're the Roughneck Raiders, and we're the best you'll ever get. I'm the guild master, the highest authority, so I'm offering to sell you our services. We've got to make a name for ourselves now that we're stuck in this world, and saving your fort from Grel is a great place to start."

Garrond stared at her a moment longer, then he shook his head in wonder. "You expect me to *pay* you to fight to save yourselves?"

"Yup," Tina said. "You've been accusing us of playing since we arrived, but doing a job for pay is the definition of *work*, and that's what we're ready to do for you."

When the commander looked at her this time, the hate in his eyes was mixed with something else. Tina wasn't sure what it was, but for the first time, she felt like they were getting somewhere.

"All right," he said slowly. "Just for the sake of argument, if I were to accept your ridiculous offer, dare I ask how much it would cost to hire your raid to kill Grel'Darm?"

"The return of all our weapons and a full resupply of food and ammo for my raid," she replied without missing a beat. "*Before* the fight. I also want a portal to Bastion for all of us after the deed is done."

That was clearly not what Garrond had been expecting. "Food and ammunition?" he said incredulously. "That's all you want? During the Nightmare, you demanded our best artifacts, relics, and gold! Now all you want is arrows and bread?" He gaped at her. "What kind of scam are you running?"

"It's not a scam," Tina said angrily. "You think we want your crap loot? We're Dead Mountain raiders! The Order's quest rewards were obsolete by the time we made it to the Once King's doorstep. And gold? I have millions of gold pieces in Bastion's central bank, and that's not even counting all the other priceless artifacts and resources I've hoarded over the years. All of my other players are the same. We don't need *money*. Supplies, on the other hand, are the most expensive things around in a war. I can't buy arrows out here for all the gold in the world, so I'm actually charging you a lot, but you're getting a lot in return. You can't kill Grel. We can. We're offering you the impossible, but you have to pay for it."

Tina was shaking with the effort of sustaining her sales pitch by the time she finished. Whether Garrond believed her or not, though, the haggling had clearly put him on more familiar ground. The guy was definitely more comfortable dealing with greedy mercenaries than demonic players, and so long as Tina could convince him that was what they were, she had a shot.

Fortunately, faking greed wasn't hard. She was sick of worrying over every spell and arrow. A resupply and the return of their weapons would lift the whole raid, not to mention make fighting Grel possible. Without their gear and food, they'd be just as dead as the rest of the Order. But as much as Tina wanted to yell at the still-silent commander to stop being such a prejudiced dick and let her save their asses, she forced herself to let him stew. The only way this plan worked was if Garrond talked himself into it. Thankfully for her, he really was screwed without them, and soon enough, the commander walked back to his desk with a sigh.

"You are very fortunate the Order is sworn to defend the higher good," he said, sinking heavily into his chair. "But before I agree to anything, let me be absolutely clear: I hate you. My men who were trapped in the Nightmare with me hate you, too. If it were up to us, all of you would already be dead. But we are servants of the Sun, sworn to protect the living, the innocent, and the just. No matter how badly I want to personally butcher each and every one of you for the hell you put our world through, my oaths will not allow it, because you are right. We cannot fight Grel'Darm as we are. You are the only weapon I have that can protect the lands and innocents that lie beyond this fortress, and so you leave me no choice."

He shoved his hand at her. "The Order of the Golden Sun offers you hire. As requested, we will return your weapons and provide you with food and ammunition such that you can fight. In return, your Roughneck Raiders will be responsible for singling out and defeating Grel'Darm the Colossal. I also expect you to participate in battling whatever additional forces remain once you've downed the giant."

Tina had to bite her lip to keep from cheering out loud. She'd done it. She'd *won*. After the last day and night, she'd almost forgotten what that felt like. But there was still one thing Garrond hadn't mentioned. "What about our portal?"

He shook his head. "We cannot reopen the portal to Bastion until the fortress is out of danger. The royal city *must* be protected at all costs. However, should you succeed in fully routing the Once King's army, opening a portal will no longer be a security vulnerability."

That was good enough for her. Before anything else could go wrong, Tina grabbed the commander's hand. He responded with the most hostile, bone-crushing handshake she'd ever received—despite being a stonekin—but Tina just gritted her teeth and bore it.

"Deal," she said firmly. Then her lips curled into a smile. "Now give me all that again in writing."

Garrond dropped her hand with a sneer. "I suppose I can't blame you for being distrustful," he said, plucking a sheet of paper from the stack on his desk. "Whom do I make the contract out to?"

Tina's smile turned into a full-on grin. "Roxxy," she said. "With two *X*s."

Garrond's eyebrows shot up, then he shook his head. "*Players,*" he huffed, his quill scratching over the paper as he wrote out their agreement.

■ ■

When Tina returned to the raid, hand still aching from Commander Garrond's menacing handshake, she was pulling two wagons piled high with crates, bags, and barrels. Everyone in the raid sat up at the sight, the sleeping members poked awake by their neighbors. They crowded in around her as she set down the ox-pull she'd been using as a handle. Tina grinned widely, kicking open the first chest to begin handing weapons back to their owners.

Shouts of joy rose as the players were reunited with their armaments. Some people actually cried, clutching their beloved weapons to their chests like lost children. As their leader, Tina reclaimed hers last, sliding her sword back into its sheath and putting her shield back on her arm with a relieved breath. The return of the familiar weight felt like reclaiming a lost limb, making her grin with glee as she grabbed one of the extra sacks from the rear of the wagon and tossed it into the crowd.

Killbox caught it one-handed, and everyone's attention fixed on him as he opened it, releasing the heavenly smell of fresh bread. Stomachs rumbled loudly, then the Berserker was mobbed as everyone rushed the food. Grinning like a maniac, Tina tossed the next sack, then another and another, flinging her hard-won loot into the eager hands of her players.

The raid tore open each bag the moment they landed, revealing quivers full of arrows, rashers of dried meat, and wheels of cheese. She cracked open the barrels next, revealing casks of fresh water and salted fish.

"What's all this?" NekoBaby asked as the people began looting the supplies.

"This is for us," Tina said proudly, lifting her voice. "Everyone, grab whatever you want! Fill your bellies, backpacks, and pockets. I'll talk after we've eaten."

Players were eyeing her suspiciously, but that didn't stop them from grabbing up all the food and munitions they could carry. Tina herself went straight for an entire bucket of water and gulped it down in one go, closing her eyes in bliss. It was just water, but after a day and a half of dry marching, the cold wetness washing the dust from her throat was the most glorious thing she'd ever put in her mouth.

The rest of the raid was having a similar reaction. The ichthyians were stripping down and dumping whole buckets of water over their heads. Anders actually climbed inside the barrel of salty brine left over from the preserved fish, dunking his green-scaled head over and over. The other ichthyians looked on, appalled, and Tina had to wonder if that was just their dislike of Anders, or if there were freshwater and saltwater variants among the fish-people.

At least she didn't have to worry about pickiness. She'd never touched a salted fish in her life, but the jubatus players leaped on them. NekoBaby piled her arms high with herrings and started tearing into them with her fangs. The elves and humans took much more normal portions of bread, jerky, and cheese, happily wolfing the food down in huge bites.

"Ha ha, go slow, guys!" SilentBlayde called, pulling down his mask to cram his own mouth full of bread. "We haven't eaten in a while. Don't make yourselves sick!"

Tina was finally hungry as well, but looking around, she wasn't sure what to eat. She picked up a fish, but it felt squishy and completely unappetizing. The bread was the same. Not bad but not something she wanted to eat. She was rummaging through crates to see what her options were when she bumped into the raid's other stonekin.

"Hey, GneissGuy," she said, pointing at the piles of unappetizing food. "You having the same problem I'm having?"

The gray-faced stonekin nodded. "Nothing here seems to be our kind of grub."

"What the hell do we eat?" Tina asked, annoyed. "It's not like I had a stone mom to teach me this stuff."

SilentBlayde came over with a concerned look. "What's wrong, Roxxy? Hey, Gneiss."

GneissGuy gave him a friendly wave, but Tina was getting annoyed. "We have no idea what we eat," she said angrily. "I don't think we do the squishy-people-food thing."

SB chuckled, earning him a baleful glare. "Sorry, sorry," he said, putting up his hands. "It's just funny. You're studying to be a librarian, but you've never read any of the lore for the game."

"I want to be a librarian because I like *good* books," Tina grumbled. "The FFO lore is ridiculous."

"What are you talking about?" SB said, aghast. "The lore is great! It's full of amazing knowledge, like what stonekin eat."

His eyes twinkled with amusement, and Tina rolled her eyes. "Cough it up, 'Blayde."

Still laughing, SB hopped up on the cart and started digging through crates. A few moments later, he came back with some heavy-looking sacks and a wicked smile. "Here you go," he said, handing a bag to each of them. "*Bon appétit!*" Then he darted away, safely out of her range, to go talk to Frank.

Tina and GneissGuy looked at their bags with trepidation. Finally, Tina untied the top of hers and peered inside, hoping against hope that it wasn't the bag of rocks it felt like.

"Crap," Tina said, pulling out a fist-sized stone laced with faintly glowing, obviously magical white lines. "It's just rocks all the way down with us, isn't it?"

"At least they smell nice," GneissGuy said.

They *did* smell inviting. Cool and earthy, like a stone dug out of a garden. She was giving the one in her hand an experimental sniff when GneissGuy popped an entire stone nugget into his mouth and began to crunch. Tina watched in horror as sparks flew off his huge marble teeth. Then he swallowed with the sound of gravel going down a mine chute, and his granite face split into a grin.

"It's good!" he said, digging into his bag for another. "Try it before it gets warm."

Tina didn't see how temperature was going to improve the *rock* in her hand, but GneissGuy had already shoved two more into his mouth as he walked away to sit down with the other Knights. The humans stopped stuffing their faces long enough to watch him crunch another magical stone into rubble between his teeth, then all the Knights had a good laugh before returning to their food.

Tina looked back down at her rock with a sigh. "When in Rome," she muttered, shoving it into her mouth.

The rock broke apart under her teeth like the hardest, crunchiest granola that had ever been. The glowing white veins were softer with a lively acidic, metallic taste. But as strange as it was to be grinding ore into sand in her mouth, the rock tasted pretty good. More importantly, it *felt* right, which was a first. Tina hadn't realized how hungry she'd been until she bit into the food her new body actually wanted.

Grabbing another rock from her bag, Tina sat down on her cart to eat and watch the raid. People seemed much happier now that they had food. Color was coming back to scales and skin. Everyone was still dusty and torn but much less beaten down.

After they ate, several of the casters got up and started healing minor injuries they hadn't had the resources to take care of earlier. There were cheers and thanks as bruises, cuts, and gashes were washed away by the euphoric golden-and-green light. When the whole raid was healed to full, the casters sat back down and stuffed themselves again to replenish their mana.

As the pig-out finally started to wind down, Tina decided that now was the time. She climbed up on a crate and clapped her hands to get everyone's attention, but the noise wasn't actually necessary. The moment she got up, everyone turned to look at her, their eyes worried.

"This should be good," KuroKawaii called before Tina could say a word. "Who'd you blow for the food, Roxxy?"

Tina shut the Assassin down with a murderous glare and turned her attention back to the raid as a whole. "Before anyone gets any stupid ideas, I want to start by saying again how sorry I am for how I've treated you. Even though I only met most of you a day ago, I've gained a ton of respect for every member of this raid during the march here.

I'm sorry I haven't shown it, and I promise to do better going forward."

Many of the raiders looked embarrassed by that, but the flushed faces were generally smiling, which Tina took as a good sign.

"We haven't talked about this yet," she went on. "But if you aren't in my guild yet, congratulations. You're a Roughneck if you want to be. You've all certainly earned your place among our ranks. That said, if you've seen enough and want to quit, now's the time. This includes the older members."

There were a lot of hurt looks at that, and Tina held up her hands. "I'm not trying to get rid of anyone," she said quickly. "Just hear me out. The Roughneck Raiders have always been a hardcore raiding guild, but that part of things is over. This is our reality now, and the old guild stuff isn't applicable anymore. Hell, ninety percent of the Roughnecks' roster isn't even here. Which is why, starting now, I'm forming a new guild."

She reached into her bag and pulled out the signed contract she'd had Garrond write up, then unfurled the scroll and held it up so they could all see. "When I started the Roughnecks, we all agreed that if we ever moved to a new game, we'd re-form the guild. This is *definitely* a new game, so I'm re-forming the Roughnecks here and now to be what we need it to be."

"What's that?" NekoBaby asked.

Tina grinned. "A mercenary guild."

The raid began to buzz. "Why mercenaries?" called someone from the back.

"Seemed like the right fit," Tina said with a shrug. "Some of you started as Roughnecks, but the vast majority of us are still strangers. There's definitely no bonds of blood or camaraderie. Hell, most of us don't even like each other."

"So?" yelled Killbox.

"*So*," Tina said, "when your brother hits you, that's a dysfunctional family. But when two mercs get in a fight, they're still shoulder to shoulder on the battlefield the next day. Mercenaries can be friends, enemies, lovers, even strangers, and it's all good so long as the fighting gets done right. I think that's the model that fits our group best right now, so that's what I've got."

She paused to let that sink in. Frank looked delighted by the idea. So did SilentBlayde. Even Zen was nodding, talking quietly with the

291

other Rangers. Not everyone was happy, but the general atmosphere was more positive than Tina had seen since this started, and she decided to go for the final blow.

"Going forward, I'm not asking you to like me," she said, raising her voice over the whispers. "We can spit and cuss and fight each other as much as the enemy if we need to. But if you decide to stay, I expect one thing from you, and that's to never forget that it's us against the world. When someone out there threatens one of us, they threaten *all* of us, which means we band together and shut them down. That's what it means to be a Roughneck now, so if you're in, I'm with you."

The players' corner of the yard was silent when she finished, then KuroKawaii stood up. "This is ridiculous," she said, sneering at Tina. "What's the point in making a new guild? We're all going our own way once we hit Bastion. Most of us are already in our own guilds, anyway. Why would we leave them for you?"

"Because they're not here," Tina said grimly, pointing at KatanaFatale, who was still stuffing his face with bread. "He's the only other player we've seen alive since this started, and he barely escaped with his life. I hate to be Captain Bring-Down, but if your old guild got caught in this, they're probably dead. The only reason we're still alive is because we've stuck together, and that's what I mean to keep doing. Again, if you want to leave, I'm not going to stop you, but why mess with what works? We've come this far by working as a team. If we just keep sticking together, there's nothing we can't do."

"You mean nothing we can't do for *you*,'" Kuro said, narrowing her eyes. "This isn't about what's best for us. You're just looking for a way to stay in charge."

Tina's fists clenched. After everything she'd done for this raid, that was a low blow. But as satisfying as it would be to punt the tiny Assassin over the walls and into Grel's approaching army, that wasn't how responsible guild leaders behaved. She did not, however, see any point in being nice.

"You think you've got something better?" she asked coldly, looking down on the much-shorter KuroKawaii from her full, towering height. "What are you going to do when you get to Bastion, huh? Go it alone? Find a way home? We don't even know how we got here or if there *is* a way back. We don't know shit about this new world, but it's pretty damn clear that if we want to survive long enough to find out, then we're going to have to fight for everything we need. Food, water, safety, knowledge—no one here is going to give us those things. We have no rights and no country, and everyone we've met so far hates our guts. Everything we have is in this courtyard right now. We have *each other*. We're all veterans who've played *way* too much FFO. Some of you are questing badasses, some are PvP nightmares, some are world-first raiders, and others are crack explorers and lore masters. I don't know how many other players got swept up in this, but I bet there's no other group that can match the geared, top-notch people we've got right now. Right here."

She pointed at the ground at their feet. "*That's* why I want us to stick together, because we're already the most any of us could want. As mercenaries, we'll be able to go anywhere, do anything, be whatever we have to be to find our way back home and earn what we need to survive while we do it. *That's* what I'm offering you, so before you listen to others spouting bullshit about what I want, listen to me, 'cause I'm straight-up telling you: I want *this*." She waved her arm across the gathered raid. "My only scheme here is to take what we already have and make it *better*. If that's not for you, then you're free to go. But if you see the same potential for awesome that I do, I'm happy to welcome you to the new Roughnecks."

The crowd began to buzz as she finished. Maybe Tina was being overly optimistic, but she thought it sounded like excited chatter. Then Zen raised her hand.

Tina winced internally. "Got a question about something I said, Zen?"

"No," the Ranger replied, standing up. "It was a good speech, Roxxy, but you never did answer Kuro's question."

Tina arched an eyebrow. "What'd I miss?"

Zen pointed at the crate Tina was still standing on. "Where'd you get the food?"

CHAPTER *14*

James

As befitted a final boss, the lich's chamber was an enormous vaulted cavern carved into the red stone of the canyon itself. The towering walls were engraved from floor to ceiling with sharp, unpleasant-looking runes that flickered with the pale blue-white glow of ghostfire. Most of the floor space was taken up by worktables and alchemical benches covered in scrawled papers and bubbling magical experiments, but there was a large clear spot in the middle for player parties to arrange themselves before starting the encounter.

At the far end of the room was the three-tiered dais where the lich traditionally waited while players got ready to kill him. He wasn't there now, of course, but everything else was, including a metal stand in the shape of a bony hand that was holding an inky-black orb the size of a beach ball.

James's breath caught. *"That's it!"* he hissed, grabbing Arbati's arm. "That's the control orb we have to break! All we have to do is get up there and—"

He was cut off by the sharp *tack* of a metal boot heel striking stone as the lich stepped out from behind a large rack of alchemical tanks at the rear of the dais. The undead Sorcerer was a towering figure in decaying silk robes, his elven beauty long lost to the rot of his unholy existence. He actually looked even more decrepit now than he had in the game, which struck James as a good sign. Not only did the lich look dead on his feet, but he was standing on the opposite end of the dais from the orb they needed to break.

"Welcome," the lich said grandly, spreading his arms wide. "My most annoying—"

James cut off the opening dialog by immediately casting Stone Grasp.

As he scrambled to shape the magic, he couldn't help but think it was a waste. Under different circumstances, he would have loved a chance to talk with an original inhabitant of the Unbounded Sky. Unfortunately, Lilac had no time for his curiosity. There were only a few minutes left before the sun rose and her corruption was complete. Arbati was already halfway across the room, racing toward the orb with his sword raised to slice it in half.

Letting the warrior draw the lich's attention, James finished gathering the flows of earth into a stone hand, but not beneath the lich. Despite the setup for a grand battle, they didn't actually have to beat the necromancer to win. Breaking the orb was the only thing that mattered, so James ignored the undead elf and conjured his Stone Grasp spell under the other side of the dais where the hand could rise up and crush the cursed ball to splinters.

He was placing the final line of earth magic when a razor-sharp line of mana shot into him, tangling his spell and scattering the magic he'd gathered. James jumped in confusion, head shooting up to see the lich smiling at him. The ancient sorcerer waggled his finger in a "no, no, no" gesture before turning to crook his hand at Arbati, who was lunging up the stairs at the orb. A ghostly light flashed, and Arbati went flying across the room, crashing through a row of alchemical tables beside the door.

The warrior was back on his feet in an instant. Moving faster than James had ever seen him go, he charged the orb again. This time, the lich walked forward to meet him, blocking Arbati's two-handed overhead swing with a lazy gesture of his black metal staff.

James's heart sank as he watched the lich parry Arbati's attack one-handed. The necromancer deflected the warrior's next attack with similar ease, keeping Arbati trapped on the stairs using nothing but his staff and his insanely fast reflexes.

Swearing under his breath, James started on another Stone Grasp spell, but he'd barely gathered enough magic to make a dirtball when the lich flicked another counterspell at him. Once again, the line of mana shot through him, slicing the building magic to ribbons and ruining his spell. Then for an encore, the ancient elf caught Arbati's blade in his skeletally thin hand and yanked, hauling the jubatus up by his own weapon before flinging him off the dais yet again.

The warrior landed in a snarling, yowling heap beside James, who was already working on his *third* attempt at a Stone Grasp spell. The lich broke his casting without even looking, flicking a finger at James over his shoulder while he turned to examine the orb for damage.

James hissed in frustration as his magic fell apart yet again. This was bullshit. All counterspell abilities, bosses' included, were supposed to have at least an eight-second reset time. That should have made this kind of total casting lockdown impossible, but apparently they weren't the only ones who'd been freed from the game's rules. The lich clearly had no problem disrupting James's magic whenever he liked, and he had no idea what to do about it. He was still fuming when the lich finished inspecting his orb and turned to face them again.

"What is this?" the ancient sorcerer said, his dry lips cracking as he laughed at them. "Such faces! Is the twisted child surprised?"

Arbati snarled and charged again in reply, but the lich wasn't even looking at him. His ghostfire eyes were locked on James, their flames dancing with cruel delight.

"Poor misplaced soul," he said, smacking Arbati back across the room without so much as a glance. "You think that because you can cast, you understand what it means to have magic? I was born before the sky knew limits—before our wings were burned. I was a *true* sorcerer, and now that your game is no longer forcing its clumsy idea of how mana works upon me, I am free to be one again. But not you." He shook his head in pity. "Poor miserable creature. You've been given so much power, but you're still too bound by the old assumptions to use it, which is why you will never win."

James clutched his staff. Never win, huh? He'd show this level thirty what it meant to have power. But as he pulled magic through his weapon in preparation to start grabbing up air magic for a lightning spell fast enough to beat the counter and big enough to turn the undead elf into a lich-roast, his vision began to go dark.

James paused, holding his magic tight on the off chance that he'd been hit with some sort of counterspell he'd never seen before. A heartbeat later, though, he knew that wasn't it at all. Whatever this darkness was, it was coming from inside his head, and with it came a voice.

Why fight?

He blinked in confusion.

Why fight? the voice asked again. *There's no point.*

Anger washed through him. Of course there was a point! Lives were riding on this. His life, Arbati's, Lilac's, the gnolls', all the jubatus of Windy Lake's—they would all die if he didn't win.

So what? the voice whispered as the Eclipsed Steel Staff grew cold in his hands. *Life is meaningless. An accident, a tragedy. To live is to suffer, to be bound by pain. Only the dead are free.*

There was something lovely and sad in those final words, a sense of yearning like nothing James had ever felt. Listening to them, James couldn't help but yearn, too. All this work, the constant dangers in his life here and all his troubles back home—what was the point? Even if he won this fight, all he'd get in return was more work. More trouble and pain.

Life is pain, the staff agreed. *You're doomed to die anyway. Why not save yourself all that suffering and end things now, while the choice is yours?*

It would be easier, James thought. If he rushed the lich now, the old elf would kill him, but not before he smashed his staff through the orb. He could die a hero, saving everyone, including himself, because if he was dead, he wouldn't have to worry about this world and its rules anymore. He wouldn't have to worry about going home, either. He'd finally be free of his debts, free of working like a dog every single day, free of Tina's scorn, free of his guilt.

You would be free, the staff agreed, its voice as sweet as sandalwood smoke as a blissful, numbing coldness began to spread through James's body. *That is the gift I give. I can make your death easy, painless, and heroic, and all you have to do is let me.*

James frowned, considering, but it was hard to think when everything was so dark and cold. He could barely make out Arbati anymore. The warrior had lost his sword and was now fighting the lich with his claws, screaming at James to wake up. That Lilac only had a few seconds left.

He blinked. That was right. *He* could choose death, but Lilac hadn't had that luxury. Her life had been taken, just like Thunder Paw's grandson's. Their deaths wouldn't be easy or heroic. They'd be terrible, the eternal pain of ghostfire and the devastation of those left behind. He thought of his parents, who'd be screwed by his mistakes if he never returned. Of Tina, who'd cry—

You really think she would cry over you?

His throat closed up.

You've been nothing but trouble to her, the staff whispered, angry now. *You ruined her future with your selfishness. You're a bother to her, not a brother. Everything would be better if you died.*

James slumped. Maybe it was the sleep deprivation kicking in, or maybe he'd just dealt with too much since he'd woken up in the yurt yesterday morning. Maybe it was Tina and the endless mess of his emotions surrounding what he'd done to her, but when James reached for the courage to live, there was nothing there. There was *nothing* for him to look forward to, not in this world or back home. If he died here, though, there was still a chance he could do some good. Arbati was getting nowhere, and with the lich locking down all his casting, James was useless as well. As useless as he'd *always* been. But this way, at last, he had a chance to do something right, so James dropped the magic he'd been gathering with a ragged cry and charged the dais instead, swinging his Eclipsed Steel Staff like a bat straight for the orb.

Good boy.

Rotten lips curled in amusement as James hurled himself up the dais stairs. With one hand, the ancient sorcerer tossed Arbati away before turning to parry James' charge, knocking his staff to the side. As James stumbled, the lich's other hand shot out and grabbed him around the throat.

It should have hurt. The lich's fingers—more bone than flesh—were cutting into his neck like garrote wires, but the staff's cold numbed everything. James relaxed into the nothingness, his body going slack as it welcomed its end.

See how wonderful death is? the staff whispered kindly.

"See how wonderful death is?" the lich said at the same time, much less kindly. Then the old elf froze, his ghostfire eyes growing wide. For several seconds, his rotting face was twisted in confusion, then he looked down at the staff James was still clutching in his hands and began to laugh.

"You fool," he said, dropping his own weapon so that he could rip the Eclipsed Steel from James's hands. "You precious, *precious* fool. This is a treasure of the Once King himself, and you brought it *here?*"

Cackling with delight, the lich twirled the Eclipsed Steel Staff joyfully with his left hand then pointed it at James's chest. "Thank you, player," he said mockingly. "You will make me a wonderful servant."

James wrenched his head up with a gasp. The beautiful numbing cold had vanished when the lich had taken his staff, leaving him clear-headed and furious. What the hell was he thinking? He couldn't die here! The orb wasn't smashed yet, which meant Lilac wasn't saved. Thunder Paw and the gnolls were still sealed in a cage match against the armored undead they'd left trapped at the door. Tina was out there, and he needed to find her. He had so much to do, so many people relying on him. How could he even consider giving up?

Red-hot shame burned the last of the cold from James's body. He grabbed the lich's hand and started ripping the rotting fingers from his throat, but it did no good. The staff was already pressed into his chest, its tip a blazing inferno as the old elf prepared to fill James with ghostfire. He was kicking his legs in a last-ditch effort to kick it away when he saw Arbati moving out of the corner of his eye.

As quiet as the cat he resembled, Arbati snatched up his dropped sword and prowled back up the side of the dais. Cackling over James, the lich hadn't spotted him yet, and James's hopes soared as Arbati reared back as if he was going to throw his sword at the orb. Hopes that immediately crashed when he realized his own body and the lich were between the warrior and his target.

Arbati hurled the blade anyway, flinging the sword straight at James. Watching it fly, James was certain that Arbati meant to kill him before he was turned undead, but the six feet of glowing-green enchanted steel didn't land in his side. Instead, it whirled through the air beside him to crush the elbow of the lich's outstretched arm.

The rotting sorcerer cried out in pain, dropping his staff and the ghostfire inferno surrounding it. He dropped James as well, leaving him to tumble down the stone steps.

James was still seeing stars when Arbati grabbed his shoulders and bellowed in his face.

"*Cast!*"

The head warrior hurled himself into the lich after that, leaving James reeling. Arbati fell on the ancient elf in a whirlwind of snapping teeth and flashing claws. The lich shouted again in surprise and pain, then his body erupted in a pillar of white-hot ghostfire. After that, it was Arbati's turn to scream as the two of them fell off the dais, struggling and pummeling each other in the heart of the blaze.

James didn't dare look to see where they landed. He didn't even push himself off the floor. Everything he had was focused on casting one more Stone Grasp spell, keeping the image of Lilac crystal clear in his mind as he wove the magic faster than he ever had before.

One second later, a massive hand of gray stone erupted from the platform, knocking over the metal stand and catching the necromantic orb in its palm. Making a fist, James commanded the granite hand to close, crushing the delicate orb in its stone grip. An explosion of death magic followed, shooting shards of black crystal in all directions. One of them left a nasty gash on James's shoulder, but he barely felt it. The rush of victory overwhelmed everything else, sending James straight up to his feet. But as he turned to shout the good news to Arbati, he saw his friend was down on the floor, his face pressed into the stone underneath the lich's tattered boot.

James froze, the shout dying on his lips. The warrior's eyes were closed in agony, and his body was covered in smoldering patches of ghostfire. When James tried to get closer, the lich gave him a ghastly grin and pressed his boot down harder, grinding Arbati's face into the floor.

"You've won nothing," the undead elf growled, reaching up to shove the jaw Arbati's punches had broken back into place. "My orb might be shattered, but your friend here is now the property of my king. You can't save him, and you can't beat me. You have nothing, player."

Rather than answer, James turned and grabbed the Eclipsed Steel Staff off the ground where the lich had dropped it. When he came up again, the ancient elf was sneering at him.

"Surely you don't think that's going to work," the lich said. "That staff is as much my king's as your cat here. You can't use it against—"

James flipped the staff in his hands and swung it as hard as he could, savoring the look of surprise on the lich's face as the black steel knob landed in the side of his skull. The blow knocked the sorcerer off Arbati and onto the floor. He was trying to push himself back up when James marched over to kick his decrepit hands out from under him.

"This isn't a game anymore, but that orb was still the source of your power," he said, flashing the lich an evil grin. "Now that it's gone, you're a one-skull, buddy."

"*Ahh!*" was all the ancient sorcerer got to say before James brought his staff down again. Without necromantic fortification, the lich's millennia-old bones shattered easily. A few more hits, and even his ghostfire snuffed out, vanishing into the dark as James crushed what was left of his mummified husk into powder.

Panting, James stepped back from the pile of dust and robes that was all that remained of the very old, very *dead* celestial elf. When he was certain the white fire was gone and the lich wasn't going to rise from his ashes, he dropped his magical-staff-turned-beat-stick and ran to Arbati.

The warrior looked bad. The fight with the lich had left him even more beaten up than his duel with James, but the real problem was the ghostfire that was rapidly consuming his body. Once it spread to the lifelines of his magic, there'd be no getting it out. He'd be bound to serve the Once King forever. James was scrambling to think of how to stop it when Arbati's eyes flickered open.

"You really will have to kill me now," he whispered through clenched fangs. "I will not serve the enemy."

"You aren't gone yet," James said angrily, standing up. "Hold tight. I'll be right back."

Leaving the warrior writhing on the floor, James ran across the dais to the tanks the lich had appeared from when they'd first entered. Behind them was a large desk covered in what was clearly the lich's personal papers. Everything was written in ancient elvish, but otherwise, it looked like any other cluttered desk James had ever seen. Fortunately, he'd killed and looted this lich a hundred times back in the game, and he knew exactly where all the good stuff was. Sure enough, when he opened the bottom-right desk drawer, there was a stone box inside, its lid sealed by an enchanted golden lock.

Cradling the box carefully, James ran back to the sad heap of crushed bones and grabbed the lich's robe, riffling through the pockets to find the golden key that matched the box's lock. The whole process couldn't have taken more than forty-five seconds, but by the time he fitted the key in and got the box open, the ghostfire had completely covered Arbati's body, making the head warrior convulse and scream as the blue-white flames began to eat into the magic that gave him life.

As fast as he could, James grabbed one of the four pan-elixirs inside the lich's box and dropped to his knees beside Arbati. When he grabbed the warrior, the ghostfire jumped to him, scorching his flesh with fire that was burning hot and searing cold at the same time. Far worse than the pain, though, was the rage. There was anger in the ghostfire that was very different from the numbing, almost sorrowful cold of the Eclipsed Steel Staff. That difference felt significant, but James didn't have time to explore it. He was too busy cramming the pan-elixir into Arbati's mouth, tilting the warrior's head up so he wouldn't choke on the rainbow-colored liquid inside.

The warrior sputtered as the elixir splashed into his mouth. The cure-all shone with prismatic light as it ran down his throat, then all the white fire on the warrior's body snuffed out in an instant, leaving him whole and gasping on the floor.

The shock lasted only for a heartbeat before Arbati's hand shot up and grabbed James by the collar.

"*What happened to you back there?*" he roared. "Why did you throw yourself at the lich like that?"

Choking, James slapped his hands against Arbati's until the warrior let go. "It's the new staff," he gasped when Arbati let him breathe again. "I think it's made from some kind of cursed metal that has a connection to the Once King."

"Then you should stop using it," Arbati said at once, glaring at James's dropped staff with a hiss. "That thing almost got us killed!"

James dropped his eyes. "It wasn't all the staff," he said quietly, rubbing the back of his neck. "It spoke to me, yeah, but it didn't take me over or force me to act. It just…got into my head. I'm the one who actually screwed up." He bent lower. "I'm sorry, Arbati. Deep down, I guess I really am just a coward who causes trouble for—*ow!*"

James jumped back, rubbing the back of his head where Arbati had cuffed him. "*What was that for?*"

"For telling lies," the warrior said, lifting his chin. "I've fought at your side for a night and day, and I have seen no sign of cowardice. Quite the opposite. You've stood with bravery many times when a smarter man would have run." He shook his head. "You have many, many flaws, James Anderson, but being a coward is not one."

James gaped at him, touched. "Thank you."

"You should be apologizing for telling such a blatant lie to my face," the warrior said, fur bristling. "But that cursed weapon of yours is clearly a tool of our enemy. You must swear on your honor to get rid of it at the first opportunity."

Just the memory of the cool, smooth voice whispering through his thoughts was enough to make James shudder. "I'm sorry," he said, nodding rapidly. "The first opportunity I get, it's gone." The moment he figured out how to unbind it from his magic, he was pitching the hunk of black metal into a volcano.

"Good," Arbati said, then for the first time, he smiled. Not a cruel grin or a bloodthirsty smirk, but an actual, joyous smile. James was still staring at it in shock when the muscular jubatus clapped him on the shoulder hard enough to make him stagger. "We won!"

An even bigger smile spread over James's face. "You're right," he said, looking at the black glass shards that were all that remained of the orb. "We did it. We *won!*"

Maybe it was relief, or maybe they'd both had too much tonight, but that statement sent both James and Arbati collapsing into a heap. They lay on the dusty stone, laughing until their sides ached and their faces were wet with tears from the pure joy of having survived. They were still on the floor when a peal of thunder rumbled through the ground beneath them.

"The gnolls!" James said, sitting up in a rush. "They're still fighting!"

He and Arbati shot to their feet and ran for the door. When they reached the stairway where they'd dropped the portcullis, James heard the clash of steel and the twang of bowstrings. Rushing down the stairs, James almost slammed into the iron grid of the lowered portcullis. This turned out to be a good thing because beyond the dark grid was a raging battle.

The long hallway was a graveyard of shattered skeletons and dented armor, but the remains of the undead were far outnumbered by the bodies of injured and dead gnolls. At the opposite end of the long hallway, back by the stairs where they'd collapsed the ceiling to cut off the rest of the bosses, a desperate knot of hyena Naturalists were standing with their backs to the shattered stone, facing off against a huge pack of armored undead.

"We have to get in there!" Arbati said, throwing his shoulder against the portcullis. James grabbed the bars and heaved as well, but the gate wouldn't budge thanks to the gear mechanism they'd jammed earlier. Arbati was trying to cut the entire thing in half with his sword when James smacked himself on the forehead.

"I'm being so dumb," he said, face heating. "Watch this."

During the whole battle through the dungeon, he'd avoided using magic as much as possible to save himself for the lich at the end. But that fight hadn't used nearly as much mana as he'd anticipated thanks

303

to the constant counterspells, which had only dispersed his magic, not wasted it. This meant he was still close to full, and since now was the time to use it or lose it, James decided to use it all.

Careful not to pull too deeply off his cursed staff, James lifted his hands in a dramatic arc and began casting his favorite spell in the entire game. It was so large that the casting motion was practically a dance. Flowing back and forth, he hooked huge streamers of life, water, and air magic in his arms, filling the hallway with vibrant golden light as bright-green vines grew from the cracks in the stone to form a magical circle around him. Golden flowers burst from the stone floor, and glowing leaves floated down from the ceiling, making Arbati jump in alarm. Grinning, James continued to build the power, spending his mana indiscriminately to pull in the thick ropes of energy until he felt high on magic.

When the euphoria was at its peak and his head was swimming with the intense feeling of being more alive than he'd ever been before, James let the spell go. The rush of magic that followed was so heady and glorious, he couldn't help but yell out the spell's name.

"*Verdant Glory!*"

Hundreds of bright-green roots shot out from the circle at his feet, snaking through the portcullis to carpet the walls and floor of the hallway the gnolls were fighting in. Glorious, emerald light banished the dark as James, Arbati, and every gnoll within line-of-sight were suffused with healing magics. Poisons and wounds were washed away in an instant. Severed limbs picked themselves up and moved to merge with their owners. Armor and weapons were not repaired, but all the injured gnolls on the ground suddenly shot to their feet, barking with joy as the wave of resplendent life washed over them.

In an instant, the remaining undead went from winning to being grossly outnumbered. Howling with renewed fury, the gnolls swarmed over them, hacking the skeletal knights to pieces. When the last one went down, yips and bays of victory filled the tunnel, echoing off the stones as the magical greenery finally vanished.

Mana spent, James sank to his knees. He was so tired but so happy in this moment. Twisting around, he gave Arbati a thumbs-up, but the head warrior was staring slack-jawed, looking at James as though he'd never seen him before.

"*What was that?*" he cried at last.

"Verdant Glory," James said, brushing the last of the glowing flower petals from his clothing as he stood up. "It's my big raid heal and cleanse. Really fun to use, I gotta say. Too bad it takes my entire mana pool to cast."

Arbati's eyes didn't get any smaller. "I've never seen a player do that before."

"Well, to be fair, I don't know why you would have," James said. "Players low enough to need the Windy Lake quests don't have spells this big yet, and geared level eighties can one-shot anything in the zone just by swinging their weapons around. No one PVPs here, either, so I can't think of a time when you would have had an opportunity to see a max-level player go all out before now."

He finished with a shrug, but Arbati looked more upset than ever.

"Are the Four Clans really that weak?"

The question had a very un-Arbati-like tremble to it, and James suddenly felt sorry for all the non-player characters who were now having to deal with the consequences of FFO rewriting their world. "The clans are mostly level twenty and below," he answered honestly. "Only you and Gray Fang are higher."

Arbati kicked the portcullis in anger. "Even the gnolls are stronger than us now!" he snarled. "How could this have happened? We stood proud before your game ruined everything!"

Despite the cursing of "his game," James didn't take offense. It sucked to suddenly have your entire existence shoved onto a number scale then discover that you were at the bottom. But just because the jubatus clans had gotten the short end of the level stick didn't mean they were defenseless.

"I can help," James said, offering his hand to Arbati. "I don't know if it's possible to level up anymore, but my home country was really warlike. We've invested a lot of our intelligence and creativity into finding new ways to fight each other. We even make games about tactics and strategy so that we can wage bloodless wars against each other for fun. I've played a lot of them, which means I know battle tactics that I'm pretty sure no one in this world has experienced yet. If I teach this knowledge to the Four Clans, you'll have tricks no one else here knows. Even if you are lower level, that's a hell of an edge."

This promise earned him an eager grin from the head warrior. "I'm glad you're applying to join the clans!" Arbati said, clapping him on the shoulder. "You will tell us all your secrets, and when we get back, you will teach me how to fight like you do!"

The thought of having to spar for real with the much-stronger warrior made James wince. Fortunately for him, he hid it quickly. "I'd love to. First, though, we have to get out of here."

■ ■

James and Arbati were back by the winch, pondering how to open the wrecked portcullis, when ten large stone hands rose from the earth to smash the metal gate straight into the ceiling. Moments later, a wave of gnolls began rushing up the stairs. James and Arbati had to step back into the lich's chamber to make room as the shoulder-high army, led by Thunder Paw, flooded inside.

When they saw the shattered body of the lich and the smashed orb, they began to howl with joy. The gnolls tossed down their weapons and their hacked-up, arrow-riddled doors then grabbed each other in huge hugs, laughing and braying in their new freedom. There was one sour face among the jubilant crowd, and James held his breath as Thunder Paw approached with the utmost of seriousness.

"Chieftain James."

"Yes, Thunder Paw?"

The old gnoll tilted his head back, peering into James's face with his one eye. "Have Me followed you well?"

James nodded. "You've followed me incredibly well."

Thunder Paw nodded back. "It your turn to follow Me then."

James gulped. He'd known this was coming. He just hoped it wouldn't hurt too much. He didn't have the mana for another heal.

"What are you two talking about?" Arbati asked suspiciously.

"Just back up, please, Arbati," James said. "This is between Thunder Paw and me."

When the cat-warrior stepped back, James picked up his staff from where he'd set it down and clutched it in his hands. The celebration around them cut off as he straightened up and turned to face the snaggletoothed Naturalist with a determined glare.

"Chief James Anderson!" Thunder Paw cried, his hideous collar pulsing as it translated the barks. "Crisis is over, so Me will not tolerate a jubatus ruling us anymore! Me, Thunder Paw, Speaker of Storms, challenge you for the right to lead Grand Pack!" The hunched, one-eyed gnoll twirled his new staff with a flourish, and the gnolls quickly scampered back, clearing an empty circle around them to make room for the fight.

"I will never let you have it!" James announced, slamming his own staff into the stone floor with an echoing *tak*. "Come at me, then, if you wish to die!"

It was really hard not to cringe at that last line. He sounded like a bad action-movie villain, but the gnolls were eating it up. The whole room was barking and howling as a tough-looking warrior gnoll pulled a bandage off his arm and walked into the empty space between James and Thunder Paw. After a look at each of them, the gnoll threw the cloth high into the air and dove for the sidelines, wiggling back into the crowd.

The moment the bloodstained cloth fluttered to the ground, James yelled and charged, holding his staff like a club. He ran slowly and dramatically, giving Thunder Paw time to wind up a suitably impressive-looking—but not actually painful—spell. The old Naturalist didn't seem to be on the same page, though. He gathered up a massive staff full of lightning and let fly, hitting James with a flash that left him blinded.

The blast threw James back ten feet. His muscles were locked from all the electricity, so he didn't even land on his feet, crashing hard into the line of gnolls behind him. The impact knocked the breath right out of him. By the time he got it back, Thunder Paw was on top of him with a dagger pressed into his throat. For a second, James felt real panic, then he remembered his role.

"I yield! I yield!" he cried, raising his legitimately shaking hands.

The old gnoll nodded and hopped off him. James rolled back to his feet with a wobble then dropped down again to kneel before Thunder Paw. "All hail Thunder Paw, Chief of Chiefs!"

There were several moments of silence, and James began to sweat, terrified that the others weren't going to accept this farce of a fight they'd just put on. But then the gnoll army burst into cheering and partying again, hoisting Thunder Paw onto their hunched backs as they marched around the room.

He let them carry him around for a few moments, then the new Chief of Chiefs got everyone's attention with another crack of lightning.

Ears ringing, James just watched as Thunder Paw stuck his fingers into his collar to separate it from his throat. The moment the black metal was no longer touching his skin, the device stopped translating, leaving Thunder Paw free to give what James could only assume was a stirring speech in the gnolls' language without letting the jubatus listen in. When he finished, the gnolls let out a roar that shook the canyon, and the army burst back into motion, picking up their weapons and getting into groups as they marched toward the tall blue teleportation crystal in the far back corner of the lich's chamber.

As the gnolls were teleporting to the front of the dungeon, Thunder Paw resettled his collar and came over to James and Arbati. "We must go defeat the undead who were cut off by the cave-in earlier. You with us?"

James shook his head. "You don't need me. Now that the orb is broken, all the monsters from this lab are one-skulls, including the bosses. You guys should have no problem taking them down."

Thunder Paw nodded. "What will you do, then?"

James pointed back toward the stairs. "With the hallway to this place caved in, the teleportation crystal is a one-way trip. It'll be a long time, if ever, before someone comes to this room again, so I need to investigate a few things before I leave. But wait!" He ran over to the dais steps and grabbed the lich's lock-box with the three remaining pan-elixirs inside. "Here," he said, handing the box to Thunder Paw. "These are yours, as promised. Go cure your grandson."

Thunder Paw almost dropped the box as his old paws started shaking. When James reached out to help, the old gnoll pulled him into a hug.

"Thank you, James."

The translation collar issued the words flatly, as always, but the wetness in Thunder Paw's one eye said it all.

"My pleasure," James replied, patting the Naturalist on the back. "My pleasure."

CHAPTER *15*

Tina

"Where'd you get the food?"

Tina blew out a long breath, choosing her next words very carefully. "These supplies are payment," she said, holding up the scroll she'd signed with Commander Garrond for everyone to see. "As guild master of the new Roughneck Mercenaries, I've taken a job to kill Grel'Darm for the Order."

Zen didn't look surprised by that at all, but everyone else erupted.

"We can't!"

"We're killing Grel for food? That's bullshit!"

"Did she have a sign? 'Will raid for food?'"

"We're going to die!"

"We're not going to die, and we're not killing him for cheap!" Tina said fiercely, raising her voice over the din. "The Order can't kill Grel. We can. I used that as leverage to get our stuff back, plus food, ammo, and a portal to Bastion once this is over. That's everything we came here to get in the first place."

"Except it's suicide," ZeroDarkness called out. "You death-marched us here running *away* from Grel'Darm! You think getting a few loaves of bread makes it okay to draft us all into a new guild that you've already signed up for an unwinnable fight?"

There was lots of angry muttering at that, and Tina banged her gauntlets together for silence.

"Chill out!" she boomed. "I haven't drafted anyone for anything! The commander hired the *guild*, not you personally. I'm not going to make anyone fight if they don't want to. As I already said *multiple times*, anyone who wants to go is free to leave."

"But we already got paid!" NekoBaby said. "What are we supposed to do if we want to bail? Cough the fish back up?"

"The food is free," Tina said with a wry smile. "Think of it as part of my apology. The same goes for your weapons. But the rest of the contract stands, and I'll fight Grel'Darm alone if I have to in order to honor it. The Roughnecks can be a guild of one if that's what it takes. Once I engage the enemy, the rest of you can take what's left in this cart and run for the Verdancy while the Order deals with the undead."

"Hold up," Neko said, cat eyes wide. "So you're saying you'll go out there and die *alone* if no one joins your guild? Like, for serious?"

"For serious," Tina said firmly. "You didn't have a choice when this started. Out there, it was stick together or die. But despite what some people have said, I'm not a dictator, and I'm done kicking people down roads. If you want to go, then go, but for what it's worth, I still think everyone's chances are much better if we stay here and work together. This world is full of unknowns, but I've beaten Grel'Darm lots of times. All we have to do is beat his ass once more, and we'll go from hated outcasts to...well, probably not heroes, but at least we'll get some respect. I'll take that over slogging through a swamp any day, but that's my choice. I'm not forcing anyone to make it with me."

"Roxxy..." SilentBlayde whispered, his eyes terrified above his mask, but Tina held up her hand.

"Anyone who wants to stay and fight as one of the new Roughnecks can sign up now," she said, placing Garrond's contract, plus the quill and ink she'd nabbed from the quartermaster, down on the wagon beside her. "You'll get a share of any earnings or spoils just as you would in a raiding guild. Before you decide, though, let me say one more thing."

The raid looked at her curiously, and Tina flashed them a cocky grin.

"This isn't going to be like it was on the hill. I have a plan to kill Grel'Darm. Long story short, we're gonna cheat, cause this isn't a game anymore, and I don't mean to play by the rules. So if you want some payback for last night, sign up and help me take the bastard down. If not, good group and happy trails. See ya around."

With that, Tina hopped off the cart and walked away. The urge to keep talking until they were all convinced was overwhelming, but she kept her mouth stubbornly shut. She was done forcing people to pull their weight. From here out, if someone was fighting at her side, it was going to be because *they* wanted to. She'd given them the information. Now it was up to them to decide, so Tina forced herself to sit down and wait, stopping her mouth with another magical rock as she watched the others deliberate.

They were still talking when SilentBlayde came over.

"Damn it, Tina," he whispered, thumping down on the crate beside her. "Why'd you have to do it this way?"

"It was the only way to make new options," she replied with a shrug. "I'm not going to let everyone die when I can do something to stop it."

"But why *this?*" he hissed, clenching his gloved hands. "Why did you have to pick the *one path* that puts you in front of that monster?"

"I'm a tank," she said, doing her best to sound confident. "Being in front of the monster is what I do. And for the record, I think we can beat him."

"Not if everyone abandons you!"

"It won't be that bad," she said flippantly. "Even if half the raid turns me down, we've still got a whole fortress full of possibilities. I'll figure it out."

"You're betting your life on an unknown," he snapped, glaring at her over his mask. "You can't beat Grel without a raid, and you just gave everyone a free pass to turn their backs on you!"

His vehemence made Tina jerk.

"Dude, I had to," she said, taken aback. "We were cornered, and this was the only way to get the raid out alive. But I had to give people a choice, or I really would be what Kuro says."

SB turned away, and Tina's copper brows pulled into a scowl.

"What is with you?" she asked. "Why are you so mad at me?"

"I'm not mad at you," he snapped. "I love—" He stopped, leaving the breath frozen in Tina's throat. "I love how brave you are," he finished a second later. "You're fearless and heroic and everything a leader should be, and I'm mad because someone like you shouldn't have to die saving a bunch of cowardly ingrates."

He shot a venomous look at KuroKawaii, and Tina exhaled with a smile.

"Thank you," she said softly, putting a hand on his shoulder. "But I'm not planning to die, you know. It's just Grel. We kill him every week."

"Sure, back when we were a proper raiding guild," SB said tensely. "Back when we had fifty people who knew what they were doing and could follow instructions. But I don't know how we're going to survive this if the whole group doesn't come, and I'm not enough to save you from Grel'Darm by myself!"

His voice was shaking by the time he finished, so Tina turned and leaned over, bending down until her forehead was resting on the top of his helmet.

"Thank you for always having my back," she whispered. "We wouldn't be standing here right now if not for all the times you filled in for my failures, but I need you to trust me. We can do this. I promise."

He looked up at her, his blue eyes full of so many tangled emotions, Tina couldn't pick them apart. She'd never actually seen his eyes this close before. Sitting as they were, side by side on the boxes with her head resting on his, there was only an inch of air between their faces, closer than they'd ever been.

Tina's heart started to pound. SB must have noticed their position at the same time, because whatever he'd been about to say slipped off his tongue as their physical proximity took over the conversation. Breath quickening, Tina couldn't help but wonder what it would be like to get even closer. Her eyes dropped to his ever-present mask. All she'd need to do was pull it down, and there'd be nothing left between them.

It was something she never would have considered back when this was still a game. Now, though, with everything so different and deadly, crazy ideas didn't sound so crazy. For all her bravado, there was still a good chance she'd be dead under Grel'Darm's boot in less than an hour. Why not take a risk?

That felt like the best idea she'd had in a long, long time. With an excited breath, Tina started easing herself closer to SilentBlayde's warmth. But just as she was about to close the final distance, something in her stone body vanished.

It was a small change, but once it settled into place, everything felt wrong. The sky-blue eyes she'd been admiring only seconds before now struck her as soft and moist. *Fleshy.* His tall, lanky frame was suddenly too narrow and flimsy, the long fingers of his gloved hands too spindly. As she stared at him now, all the effortless elven grace she'd always secretly loved to watch suddenly seemed like weakness. Even the paradise scent of his golden hair had soured. Not because it was not beautiful, but because it smelled of the sky, not the ground.

Not like her.

Tina fought the impulse for as long as she could, searching his familiar face for the parts she'd liked best back when she'd been human.

But she wasn't human anymore, and in the end, her stonekin revulsion won out, forcing her to pull away.

SilentBlayde jumped when she moved. He blinked for a second as the spell between them broke, then the half of his face Tina could see flushed red all the way up to his golden eyebrows.

They both looked away in embarrassment, but Tina's quickly turned into disgust as she touched a hand to her face. Her stone skin was flexible under her fingers, but her cheeks were cold, and her lips were as rough as granite. Sitting next to the graceful, dancer-like elf, Tina felt enormous—a hulking, stomping, elemental monster. A being who lived underground and ate rocks and disdained all of the normal, soft, physical things the squishy races did.

And she hated it.

"So," SB said when the silence had become unbearable. "You said you had a plan for beating Grel'Darm?"

Tina grabbed her bag of "food" and popped a rock into her mouth, crunching so loudly, people twenty feet away jumped at the noise. It took two more rocks before she felt together enough to reply. Even then, she could only recite the facts.

It was a cold, awkward sort of conversation, nothing like they usually had, but SilentBlayde at least was back on his game. He listened intently, asking smart, pointed questions until she got to the crux of it. He made her explain that part twice, then he burst out laughing.

■ ■

Ten minutes later, gongs sounded on the fortress walls. Soldiers poured from their barracks at the sound, grabbing weapons and shrugging into armor as they ran to join the units forming in the courtyard. Moments later, Garrond himself appeared, marching down the lines of soldiers with an even grimmer expression than usual on his dour face.

In the players' area, Tina pushed herself up with a sigh. Dawn had broken while she'd been going over the plan with SB, changing the Deadlands sky from oppressive black to oppressive gray. The faint light illuminated the faces of her raiders as well, highlighting the dark circles under their watchful eyes as Tina walked over.

There was no need to bang on anything this time. The whole

313

raid's attention was on her the moment she climbed into the cart, watching her like a threat as she placed her hand down on the guild sign-up sheet.

"It's choosing time," she said, looking around at the now-familiar faces. "SilentBlayde has told you the plan, so there's not much else for me to say. You know what's coming. If you want out, step forward now."

KuroKawaii hopped up immediately. "Sorry, Roxxy," she said with a shrug. "It was a good try, but I'm not willing to die for this shit." She turned to the others. "If you're smart, you'll follow me, and we can give these Order jackoffs the backstabbing they deserve for being so snooty."

Tina's jaw clenched. She'd known this was coming, but the desertion still stung. Even so, she kept her word, holding out her hand to the Assassin. "Good luck, then."

KuroKawaii rolled her eyes at the offered handshake and walked away, snagging a bag of bread as she left. "Come on, Zero," she said, swinging the bag over her shoulder. "Let's get out of here."

But ZeroDarkness didn't move. When she realized the other Assassin wasn't behind her, Kuro whirled around with a furious scowl.

"What the hell, man? I thought we were together on this!"

"We are," the jubatus said, pulling down his face mask. "But I'm staying, and you should, too."

"What is wrong with you?" Kuro demanded, stomping over to the other Assassin, though she had to stand on her tiptoes to get in his face. "Roxxy's plan is nuts! You and I left the first time because she was going to get everyone killed."

"But Roxxy didn't get everyone killed," ZeroDarkness said angrily. "She got them here. We were the ones who had to beg to be let back in!"

Kuro scowled. "But—"

"I came with you the first time because I didn't want you to go alone and die," he said, scowling down at her. "But that was before we knew the whole world hated us. I think we have a better chance if we all stay together."

Kuro's eyes narrowed. "And if I go alone?"

"Then you go alone," he said, crossing his arms.

KuroKawaii made a frustrated noise, but he didn't budge, and in the end, she dropped her bag of bread with a huff. "Fine," she said, glaring at Tina. "But screw your guild! I'm bailing the moment this loony-bin plan of yours goes south."

Tina let out the breath she'd been holding. "Fair enough," she said, looking around at the silent raid. "Anyone else?"

Zen stepped forward, and Tina cursed under her breath. No one liked KuroKawaii much, but Zen was respected by the raid at large. Losing her would be a huge blow, and Tina was scrambling to think of how she was going to mitigate it when Zen said, "I'm not bailing."

Tina blinked in surprise. "Okay," she said, trying not to show how relieved she was. "Is there something else you want to say, then?"

"Yes," the Ranger replied, holding her head high. "I like this plan, and I like the idea of being a mercenary company, but I don't want to follow you."

It hurt her to hear it, but there it was, and Tina couldn't say she didn't deserve it. "So this means you aren't in, then?"

"Correct," Zen said. "And the rest of the Rangers are with me."

Tina felt like she'd just been punched in the gut. Losing Zen would have been bad enough, but losing all six Rangers could collapse everything. She was desperately trying to think of something to say to change their minds when Zen continued.

"We're not content to follow you as we have been," she said. "We've all discussed it, and we've agreed that none of us want to be part of *Roxxy's* Roughnecks or *Roxxy's* mercenaries."

"Then what *do* you want?" Tina said, confused. "My name's kinda already on the contract."

"It's not about the name," Zen snapped. "We're willing to stay and fight, but only if we get a say in how the guild is run from here forward. We're not going to sit back and blindly take orders from Queen Tina anymore."

"Is that what you think I'm doing?" she demanded. "Did you even listen to my apology? I only acted like that because I couldn't just stand there and let you get yourselves killed!"

"That's the problem!" Zen shouted back. "You treated us like we were stupid. You're still treating us that way, but we're *not*. We were confused, sure, who wouldn't be? But we still carried out orders every single time. Even when you were unconscious, we made it work, and yet you still—*still*—treat us all like children!"

"Because I had to!" Tina cried. "We were running for our lives, and you weren't getting with the program fast enough! What was I supposed to do? Ask Grel to wait while we held a conference?"

"You could have listened," Zen said sharply, folding her arms over her chest. "Since hour one, you've treated us like children and idiots. You never properly told us what was going on or asked our opinion about what the raid should do. It was just orders, orders, orders. And whenever anyone *did* speak up, you threatened them until they backed down!"

"I did what I had to do," Tina snarled. "If I hadn't been the fire under your heels, we'd all be under Grel's."

"You saved us from the Dead Mountain," the Ranger admitted. "Everyone knows that, which is why there hasn't been a mutiny. But everything since has been us scrambling to escape problems *you* caused, including the one we're standing in right now."

She pointed up at the Order fortress, and Tina flinched.

"Maybe getting the Order's help didn't work the way I'd hoped," Tina admitted grudgingly. "But it was our only valid move, and it's *not* over. While you were curling up in the courtyard to die without your bow, I was in Garrond's office, putting my ass on the line to get us a fighting chance!"

Her voice rose with every word, booming until it rattled the paving stones. "You don't like what I've done or how I've treated you? *Too bad!* I've kept us all alive despite constantly being stabbed in the back for it. That's why it's *Roxxy's* Roughnecks, because I'm the only one willing to kick your asses until you agree to help me save them. I'm the only one here who has done *anything* that has gotten *any* results!"

"*Because you never let anyone else try!*" Zen screamed at her, standing on tiptoes to get right in Tina's face. "Every time *anyone* has suggested *anything*, including me, you've shut us down with condemnation, extortion, and violence!"

"Because all your 'help' was going to get us killed!" Tina yelled back.

"We didn't think so!" Zen cried, shaking with fury. "Damn it, Roxxy! You can't say we're veteran bad-asses one minute and tell us we're all idiots the next! If that's the case, then us *idiots* are out! We'll take our chances in the swamp because we're *Rangers* and wilderness survival is *what we do!*"

As furious as Tina was, that one got to her. She'd sold this plan to Commander Garrond on the premise that she was leading a crack team of veteran raiders, but she'd treated them as anything but. She still thought Zen's idea of going through the swamp had been stupid, but considering the mess she'd landed them in, Tina couldn't say shit. Lots of mistakes had been made, mostly on her end, but this one was one she couldn't keep making. She had to decide right now if her raiders were professionals or children, because they couldn't be both. But while Tina wasn't sure which was actually correct, she knew which one she wanted.

"Okay," she said quietly, swallowing her resentment. "You're right, Zen. I acted like an ass, and I'm sorry. What's it going to take to keep you?"

Zen had clearly been thinking about this for a while, because she answered immediately. "We want a voice in how the guild is run."

"You mean like a democracy?" Tina scowled. "We don't exactly have the time to set up something complicated. Also, mercenaries are a military operation. That means one leader with the ability to make quick decisions in the field. We can't be taking a vote on every little maneuver."

"Don't care," the Ranger said, crossing her arms. "Either we get a say in decision-making, or we go."

"Grel'Darm is about to walk into us!" Tina said, pointing at the walls, where soldiers were beating the alarm gongs nonstop. "Can we just agree to figure something out after the battle?"

"*No,*" Zen said angrily. "The expediency argument isn't going to work anymore. There's *always* something going down in this shit-fest of a world! That's why we need your word *now.*"

Tina gritted her teeth. "This is extortion."

"Shoe's on the other foot, isn't it?" Zen said, lifting her chin.

Tina ground her boots into the stone, scrambling to think of a way to share power that wouldn't result in chaos or lose her all control over her guild. She could already feel Grel's footsteps rumbling through the ground. If they were going to do this, they needed to move *now.*

"What about if we used the guild officers?" she asked. "I'd still be in charge as guild leader, but Assassins, Rangers, Sorcerers, Knights, Berserkers, and Naturalists would each get one vote on a council that can overrule my decisions. Would that work?"

The Ranger frowned. "I was hoping for something more flexible."

317

"Zen, we are legit out of time," Tina said desperately, pointing at the rumbling ground. "You're getting the power to fix things to your liking in the future, but if you don't work with me now, there won't *be* a future."

The elf looked back at the other Rangers, most of whom gave her the thumbs-up. "Okay," Zen said. "We'll take it. But now we've gotta vote."

Tina rolled her eyes. They didn't have time for this, but the class-leader thing had been her idea, so she stomped her impatience down and turned to address the rest of the raid. "You heard the agreement," she said. "If that's cool with you, then sign the paper and group up by class. Once you select your officers, we'll hold a vote and get this show on the road. Just make it snappy. Grel's almost here."

Zen smiled and picked up the quill, signing her name below Roxxy's on the Order's contract that had formed their new guild. Once she'd signed, the other Rangers ran up to sign as well. More players followed, and soon, with the exception of KuroKawaii, everyone had signed on. That was much better participation than Tina had hoped for, and she would have grinned with relief if she hadn't just been forced to give control of her guild away to a bunch of ingrates.

Once they'd signed, all the players broke up into their class groups. Tina was tapping her boot, waiting impatiently for the others to finish, when she felt the imposing presence of Commander Garrond behind her.

"Taking a vote?" he asked suspiciously when she turned around. "I thought you were the 'highest authority' of this mob."

"I am," Tina snapped. "We're just handing out some long-overdue promotions while we wait for the battle. And speaking of battle, are *you* ready?"

"The Order is always prepared to come to the defense of the innocent," Garrond said pompously, nodding over his shoulder at the perfectly square squadrons of gold-and-white soldiers arrayed in the yard behind him. "Have you decided where you will fight Grel'Darm?"

Tina nodded and pointed at the keep's inner door. "We're going to trap him between the inner and outer gates," she said. "The same place you cornered us when we came in. That should keep him boxed up good and tight, and the narrow door will keep us from getting too overrun by the rest of the undead. Once we engage, make sure you keep all your men back at least a hundred feet. His Chain Fire can go forever so long as it has new targets, but it can't leap more than that. If you stay out of range, it should keep the Chain Fire out of your fort."

Garrond looked at her as if she were mad. "A *hundred feet?*" he cried. "You're talking about my front door! I can't just leave the front of my fortress unguarded during a siege!"

"Do you want Grel dead or not?" Tina snapped back. "Don't worry about the front. We're going to be jammed in between the gates. Nothing's getting past us."

"It had better not," Garrond said impatiently. "I just hope you're actually as good as you boast, Roxxy of the Roughnecks. There are a lot of lives counting on you."

"Don't worry," Tina assured him. "This kind of encounter is our bread and butter."

Garrond didn't look convinced, but he must have finally realized just how screwed he was, because he nodded anyway. "Just make sure you get into position soon. Grel'Darm and his army are only half a mile away."

The commander strode back to his troops after that, and Tina sighed with relief, turning back to the class groups to see whom she was going to be running her guild with.

Fortunately, the selection process didn't take long. One by one, the new officers left their groups and came forward. Even though there were only two of them since Kuro had declined to join the guild, Tina was beyond relieved when SilentBlayde came forward as the leader of the Assassins. The Rangers, of course, chose Zen, though Tina was shocked when NekoBaby won the Naturalist vote, and even more surprised when the Clerics chose Anders.

"Instant disaster, just add mob rule," she muttered as Neko bounced forward, shooting Anders a murderous glare when he stepped up beside her. Thankfully, any potential incidents were nipped in the bud when Killbox, now the officer of the Berserkers, elbowed his way between them.

KatanaFatale came up next, practically shoved to the front by the other Sorcerers. When Tina asked how he'd gotten elected given that he'd only been with the raid for a few hours, the poor man had muttered something about new guys getting the shit job. Finally, and most surprising of all, Frank came over.

Tina thought she was seeing things when the newbie tank walked out of the Knights' circle, and she wasn't the only one. All the officers were staring slack-jawed as Frank took his place in the circle, pushing up his visor to smile sheepishly at them.

Tina broke the awkward silence first. "Please don't take this the wrong way, Frank, but how did *you* get elected to lead the Knights?"

"You still don't know what cooldowns are!" Neko blurted out. "What gives?"

"That's what *I* said," Frank replied, shrugging his huge shoulders. "But once they found out I used to be chief engineer at an ammonium plant, they told me I had to take the gig. Seems I'm the only one with actual managerial experience."

"Can't argue with that logic," Tina said, relieved that she had someone she liked for the Knights. "Okay, folks, you know the plan. As always, SB's in command if something happens to me, but otherwise, you guys are the bosses. You're in charge of making sure all your people are okay and doing what they're supposed to be doing. Got it?"

Everyone nodded as horns began to sound from the walls of the fortress. In the courtyard, Commander Garrond thrust his sword into the air. "The undead are upon us!" he cried at the top of his lungs. "Everyone to their positions! *For the living!*"

The Order roared back as one, "*For the living!*"

"That's our cue," Tina said, thrusting her fist into the air. "*Roughnecks!* Let's go show this world just how destructive we can be!"

A deafening cheer went up from all the players as they jumped up and started running toward the gates.

■ ■

As Tina had discovered the hard way in her attempt to storm the place, the front of the Order's fortress made a good trap. The walled-in corridor between the inner gate and the outer gatehouse that stuck off the fort's main body like a gooseneck was a perfect kill box—narrow, tall, and walled in by stone on all sides. The front gatehouse especially was a massive defense of heavy walls and stone archer towers, all of which were emptying of soldiers at Garrond's command as Tina and her Roughnecks took up position between the gates.

"*One hundred feet!*" Tina yelled at the Order soldiers running along the walls above them. "You stay one hundred feet away from us, or your whole fort turns into a Chain Fire bonfire!"

Satisfied she'd done her due diligence, Tina turned to examine her battlefield. She'd chosen to fight here for a lot of reasons, but the relative narrowness and the thinner-than-average stone walls that formed the gooseneck's sides were the two biggest. Once the raid was inside, the Order locked the inner gate behind them, the giant doors closing with an ominous *boom* as teams of soldiers lowered the heavy crossbeams into place.

"Positions, everyone!" Tina yelled. "Ranged damage and healers line up in the back! Melee fighters to the left and right! Frank, you're up front with me!"

Everyone scrambled into place as she yelled out positions, and Tina grinned. *Finally*, they were starting to look like a real raid. She was ordering the back line to group up closer when a giant tremor shook the ground, and the whole fortress groaned.

"Minds on what you're doing, people!" Tina shouted when everyone's heads whipped toward the still closed-and-bolted outer gate. "Weapons out! Remember your jobs!"

The ground shook again as she bellowed the orders, and Frank gulped beside her.

"Roxxy?"

"It'll be okay," she said, turning to face the shaking doors in front of them. "Just do your job."

"About that," he said, voice quivering. "Can you please tell me how we are tanking this guy again?"

She'd already explained the fight to him several times on their way up here, but it was his first big boss encounter. Tina wasn't about to begrudge him anything right now.

"Sure, man," she said, giving him a reassuring smile. "Grel'Darm is what we call a 'Massive Blows' boss. That means he doesn't attack fast, but when he does hit, he hits for a *lot*. You need to be prepared to use your defensive cooldowns every time you get hit. But the main thing we have to watch out for is Howling Strike. It does ridiculous damage, so you never want to get hit by more than one in a row."

"And that's why we're trading off tanking him?"

"Yup," she said, nodding. "It's all about using Steady Ground. That's our anti-knock-back ability. When you take a really big attack like Howling Strike, the force can send you flying. If you're not prepared, you'll splat against the back wall like a bug on a windshield. That's where Steady Ground comes in. When you hit it, it'll lock you in place so Grel can't punt you away. The ability will give you ten good seconds of guaranteed feet on the ground, but once that's over, there's a twenty-second reset time before you can Steady Ground again."

"And that's why we're taking turns."

"Exactly," Tina said. "I'll hit Steady Ground for the first Howling Strike, then we'll switch places, and you'll use it, then me again, then you again, and so on."

"I see," Frank said slowly. "But Roxxy—and I mean no disrespect cause I'm sure you know what you're doing—ten seconds of Steady Ground plus twenty seconds of waiting for it to reset is only thirty seconds. If I understand all this 'cooldown' stuff right, that means we only get four uses of Steady Ground per minute between the two of us. What if he Howling Strikes more than that?"

"That's where my plan comes in," Tina said, nodding at the melee teams who'd taken up position against the box courtyard's walls to their left and right. "If everything goes like it should, you and I will only have to tank Grel long enough to get him into position. Once he's there, all we have to do is keep him in place for a minute while the melee does their job. After that, there should be no more tanking needed."

Frank didn't seem reassured, so Tina changed the subject. "Show me your Hunched Stance."

"That's the one where I angle my shield for the Big Boot, right?" Frank said, crouching down with the top of his shield braced against his shoulder and the base on the ground.

Tina nudged the bottom of his shield out farther with her boot. "Remember, the angle has to be forty-five degrees or lower. This is a deflection move, not a block. You want the force to slide over you, not into you." She adjusted his shield again then stepped back to check his form. "Looks good now. Just do it that way every time, and you'll be fine. Oh, and remember to keep your head down. Even us tanks can get KO'd by a bad blow."

Frank nodded nervously, dancing from foot to foot as he straightened up.

"Hey," she said, putting a hand on his shoulder to steady him. "It'll be okay. I'm right here beside you, and there's an entire raid of people behind us. None of us are doing this alone."

"But if I mess up, we're all going to die, right? The other Knights were saying this guy is really unforgiving."

Tina smiled as warmly as a stonekin could. "He is, but don't worry. I've done a *lot* of tanking in my time, and I have plenty of tricks up my sleeve. The same goes for all the players behind you. Don't underestimate how much FFO we've played. If you slip up, we'll be there to catch you."

"But what about The Contagion of the Great Pyre?" he asked in a panicked voice.

Tina frowned. "The Contagion of—*Oh!* You mean Chain Fire!" She laughed. "You've been talking to SB, haven't you? Contagion of the Great Pyre is what Grel's big ability is called in the lore, which is cool to know if you're an FFO history junkie like SilentBlayde, but no one actually calls it that. If we had to yell 'Contagion of the Great Pyre!' every time it went off, we'd be burned to a crisp before we finished talking."

That was supposed to be a joke, but Frank was too anxious to notice, so Tina just moved on.

"Okay, Chain Fire, real quick. Two times during the fight, once at half health and once as a quarter, Grel will unleash a massive-damage ghostfire attack that jumps from player to player. The attack splits with every jump, so it'll hit the two of us first then split into four, then eight, and so on forever until there are no more targets in range. Each hit does a shit-ton of damage and can't be blocked, so you just have to suck it up. That's why I've got everyone else grouped up in the back for—"

She stopped as the ground shook again, nearly knocking her off her feet. "You know what? Don't even worry about it. It's the healers' job to deal with Chain Fire."

"But you said it was going to take all their mana to heal the Contagion...I mean Chain Fire," Frank reminded her. "That's why we're not getting heals during tanking phase. They need to save their mana to put out the fire, right?"

"We're going to *try* to go without heals," Tina said. "I can still call for help if we need it, but we're geared tanks! We've got over six hundred thousand health each. We should be able to take a few whacks without needing a patch-up."

She kept her voice cocky so as not to scare him, but the reality was that their healers didn't have the mana to keep two tanks topped off *and* keep the entire raid alive through two Chain Fires. If everything went to plan, that wouldn't be a problem, but Tina still intended to save all non-Chain Fire healing for absolute emergencies. Otherwise, healers would go OOM, and people would die.

"We'll be fine," she said, slapping Frank on the shoulder. "All we have to worry about is keeping each other alive and the boss in position. The raid will handle the rest."

Frank nodded with a gulp, lowering his visor again as the rumbling in the ground increased. Feeling the paving stones rattle under her boots reminded Tina that it wasn't just Grel'Darm coming to get them. It was an entire army of the undead. That was the other reason she'd chosen to fight between the gates. In this narrow place, they could eliminate the Once King's numbers advantage, forcing the army to fight them in small, manageable clusters rather than all at once.

Or at least, that was the idea. Tina was going through everything again in her head one last time when she heard dozens of people gasp behind her.

She whirled around, sword up, but all she found were a bunch of casters staring at the sky. Confused, she looked up as well, but all she saw was the early-morning version of the endlessly cloudy Deadlands sky.

"Anders!" she hollered. "What's going on?"

Anders blinked his huge fish eyes at the sky. "Death magic…" he said, voice shaking. "Floating above us on the wind. There's so *much* of it."

As creepy as that was, magic in the air wasn't an attack, so far as Tina knew. It was distracting her back line, though, so she banged obnoxiously on her shield until all the robed spell casters were looking her way again.

"Keep it together, folks!" she yelled. "Nothing new here, just another day and another boss fight. We can do this! We even get to cheat this time, so cheer up!"

As she said that, drums began to pound outside the walls. Huge, booming, discordant war drums that beat in a frenetic rhythm. These were followed by the high-pitched wailing of thousands of hollow, ghostly voices. Listening to them was like hearing an entire country being slowly murdered. The sound plus the now-constant rumbling in the ground was enough to make even Tina quake in her boots, keeping her eyes fixed on the fortress's closed front gate.

"*Archers ready!*" the booming voice of Commander Garrond rang out behind them. He was standing on top of the fortress's northern tower—a hundred feet from the raid, as promised. Even from so far away, though, Tina could see the strain in his face, which she took as a sign that the undead were even closer than she'd realized. Then without warning, the rumbling under her feet stopped.

Tina froze. The drums and wailing continued, but the ground was still, and she cursed the closed outer gates that kept her from seeing what was going on. Locked between the walls and the two doors, the raid was essentially packed inside a box. A very useful and strategically critical box, but it was still annoying. Behind her, she heard the Rangers whispering about going up top to take a look, but though she was dying to know what was going on outside, Tina shook her head.

"Hold position!" she ordered, shifting her fingers nervously on her shield grip. "Remember the plan. Let them come to us."

The words were still leaving her mouth when she heard the *wha-chunck* of catapults. Ghastly screaming filled the air as two huge balls of ghostfire flew over their heads to smash into the fortress behind them. Massive conflagrations of blue-white flame shot up when they landed, the flames rising so high, Tina could see the tops of them over the fortress's sixty-foot walls. The air was filling with the screams of the Order soldiers when another round of *wha-chuncks* echoed through the air.

These sounded even closer, and Tina flung her shield over her head to brace for impact. But the new shots didn't fly over the walls. Instead, they crashed into the gatehouse directly in front of them.

The heavy oak-and-iron doors had no chance against the undead's magical ordinance. Tina barely had time to get her shield in front of her again before the Order's forty-foot-tall front gate exploded inward, shooting spear-sized splinters of wood into the raid at lethal speeds. One bounced right off her shield, pushing her back several feet as she hunkered in the shadow of her god-forged steel.

The rest of the raid wasn't so lucky. Cries of pain sounded behind her as the debris hit the back wall. Glancing quickly over her shoulder, Tina saw that KatanaFatale had a two-foot-long javelin of wood going straight through his recently healed leg. The Sorcerer wasn't alone in getting skewered, either. Two other casters were also down with shrapnel, moaning in pain as they began to bleed out.

"*Anders!*" she bellowed. "Healing approved!"

The Cleric raised his staff, and Tina felt the cold air grow warm as golden healing magic began to rain down on the back lines. Satisfied they hadn't just been taken out before the fight began, Tina turned back around to face the blasted-out gates...

And saw the enemy properly for the first time.

She froze, shield almost slipping from her limp hand. Down the hill, the entire pass through the mountains was choked with undead. This wasn't a bunch of monsters glimpsed through a forest in the dead of night or a dusty cloud seen from five miles away. This was an *army*. A massive, sophisticated, orderly military force with clearly demarked units. There were skeleton infantry and archers, zombie shock troops clad in crude plate armor, hulking monstrosities crafted from sewn-together corpses, and large undead animals filled with ghostfire, and that was just what was out in front. There were more troops behind those, a great, dark mass that filled the wide pass of the Deadlands for as far as she could see, and at their center, towering a good eighty feet above the rest, was Grel'Darm the Colossal.

Tina swallowed against the sudden tightness in her throat. She remembered SB telling her once that Grel was the animated remains of a giant from FFO's ancient past. Seeing him now, Tina believed it. He looked even bigger out here in the open than he had in his boss room, his eyes burning white like ghostly funeral pyres as he stared through the hazy dust of his army at the fortress's broken gates.

Straight at her.

"Roxxy," Frank whispered, his armor rattling, "do you see—"

He never got to finish, because that was the moment when the undead army started to charge. The line was so long, Tina couldn't begin to count them, but she felt them coming like a tide through the ground, the pounding of their distant feet making the whole fortress vibrate.

"*Ranged to the center!*" she shouted, bolting out of the way to join the rest of the melee against the walls.

As she and Frank ran out, the Rangers and other casters ran in, aiming their staffs and bows at the now-clear doorway. Watching them move, Tina was really, *really* glad that they'd practiced fighting as a group. Running out of mana and ammo had sucked on the road, but at least now she was reasonably sure they could fight together without killing each other. At least, she was until an arrow sailed out of the Ranger group, making her worry she'd spoken too soon.

"*Hold, dammit!*" she yelled as the arrow stuck, quivering, in one of the wooden splinters that was still hanging off the sundered doors. "Wait for my order!"

Outside, the undead army had almost made it up the hill to the fortress. Risking a peek, Tina saw that they were all zombie shock troops—fast-moving and deadly but not particularly tough. They were still too far away for the raid's fire to be effective, though, so she kept her hand up, holding her people back to prevent wasteful attacks. But while she watched the zombies race in, her real attention was on Grel'Darm.

These minor undead were just annoyances. Their *real* target was the building-sized armored skeleton boss behind them. For some reason, though, Grel hadn't joined in the charge. He was still calmly standing in the middle of his army, watching the fortress with those flaming eyes as if he was waiting for something.

With a horrible screech of bone on bone, the shock zombies made it to the top of the hill and started pouring through the blasted-out gates. Thankfully, while the catapults had taken out most of the double doors, there was still enough charred metal and smoking wood left at the bottom to force the human-sized zombies to climb. Grinning, Tina waited until the first wave hit the ground inside before dropping her hand.

"Now!" she cried, pressing her body flat against the wall. "*Fire!*"

"*Fire Storm!*"

"*Acid Arrow!*"

"*Chain Lightning!*"

The ability calls echoed off the stone walls as glowing arrows and elemental destruction landed on the zombies who'd made it through the gate. There was a series of explosions, whirlwinds of fire, and blinding lightning as the masses of undead were turned to ash, dissolved, and blown apart. Only a single half-burnt corpse made it far enough inside for Tina to hit it, and it crumbled to ash before her sword could pass all the way through.

A round of cheers rose from the raid only to fall silent as more undead began to scramble over the broken doors.

"Fire at will!" Tina yelled, pressing herself against the wall again as a steady stream of spells and arrows began flying past.

And so it went. There was no sun to be seen in the Deadlands, so Tina wasn't sure how long they fought, but it felt like forever. Channeled into such a narrow space, the undead could never mass enough numbers to overcome the damage the Roughneck's casters and archers could put out. Even the massive undead battle boars were turned to ash by the time they climbed through the broken doors. With full mana and a whole cartful of arrows for the Rangers, the space between the gates was a glorious corridor of endless zombie destruction, but Tina couldn't enjoy it. Her eyes were still on Grel'Darm, who had yet to budge from his safe position at the back of the endless army.

"Why isn't he moving?" she hissed.

"Maybe he likes it back there," Killbox said beside her, glowering at the never-ending stream of arrows and spells flying through the boxed-in courtyard. "I'm more interested in when *we* get to fight. I haven't gotten to chop a single zombie!"

"You'll get your chance," Tina promised, leaning out to try to get a better look at what was coming next. "He has to move some—"

A ghostly horn cut her off. The mournful cry was answered by several others blowing from all directions, then Tina heard the scrabble of bones as a new wave of undead crashed into the main fortress walls.

"*Crap!*" she cried, leaning out so far she nearly lost her head to a fireball. "They must have piled up on the rest of the fortress once they realized they couldn't get in here!"

She'd barely finished when the gongs on the Orders' battlements began sounding behind them, and Tina heard Commander Garrond shout the attack. When she looked up to see where, though, the commander jumped off the tower he'd been watching from, falling eighty feet to the courtyard below. She was wondering if he'd just jumped to his death when Garrond suddenly leaped up to join the soldiers on the fortress's southern battlements where the undead had wheeled in a siege tower. Another leap took him right off the edge into the undead army, then there was a flash of golden light as the commander sliced the iron siege tower in half.

"Damn," Tina said, eyes wide. "That's a four-skull for you. Glad we didn't try to fight him."

"Too bad there's not more of him," Killbox said, nodding at the wall opposite the one Command Garrond had just one-man-armied off. Sure enough, the soldiers up there were already going down to the undead's arrows. They kicked the siege ladders off the moment they landed, but with so many attackers, it was only a matter of time before the defense folded.

It was a truly bad position. The Roughnecks were holding the front gate, but with so many attackers, the undead army didn't need to go in through the doors. They could just go around the gooseneck, taking the fight straight to the fortress itself.

But as screwed as they'd all be if the fort went down behind them, the walls were not Tina's problem. Her job was to kill Grel, and she couldn't do that if he stayed in the back. As proud as she was of the hellish damage her raid was unleashing on the undead coming through the gate, they weren't here to kill crap zombies, and she didn't want them running on fumes by the time the main show finally decided to grace them with his presence. Something had to be done, so she turned and yelled for the person who could do it.

"*Zen!*"

The name was barely out of her mouth when the dark-skinned elf practically materialized next to her. "I'm here," she said, panting. "What's up?"

Tina scowled but saved the lecture. Zen knew the risks of abusing her speed better than anyone except SB himself, and frankly they needed a little fastness right now.

"Take the Rangers and get to the towers," she ordered, pointing at the two forward archer towers bracketing the gatehouse in front of them. "The undead are all over the walls, so you'll have to climb, but that shouldn't be a problem since you're all freakishly agile. Get up as high as you can and see if you can hit Grel'Darm. It doesn't have to be for good damage. We just need to get his attention. Once he's in range, I'll peel him off you."

"We can try," Zen said, glancing nervously through the broken door at Grel, who was still standing at the back of his army. "But we don't have taunts like you do, Roxxy. What if he doesn't take the bait?"

"That's why *all* the Rangers are going," Tina said with a smile. "If he won't move, go full bore on him until he does. Who knows? Maybe he's stupid enough to stand there and let you guys kill him for free." She didn't think that it'd be that easy, but putting the enemy in a damned-if-you-do-and-damned-if-you-don't situation was always a good move. "Just make sure you get back down here ASAP the moment he gets mad," she added, tapping her finger on the wall next to them. "Once the plan kicks into action, those towers aren't going to be safe."

"We're on it," Zen said, then put her fingers in her mouth to blow a high-pitched whistle.

The raid's five other Rangers whistled back, then all of them darted away so fast, Tina's eyes couldn't follow. The next time she saw them, they were climbing the weighted chains that used to open and close the fort's massive front gates, scrambling up the tire-sized iron links as nimbly as squirrels to the towers above. Whistling at their incredible speed, Tina felt foolish for not using them earlier. SilentBlayde had been right. She just needed to embrace the awesome they all had.

Now that she'd sent all eight Rangers on a mission, the raid's ranged damage output had been reduced by half, which meant tougher zombies were starting to get through the gates. She was hefting her shield to go and pick them up when Killbox and the other Berserkers bowled her over, crushing the corpse monsters beneath their massive axes while fireballs rushed by over their heads.

"Good work," Tina said, pushing herself back up as the melee finished off the undead. "Now get back in position. We don't know when—"

She cut off with a jump as something elf-like flashed by her.

"He'scomingRoxxy!" said the blur that was Zen. "Holycrap. HeisFAST!"

She and the other Rangers were going so fast, they almost crashed into the door at the back. They skidded to a halt just in time, all of them gasping for air as they sank to the ground. Tina smashed a half-dead zombie out of her way and got back in position at the center of the box, yelling at Frank to get beside her as she turned to face the broken gates.

And nearly dropped her shield.

Grel'Darm the Colossal was coming up the hill at them like a crashing plane. As she watched him charge forward, all Tina could think was how foolish she'd been. Grel had never been the slow one. He'd been held up by the catapults and the army he was escorting. That was how he'd caught them with their pants down on the hill. He'd just run up it before they could hear him coming.

But there was no time to stew on past mistakes. Grel'Darm was almost to the gate. The giant skeleton was as tall as the front towers, a good twenty feet too tall to go through the broken door of the front gatehouse. Tina was wondering how he planned to get inside when then the giant turned and shoved his armored shoulder forward, charging like a linebacker as he picked up even more speed.

"Holy shit," Tina said, taking a step back. "He's gonna ram the gatehouse!" she yelled, throwing up her shield as she scrambled backward. *"Everyone collapse!"*

The whole raid fell back into a knot around the spell casters. When they were all properly bunched together, Tina gave the command.

"Anders! Sanctuary!"

The fish-man Cleric was already in position at the center of the clump. He gave her a quick smile and spread his scaly arms wide, his golden staff blazing. "Sanctuary of the Four!" he shouted as the air filled with warm sun-colored magic. It was still building when the fish-man's smile turned into a grin. *"You shall not pass!"*

He slammed his staff down dramatically, and a spinning golden circle filled with sacred geometric patterns appeared on the ground below their feet. At the same time, a dome of golden light dawned above their heads, creating a transparent but impenetrable barrier of holy magic just in time to bounce the wave of broken stone and shattered iron that crashed over them as Grel's shoulder collided with the fortress's heavy stone gatekeep.

The fortification didn't even slow him down. Car-sized chunks of masonry bounced off the golden barrier as Grel'Darm blew right through the reinforced archway above the destroyed gates. An entire half staircase slammed into the ground in front of them, tearing through the stone tiles like a plow before crashing into the barrier and exploding inches from Tina's face.

If the golden wall hadn't been there, they all would have been flattened. But the Cleric's barrier only lasted for five seconds. As the golden magic faded, Tina gulped in fear.

This was her moment, but suddenly, her feet didn't want to move. She was supposed to pick up Grel and keep him busy while everyone else got into position, but now that the eighty-foot-tall giant was towering over her, all she could think about was how he'd flattened her last time. Of course, she'd been unprepared back then, but that didn't help the knot of fear in her throat as Grel'Darm's dented steel boot filled her vision.

"*Tina!*"

SilentBlayde's shout rang in her ears, making her jump. They were all still bunched up for the barrier spell. It Grel's foot landed in the raid now, he'd hit everyone, and that would be the end. The sheer stupidity of that was enough to beat back her fear, and Tina launched forward with a roar.

"Team Hulk, go!" she yelled as she ran back to her position at the center of the box between the gates. "Ranged, get to the back! Frank, with me!"

The Knights and Berserkers bolted to their positions on the walls to Tina's right and left. The Rangers and Sorcerers ran, too, re-forming their back line in front of the fortress's inner door as they resumed fire on the gates, shooting arrows and fireballs over Tina's head to disintegrate the undead that were still pouring in through the now-smashed gatehouse behind the boss. Everyone seemed to be doing exactly what they were supposed to, but Tina didn't have time to check, because in the heartbeat it had taken to shout the orders, she'd finally reached Grel'Darm.

Or maybe he reached her. It was impossible to say who got there first as the giant's massive boot landed in front of her, filling her vision and cratering the ground. Tina dug her own boots into the cracking stone and stomped back, clipping Grel'Darm's foot with the glowing power of her area taunt. She was about to stomp again to make sure she'd gotten his attention when Grel'Darm's boot vanished.

Tina's eyes grew wide as her head snapped up, neck creaking backward at an almost ninety-degree angle to watch as Grel'Darm launched himself into the air. He leaped so high that, for a heart-stopping moment, Tina was terrified her taunt hadn't worked. That he was jumping *over* her to land on the casters. But as the giant's leap reached its peak, his ghost-fire eyes swiveled in his skull to look straight down at her, then he began to howl, filling the battlefield with his bone-chilling, discordant wail as he swung his charter-bus-sized club over his head.

"Shit, shit, shit!" Tina said, ducking behind her shield. Howling Strike already? She'd thought she'd get at least a few normal hits before he pulled out the big guns. Using her cooldowns this early in a fight was never a good move, but the bus-sized club was falling like a meteor straight toward her head, so Tina sucked it up and activated her big defensive abilities. All of them.

"Earthen Fortitude! Iron Wall! Steady Ground!"

She yelled each ability at the top of her lungs so Frank and the healers would know she'd just blown her full stack. Shield over her head, Tina hunkered down and braced on her sword as her skin hardened her into place and the broken pavement beneath her feet turned into a pillar of bedrock going straight down to the world's roots, locking her in place as the full force of Grel'Darm landed on top of her.

The monster's club collided with her shield like a train crash. Above her head, Tina could hear the magically imbued metal groaning as it fought to keep itself together. Her hardened body cracked and popped as the energy of Grel'Darm's strike traveled through her into the bedrock pillar her stonekin racial ability had created. All around her, giant cracks opened as the ground split from the force, the fissures spidering across the pavement to run up the stone walls on either side. Even the oppressive gray clouds overhead split briefly, allowing a glimmer of weak sunlight to gleam across her dusty armor before closing up again.

For three entire heartbeats, the ringing gong of the giant's blow was all Tina could hear. Then the noise of battle resumed, the shouting and clanging of steel on bone creeping back into her consciousness as Grel'Darm's weight lifted.

Her abilities wore off a second later, and Tina staggered to her feet. Silvery blood dripped from her gauntlet as she lowered her shield, and her left eye could only see the world in a white haze. She was blinking rapidly in an effort to clear it when something enormous and heavy crashed beside her. Jumping at the impact, Tina lurched her spinning head to the right, but it took her several moments before she realized that the car-sized hunk of dark wood lying on the ground next to her was the upper half of Grel'Darm's wooden club.

"*Ha!*" she shouted, staggering backward. "*Ha ha ha! A ha ha ha!*" Punch-drunk laughter bubbled out of her as Tina stabbed her sword at the giant, who was standing in front of her, looking at his broken weapon in stupid confusion. "That's right! Don't mess...with...the ROUGHnecks!" she slurred.

She made a rude gesture with her free arm that Grel'Darm didn't see or care about. He just tossed his shattered club into the fort behind her and reached down to grab a boulder-sized chunk off of one of the gatekeep's broken towers. While the monster hefted his new weapon, Tina shook her head to clear it and turned to see if "Team Hulk" was still on mission or if they'd all been flattened by Grel's weapon-breaking strike.

She should have had more faith. Though knocked back by the blast wave of Grel's attack, all of the raid's Berserkers and Knights were back on their feet and back on task, lined up against the walls to her right and left where the huge chains that had once operated the fortress's massive front gate now dangled broken from their busted housing.

Not counting Tina and Frank, there were twelve Strength-based players in the raid. As Tina had discovered personally when fighting Killbox, each one was as strong as Hercules, and that crazy strength was the core of her plan. Just as she'd told them to, they'd divided themselves into two groups, one for each side of the boxed-in courtyard. Like two halves of the same whole, they ran to the broken chains, grabbing up one foot-long iron length each. Once they had the chains in hand, they began to pull, unspooling the chains from their gears until they'd dragged the oxen-sized solid-iron counterweights that opened the gates all the way up to the top of the pulleys, where they caught.

Too big to pass through the ring of the pulley and too sturdy to break off, the massive iron counterweights were trapped inside the gear boxes, which were themselves trapped inside the walls of the still-standing corners of the gatehouse. This meant the chains were now stuck inside the stone, creating an anchor for the Berserkers and Knights to pull against, hauling on the chains with all their strength until the stone cracked and the towers themselves began to groan.

Tina watched the whole thing with glee. This was the "no tanking" plan. In front of her, Grel was exactly where she wanted him—in the middle of the gooseneck, halfway between the inner and outer gates, where the side walls were weakest and the gatehouse's guard towers were directly above him. At Killbox's command, Team Hulk dug their feet in and pulled on the locked chains with vein-bulging might. The masonry groaned and popped as the cracked towers they were hauling against began to tilt backward toward Grel's skeletal head, and for a soaring second, Tina thought they were going to get this in one. But then a red-faced Knight suddenly gasped for breath, and his grip on the chain slacked. He was followed by several others as both pulling teams reached their limit.

They were all huffing for breath when Killbox yelled, "Heave *HO,* chumps!" and they all sucked in their breath for another try.

But though they were all clearly pulling with every bit of their might, the listing towers and cracked walls didn't budge again. Tina was opening her mouth to yell at them to keep trying, that they were almost there, when a shadow fell over her.

She turned back to Grel'Darm with a curse. After several tries, the giant had finally located a truck-sized piece of rubble that would suit his purposes. He was raising it to crush her when Tina suddenly remembered that she had nothing left.

"*Frank!*" she cried, stepping to the side. "You're up!"

Frank was there at once. He shoved his way in front of her and smacked the skeleton's giant, ironclad foot with the flat of his sword. "You've got osteoporosis!" he taunted.

With the same ghostly howl as last time, Grel slammed his stone down. Tina barely had time to jump clear of the impact zone before the blow landed. "*Steady Ground!*" Frank yelled, hunkering down as the boulder exploded against his shield.

It looked like a good defense until Tina looked over her shoulder and saw Frank's head wasn't low enough. As a result, the full force of the hit drove Frank's shield straight onto his skull rather than his shoulders, and he crumpled like a crushed paper cup.

"*Shit!*"

Tina hurdled over the remains of the boulder that was now crumbling out of Grel'Darm's hand to grab the still form of the other tank. When he didn't even groan, she turned and yelled over her shoulder at the casting camp. "Frank's unconscious! Healing approved!"

The order was barely out of her mouth when she rushed forward to taunt Grel'Darm again. The giant responded by pulling his foot back for the Big Boot attack. Skidding to a stop on the broken stone, Tina frantically slammed her shield down for the deflection. It was only the year of fighting Grel that allowed her to land the perfect forty-five degree angle in time before the wall of Grel'Darm's ironclad toes smashed into her.

Tina smiled at the sparks flying over her head as the majority of the force went up and over her, but even with the perfect deflection, her shield arm still exploded in pain. Flexing her fingers to make sure they still worked, Tina risked a look back at Frank. Golden-and-green light was exploding like fireworks over his body as the healers showered spells on him, and he stirred with a groan. But as happy as she was to see he wasn't dead, there was no way Frank was getting up in time to catch the next attack. Grel'Darm had already found a new rock and was raising it over his head, his giant jaw opening for another of those horrible howls.

Cringing at the sound, Tina forced herself to her feet. To do what, though, she wasn't sure. It felt like ages since Grel's first Howling Strike had broken his weapon across her shield, but it couldn't have been more than thirty seconds, because she could still feel the weakness in her chest that meant her key abilities were still on cooldown.

Frantically, she looked at Team Hulk. They were still pulling on the chains exactly as she'd told them to, red-faced and clearly giving it everything they had. But though the stone walls on either side of Grel were buckling inward, neither had reached the point of collapse yet, and that was a serious problem. Tina had never expected this to be an easy win, but those walls were *really* supposed to be down by now.

Cursing under her breath, she looked down at her battered armor. Back in the game, she could have tanked Grel's normal hits forever, saving her special abilities for the really big stuff. Now, though, every blow felt like getting hit by a bus dropped from orbit, and with all the damage she'd already taken, Tina was depressingly certain that whatever hit he landed next—special or otherwise—would probably be fatal.

"Stupid physics," she muttered, clutching her shield. "Stupid hundred-ton monster."

Above her, Grel'Darm appeared to have given up on finding a new weapon, or maybe he just wanted the pleasure of crushing her with his own hands. Either way, he didn't grab another rock. He just curled his giant iron-gauntleted hand into a fist and punched straight down. As the shadow of his hand enveloped her, Tina realized there was no "probably" about it. When that thing hit her, she was going to die. She lifted her shield anyway, just to keep up appearances, but when she glanced over her shoulder for a final look at SilentBlayde, she found him in the caster camp, pointing at her and yelling at the top of his lungs.

"*External!*" he screamed. "External on Roxxy *now!*"

NekoBaby raised her staff in answer. *"Circle of Thorns!"*

Green-and-brown light sprang up from Tina's feet as a dense hedge of thorny ironwood vines surrounded her. They'd barely finished growing before the giant fist smashed into them. Black vines as thick as Tina's waist splintered under the force, but by the time the monster's fist crashed through the barrier into her shield, the remaining force couldn't do more than drive her to one knee. When Grel tried to pull back to hit her again, his armored hand got caught in the hedge, pulling the whole ironwood thicket up with it. Rumbling angrily at his tangled hand, the giant stopped attacking to rip the vines from his fingers, giving Tina a chance to push herself back up.

"Thanks, guys!" she yelled, grinning at Neko and SB over her shoulder. "I can't believe you remembered!"

During the Roughnecks' early raiding days when they'd had fewer abilities and much worse gear, they'd had to rotate defenses across the whole raid to survive. The term "external" meant that the tank was out of tricks and needed another player's defensive ability cast on them. It had been five years at least since they'd had to use it, though. She was amazed that SilentBlayde and NekoBaby had remembered, but the fact that they'd had to was a bad, bad sign.

"Plan's not working!" she yelled, keeping her eyes on Grel as she pointed her sword at the straining Team Hulk. "The wall's too strong!"

"I know!" SB yelled back. "What are we going to do, though? Mana's running low over here. We're gonna be neck deep in zombies if we don't end this quickly!"

"Why don't we use the last of our mana to blast the boss?" KatanaFatale yelled. "Maybe we can burn him down!"

"No!" Tina roared. "Keep all ranged DPS on those gates!"

The constant stream of fire was the reason she was only fighting one boss and not one boss plus every-other-undead-in-the-Once-King's-army. There was no way their ranged damage could burn down the Great Wall of HP that was Grel'Darm before the zombie hordes they'd been keeping back overwhelmed them. Once the walls fell and Grel was buried under thousands of tons of rubble, they'd have time to kill him *and* keep the small fry under control. Until that point, though, they were stuck. Those walls *had* to come down for the plan to work, and as the *wha-chunck* of the catapults sounded again, lobbing two more ghostfire shots over their heads, Tina knew just how to do it.

"*SB!*" she yelled as Grel shook the last of the ironwood vines off his hand. "Take the Assassins and go capture those catapults!"

She didn't have time to say more. Fortunately, with SB, she never needed to. He'd already given her a thumbs-up and turned to the other Assassins. After some quick pointing, all three of them vanished into the shadows. Satisfied that her second was on top of the situation, Tina turned her attention back to Grel'Darm.

The monster had freed his hand and was using it to pick up the long iron bar that had once held the front gates together. He turned back to her, hefting the twisted beam menacingly. Tina raised her shield in reply, sighing in relief as she felt the first of her defensive abilities come back for use again. Behind her, Frank finally staggered back to his feet. He tried to take her place, but Tina waved him back, lifting her shield instead.

"*Steady Ground!*"

The ground under her feet hardened as Grel slammed the iron bar down on her like a whip. She winced as the blow went through her, leaving her head ringing. Swallowing the silver blood that pooled in her mouth, Tina stepped aside to let Frank pick up the next one, hoping against hope that they could hold out long enough for the Assassins to save their hides.

CHAPTER *16*

James

"**A**re you done yet?" Arbati growled.

"Almost," James said, moving yet another letter to the neat pile he was making in his lap.

It had been over an hour since Thunder Paw had left with the gnolls to clear out the rest of the dungeon. James had spent the entire time in the lich's chamber, sorting through the pile of papers that covered the ancient sorcerer's surprisingly non-magical, very cluttered desk. Anything that looked important got added to his pile. The rest he swept to the side, possibly to be burned. James hadn't decided yet, but research notes on how to make corrupted elements definitely didn't feel like knowledge that should be kept around.

He kept himself moving quickly, reading just enough from each paper to determine whether or not it was worth keeping. Even so, it was exhausting work. The papers were endless. Apparently, this lich had been quite prolific, and he'd been down here for a very long time.

"What are you even looking for?" Arbati demanded, tipping backward in the chair he'd snitched from one of the alchemy tables. "It's not like you're planning to become a necromancer. Burn it all, and let's go."

"I would," James said. "But it's not just research notes." He held up a letter for Arbati to see. "There's lots of quests in Bastion relating to the Once King's spies and plots, including several involving this lich. I was hoping to find a letter I could use as proof, maybe something with some names, but I keep finding letters to new collaborators and reports from new spies. I need everything so I can tell the Royal Knights who the traitors are when I go to Bastion."

That last part was key, because after what had happened in Windy Lake, James was certain he'd be attacked or arrested on sight the moment he set foot in the royal capital. He really, *really* wanted to have something of value to use as leverage for his safety when that happened, and vital military intelligence was as good as it got.

"There's also this stuff," he went on, pointing at the third stack he'd made of ancient-looking papers. "Those are written in old elven, as in the Unbounded Language. I'm not educated enough to read what they say, but someone in Bastion is. These papers definitely weren't here in the game, because you can read everything on the lich's desk, and I've never seen a mention of them on the wiki. That means they're new information that no one, not even players, knows about. I'm betting that's important."

"Fine, fine," Arbati said, tail lashing in irritation. "Just tell me when we can *leave*."

James was about to say it wouldn't be long when he opened the last drawer and spotted a sealed scroll covered in silver-inked runes.

"Bonus!" he cried, holding it up with a grin.

"Is that the last one?" Arbati asked hopefully.

"Better," James said, tucking the scroll carefully into his bag. "It's a portal scroll to Bastion!"

The warrior blinked. "A what?"

"A transportation spell," James clarified. "When you break the seal, the scroll will open a portal that can take up to fifty people to the Room of Arrivals on the east side of Bastion. They're *super* expensive to make, which makes them hella rare."

Arbati shot up from his chair. "Into the center of the royal city? As in past the walls and the guards?" When James nodded, the warrior's eyes narrowed. "Why did the lich have this?"

"To invade with, I'd wager," James said grimly. "I keep telling you, everything going on out here in the questing zones was part of the larger plot. This lich was just one cog in a multistage effort to isolate, infiltrate, and eventually invade the capital city of Bastion. According to his papers, and his questline, the lich of Red Canyon was supposed to corrupt the gnolls, use them to conquer Windy Lake, then turn all of the important characters—including you—into boss-level undead that he would then send straight into the heart of the city using this scroll. And he's not the only one. Every zone in the game has got some undead baddie planning a different version of the same thing. It's all set up for the Invasion of Bastion plotline that was supposed to be the culmination of the Once King's expansion, but—"

"Then why are we sitting around here?" Arbati cried. "We're on the brink of war! The undead could be ready to invade Bastion as we speak!"

"I know. That's what I've been trying to tell you," James said. "But if it makes you feel better, we've ended the threat here in the savanna. With the lich gone, his minions are mindless and easily killed, but his spies in the city won't know they've been found out for a while yet." He picked up his stack of letters. "If we move fast, we can get to Bastion and give this information to the king in time to shut this whole thing down. Meanwhile, I have a plan to help you and the rest of the clans strengthen the savanna against what's coming."

The head warrior scowled. "What plan is that?"

"One that's already in motion," James said with a grin, carefully placing the letters—and the lich's mysterious ancient elven writings—into his bag as he walked over to touch the teleportation crystal. "Come on. Let's go talk to Thunder Paw."

There was a bright flash and a moment of disorientation, then James stumbled as his feet touched down in the open ravine at the bottom of the Red Canyon. His eyes were still adjusting to the bright morning light when Arbati arrived with a flash of his own and started immediately up the switchback trail to the canyon's rim.

The gnoll village was already looking a lot better when James and Arbati made it to the top. Under Thunder Paw's direction, the Grand Pack was quickly sweeping away all vestiges of undead rule. Orderly patrols and guards were everywhere, and despite being a famous former chief, James was challenged at every checkpoint he passed. Eventually, they found Thunder Paw and his newly appointed chiefs holding a council in the village's largest building, a tall, open-fronted lodge on top of a stony hill that overlooked the entire city.

James and Arbati were quickly whisked aside to meet with Thunder Paw in private. They didn't have to wait long before the old Naturalist shuffled in along with his grandson.

The gnoll pup ran over to give James a hug and a high-pitched yip of thanks, making him struggle not to melt on the spot. The kid had all the cuteness of a puppy *and* a happy child rolled into one floppy-eared, big-eyed package. It was a real fight not to grab him and say, "*Who's a good boy?*" but James restrained himself, though nothing could stop him from pointing at Arbati as he leaned down, whispering in the pup's ear, "He helped you, too."

The child dove at Arbati with a yip. The warrior went stone-still when the child hugged him. So did Thunder Paw. But the gnoll pup was completely oblivious to the adults' apprehension. He just kept wagging his little tail and yipping happily until, at last, Arbati stiffly leaned down to hug him back.

James wiped the smile off his face just in time as Arbati shot him a death glare. Thunder Paw coughed uncomfortably and escorted his grandson out of the room, handing the pup off to someone outside. "You had a request of Me, James?" the one-eyed gnoll asked when he came back, his collar translating the barks and growls into curious words.

"Yes," James said, clutching his precious sackful of the lich's papers. "I have a plan if you will follow me this morning."

That earned him a tilted head from Thunder Paw. James knew his phrasing was awkward, but he prayed the savvy old gnoll would hear the hidden message and roll with it.

"Our gratitude for you is deep," the chieftain said at last. "Tell us what you need. If it is within our power, we will help."

Thunder Paw said this with heavy formality, and James nodded gratefully. That had gone as well as he could hope. Now it was time to play his card. It wasn't going to be a popular one, but it was the best shot he had, so James laid it out.

"I want you to send a peace delegation to Windy Lake to negotiate an alliance with the jubatus."

Sure enough, Thunder Paw's eye narrowed, but it was Arbati who exploded to his feet. "This is your plan?" he cried angrily. "Ally our clans with scavengers? With *thieves*? We would never agree to peace with the likes of them, not even if they begged us!"

"Arbati..." James said tiredly.

"*No!*" the warrior snapped. "The gnolls took our ancestral lands! They've raided my people's herds and homes for two centuries! They even sold out to the undead for the power to try to take the savanna from us!"

That was all in the game's lore, so James wasn't surprised by any of it, but it also wasn't the whole story. "And I'm sure Thunder Paw can recite an equally long list of thefts, murders, and attacks that the clans of Windy Lake have committed against his people," he said calmly. "Even I know about the Thorn Ravine Massacre, and I'm not even a

342

real jubatus."

He looked over at Thunder Paw, who nodded in agreement, but otherwise the gray-furred gnoll didn't interfere. He just watched Arbati carefully, which James took as a wise move and a good sign.

"So what?" Arbati cried angrily. "Everything we've done to the gnolls has been in retaliation for crimes *they* committed! We will not rest until we have driven them from our savanna!"

"Then why are they still here?" James asked, pointing out the window at the city below. "This village is bigger than Windy Lake. The Nightmare was only for eighty years, but you claim the gnolls have been a problem for centuries. If you're the true rulers of the savanna, why didn't the pre-Nightmare generation of jubatus get rid of the gnolls? Or the generation before that?"

"Because they are cowardly and they breed fast," Arbati spat. "And their hit-and-run tactics make them hard to pin down for a real fight."

"They have a fortified *town!*" James yelled. "It's not a secret camp that moves around! *We* found this place in less than a day!"

"And when I return to Windy Lake, I will gather our warriors and destroy it!" Arbati cried. "We will have peace that way!"

James looked at Thunder Paw out of the corner of his eye. Thankfully, the Naturalist was still sitting calmly, but he wasn't watching Arbati anymore. His one eye was locked on James, who took a deep breath.

"You can't," he said, turning his attention back to Arbati. "Your ancestors couldn't exterminate the gnolls, and you can't do it, either. That's why there's an entire city here despite your campaign against them. Because no matter what you do, no matter how they got here, the gnolls are part of the savanna now, and you can't force them out."

Arbati was red-faced when James finished, his hackles standing straight up. For a second, James was worried he'd just signed himself up for another fight, but then Arbati crossed his arms stubbornly over his chest.

"Say what you will," he growled. "But I'm still the head warrior of the Four Clans, and I say we will never shake hands with them. Not while they have what is ours."

"That's a choice you can make," James said. "But it's not the *only* choice. The way I see it, there are two paths before you. You can keep wasting lives and resources, fighting the gnolls as your ancestors did.

Or." James paused for dramatic emphasis. "You can take this once-in-several-lifetimes chance to try something different."

"And you've just shown how little you understand," Arbati snapped. "We might have worked with the gnolls to win a victory over the undead today, but nothing has actually changed between our two peoples."

"That's where I disagree," James said. "There *is* something different, something that has never been before in the history of the savanna."

"What?" Arbati demanded with a contemptuous snort. "*You?*"

"No," James said, nodding at the still-silent gnoll sitting beside him. "Thunder Paw."

Arbati looked confused, and James pointed at the void-black choker that was still locked around the old gnoll's throat. "You have the only gnoll *ever* who has the physical ability to speak the Language of Wind and Grass. Your two peoples have a long history of bad blood to be sure, but you've also never had the ability to reconcile your differences because, before now, you could never *talk*. Now, though, you have something none of your ancestors had—a gnoll who can not only speak your language, but is willing to negotiate. I doubt we could arrange for more collars from the undead or find gnolls willing to wear them even if we could, so this is probably the first and last time a situation like this will *ever* occur, and you've never needed it more."

He held up his bag full of stolen letters. "This world—this *part* of the world specifically, since the savanna is only three days' ride south of Bastion—is about to fall into chaos and war like no one has ever seen. Do you want the enemy to find the savanna divided and ripe for conquest? How much will all of that ancestral land matter when you're undead and the grasslands are trampled under the Once King's armies?"

"It will not come to that!" Arbati hissed.

"Tell that to Gore Maul!" James yelled, remembering the look of ultimate regret he'd seen when he'd executed the undead gnoll chieftain. "You've got a chance at everything here, Arbati! An end to two hundred years of pointless violence and a chance to survive the war that's coming. *Or*, you could keep doing what's never worked and look up from fighting the gnolls just in time to watch everything you love burn. That's not even a choice in my book, so why aren't you considering it?"

"*Because I hate them and I want them gone!*" the warrior yelled, his

344

eyes flashing with animosity that had nothing to do with logic, strategy, or good decisions. This was about hate, hurt, and anger, and those, James realized suddenly, required a different angle.

"You fought alongside them last night," he said, switching tactics. "Do you still want to kill them all?"

"Yes," Arbati said without hesitation. "They killed my cousins before the Nightmare. I wish they'd all died to the undead last night!"

"What about Thunder Paw's grandson?" James pressed. "If you want to kill them all, are you going to slay the children, too? Did we save that pup from the ghostfire just so he could be murdered by you?"

Arbati's mouth opened then closed again, and James turned to Thunder Paw. "How old is your grandson?"

"He is six years old," Thunder Paw replied quietly.

James nodded and turned back to Arbati. "There you go. Are you going to kill a six-year-old boy? It won't be hard. I think your sword is bigger than he is. How about you just rip his throat out with your claws?"

"Of course not," Arbati said, recoiling. "I'm not going to butcher a child!"

"But his parent and caretakers are okay? You're willing to kill Thunder Paw and leave that pup an orphan, alone and uncared for?" He shook his head. "That's a pretty sick thing to do."

Arbati's ears went back. "That's not what I—"

"Do you hate Thunder Paw enough to kill him?" James kept on, merciless. "He's right here, the Chief of Chiefs, no less. There nothing stopping you from doing it."

As he said this, James would have killed for a mirror or a shiny surface, anything he could have used to shoot Thunder Paw a wink. He was uncomfortably aware of just how much blind trust he was demanding from a person he'd only met last night, but he didn't dare take his eyes off Arbati.

"You twist with words, James," Arbati growled. "There's nothing wrong with killing thieves and murderers!"

"Okay, so you want redress, then," James said, pointing back at Thunder Paw. "He's the gnoll leader, so why don't you challenge him right now for things his ancestors did to yours? He's only an old, one-eyed caster who's half your size and twenty levels lower than you. Heck, after last night's battle, he's even *out of mana*. That's your favorite kind of opponent, right?"

Arbati's face went so red it showed under his fur, and James thought for sure that he was about to get punched through the wall. He shifted his weight to the balls of his feet, just in case, but no punch came. Instead, Arbati dropped his head. "I am done with dishonorable fights. Damn you."

"So you won't kill Thunder Paw?"

Arbati sighed. "No."

"What about his grandson?"

"Of course not."

James crossed his arms over his chest. "What are you going to do, then? It seems your plan to 'kill everyone' suddenly has a lot of caveats."

"Just because I won't kill children and the elderly doesn't mean I've given up!" Arbati yelled at him. "There are many here who are guilty of crimes against my people!"

"Which ones?" James asked, pointing out the window at the village, which was still cleaning up the death and destruction the lich's rule had left behind. "That soldier over there, crying over his dead brother? Or maybe the old woman looking for her lost mate among the dead? How about the kids who had to put down their own undead fathers last night? Which of them will you kill?"

"We take names!" Arbati snapped. "Raiders, rustlers, and the like!"

"Is that so?" James said, crossing his arms over his chest. "Then name them, because so far, all I'm hearing is 'Kill these gnolls. Don't kill those gnolls.' Were you just playing at the idea of 'ending the gnoll menace on the plains,' then?"

It felt so *good* to throw Arbati's words back at him, but as much as James wanted to enjoy his victory, this was too important. "What will you do?" he pressed. "Whom will you kill?"

"*I don't know!*" Arbati roared, stabbing his claws down at the village outside. "They stole our land! If we don't fight them for it, we give it up forever!"

"But if you *do* fight them, then we're right back to square one where everyone dies again," James said. "If you war amongst yourselves while the undead invade Bastion, the Once King will win. His forces will arrive to find a weak and divided zone that's easy to conquer, which is *exactly* what the lich was sent here to do. Are you going to do the undead's work for them, or do you want to save your home?"

Arbati was growling deep in his throat when James finished, then the warrior turned and smashed his fist into a small table so hard, the wood snapped in half. "It's not fair!" he cried. "Why should we have to give up what's ours just because there's a new enemy?"

"What if they didn't steal anything?" James asked.

"They did!" Arbati snapped.

"How do you know? Were you there?"

The warrior bared his teeth. "Of course not. It was two hundred years ago!"

"It was," James said calmly. "But do you know how or why the gnolls came to the savanna in the first place?"

"No," he snapped. "And it doesn't matter!"

"I think it does," James said, turning to Thunder Paw. "Why did your people come to this place all those years ago?"

The old Naturalist jumped at the sudden question. "The songs and weavings say that we used to live in a place much like this. Then an evil took hold. It corrupted our lands, and our ancestors were forced to flee. The Grand Pack wandered for many, many years before finding the savanna, the only land we were suited to live in."

James already knew as much from completing the gnoll questline in the next zone over, but he'd wanted to hear it in Thunder Paw's own words, and he nodded his thanks before turning back to Arbati. "Which truth is better, Arbati? That evil, no-good gnolls stole your land, or that Windy Lake took in desperate refugees and gained Bastion a useful ally?"

"That's not what happened!" Arbati cried.

"But it could be," James said patiently, moving closer. "The jubatus have fought the gnolls for a long time, but all your ancestors who had firsthand claims against the gnolls are dead. You don't have to answer to them, but you will have to answer to your children. Will they say that you were wise, the voice of reason who united the savanna and built a safe, strong future? Or will you have to explain how a two-hundred-year-old grudge was so important that you passed over your *one-time-ever* chance at peace so you could keep fighting gnolls while the Once King turned this world into a grave?"

James stopped there, waiting for his answer, but for once, Arbati had none. The whole room fell silent as the warrior wrestled with himself. Finally, in a small voice, he whispered, "But they have to pay."

"They have paid," James said quietly, grabbing the jubatus's shoulder. "Look."

Arbati dug in his heels, but James made him walk forward, dragging him out onto the lodge's open balcony. He snared a bit of wind magic as he went. Not enough to cast, but enough to shift the breeze so that the stench of burning flesh and fur reached Arbati's nose.

At the center of what had been the spike pit for executing players, the gnolls had built a twenty-foot-tall pile of furry corpses. They'd dug out the remaining spikes as well, using the logs to build a pyre around the dead. The blaze was just getting started, but already a black plume of smoke was rising to the sky. Around it, gathered along the edge of the drained lake, were hundreds of grieving gnolls. Their whining rose like sad, atonal music, drowning out even the ceaseless wind of the grasslands. Occasionally, one of the crowd would step up and throw a memento onto the fire, whining and crying with grief that needed no translation.

"What could you do to them that would be worse than this?" James asked quietly, his eyes locked on the pillar of smoke. "How much more death could you want?"

Arbati raised his hands to his face. "But..." His strong voice cracked. "But why does it have to be *me*? You did my quests. The gnolls captured me. They *tortured* me. Why do *I* have to be the one who forgives them?"

"Because you're the one who's here now," James said. "This is when it has to happen, and you're the only one who has the power to do it. You're the head warrior. You can give Thunder Paw safe passage into Windy Lake to start the peace talks. No one else could make that happen. No one else could be trusted. But everyone knows how much cause you have to hate the gnolls. If *you* lead them to Windy Lake, the other jubatus will listen. I can't do that. Only you, but you have to choose." He smiled. "What songs will they sing of you, Arbati? Will you be just another head warrior put there by his father? Or will you be the hero who ended ten generations of bloodshed and brought peace to the savanna?"

With that, James returned to his seat by Thunder Paw, leaving Arbati staring at the black smoke from the pyre. The silence stretched on for several nerve-wracking minutes before Arbati suddenly lashed out, grabbing the wooden railing so hard it splintered. Cursing silently, James shot to his feet. He'd *really* hoped that would work. But just as he was moving into position to tackle Arbati before he could do anything regrettable, the tall warrior turned around.

"Chief Thunder Paw," Arbati said, speaking each word as if it were being carved out of him with a knife. "As the Leader of War for the Four Clans, I offer the Grand Pack a temporary truce and safe passage to Windy Lake so that we may…talk."

Thunder Paw nodded gratefully, the crystals in his fur chiming softly. "As the Chief of Chiefs of the Grand Pack, Me accept your offer and will honor your truce." Then the gnoll gave Arbati a tough look. "Me not agree to any unfair treaties, though. Me only offering hand, not whole arm."

Arbati nodded, and James let out a huge breath. They all did. When it was over, Arbati turned to James. "You got what you wanted," he said, his voice tired. "But remember, I don't actually handle treaties. That's up to Gray Fang and the clan heads. All I can do is bring them face-to-face."

"I couldn't ask for anything more," James said, trying his best not to smile like a maniac and ruin the somber and serious air of what was happening. "Thank you, Arbati."

The warrior waved his words away and sat back down on his pillow, out of the way of the reeking, smoky breeze drifting in from the pyre.

CHAPTER *17*

Tina

"**K**eep pulling!"

The morning was crawling by, but still nothing had changed. The Knights and Berserkers heaved with all their might, skin flushed and muscles bulging as they fought to bring the walls down. Killbox had even tried moving all twelve Strength classes to one side to double their pulling power, but the damn stones still weren't budging, and Tina was rapidly running out of tricks.

At least Frank was back on his game. Once he'd recovered from being knocked out, he'd hit every switch perfectly, taking his share of Grel'Darm's Howling Strikes without so much as a wince. Unfortunately, there were still only two of them, and Grel'Darm had found a new formidable weapon in the iron bar that had once held the gates closed. It was shorter and lighter than the club he'd broken on Tina's shield, letting the giant hit faster than ever before. Faster than their abilities could keep up with.

"*Frank!*" Tina yelled as she deflected another crushing blow off her shield. "Change of plans! Neither of us has the abilities for this many hits, so we're gonna try to split the damage. My Steady Ground is up now, so I'll go first. You hit yours the moment you're off cooldown."

Frank nodded and stepped in beside her. When he got close, though, Tina realized he was shaking.

"Stay with me, man," she said gently, using her shield to bump his back to the correct angle. "We can do this."

"I know," Frank said, his voice cracking, "It's just…I thought I'd come to terms with dyin' years ago, but I just can't stop shaking."

"It's okay," Tina said, bracing her feet as Grel raised his iron bar again. "Just remember: you're a superhero covered in magical equipment that was forged by ancient gods. Compared to you, this guy ain't shit."

Frank cracked a nervous smile behind his helmet. "I don't feel particularly super right now."

Neither did Tina, but she knew better than to let that show. "We got this," she said firmly, preparing her shield for the iron bar that was now high in the gray sky above their heads. "Just follow my lead."

With a ghostly howl, the colossal skeleton hammered his iron beam down on top of them. They braced their shields on their shoulders and locked the edges together, then Tina grabbed Frank around the waist with one arm and leaned into him as hard as she could.

"Steady Ground!"

The earth beneath them hardened into a column of bedrock as the iron bar slammed down with the sound of a plane crash. The impact vibrated down through shields, armor, bones, and finally into the ground itself. Both Tina and Frank were driven to their knees before it was over, but the hit didn't make them bleed this time, and Tina's spirits lifted. It had worked!

Then Grel'Darm tried to kick them.

"Fuck!" Tina yelled, yanking her shield down. "Big Boot! Angle shields!"

Frank followed her lead, slamming his shield into the ground next to hers at the exact right angle seconds before Grel's boot hit the combined wall of their bulwarks and slid up, perfectly deflected. Grel howled with rage and brought his iron bar up again, but he'd moved so fast that Tina's Steady Ground was still going, and she yanked Frank back into position beside her. They threw up their shields to take the hit again.

The blow hammered them both into the stone again, only this time, it didn't stop. Grel just hauled back and kept hitting, slamming the iron length down on them again and again like he was trying to jackhammer them into the pavement. Frank used his Steady Ground the moment Tina's ran out, but the attack showed no sign of slowing. The giant skeleton just kept going, beating them farther and farther down into the pulverized stone of the fortress's entrance.

As Frank's defense ticked down, Tina focused all her strength on her shield and prayed for the sound of a catapult. This kind of beating was *not* part of her plan. If things didn't turn around soon, something was going to break. Tina was terrified that it would be her, but reality turned out to be much, much worse.

Between her team-up with Frank and Grel'Darm's new super-speed mode, Tina hadn't been able to keep an eye on the casters, but she still knew the moment they ran out. All of a sudden, the constant stream of fireballs and lightning that had been shooting past her to blast the lesser undead pouring through the broken doors behind Grel began to dry up. The arrows were still flying, but eight Rangers weren't enough to hold the door by themselves, and as the barrage of magic fell silent, the rattle of bones in armor grew louder.

"Shit," Tina whispered, peeking around her shield. "Shit, shit, *shit—*"

She cut off with a gasp as an enormous undead boar jumped through the shattered door and ran between Grel'Darm's feet, straight at them. As braced as they were for the boss's overhead assault, neither tank was in position for an attack from that direction, which meant Frank's front was wide open when the boar plowed into him, its giant tusks stabbing right under his raised shield and into the heavy armor of his chest.

Smashed by the boar's shoulder, Tina was flung to the ground. Fortunately, Frank's armor was good enough that the boar's tusks shattered instead of sinking into his chest, but the blow still threw him into the caster camp, forcing the Rangers to scatter as he crashed into the fortress's bolted inner door. The moment they got clear, they turned and started pouring arrows into the boar as it charged after Frank. The undead beast went down with a scream, but Frank was still stuck in the door, leaving Tina alone with Grel.

"Pry him out!" Tina screamed, scrambling to her feet. She'd barely made it up before Grel'Darm slammed his massive iron bar down again. This time, though, she had nothing left to take it.

"*External!*" she yelled as the black plank of iron filled her vision. "External on me *now!*"

Both a circle of thorns and a sanctuary appeared around her, and the attack bounced off. Cursing the waste of two big abilities, Tina got her shield up to prepare for the next attack only to discover it was already coming, and she *still* had nothing to stop it.

"External!" she yelled again.

Another golden shield appeared above her, blocking the attack, but Grel was back to his insane rhythm, slamming the bar into her so fast, it sang in the air.

"External!" Tina cried as he hammered her. "Keep it up!"

Again and again, the raid found new ways to stay her execution, but Tina knew it couldn't last. Only a handful of classes had big-damage shutdowns, and most of those had an hour reset. One of these attacks, she was going to call for an external, and there wasn't going to be one, but there was nothing she could do. Now that the damage casters were dry, Frank was stuck in the back, keeping the undead off their healers. The moment they'd gotten him out of the door, he'd had his hands full, grappling with another giant boar *and* a pack of zombies. If the casting camp folded, they were all done for, so Tina sucked it up and set herself to facing Grel alone, keeping her shield high as he slammed her down with blow after blow.

"Exter—" she started to yell then cut off as her heart skipped a beat. This was it. How she knew, Tina wasn't sure. Maybe it was instinct from nearly a decade of tanking, but she *knew* in her bones that there wouldn't be anything coming to save her this time.

Sure enough, no golden feathers or ironwood vines blossomed in the air above her head. The healers were out of big abilities. She was on her own.

"*Earthen Fortitude!*" she yelled, bracing her shield. "*Iron Wall! Steady Ground!*"

The time being supported by Frank and the rest of the raid had given her best defenses time to reset. She'd been hoping to limp through this using only one at a time, but Grel was howling again, which meant this was going to be a big hit. There was no way she was getting through that alive, *alone*, without her best shit. If she died, everything was over, so Tina blew her full stack again as the bar crashed down.

Tina had taken a lot of hits from Grel at this point, but the force of his blows never ceased to amaze her. He crashed his bar into her shield with the force of a rocket. Metal screamed as the iron length bent across her shield, smashing her to the ground. It hit so hard, her vision went dark for a moment. Then the weight lifted, and Tina staggered up from her knees.

She was shaking her head to clear it when the bus that was Grel's boot suddenly filled her vision. There was no time to react, but Iron Wall—the ability that guaranteed her a perfect defense no matter how badly she messed up—must have still had a second left, because her body moved on its own, slamming her shield down at the perfect angle to send the fight-ending kick up and over her head.

For a glorious moment, Tina felt the rush of victory. Then the supernatural confidence of Iron Wall faded, leaving her heavy, sore, and alone. Above her, Grel regained his balance and lifted his bent weapon high over his head. With nothing left, Tina raised her shield to meet him, hoping more than believing she had enough health left to soak up an attack with no defenses. But then just when the warped bar was all she could see, Frank appeared at her side, locking his shield with hers as the massive iron bar crashed into them.

"Iron Wall!"

Gasping, Tina clung to Frank as his shield deflected blow after blow. Iron Wall's perfect defense made up for his lack of experience, but beneath the perfect movements, Tina could feel him shaking inside his armor. Or maybe it was her. Either way, it was clear neither of them could take much more of this.

"We need to kill this guy!" Frank yelled desperately. "The Rangers are ready. They've killed off all the undead on the back lines. Zen said she can—"

"No!" Tina yelled. "We stick to the plan!"

"But the plan isn't working!" Frank cried, his voice pleading. "We gotta kill him *now!"*

"I know, but we *can't,"* Tina said angrily. "Grel has more HP than any boss in the Dead Mountain except the Once King himself! Even when our casters were full, we never had the damage to burn him down before he killed us because we were *never a full raid!* This group would have struggled to kill him back when this was a game, and that was before we lost two people. That's why I came up with the plan in the first place! If we bury him in rocks, it won't matter how long it takes us to kill him, but if we try to go all out now, the undead will flood us under, and *everyone* will die!"

"Looks like we're going to die anyway," Frank said, but he kept his shield up, looking to her for their next move. Tina wasn't sure if she was impressed or terrified by the amount of trust he was giving her, but she was determined not to fail him.

"We can tank this," she said, locking her shield more tightly with his. "Just stay together!"

Above their defense, Grel'Darm was swinging harder than ever, his ghostfire eyes flaring with rage. But while the boss was doing fine, his improvised weapon was looking sadder with every hit. Now that Tina's shield had bent it out of shape, the metal beam was warping all over, growing hot and pliable until it was moving more like a whip than a sword. As he kept hammering anyway, Tina realized with a start that Grel'Darm wasn't smart enough to go for a better weapon, which was probably why they weren't dead. Frank's Steady Ground had faded ages ago, but though Grel was as strong as ever, his weapon was no longer transferring that strength into his targets. Attack after attack, the squishy iron was the only thing saving them from obliteration.

It was still a pounding, though. They didn't need externals or cooldowns, but every hit still took a chunk out of their health. The constant clang of metal left Tina deaf and numb, and her shield arm felt like it was going to fall off. They *had* to get this plan to the next phase, but the catapults outside were still silent. Tina clenched her teeth as she took another hit. Where the hell was SilentBlayde?

A few hits later, Tina began to fear it didn't matter. She didn't dare take her eyes off Grel, but every time the clanging cleared from her ears, she could hear the rattle of bones all around them. With the Sorcerers out of mana, the Rangers had been keeping the undead back by themselves, but they were starting to fall seriously behind. When Tina risked a look over her shoulder, she was horrified to see the undead were behind them now, as well, only a few feet from the caster line. The only thing that kept them off the tanks was the fact that Grel's constant pounding was crushing them as well, pulverizing any skeleton or zombie that got too close.

That wouldn't save the casters, though. Some undead were too stupid to get out of Grel's way, but plenty more were running around him, building up on the line the Rangers were holding with their frantic arrows. Frank could help clear them out, but then Tina would be alone and flattened. If they didn't do something, though, the whole fight would fold.

The bitter bile of defeat began to rise in her throat. On either side of the walls, Team Hulk was red-faced and flagging. Some of them weren't even pulling anymore, turning instead to help keep the undead off the others. There was no sign of SilentBlayde or the other Assassins. For all Tina knew, she'd sent them to their deaths by ordering them to take catapults in the middle of an enemy army. She might have just gotten them *all* killed, because the walls weren't coming down, and without external help, Grel was too much for them.

The ugly truth sank into her stomach like a rock. It was over.

They'd lost. *She'd* lost, and if she wanted to save anyone, she was going to have to call the retreat. If she gave the order now, there was a good chance the healers and other casters would escape. The Rangers were fast, so they'd be fine, and if she did her area taunt to get all of the zombies on her, she might able to buy enough time for Team Hulk to get out as well before she went down.

It was a long shot and a deadly one for her, but it was the least Tina could do after miscalculating so epically. But just as she raised her voice to give the command to fall back, she was drowned out by a huge, fiery explosion as something crashed into the gooseneck's left-hand wall from the outside.

The resulting force wave was enough to make even Grel'Darm stagger. As he listed sideways, his blow went awry, the metal bar sticking deep into the stone on Tina's right. He was yanking it back out when a second, equally huge explosion hit the stone box's right wall, opening a sprawling crack right down the middle. As she watched the stone crumble, Tina felt her strength kick back in. The Assassins had done it! They'd captured the undead's catapults and fired them at the walls! They weren't defeated after all!

She shot to her feet and turned to Frank in a rush, sheathing her sword so she could yank him up. "Go help Team Hulk!" she yelled in his face. "They're out of gas!"

He stared at her like she was crazy. "But you'll be alone with—"

"*Go!*" she shouted, shoving him toward the cracked walls before turning back to Grel. "This is *it*, people!" she bellowed, raising her voice until it bounced off the crumbling stone. "Healers, snares on Grel'Darm *now!* Do not let him move!"

A flurry of magic went off behind her, and Grel was suddenly draped in golden chains and stone hands as six snares went off at the same time. The giant looked down in confusion, but no matter how hard he pulled, his feet stayed rooted.

The moment Tina was sure he wasn't going anywhere, she ran to help Killbox. The snares would only last on a boss that big for six seconds at most, but if this worked, six seconds would be enough. Bashing undead out of the way with her shield, she grabbed the end of the iron chain. "Now, Team Hulk!" she screamed. "Bring these walls *down!*"

"*You heard her!*" Killbox shouted, bracing his trunk-like legs. "*Pull!*"

Everyone heaved together, pulling on the chains until their eyes bulged and their veins practically burst. Tina leaned back with all her weight, putting every bit of the strength she had left into her arms as she tugged on the giant chain. For a terrible second, nothing happened, but then the crack on the left slipped sideways with a *crunch*, and the whole wall began to fall inward. The right wall gave a second later, and suddenly the air was full of dust as the gooseneck's stone walls—and the towers attached to them—began to cave in. Tina and the rest of Team Hulk jumped out of the way as the massive chains they'd been pulling ripped free. Giant gears and pulleys rained down as the counterweights tore through the side of the falling towers, the giant iron blocks hurtling down straight toward Grel'Darm's head.

"*Run!*" Tina screamed as the shadow of the falling wall closed over their heads.

There was no need for an order. Everyone was already sprinting as fast as they could toward the casters as the artificial canyon that was the gate yard collapsed in on itself, burying the undead—and the boss who was still trapped in the middle—under a mountain of man-sized white granite blocks.

As the walls fell, Tina finally saw why they hadn't been able to topple them themselves. The sidewalls had *looked* small in comparison to the rest of the fort, but the support stones inside were the size of cars. Now that they were down, though, the miscalculation actually worked in her favor, because the same weight that had defeated Team Hulk was crashing into Grel'Darm.

The collapsing wave of stone knocked the giant from side to side like a pinball. He reached out a bony arm to grab what remained of the front gatehouse in a last-ditch attempt to keep his balance, but with the towers on either side gone, that was collapsing as well, sending the monster flat on his face as the stone landed on top of him.

The undead army that had swarmed in was crushed out of existence as well, the zombies, skeletons, and undead boars collapsing like paper dolls under the tremendous weight of the rock. It would have crushed the raiders as well if Tina hadn't ordered everyone to stand inside the lee of the fort's inner gate.

Pressed against each other with their backs to the heavy wooden doors, they were protected by the main fort's wall as everything else came down. Tina and the other heavily armored knights made a wall in front of the rest of the raid to protect them from any stray stones, but it almost wasn't necessary. Once they'd started to fall, the walls landed exactly where Tina had wanted, leaving the raid staring at a forty-foot-tall mound of rubble with Grel'Darm's arms and legs just barely poking out from the edges.

For a heartbeat, everyone just stood there, staring in wonder, then the entire raid broke into cheers, hugging each other and jumping up and down. Tina would have jumped, too, if her armor hadn't felt so heavy, but it wasn't time to celebrate yet. Grel was already stirring beneath the stone, reminding her that the actual *fight* part of the fight was just beginning.

"All right, everybody!" she said, holding up her sword. "Time for phase two! Let's kill this bastard!"

The raid cheered even louder, swarming over the mountain of rubble to start hacking, shooting, and beating on the giant trapped below. Even the spell casters who were out of mana whacked at him with their staffs, pounding on whatever part of Grel'Darm they could find under the stone. The giant shook and roared, but it didn't do a damn thing. Grel'Darm the Colossal had finally met a force even more colossal than him. Trapped and crushed flat, he could do nothing but struggle futilely as three dozen Roughnecks chipped him to death.

Tina left the work to the others and climbed up on top of the pile to look around. While they'd been fighting in here, the rest of the undead army had spread out to attack the rest of the fortress. Dismantled zombies and skeletons were piled high at the base of the walls, and Garrond himself was running back and forth along the battlements, slaying huge groups of undead single-handedly with his blazing golden sword.

But while he made quite the impressive one-man army, the rest of the Order was in *way* over its head. The soldiers on the battlements were barely keeping the undead off the walls, and the archers' fingers were bleeding through their gloves because of how many times they'd pulled back their bowstrings.

It was a staggering sight but also wasn't Tina's problem. *She* was worried about what would come to attack them next. But her raid must have killed more undead than she'd realized, because though the walls were still swarmed, the field in front of the fortress was almost empty.

Satisfied that no more threats would be coming from that

direction in the immediate future, her next thought was to look for SB. She didn't have much hope—trying to spot an Assassin who walked through shadows was a pretty foolish thing to do—but she looked just the same. But though she spotted the catapults, she didn't see any sign of her friend, and she couldn't go looking for him until Grel was dead. Telling herself he'd be back soon enough, she whirled around and stomped back down the mountain of rock to stab her sword angrily into the top of Grel's skull, the only bit of the boss she could see.

The exhausted raid pounded on their trapped prey for a comically long time. The sun was never visible in the Deadlands, so Tina couldn't say how long exactly, but seeing how much abuse Grel'Darm could soak up made her feel *very* validated for insisting they stick to the plan. There was no way they could have done this much damage while actively defending against the rest of the undead at the same time.

Finally, their endless hacking was interrupted by a sudden white glow. Heat began to creep up through Tina's boots next, then actual tongues of ghostfire appeared, the white flames blazing up through the stones brighter and hotter by the second.

"Get ready!" Tina cried, looking around to make sure no one had any unhealed damage except her and Frank. "Here comes the suck!"

The raid replied with a chorus of yelled-out personal defensive abilities. Wards, personal shields, and magical barriers lit up the dreary afternoon as everyone braced for Chain Fire. Seconds later, two pillars of white-blue fire blasted out of Grel's cavernous eye sockets and through the rock like geysers to jump into the raid. The flames hit NekoBaby and Zen first, making them both scream in pain as they lit up like torches. A heartbeat later, the ghostfire jumped to four more people, then eight, on and on until the whole raid was burning.

It leaped to Tina last. The white flames covered her stone skin beneath her armor in an instant, bringing both horrible pain and sudden hatred of all life. For a few seconds, she was consumed by the overwhelming urge to murder everything. The world was a sin that needed to perish, and she would be the one who swung the righteous sword. She was already turning to strike the player next to her when the flame fluttered out, and Tina sagged to her knees, closing her eyes as the urge to murder the living faded, leaving little else behind.

Hand shaking, she reached up to rub the burns that covered her stony face. That had been close. *Too* close, and not just because of the new murder impulse. That was a side of Chain Fire she'd never seen in the game, but as scary as it had been to suddenly hate everything, her death was what Tina feared the most. She couldn't see her hit points anymore, but the strange, crumbly stiffness in her body told her she'd pushed it down to the wire. A few more seconds of burning, and the fire would have killed her.

It hadn't, though. She was still alive, and now that they'd made it through the first big hurdle, things would get a lot easier.

"Okay," she said, turning to her gasping, burned raid. "*Now* you can heal."

Cheers went up as the Clerics and Naturalists began casting spells as fast as they could go, lighting up the raid in a fireworks show of green and gold. Tina sighed with relief as the blessed healing magics swept through her. She'd never been healed for this much before, and the experience was utterly euphoric. She felt like she was swimming through golden clouds as her wounds closed and her shield arm grew light again. The cascades of silver blood vanished from her armor, and her vision cleared completely, revealing a world that was alive and full of color. Then suddenly, it was over, the healers cutting off early to save mana for the final Chain Fire.

"All right," Tina said, trying not to shudder at the loss of so much bliss. "That was the halfway mark. Let's burn down the rest of him!"

The renewed raid cheered and returned to bashing and stabbing the pinned Grel'Darm with utmost vigor. Tina got back to work as well, picking a large finger this time to gleefully hack her way through. It was immensely gratifying to finally cut off a piece of the giant she'd had to take such a beating from, and she savored every resounding *thwack*.

"Forty-five seconds, Roxxy!" Anders called out a few minutes later. Tina looked up in confusion, then she remembered that the ichthyian and all the other Intelligence-geared players now had razor-sharp time-tracking and calculation abilities. Anders must have done the math to figure out how long it had taken them to get Grel to fifty percent and used that number to estimate how long it would take to get him to the final twenty-five percent.

"Last chain fire incoming!" she yelled to the raid. "Use 'em if you've got 'em!"

The words were barely out of her mouth when the rubble pile began to heat up again. Grel'Darm bellowed again, shaking the entire rubble pile as his broken eye sockets lit up with the great ghostfire of the Once King. The flames rose through the broken stones and jumped to the closest players, engulfing Frank and one of the Sorcerers in blue-white fire. Everyone around them started calling out whatever was left of their defensive abilities, bracing for the ghostfire as it split again, spreading like a virus through the raid.

Just like the first one, the second Chain Fire ripped through everyone in quick succession. Some people cried, and others howled damnation for the living. Tina was forced to duck as a burning Killbox turned on her, his eyes blazing with the white fire as he swung. Thankfully, he lacked his usual precision, and the ax flew over her head, but it was still terrifying.

He was about to swing again when the golden light from a Cleric's spell washed over him. The Berserker's burning eyes cleared, and he dropped his ax in horror. "Sorry, Roxxy," he said, staggering away from her. "I don't know—"

She cut him off with a grin. "It's all good," she said, scooping his ax off the ground and handing it back to him. "No slacking. We've still got twenty-five percent left to go, so get back to chopping."

He gave her a shaky grin in response and saluted then turned around to bury his ax deep in the exposed bone of Grel'Darm's wrist.

After that, there were no more hurdles. Tina and the raid hacked, kicked, pounded, and stabbed the massive skeleton boss into bony bits. It was tedious, backbreaking work that took much longer than anyone could have expected, but at last, the ghostfire vanished from Grel's pulverized skull, and the shaking stones fell still.

The moment it was over, everyone collapsed into the mound of rubble. Tina thrust her sword into the air, and the raid joined her in a joyous—if ragged—cry of victory. As predicted, Grel had been the army's burning heart. Once he was gone, the undead assault on the rest of the fortress quickly fell into disarray, allowing the Order to finally gain the upper hand. The undead, as was their nature, still fought to the last twitching limb. Without their general, though, the mindless skeletons were little better than dangerous cannon fodder, and the one-skull Order soldiers made short work of them. When it was over, Commander Garrond himself walked out into the battlefield, marking dead soldiers for burial and dealing personally with any remaining troublesome undead monsters.

Tina was right behind him.

She was exhausted, and she still hadn't been healed to full, but SilentBlayde and the other Assassins still hadn't returned. Now that Grel was dead, finding them was Tina's top priority. The rest of the raid was still healing up, though, so she'd left them with orders to get back in fighting form, given Neko a loaf of bread, and told her to get onto her back. Once the Naturalist was safely eating on her shoulder, Tina marched them both out through the blasted front gates to start the search.

The hill leading up to the front of the fortress was a scarred battleground. Tina hadn't even heard them going off in the chaos, but the Order's own catapults and ballistae must have been going nonstop. The ground out here was a pockmarked mess of blasted craters and huge bolts stuck deep in the gray dirt.

The rest of the debris belonged to the undead army. Broken ladders and siege towers lay in heaps all over the field. Pushing the crushed gray wood out of her way, Tina made a beeline for the closest of the undead's catapults. It must have been put together quickly for this assault, because it was lacking the usual decorative skulls and bones, but it was pointed at their position between the gates and surrounded by dead zombies. That gave Tina hope, and she started running toward it, forcing NekoBaby to cling to her shoulders.

As she got closer, she saw that all the zombies had been dismembered, their bodies cut apart by a sharp blade. They were piled everywhere, but the biggest heap was at the back of the catapult by the firing lever. Nothing was moving, though, and Tina's heart began to pound as she grabbed the bodies and started flinging them aside, digging her way down to the firing position underneath. Then halfway to the bottom of the stack, she saw something gleam silver.

It was the tip of a sword poking out the back of a zombie. Scrambling, Tina grabbed the body and tossed it over her shoulder. Then she tossed the one below it, finally clearing the way to see what she feared.

At the very bottom of the pile, a shredded and bloody SilentBlayde was lying with one hand on his sword and the other curled around the catapult's firing lever. She'd already grabbed Neko to demand another Raise Ally spell when his blue eyes cracked open.

"Hey, Roxxy," he wheezed. "Did we get Grel?"

It took everything Tina had not to grab him in a crushing hug. That might have killed him, though, so Tina settled for digging the rest of him out instead. "Yeah, man, we did it, thanks to you. I'm so glad you're alive! Now tell me how you ended up covered in..."

Her voice trailed off when she got to his legs. She'd wondered why SilentBlayde hadn't Shadow Walked his way back after completing his mission. Now she knew. He'd been stapled to the catapult by no fewer than four barbed spears.

"Holy shit, dude."

"It stings a bit," he said weakly. "But I couldn't leave the job undone, could I?"

Considering he'd saved them all with that catapult shot, Tina couldn't argue, but that didn't stop her hands from shaking as she began pulling the spears out. SilentBlayde gasped as the barbed points ripped free, then NekoBaby bathed him in soothing green light, and his eyes grew delirious as the bliss of the healing magic washed through him. Tina took advantage of his altered state to rip out the last and deepest of the remaining spears and caught SB as he collapsed into her arms. More healing poured over him, and the elf shuddered in relief before putting his weight on his legs.

"Wow," SilentBlayde said, giving himself a shake. "That's the *good* stuff. Thanks for the save, guys!"

"That's our line," Tina said, grinning so hard her face hurt. "You Assassins were the heroes today. We'd all be dead if you hadn't landed those shots." She glanced at the fortress on top of the hill, several hundred feet away. "How'd you even hit the wall from this distance?"

SB began to preen. "Turns out Agility makes me deadly accurate as well as superhuman fast."

Tina's eyes grew wide. "You mean like it does for the Rangers? Cooooooooool!" She was about to ask what else he could do when she realized something else was missing. "Wait, where are the others? Surely you didn't fire both of those shots yourself?"

SilentBlayde's expression darkened. "Zero's probably still at the western catapult, but you won't find KuroKawaii." He clenched his fists, looking angrier than Tina had ever seen him. "She bailed on us!"

"She ran?" NekoBaby said, horrified. "In the middle of a fight?"

SB nodded. "We tried to give her the benefit of the doubt, but once it became clear she wasn't coming back, Zero and I had no choice but to split up to save time. I came out of the shadows by myself here and made it work but wound up in that predicament. I don't know what happened to Zero."

"I can't believe she left Zero," NekoBaby said, baring her fangs. "That dirty little *traitor!*"

"Don't worry. She'll get hers," Tina promised, cracking her knuckles. "But we've got more important things to deal with right now." She turned, waving for them to follow. "Come on. Let's go find ZeroDarkness and get back to the fort to collect our ticket out of here."

SB and Neko nodded together and ran after her as Tina strode across the battlefield toward the western catapult. They'd barely made it halfway when ZeroDarkness climbed out of the corpse of the undead boar he'd been hiding inside, waving his bloody arms wildly at Neko for a heal.

■ ■

"You call that a victory?" Commander Garrond snarled. "You did more damage to my fortress than the enemy did!"

Tina laughed haughtily at that. It was an hour after their victory, and she'd come to Garrond's office to negotiate the opening of their portal to Bastion. She'd expected the commander would be a little pissed about the destruction of his gate, but after what she'd just been through with Grel, the four-skull's anger didn't even faze her.

"We just killed the twelfth most dangerous creature in the entire *world*," she reminded him. "Grel'Darm the Colossal is—or *was*—the Once King's greatest siege weapon, and you're bitching about some broken masonry?" She snorted. "It's only because of us that you have a fort left to fix."

Garrond huffed through his mustache. "You've left us defenseless! With the outer gatehouse demolished, we have nothing to prevent—"

"And nothing to attack," Tina snapped. "The enemy is dead. Re-dead, really, but the point is we *won*. The Once King's army is demolished and Grel's a pile of bone meal on your front door. You can't say we didn't do our job, so when are you going to open our portal?"

Garrond gave her a hard stare. Tina met and held it, unblinking. It was a fun trick she'd come up with once she'd discovered that stonekin didn't need to blink half as often as the fleshy races did, and it worked like a charm. After almost a minute, he was forced to drop his eyes and shuffled his papers as he glared at his desk. "I can't give the order until tomorrow."

Tina's glare grew sharper. "I hope you're not trying to play me, asshole, because—"

"You misunderstand," the commander interrupted. "I would *love* to kick you out today, but opening the portal to Bastion takes a great deal of magic, and my entire base is out of mana. You'll just have to wait."

Given that none of Tina's people had been able to open a portal since this thing began, she was very interested in knowing how the Order still could. "Could we help?" she offered, hoping he'd take the bait. "I have a lot of skilled Sorcerers."

"You have *five* sorcerers," Garrond said. "All of whom are exhausted, by the way. It takes a lot more than that to open a Bastion portal from this distance, so as great as you players are, I'm afraid you'll just have to wait."

Tina sighed, disappointed. Clearly, opening portals across the world took a lot more magic now than it had in the game. If it was just a matter of getting enough Sorcerers together, though, that didn't mean they were out of reach, especially once they got to Bastion and she could rally more players. Still, it looked like they were stuck here for at least another day, and if they had to put up with a bunch of glowering Order stiff necks, Tina intended to make the most of it.

"Fine," she said, stabbing an armored finger down on his desk hard enough to dent the wood. "But we're dining on your dime as long as we're here."

"Very well," Garrond said, then he stood up and offered his hand. After a moment's hesitation, Tina took it, watching the commander suspiciously.

"What's this about?"

"Appreciation," Garrond replied, folding his hands behind his back. "For all that I still hate you players, you fought like legends today. I don't like your methods, but I cannot question your courage. Your guild may sleep in one of the empty barracks tonight instead of the courtyard, and if any of your people ever want to join the Order of the Golden Sun, I would welcome them. We need fighters of your caliber out here on the front lines."

It took everything Tina had to keep the smug grin off her face. Her brother, James, always said she was a bad winner, and maybe it was true, because the urge to rub just one "I told you so" in Garrond's face was overpowering. But that wasn't the sort of behavior that would get her new mercenary company a good reference, so she bit her tongue until she came up with something more politic.

"Thank you," she said instead. "You aren't an easy man to please. I hope you'll remember this when you speak of us to others. Roxxy's Roughnecks are always looking for good paying work."

Garrond arched an eyebrow at that. "You've certainly taken to your new role," he said, sitting back down at his desk. "I'll keep it in mind."

Grinning at the implicit compliment, Tina turned and headed downstairs to the courtyard, where the rest of the Roughnecks were waiting.

"All right, folks!" she said as she emerged. "We head for Bastion tomorrow, but tonight we get to sleep in real beds and eat the Order out of house and home!"

Hearty cheers rose up at that. Tina lifted her fist in reply and turned to lead them toward the fortress's meal hall, hoping that maybe she'd get a hot rock to eat this time.

CHAPTER *18*

James

James was riding on a magical wagon, and it was *awesome*.

Since war was an any-day-now proposition, the brand-new gnoll peace delegation had departed for Windy Lake as soon as possible. Given how gnolls usually traveled, James had assumed this meant running. Then Thunder Paw had rolled out a wind caravan, a long train of wagons chained together and decked with sails so they could be blown across the grasslands by wind magic.

The Naturalists of the Red Canyon had a tradition of working big magic together since long before the undead. At Thunder Paw's order, they'd performed a ritual to summon a strong wind from the west. Now, with that endless magical gale at their backs, James was clinging to the railing of the craziest wagon ride of his life, bumping down the old trade road toward Windy Lake at an astonishing, almost terrifying speed.

At his suggestion, the wagons had been loaded with all manner of diplomatic "ammo," including tents for all the gnolls who'd come along, exotic food and drink, musicians, and gifts galore. He wasn't sure if Thunder Paw knew how to use it all, but James felt like he and the new Chief of Chiefs were getting pretty good at backing each other's plans on the fly. Running peace talks was a bit above his pay grade, but James was delighted to finally put his seven years of Political Science classes to use.

Since Arbati had claimed the front wagon for himself, James took the chance to hang out with Thunder Paw in the surprisingly spacious Chieftain's Wagon. With its rugs, sitting cushions, and a heavy canvas canopy, the covered caravan was practically a medieval mobile home. This was great, because it finally gave James a chance to talk with the old Naturalist in a non-life-or-death setting.

He was delighted to discover that Thunder Paw had an incredible understanding of nature magic outside of the game's mechanics. Now that James was no longer strictly limited to his class's abilities, he was eager to geek out about magical theory. They were discussing the finer points of how earth magic grounded lightning magic when James suddenly remembered something that he'd been burning to ask since the night before.

"Thunder Paw," he said, moving closer to the old gnoll, who was cosseted inside a nest of pillows to cushion his "old bones" from the bouncing of the wagon. "When we first met, you said you were *told* about the Nightmare. Does that mean you weren't caught up in it?"

The chief nodded. "Me was spared," he said, collar flashing.

"So what happened to you these last eighty years, then?" James asked excitedly. "Where were you?"

"Me not sure," the chief said with a shrug. "Me go to sleep one night, wake up the next morning in an ancient graveyard in the hills with everyone else. We all very confused."

"How many gnolls were there when you woke up?"

"Most all of Red Canyon was there. Nine out of ten. Only some missing. No undead chiefs."

That made sense.

"What did you do after that?"

"We went back home," Thunder Paw said. "Red Canyon was not far. It was a sad return, though. The town was different. Many more undead, and much stronger. They put us back in line before we could rebel."

Thunder Paw looked sad as he finished, but James was almost bouncing with joy. "This is huge," he said excitedly. "I thought this world had been through Armageddon, but if what happened to you happened to others too, then all those missing jubatus from Windy Lake might not be missing after all!" He shot to his feet. "I need to tell Arbati!"

James thanked him as he left and scrambled over the jostling, bouncing connections between wagons toward the front. When he reached the first wagon, though, the head warrior wasn't there. "Where's Arbati?" he asked the driver.

The gnoll jerked a clawed thumb backward into the canvas-shadowed depths of the lead wagon.

"Thanks," James said and opened the flaps to climb down into the dark wagon bed. It looked empty at first, but then his jubatus eyes spotted Arbati in the far back, curled up into a ball behind a crate.

"Hey, are you okay?" James asked, walking over to place a hand on the cat-warrior's shoulder.

Arbati curled himself tighter. "Do you know how many times I've died?"

The words came out in a whisper, and James frowned. Thanks to the Intelligence from his staff, the calculation was fairly simple. He just needed to take the number of times per day Arbati's questline started, subtract the likely completion rate to remove the times when players saved him, then multiply by eighty years. But while his boosted brain had already come up with a likely number, he didn't think that was what was actually needed here.

"How many?"

Arbati wrapped his arms around his knees. "Thousands," he whispered. "Maybe tens of thousands. I don't know. For eighty years, I was tortured and killed over and over and over. First by the gnolls, but mostly by that damned undead lich. He was trapped in the Nightmare the same as the rest of us, but I know he enjoyed it. I've thought of nothing but revenge for eight decades. Revenge on the lich, on the gnolls, on the players. But now…"

He trailed off with a shuddering sigh, and James sat down next to him. He still wasn't entirely comfortable around Arbati, but it was impossible to hear a story like that and not feel sympathy. It was a miracle the warrior was still sane after what he'd been through, and though James was itching to defend himself and the other players, that wasn't what Arbati needed from him right now. So he kept his mouth shut, waiting silently until, at last, Arbati continued.

"Now you, a *player*, are going to join the Four Clans. We killed the lich and saved my sister, and *I*, the Ar'Bati, have personally invited the gnolls to talk of *peace*." He dug his claws into his arms. "Everything is moving on, but I can't forget all the times I was skinned alive. I'm still so *angry*. While I was frozen in place, it was easy to pour everything into my hate and plot revenge, but where do I send my anger now? There's no one left to take it."

The warrior lowered his head with a breath that sounded dangerously close to a sob, and James shifted uncomfortably. He had some experience with counseling, but this was *way* out of his depth. All he could do was to put an arm around the jubatus's shoulders and give him an awkward sideways hug.

Arbati jumped at the contact, but he didn't jerk away. Instead, James felt a burst of shaking, then another. The quivering reminded him of the time he'd picked up his mom's traumatized cat from the vet. There was nothing to say, though, so he just held Arbati in a one-armed hug as the wagon bounced down the road.

Several miles later, the quivering stopped, and awkwardness set in. James was trying to decide if he should let go when the head warrior beat him to it, shrugging out of James's arm with a self-conscious cough.

"Can I ask you a question?" James said to break the uncomfortable silence. "Why did you call yourself 'the Ar'Bati' just now?"

"Because that's my rank," Arbati replied, rubbing his paw across his nose. When James blinked at him in confusion, the warrior scowled. "What? You didn't think 'Arbati' was my *name*, did you?"

"But that's… In the game, that's what was above your head! It said 'Arbati, Head Warrior of Windy Lake,' so I always assumed—"

The warrior huffed, insulted. "It said 'Ar-*bati*,' and it is *not* my name. Ar'Bati means 'head warrior' in the old tongue."

James felt like an idiot. "So I've been calling you 'The Head Warrior Head Warrior' this whole time?" He pressed a hand to his face as the Ar'Bati began to laugh at him. "So what *is* your name, then?"

It took several minutes to get an answer because the tall warrior was laughing too hard to speak. "My name is 'Fangs in the Grass'," he got out at last, wiping the tears from his eyes. "Claw Born."

"Fangs in the Grass, Claw Born?" James repeated with a wince. "No offense, but that's kind of awkward to say."

"It is a very honorable and auspicious name," Fangs in the Grass replied proudly. "One befitting the eldest son and next leader of the Claw Born clan. But my friends and family call me Fangs."

James sighed in relief. "Right on. Fangs it is, then."

"We might give you a new name when you join as well," Fangs the Ar'Bati said. "It depends on who sponsors you. And before you ask, I cannot be your sponsor because I am your trial witness."

James nodded, feeling suddenly depressed. Hearing Arba—*Fangs* talk about his inclusion into the clans as a sure thing should have been a victory, but getting something as simple as the head warrior's name wrong for two days really shook his confidence. He tried to tell himself it wasn't his fault, that he was just exhausted and bombarded by too many new things to worry about properly addressing the angry cat-man who'd been trying to kill him, but this felt like a really important mistake. One that seriously impacted his future here, which bothered him a lot, because James wasn't sure he wanted a future here anymore.

As much as he admired the jubatus of Windy Lake, he didn't actually want to live in a tribal village. He didn't want to go to Bastion and handle whatever threats and politics were waiting there, either. He didn't even want to be a magical cheetah person anymore. All James wanted right now was to go home and be in his own skin again with no fur rubbing the wrong way inside his armor, no tail to trip over, and no claws to worry about every time he raised a hand to his face. If you'd asked him last week, he'd have jumped at the chance to live in FFO for real, but that was before everything had gotten so violent, bloody, painful, and terrifying. So *real*.

Even now, as he sat in the middle of a caravan full of gnolls on the way to peace talks he'd arranged, all James could see was more trouble and drama. *Good* trouble and drama that would vastly improve the lives of everyone who lived in the savanna, but he didn't want to live here. He wanted to go home. He wanted to go back to the world of internet and air conditioning, where you could call the police if someone was trying to kill you. Even if his life there had been awful, at least it was a normal, comfortable sort of awful. Sitting here in the hot, stuffy dark with his whiskers bouncing into his vision every time the wagon lurched, James felt like an alien. Like a stranger, and he was so *tired* of it.

"I'm glad you are joining our village," Fangs said.

The quiet statement shocked James out of his self-pity. "*Really?*" he asked, astonished. Given how they'd started, that was the last thing he'd expected to hear from the head warrior. "Why?"

The tall warrior scratched his ear self-consciously. "Players are unpredictable and dangerous. I used to think that killing you all was the best way to make us safe, but now that I know how badly we are outmatched, I've realized we must learn to understand you if we are to survive. I'm glad that you are joining us because that means Windy Lake will have at least one player we can trust, and a level eighty at that." He flashed James a sharp-toothed smile. "Seems you aren't weak and useless after all."

James stared at him, dumbstruck. Even with Ar'Bati's gruff manner, the compliment meant so much to him. Almost *too* much.

He was just so used to everyone seeing him as a failure that hearing someone say they didn't—to imply that he was good, that he was worth something—made his whole body tremble, forcing James to turn his head away before he embarrassed himself.

"Thank you," he choked out at last. "That...that means a lot to me."

"Good," Fangs said with a stiff nod, then James felt a rough hand smack his shoulder. "Come on. We're almost to the village, and I need to be riding at the front so no one attacks us."

James nodded then wiped his eyes surreptitiously as they climbed out of the wagon bed and up to the front seat by the driver. He was about to ask Ar'Bati—*Fangs in the Grass*, he mentally corrected, shaking his head—how much farther they had to go when they bumped over a low hill and the outline of Windy Lake appeared, shimmering in the afternoon heat.

As to be expected given that they were in a gnoll caravan, a large mass of armed jubatus began forming on the village's edge as soon as they came into view. Ar'Bati waved vigorously at the distant crowd, but his presence—clearly free and at the front of the procession—seemed to do little to quiet the anger James saw as the wind caravan got closer.

When they were almost in walking distance, the Naturalists let the conjured wind drop, slowing their madcap speed to a gentle roll. As they slowed, the natural wind from the east took over, bringing the smell of death.

James and Ar'Bati both froze. They were very close to the village now, close enough that James could see fresh bandages and bruises on the warriors who'd come out to meet them. Shivering, he stood up on the driver's bench to get a better look, his cat eyes squinting as he searched the village and the land around it for a mass grave or a battlefield, something that would emit such an intense rotting smell.

He spotted it soon enough. On the southern shore of the Windy Lake, a score of tall posts had been driven into the ground, and tied to the wooden poles like scarecrows were bodies.

They were clearly fresh. The blood on their clothes was still red, not oxidized brown. The carrion birds had already moved in, covering the bodies in a squabbling blanket of black feathers and snapping beaks. Even through the mass of scavengers, though, James could see the closest victim was wearing a bright-yellow chest piece and crimson pants. Another wore a fluorescent-pink shirt under her leather vest, and James felt something cold go down his spine. Even ripped and smeared with blood and dirt, there was no mistaking the tragically mismatched armor that only mid-level players wore.

"Um, Fangs?" he said nervously. "Did you really mean what you said about being happy I was joining the clan?"

"Of course," Ar'Bati said with a cross look. "I would not have said it if it weren't true."

"Good," James said, cringing away from the mob that was eyeing him with naked hatred. "Because I don't think they're angry about the gnolls."

■ ■

When the wind caravan finally rolled to a stop, Ar'Bati hopped down with a confident leap. James followed more discreetly, sticking to the warrior's shadow as the two of them closed the final distance toward Windy Lake.

Despite their clenched weapons and lashing tails, the mob of jubatus villagers didn't hiss or jeer at them. They just watched, their mouths locked tight in angry, bloody silence. The gnolls clearly felt it, too, because they fell quiet as well, sticking to their wagons and keeping their hands on their weapons. This whole thing was already going much, much worse than James had envisioned, and since all the villagers were glaring at *him*, he was pretty sure why.

When they were less than fifty feet from the wall of angry cat-people, Ar'Bati held up his fist. James scrabbled to a stop, staying as close to the warrior as possible without literally hiding behind him. He was trying to figure out how to ask why they'd stopped without anyone hearing when the stooped form of Elder Gray Fang emerged from the crowd, her staff crunching on the hard-packed road as she walked out to face them.

"Ar'Bati," she said in a steely voice. "What is the meaning of this?"

She fixed the head warrior with a hard glare, but James had to give Fangs points for unlimited guts, because he flashed her a cocky grin in return. "We have returned victorious!" the warrior announced, raising his voice so everyone could hear. "The lich is destroyed, and the undead forces beneath the Red Canyon are vanquished! We have driven their evil from the savanna!"

He lifted his new magical sword high as he finished, striking a victorious pose. But while he was clearly shooting for wild applause, the crowd remained as angrily silent as ever.

"You did save Lilac," Gray Fang admitted grudgingly. "Though it was as close as these things can get. Still, you completed your mission and upheld the honor of our village. Thank you, Ar'Bati."

She gave the warrior a bow so tiny, James almost missed it. When she looked up again, though, her face was harder and angrier than ever. "Now," she growled. "What have you brought to our doorstep? Why do you travel with these *gnolls?*"

She said *gnolls* the same way someone else would say *dead skunk*, and the hyena-men in the wagons behind them began to growl. James swallowed, too. He was dying to explain that this was a *peace* mission, but the baleful glares from the crowd made it clear that anything he tried to say would only make the situation worse. So he kept his hands on his staff and his mouth shut, mentally crossing his fingers as Ar'Bati opened his mouth.

"We—"

Whatever explanation he'd been about to give was cut off by a sudden burst of yipping, and James looked back to see Thunder Paw making his way up to the road to join them. The one-eyed Naturalist was flanked by several warriors, which caused several armed jubatus to rush out from the crowd and take up position around Gray Fang. But despite the score of tall warriors that were now looking down their daggers at him, the old gnoll continued his approach, walking slowly and deliberately until he was standing beside Ar'Bati and James.

"Greetings, Elder of Windy Lake," the gnoll said, the obsidian choker clamped around his throat flashing with each word.

At the sound of his mechanized voice, several jubatus gasped and made warding gestures against evil, but Thunder Paw didn't let that stop him. He just kept going, his barking yips clearly respectful even though the collar wasn't sophisticated enough to copy that same tone into the auto-tuned words.

"Me Thunder Paw, Chief of Chiefs of the Grand Pack. Me come before you today bearing gifts and desiring peace."

He waved at the wagons behind him, which gnolls were now pulling the covers off of to reveal the food and gifts packed inside. In the village, the jubatus' ears pricked forward in attention. Even elder Gray Fang looked stunned, her carefully guarded expression lost to surprise as she stared at the old gnoll's death-magic-riddled collar.

"You can speak?" she said at last.

"Me have always been able to speak," Thunder Paw said gruffly. "Now, Me can speak your tongue as well. A 'gift' from my former masters." He touched the void-black ring fixed around his throat. "But they are defeated! Now, Me wish to use this collar to end our struggles. Many enemies are coming. If you will hear us out, we will speak of peace and cooperation against them."

Gray Fang snapped her hanging jaw shut as she tried to process what he'd just said. James couldn't blame her for taking a while. They'd dropped quite the bomb on the old cat, and in front of the entire village, no less. She was clearly still disgusted by the gnoll in front of her, but James was hoping that age and wisdom would overcome her prejudices. As the elder's face twisted again, though, he realized he'd guessed wrong. Really, he should have known. Jubatus always seemed to react to surprises with anger or violence, particularly when stressed. Thankfully, he'd planned ahead for just this sort of situation.

"*The gift,*" he hissed at Thunder Paw. "*Give her the gift!*"

Thunder Paw gave him an uncertain look, and James motioned frantically. This was no time to hold back. If they didn't want this peace process to crumble less than thirty seconds after it began, they needed to use their ace *now*. Thankfully, Thunder Paw followed him once again, pulling a small parcel out of his belt pouch and walking forward to unwrap it practically in the elder's face.

Gray Fang's guards brandished their weapons, but the elder stopped them with a wave of her claws, her slitted eyes growing wide as she saw the delicate crystal vial filled with brilliant, rainbow-colored liquid in the gnoll chieftain's paws.

"We present you with this gift as a symbol of our interest in friendship," Thunder Paw said, holding the pan-elixir out to her. "May it be the first of many good acts between us."

Gray Fang's hands shook as she reached out to take the small bottle. "A pan-elixir," she said, her voice astonished. "How did you...?"

"It is a trophy taken from the laboratory of the defeated lich," Thunder Paw said proudly, lifting his pointed snout high. "We wish for there to be healing between our two peoples. Would that it be as easy as drinking this potion."

James bit back a grin at Thunder Paw's flawless delivery. He and the old Naturalist hadn't just yakked about lightning magic during the ride over. Rare to all but the wealthiest high-end raiders, a pan-elixir was a literal miracle in a bottle, which made it the gnolls' best shot at breaking through the wall of the jubatus' prejudice. *No one* could turn down a gift like that, and Gray Fang was no exception. She was already staring at the shifting colors inside the bottle as if they were the most beautiful things she'd ever seen. She might have stood there spellbound forever had Ar'Bati not cleared his throat.

Gray Fang recovered at once, clutching the vial to her chest as she looked back down at the waiting Thunder Paw. "It is a great gift, indeed," she said, clearly struggling to find the words. "As the spiritual leader of the jubatus clans of the savanna, I, Gray Fang, offer you hospitality. We will hear what you have to say."

This raised a new round of gasps from the crowd behind her but not nearly so many hisses. Now that it was obvious the newcomers weren't going to attack, lots of villagers were shooting keen looks at the gnolls' food-laden wagons. They still weren't welcoming looks, but greed was a lot better than murderous hate, and James was happy to take it.

"Ar'Bati," the elder said, turning back to her grandson, who was puffed up with pride. "Escort our guests to the festival field so that they may make camp."

The head warrior nodded and motioned for the wagons to follow him. As they creaked forward, James let out a breath of relief. He was stepping up to walk beside Thunder Paw when Gray Fang put out her hand.

"Not you."

James froze, looking up to see the elder glaring at him. "You are not welcome here."

The words sent a spike through his chest. James shot a pleading look at Ar'Bati as the warrior was leading the gnolls away, but any hopes that he'd finally gotten somewhere with the warrior died when Ar'Bati refused to meet his eyes. He just flicked his ears at James and kept walking, leaving him standing alone with Gray Fang.

James's ears flattened in response. After everything they'd been through, the betrayal was crushing. At this point, the only leverage he had left was the bundle of enemy communications in his backpack. The letters he'd stolen from the lich contained vital information about the Once King's coming invasion of Bastion, and the jubatus of the savanna were famously loyal to the king. She might kick him out on his tail to walk to Bastion on his own, but Gray Fang wouldn't kill him so long as he knew what he knew.

At least, that was what James told himself. To be honest, the idea of trekking across the savanna just so he could start all over with a new set of prejudiced, hateful non-player characters was the most depressing situation he could think of. His whole body wilted as he imagined brandishing the lich's letters in front of new murderous faces to save his life, but from the way the jubatus were glaring at him, it was clear he couldn't stay here.

As unwelcome as he clearly was, though, James wasn't willing to let this go just yet. Not after all the pain and trouble he'd gone through to save these ungrateful cats, and *definitely* not after the total victory he'd helped bring about. He might not be able to stop them from running him out of town, but dammit, James was going to know *why*.

"What happened here?" he said, turning to face Gray Fang properly. "I kept my end of our bargain, but it seems I'm the only one. Does breaking your promise to let me petition to join the clans have something to do with that?"

He pointed at the dead bodies the village had hung out to dry on poles, but Gray Fang didn't even flinch.

"A group of five players came into our village shortly after you left yesterday," she said, her voice hard. "They announced that they were now the rulers of Windy Lake, and any who opposed them would die. They demanded tribute, servants, and women. We tried to fight them but were badly outmatched. Thankfully, our lost ones returned, and we were able to overwhelm them at last. But the losses were heavy and have made for a sad reunion."

Her ears fell as she spoke, making the gray-furred elder look even older than usual. Then her fists clenched tight. "This is why we will not tolerate your kind anymore!" she hissed, her eyes popping up to meet his with a look of pure hate. "You are all *evil*! Horrible children trapped in the bodies of gods! You have proven yourselves again and again to be selfish, greedy, wanton, immoral creatures, and *my* people have been the ones to suffer! Our only hope of survival is to kill any players on sight before you destroy us with your madness!"

"But we aren't all the same!" James said angrily, offended despite knowing better. "I've never attacked you or hurt anyone here! I just spent *two days* risking my life for you!"

"We can never forget that you are not jubatus!" she snarled. "You possess that body like an evil spirit, but you will never truly be one of us!"

James clenched his fangs, glaring at the bodies across the water. There *had* been other players *alive* in the savanna, and they'd acted like utter idiots. If only he'd been able to stay in Windy Lake a little longer, he could have met them, maybe convinced them not to try to conquer the town like power-drunk morons. If nothing else, he wouldn't be so alone. But he was. He *was* alone, and the one place that might have offered him the closest thing he could hope for to a home in this mad world was gone forever. And it was all their fault.

They are better off now, whispered the staff in his hands. *In death, they can't ruin anything else.*

He felt the voice's attention shift to the crowd of jubatus, almost as if the staff were turning its head.

You should send the others to join them. The only way to break the cycle of hatred here is for everyone to share the same fate.

Magic stirred in his hands, reminding him he was far more powerful now than he'd been the last time he'd been face-to-face with Gray Fang.

You should teach them what it means to betray you.

For a terrible second, James was sorely tempted. He was ten times stronger than those low-level idiots who'd nearly conquered the town. Why should he keep the gloves on if the jubatus were going to be honorless scum who broke their promises and spat on the feet of the man who'd risked his life to save theirs?

You should wipe them out, the staff suggested. *The living always betray you, but the dead are at peace. These people have already made it clear they're incapable of listening to reason. Why let them betray anyone else? You're a hero, aren't you? Save them from themselves. End their suffering, and you will end your own.*

Growling under his breath, James turned around and banged the stupid cursed staff on a rock to shut it up. When he looked up again, Gray Fang was staring at him in horror. He didn't know if she'd felt the dark magic of the staff or if he'd actually been standing there talking to himself throughout that entire exchange, and he didn't particularly care. James was sick and tired of trying to help nasty, angry cats who kept biting him.

"Fine," he told Gray Fang, hefting the bag full of precious letters back onto his shoulder. "Just let me say goodbye to Thunder Paw, and I'll be out of your fur."

The elder nodded stiffly, and James turned to go, but before he'd taken two steps, the crowd began to whisper, and James looked up to see two muscular jubatus pushing their way to the front. It was Ar'Bati and an older but equally tall and tough-looking male. Gray Fang shifted uncomfortably at their arrival, but the new jubatus ignored her, grinning at James instead.

"What are you doing, Gray Fang?" the newcomer asked. "What's this about sending him away? We should be begging him to join us!"

"I am against it," Gray Fang said without hesitation. "He is a player."

The jubatus man turned to give the elder a very not-nice grin. The expression highlighted all the scars hidden by his fur, and James blinked in surprise. The old cat looked like he'd been in a hundred battles and was looking to fight a hundred more. When Ar'Bati's face split into the exact same expression, James finally saw the family resemblance.

"Your objection is noted," Ar'Bati's father said sarcastically. "But this isn't your call." He turned his grin on James. "My son has told me of this one's deeds. They are most impressive! We Claw Born wish to sponsor and adopt James..." The tall jubatus scowled. "What's your full name, kid?"

"James Anderson," James said quickly.

"—wish to sponsor and adopt James Anderson into our clan," the patriarch said proudly, clapping James on the back.

James didn't think it was possible for Gray Fang to look more horrified, but the old woman managed it somehow.

"*Adopt?*"

"Of course adopt!" the elder Claw Born replied, grinning so widely that James could see every single one of his terrifyingly sharp teeth. "We'll be writing songs of his accomplishments for generations! The other clans don't yet appreciate how valuable James is, though with that said..." The scarred jubatus put his arm around James's shoulder and leaned in until they were whiskers to whiskers. "I could pay the Water Born to adopt you if you wanted to, say, marry my eldest daughter, Lilac. You saved her life, so it'd be a most appropriate reward for your deeds *and* get you started off real well here. I shouldn't say so myself, but my Lilac's a catch."

"*Father*," Ar'Bati hissed as James began coughing to cover his surprise and alarm. He didn't want to offend his savior, but he'd never even met Lilac while she was conscious, and there was no way he was getting married to someone who was being offered as a *literal* trophy wife. Worse, a trophy wife doomed to be some kind of half-widow after he found a way back home.

"I'm sorry. I can't accept a marriage," he said, thinking fast. "I'm, uh, already promised to someone back home."

"Oh yeah?" The scarred cat's ears swiveled suspiciously. "What's her name?"

"Jiujitsu."

"Fancy-sounding name," the elder Claw Born said, scratching his salt-and-pepper fur. "What family is she from?"

"Brazil," James said, hoping the old cat wouldn't see him sweating. Fortunately, Ar'Bati's father looked more annoyed than insulted.

"Hrmph, what's so good about her? Can't you ditch her for my daughter?"

James shook his head, carrying the lie as far as he could. "I'm absolutely devoted. She's an incredible warrior. Taught me how to fight when I was growing up."

"Fair enough," the old man said, squeezing his arm almost threateningly around James's shoulders. "At least we'll have ties to this Brazil warrior clan to look forward to in the future! Marriage would have been better, but adoption will be good enough." He squeezed so hard, James's joints creaked. "Welcome to the family!"

"Ahem," Gray Fang said, clearing her throat pointedly. "My word is still *no*."

"Ehh? What was that?" said James's possible-new-father. "You set this trial up yourself, Gray Fang. I know because I was there when you came out of the lodge. You *told* me you were sending this pair to save my baby girl. Now the trial's done successfully, *and* the witness has vouched for him." He glanced at Ar'Bati, who nodded, and his father turned back to Gray Fang with a wide grin. "Looks like everything here is green grasses to me. And just so you know, I had to outbid the other three clans to get first pick on this boy, so good luck getting them to side with you." He chuckled. "Looks like you're outvoted."

Gray Fang's hackles rose, and James worried for a moment that she was going to try to claw the scarred old man. Then her shoulders slumped, making her look frail and tired again. "You win, Rend," she said, turning her back on him. "But he and his kind will be a curse upon your head. The Claw Born will regret this day. Mark my words."

"You're a Claw Born too, you know!" Rend called after her as Gray Fang walked stiffly back into the village. Then to cement his apparent victory, Ar'Bati's father turned to the remaining onlookers and grabbed James's wrist. "Behold!" he cried, thrusting James's arm into the air. "This James is now of the Claw Born!"

There were only some polite claps in response as the crowd broke up and drifted back into the village. But if the lack of enthusiasm bothered James's new adopted father, he didn't show it.

"I always wanted another son," he said, slapping James hard on the back. "Come on, boys. Let's go celebrate!"

That was the best suggestion James had heard all day, but there was something he wanted to sort out before moving on. "Can we catch up in a minute? I need to ask Fangs something."

Rend's scarred face twisted into a sour expression. "All right," he said, letting go of James at last. "Just be quick about it. I need to show you off!"

"It won't take long," James promised. When the senior Claw Born finally nodded and headed back into the village, James punched Fangs in the Grass right in the arm. "*Dude!* Why didn't you tell me what you were up to? I thought I was totally screwed when you left me hanging with Gray Fang!"

This earned him a bruising punch in return. "I did *not* leave you hanging! I very clearly flicked my ears at you!"

"So? Jubatus ears twitch all the time! How was I supposed to know that one was special?"

"You spent eighty years pretending to be one of us and you don't know that flicking ears means being in cahoots?" Fangs asked, horrified. "Anyway, what else was I supposed to do? I couldn't openly defy Grandmother in front of half the village! I had to leave you so I could get to my father before she suspected I wasn't on her side!"

Then the warrior punched James in the arm again.

"*Ow!*" James cried, clutching the now very large bruise with a wince. "What was *that* for?"

"For calling me dude," Ar'Bati replied, nose in the air. "You're my brother now, but don't think you can be so informal. Familiar names like 'dude' or 'man' are only for best friends, wives, and children. Using them casually like that makes you sound like a Schtumple conman."

James's world screeched to a halt at those words. Not all of them, just the "you're my brother now" part. He'd known Rend Claw Born was Ar'Bati's father, but it wasn't until the head warrior himself had said it that the new reality finally dawned on James.

"You're my *brother*," he said, looking at Ar'Bati with a mix of awe and horror.

"I am," Fangs said, straightening up to his full height so he could loom menacingly over James. "And you're a Claw Born now. You don't know what that means yet, but there are two things you must learn here and now before you get yourself—or *me*—killed." A pair of claws was flicked out perilously close to James's face. "One! Be respectful of everyone at all times, and never give insult. Our whole family will have to deal with it if you do. Two! Do *not* embarrass us. Don't think for a second that your life is more important than the honor of our clan. If you bring us shame, we will take it out of your hide!"

"Yes, brother," James said, ears down from the intensity of Ar'Bati's lecture. "I will do as you say. Thank you for teaching me."

This deference seemed to satisfy Fangs enormously. "Come," he said, turning on his heel. "Father is waiting to bring us to dinner, and patience isn't one of his virtues."

James nodded, running after his new brother with a rush of relief. There'd been so many ups and downs today that the idea of a belly full of warm meat as he sat with people who actually wanted him around sounded like heaven. As he walked beside Fangs in the Grass, none of the jubatus gave him more than a sideways look as they marched into the village, where the drums were already pounding.

■ ■

The first thing James noticed upon reentering the village of Windy Lake was just how many more jubatus there were. This also came as a surprise to Fangs in the Grass. It took forever to make it to the center of the village because the head warrior was constantly stopping for warm greetings and tearful hugs with friends and family he'd clearly thought were eighty years dead, and James guiltily realized he'd completely forgotten to tell the head warrior about the return of the lost population. Fortunately, Fangs didn't know that he'd known, so James's sin remained undiscovered.

Even though he was in the background for these happy exchanges, James felt joyous as well. He had no idea where the game had stashed the nine-tenths of the population it hadn't needed, but he was *so* happy everyone hadn't actually ceased to exist. For their part, the new jubatus—being neither players nor non-player characters—didn't seem to know what to make of James at all. He was introduced as "James Claw Born" by his new brother, which seemed to be enough for most, but James couldn't help but notice how his presence made everyone's tails go still.

Eventually, after countless hellos and introductions, James and Fangs in the Grass made it to the center of town. The huge drum had been moved out of the way, and a giant bonfire was roaring high into the evening sky. Smaller drums and stringed instruments had been brought out, and a mishmash band was desperately trying to overpower the noise of the crowd, but it was impossible when every family was seemingly trying to outdo each other by throwing their own massive party. Large spit-roasted animals turned above dozens of cook fires, and every tent had tables set out with booze, appetizers, plates, banners, and so on. Roving partygoers moved on a circuit through the fires, greeting in the loudest voices possible and eating at every stop.

It looked so much like college football tailgating that James had to bite his lip to keep from laughing. He also had to fight not to drool over all the food. He hadn't eaten since that morning, and the smell of so much delicious cooked meat was making him salivate. He was really hoping that he and Fangs were going to make the rounds so he could try a bite from each table, but the tall warrior cut right through the middle to the center of the square, where a low platform with a wide table had been set up beneath a yellow banner marked with a black curved claw. Both Rend and Gray Fang were seated there, though Ar'Bati's father—and James's too now—was the only one who smiled.

"James, my boy!" Rend said, hopping up from his seat to grab his new son by the arm. "Come with me. We have a lot to do!"

Before James could ask what that meant, his adopted father yanked him into the crowd. For the next hour, James was dragged from gathering to gathering as Rend Claw Born introduced him to every jubatus family in the savanna. It was a dizzying number of names, titles, and faces to remember. To James's dismay, his stat-boosted memory apparently still sucked at remembering names. Worse, Rend kept them moving so fast, he didn't even get anything to eat.

Finally, they came back around to the Claw Borns' table, where James was introduced to his new extended family. Like the rest of the village, they were all very nervous to meet a player, but Rend never missed a chance to proudly proclaim his new son's amazing deeds. The old warrior's enthusiasm and joviality helped smooth out even the most anxious members of the clan, and soon they were smiling at James as well. Some even talked to him.

Finally, when all the introductions were over, James and Ar'Bati got to sit on the platform beside Gray Fang, Rend, and the other important family members. Then to his starving delight, someone brought James an entire serving platter piled high with roasted meats and his own pitcher full of something that smelled delightfully alcoholic. He immediately dug into both, but while the meat was every bit as good as it smelled, the stuff in the pitcher was not the burning liquor he'd expected. He wasn't sure what it was, but it tasted *amazing*. Sweet and slightly metallic but savory at the same time.

"Fangs," James whispered, licking his whiskers as he pointed at his already-half-empty pitcher, "what is this stuff?"

"Fermented sorghum mixed with fish blood," his new brother replied.

James's eyes grew wide as he almost horked it all back up right then and there. Fortunately, only his human side was disgusted, and all of him was more than a little tipsy. "It's good," he said, forcing a smile as he took another sip.

That earned him a raised pitcher and a grin. James grinned back, savoring the pleasant buzz between his ears as he shoved another piece of nearly raw meat into his mouth, washing it down with the delicious fermented beverage that he'd decided he wasn't going to think too hard about.

After the liquor started flowing, the party became a bit of a blur. There was dancing at some point with James being shoved into various arms for some awkward whirls around the central fire. This was followed by more food, which James ate until he felt he was going to pop. He was vaguely aware of Rend drunkenly giving some kind of speech that involved a lot of pointing at him, but James fell asleep halfway through, passing out right there in his seat with his head pillowed on the table.

He awoke to someone shaking him. Given how rough the treatment was, James wasn't surprised to see Fangs's feline face when he finally dragged his eyes open. He was still pretty dizzy, but the fires were all banked, and the partygoers were dispersing.

James was about to ask what time it was when Fangs turned away and said, "He's awake."

"Good," said Gray Fang, appearing over James as well. "It's time for business, then." She gave James a scathing look. "Cleanse yourself, and we will go inside."

James tilted his head at her, utterly confused. How was any business going to get done when everyone was as drunk as a skunk? Then he saw the bright-aquamarine glow of the Cleansing spell before Gray Fang splashed it over her head. The water magic made her shiver from ears to tail, but her eyes were much clearer when she opened them again and moved to start casting the same spell again over Rend, who was snoring in his seat.

James watched her work in wonder, his jaw slack at the brilliance of it all. Of course. Alcohol was a *poison*, which meant it could be *cleansed*.

He surged to his feet to try it on himself, but he was so drunk his first attempt fell apart. Eventually, though, the strands of magic came together, and he washed the poison out of his system.

And immediately regretted it.

Hangovers were nothing compared to becoming instantly and totally stone-cold sober. His head stopped spinning as though it had hit a wall, and his vision seesawed between sharp and blurry as the fatigue he'd forgotten about reasserted itself. After several moments of frantic blinking, his vision finally settled into a crisp black and white, which was very confusing until James remembered that all the fires had been put out. *Real* jubatus could see in almost complete darkness, so they didn't bother with torches or lights in their village at night.

The only color left was the light from the fire that was still burning in the great wooden lodge. Its orange-and-yellow light cut a swath of brilliance across the gray square. Since everyone important was heading in that direction, James followed, blinking as his eyes readjusted to the warm firelight inside.

Inside the Naturalists' lodge, a ring of hide-covered pillows had been set out around the fire along with more sedate refreshments and lots of water. Looking around for where he was supposed to sit, James realized with a jolt that everyone in here was old except for him and Fangs. He couldn't remember all of their names yet, but he recalled enough of his whirlwind tour around the fires to recognize that these were the elders and heads of the four major clans as well as those of the minor clans. He was still wondering what he should do when Rend caught his eye and tapped his claws on the pillow beside him.

Obediently, James sat down on Rend's left, while Fangs in the Grass got the right-hand pillow. James dearly hoped that left and right had the same significance in this culture as they did in his. Fangs didn't seem upset, though, so James guessed that whatever the positioning meant, it was fine. The head warrior was not good at hiding his upset, particularly with slights against his honor.

When they were all seated, Gray Fang cleared her throat and turned in his direction. "James," she said loudly.

"Yes, ma'am?" he replied reflexively. On the other side of their father, Ar'Bati winced, but Gray Fang didn't bat an eye.

"Ar'Bati has explained to me why you two invited the gnolls to come," she continued. "I find his explanation...uncharacteristic. He uses too many of *your* words, so *you* will explain to the clans why we should do anything other than slaughter this Thunder Paw and use the chaos of his death to raze Red Canyon to the ground."

James gulped. All the slitted eyes in the room were on him now, and the friendliness of the party was gone, replaced with calculation. He was suddenly all too aware of how his new father, Rends Iron Hides, had countless scars marring his fur, and that he wasn't the only one. All of the clan heads bore scars, but they still looked fit and eager to fight, their eyes gleaming golden in the firelight. A pointed reminder that he was sitting in a room full of predators.

That was enough to terrify the human in him, but James had been living as a jubatus all night, and he managed to rise to his feet. He took a deep breath as he did, looking around the circle to meet each person in the eyes. It was a habit he'd developed back in college. As a political sciences major, he'd had to take multiple public speaking classes. He'd dropped out before he could use them, but he'd never been more grateful for those experiences than now, when the fate of an entire zone depended on him not screwing this up.

"Thank you, Elder Gray Fang," he said with as much polish as he could muster. "That's a great question that cuts to the heart of the immediate threat Windy Lake now faces. To answer it, though, I must first explain the state of the savanna as it exists now."

It was going to be a brutal one. They'd defeated the lich at Red Canyon, but the gnolls were only one of multiple extinction-grade threats facing Windy Lake. That was the game's fault. FFO had divided the world into zones, and each zone into quest hubs. To make things fun for players, the area around each quest hub was in a constant red-alert crisis by design. That way, players would have plenty of problems to "solve" as they played at being heroes. As a player himself, James had loved taking part in the epic and desperate struggles to save overwhelmed towns or outposts that needed his help. Now, though, there were no more questing players, which meant all of those game-created problems would be rapidly spinning out of control.

With no more over-powered players running around fixing things as fast as they could for loot and experience, the whole world could be falling into chaos, and that wasn't even counting the Once King's upcoming attack on Bastion. The game hadn't even gotten to that part of the expansion plot yet, but everything else was in full swing, and if they didn't do something about it, it was all going to swing right into them.

Mentioning all of that would just start the player-hate up all over again, though, so James decided to keep it local, starting with the most immediate problems Windy Lake was likely to face.

"For example," he said, "if you travel twenty miles down the west trade road, you'll find a collection of burned wagons that used to belong to the Crazy Schtumple Brothers."

All the elders immediately began to mutter about "thieving Schtumples," and James paused to let the grumbles quiet down.

"As I was saying," he went on, "these brothers had an amulet, which I assume is still in their carts, that they acquired by accident. This amulet is cursed with terrible luck for the owner, and they were desperate to get rid of it. If a knowledgeable Naturalist were to accept this amulet, they'd find that the gem inside is actually a compass that points to a spot by the Northern Oasis where there's an ancient cave that was sealed long ago to trap a fledgling Bird. Not a *normal* bird. I'm talking a giant, dangerous, 'from the Age of Skies' kind of Bird. Now, recently, borers have moved into this cave and begun recklessly mining. At some point very soon, they will accidentally puncture the Bird's prison. Once freed, the Bird will enslave them all to feed its ravenous hunger, quickly growing into a menace that no one here will be able to stop."

"Lies!" cried an old, white-furred jubatus elder. "We would know if such danger existed on our lands! This is clearly made up!"

James had been so focused on mentally organizing and delivering his speech that he jumped at the sudden outburst. His rhythm broken, he shot a panicked look that happened to land on Gray Fang.

For once, she came to his aid. "What he says is true," she said grudgingly. "As a former player, James has unmatched knowledge of the world's situation."

That was a lot more support than James had ever expected from the perpetually disapproving elder. He also found it interesting that she'd called him a *former* player. He bet that was how she was dealing with him joining the village. She'd never accept a player, but a former player was a different matter. Or at least, that was what he hoped.

Gray Fang's words were backed by the nodding of Rend Claw Born, Storm of the Water Born clan, and Ar'Bati. All the jubatus who'd been in the Nightmare understood that James was describing a quest. Unfortunately, the part of the room who'd missed the Nightmare didn't even understand what a quest *was*, which prompted a round of demands that James explain how he got his information and what it had to do with Forever Fantasy Online.

"All in due time," James promised, holding up his hands. "But the Bird in that cave isn't the point. Preventing it from waking is actually very easy. Someone just needs to wear an antelope skull with a candle on it on their head. This disguise will let them trick their way into an audience with the borer prince in charge of excavating the cave and explain the situation. The prince isn't evil. He just wants a nice cave for his people to live in. Once you lay out the right incentives, he'll even agree to guard the Bird for you in exchange for getting to stay in the cave, no fighting required."

By the time he finished, the elders looked more confused than ever. Confused and *angry*, and James rushed to get to the point.

"This is just one of many, *many* new crises that exist in the savanna," he said. "There are at least thirty other completely different but equally dangerous situations going on in the lands directly surrounding Windy Lake. There *were* more, but taking out the undead in Red Canyon took care of a lot of them. The point of all this, though, is that we're not just facing one problem with one solution. *Every* dark corner and forgotten watering hole in the savanna has some kind of threat growing in it."

He started counting off on his fingers. "There are bandits with dangerous artifacts, necromantic cults corrupting animals, and one of the boneyards in the south has been taken over by the spirits of the angry dead. Every old evil or buried problem you can name from your history is on the verge of being unsealed, resurrected, or stumbled upon by some cultist, misfit, anarchist, or criminal. Unless we act quickly and decisively, all of these disasters will be out of control within the week, and chaos will engulf the savanna."

"If that's the case, then we must appeal to the king for help," Storm of the Water Born said.

"The king can't help you," James replied quickly.

"Why not?" demanded the warrior. "We Four Clans are Bastion's oldest allies! The king's ancestors swore that the Royal Knights would come to our defense in times of crisis!"

"The knights can't come, because your situation in the savanna is not unique," James said bleakly. "Every zone, town, village, outpost, settlement, farm, and island in the *entire world* is facing their own version of this exact same problem. They're all just as outmatched as you are and desperately holding together in the hopes that *someone* will come and save them. When FFO was a game, that someone was the players. Now, there's no one."

James reached down for his bag containing the lich's letters. "And there's another reason Bastion can't come to your rescue. The royal city is about to be invaded by the Once King's armies. The lich in Red Canyon wasn't an isolated incident. The Once King seeded the entire world with his operatives, and they've been building him an army on a global scale. When the Once King gives his command, that army will teleport into the Room of Arrivals at the center of Bastion and tear the city apart from the inside out. I don't know when exactly, but I have ample proof that it will happen soon. The jubatus are some of the king's oldest and most loyal allies, which is why I need your help. I must get this information to Bastion as soon as possible to make sure they're ready to defend against the attack."

"But you can't leave now," one of the minor clan heads said. "You're the only one who knows about these 'quests.' You just told us how outnumbered we are. How can you leave us alone?"

"Because you won't be alone," James said with a smile. "The jubatus of Windy Lake aren't the only ones who want to save the savanna. The gnolls of Red Canyon also want to make a home here, and that's why you need to make peace. The undead trained them into a formidable army to use against you. Now that Ar'Bati and I defeated the lich, though, they're free of his influence and a powerful potential ally. They have the logistics and strength you need to stand a chance against what's coming. The Four Clans have great warriors and unequaled ferocity, but you're not prepared for a protracted battle of this magnitude. The gnolls are. They can help you."

The room fell silent at that, and James took his chance. "I want to stay and help defend Windy Lake against what's coming," he said earnestly. "But I have to warn the king. No one else has this information, that I know of, and if the king doesn't learn of it before the undead attack, Bastion will fall for sure. I also don't believe that one player, even a level eighty, is going to be enough to protect you. Even if we did beat back the chaos that's coming to the savanna, the Once King's armies are marching. They're not going to stop at Bastion. You need strong allies now more than ever if you're going to survive the next few months, and the gnolls are willing and able. I know you have centuries of bad blood between you, but if the clans want their honor to live on for another year, you need to listen to Thunder Paw, not kill him, because he might be the only way you're getting out of this alive."

He sat down after that, panting with the rush. As he looked around the room, though, James began to worry he'd done his job *too* well. All he'd wanted was to convince them they needed to take this seriously and keep Thunder Paw alive, but the ring of leaders around him looked sick with fear. Thinking back on what he'd just said, James couldn't blame them. He hadn't realized just how bad a picture he'd painted until it was done, but between the local quests that weren't getting finished and the Once King's coming army, their situation was downright apocalyptic.

"Are we doomed?" Gray Fang whispered, her face tight. "Even if we swallowed our pride and allied with the gnolls, do we stand a chance against so many enemies?"

James wasn't sure, but before he could think of what to say, Ar'Bati leaped to his feet.

"We have more than a chance," the warrior said. "We have James!" He looked down at his new brother over their father's head. "You know how to fix all of this, don't you? Just like you knew how to take apart Red Canyon. You've done all these quests. I know you have! You can tell us how to solve these problems."

James nodded with a gulp as the room once against fixated on him. "I can list all of the questlines in this zone and tell you how to handle them, but I'm not sure how much good it will do. Now that this isn't a game anymore, everything's gone off the script, including the villains. My intel's getting older by the hour, so—"

"So we must move quickly before too much changes," finished Rend, putting a possessive arm around James's shoulders. "Fetch a scribe!"

"Fetch two scribes!" called Gray Fang, her eyes locked on James with deadly intensity. "You will tell us everything you know, and when dawn comes, we will send our warriors to complete these tasks and defend our home."

James nodded, happy to help. "And Thunder Paw?"

Gray Fang glanced at the others. "We will meet with him."

He let out a relieved breath. "Thank you."

"Thank us by saying what you know," Rend growled, motioning impatiently as a young jubatus scrambled into the lodge, carrying a quill and a stack of grass-fiber papers.

The leaders of the Four Clans grilled James until dawn. Before he could describe the quests, though, he first had to explain Forever Fantasy Online the game, clarifying terms like aggro, player, NPC, levels, and so on. Once the elders had enough shared vocabulary to understand what he was telling them, James went on to explain the situations behind each of the savanna's questing hubs as well as the enemy's levels, skull ratings, and locations of all important quest items.

By the end of it, he felt like a human wiki. Even for a hardcore

FFO nerd like him, it was a challenge to recall everything, and some of his accounts were embarrassingly vague. There were many quests that James had only done once then skipped on future replays because they were annoying, so sometimes the elders had to settle for descriptions like "that tent with the two guys who argue a lot" or "that one big lizard who ate the Schtumple wearing the bowler hat."

Fortunately, his added Intelligence gear made him great at remembering minutiae, so his descriptions never got *too* bad. Also, having been a quest giver himself, Ar'Bati knew a great deal about Windy Lake's local problems, and while his questline had been resolved with the end of the undead in Red Canyon, there were several minor quests that he knew much better than James did.

By the time the sun rose, the two scribes had recorded over a hundred different quests. Even James was shocked by the number now that he saw them all listed, but the elders looked positively defeated.

"How did things get this bad in only eighty years?" Gray Fang said.

"It was the game!" someone hissed in reply. "And the players. They're the ones all of this was for!"

James winced as another round of bile and vitriol for FFO swept the room, but at least now none of it was directed at him. It was weird sitting right next to his adopted father as the man cursed players and wished blood-chilling violence upon them with one breath only to turn and offer James a drink of water the next, grinning at him like a proud father who never got tired of showing off how useful and important his son was. But while the hate still made him uncomfortable, James couldn't help but smile back whenever the broad-shouldered jubatus beamed at him.

It was just so different. At home, he avoided his parents as much as possible out of shame, and they never sought him out. Tina didn't acknowledge him unless she needed a healer for her raids, and even among his extended family, no one ever asked him, "How's it going?" because the only direction James ever seemed to go was down. That was why, as strange as it was having an adopted family of magical, bloodthirsty cat-people who'd wanted to kill him less than eight hours ago, James found himself enjoying every second.

Even with the reality of just how screwed Windy Lake was looming over their heads, the sheer joy of not being a failure for once—*especially* when his success involved his crazily in-depth knowledge of

FFO, a hobby he'd always felt guilty for loving because it seemed like a waste of time—was indescribable. He could have sat there rattling off quests forever, but as the dawn crept higher in the sky, the questions got harder to hear. By the time the sun broke through the flap covering the lodge's door, James realized suddenly that he couldn't remember what anyone had said for the last several minutes. He was trying to get himself back together when Rend's hand landed roughly on his shoulder.

"James!"

"I'm awake," he said reflexively.

"But you shouldn't be," Gray Fang said, standing up stiffly from her large pillow. "We need to end this. We already have much to do, and it's been two days since these two"—she pointed at James and Ar'Bati, who'd fallen asleep sitting up—"last slept. They need rest if they're to be any use to us, but we've learned what we need. Today, our war parties will ride out to deal with those threats they can manage while we clan leaders talk with the gnolls of Red Canyon. Everything else will flow from there."

There were lots of nods and noises of agreement as the group of elders stretched, yawned, and dispersed. As they left the lodge, their assistants were given piles of written orders to deliver to the warriors who'd be running quests. Meanwhile, James woke up Fangs in the Grass, and the two of them wearily followed their father back to the Claw Born family's collection of yurts near the town center.

Once inside the spacious tent, James barely managed to greet the rest of his new extended family before falling face-first onto the bed Rend pointed at. The moment he hit the soft hides, he was out, his Eclipsed Steel Staff falling from his limp fingers as he sank into a deep, dreamless sleep.

CHAPTER *19*

Tina and James

James woke up what felt like only moments later with an elegant older jubatus lady he didn't know in his face.

"Up, James. Up!" she said briskly, whipping off his blankets.

Alarmed, James staggered out of bed. He was still trying to figure out what was going on when his chest armor was politely shoved into his hands. His *cleaned* chest armor. James didn't know how it was possible, but all the stains of blood and mud were gone from the leather, and the scuffs had been buffed out. Even the damaged stitching had been replaced with magically appropriate thread. The armor had also had a large yellow claw insignia added to the front and back, taking up most of his torso.

"Dress, quick, quick!" the jubatus lady said. "The sun is high, and there's a lot to do." A young girl entered with two plates of fish as she finished, eyeing James nervously before setting them down and scurrying away. The lady smiled and pointed at a sitting cushion in front the food. "Eat!"

James put on his newly marked armor, then sat down where she ordered. "I'm sorry," he said as politely as he could. "But who are you?"

"Don't be silly," the jubatus lady said with a charming laugh. "I'm your mother, Acacia Claw Born."

James almost choked on his bite of fish. The elegant woman in front of him was nothing like the jovial, casually violent Rend. Every hair and whisker was in place, and her red-and-gold robe was scarfed and belted perfectly at all points. Even the kohl outlining her golden eyes was flawlessly pointed at the tips. Everything about her screamed formality and class, which left James wondering how in the world a woman like this had ended up with Ar'Bati for a son.

"Keep eating," his adopted mother scolded. "There's not much morning left, and yours is full! First, you have to be apprenticed to Elder Gray Fang. Then you'll be joining your father for the clan heads' meeting with Thunder Paw. Once that business is settled, you'll be sent to Bastion as our emissary to deliver the scrolls you found to the king. I'd prefer to come with you since I am the clans' appointed ambassador to Bastion, but I can't leave Rend alone to conduct peace talks. I don't want to return and find Lilac married to a gnoll!"

She chuckled at that, then her face grew serious again. "I know you have no idea how to represent us properly, so I'm sending your brother Fangs in the Grass with you. Rend can lead the warriors in the Ar'Bati's absence. He'll enjoy that."

She smiled at James, whose head was spinning from so much information at once. "Thank you for arranging everything," he managed at last. "And for cleaning my armor."

"But of course, dear," Acacia said. "We couldn't have you running around looking like a bandit! You're a Claw Born now. Your actions and appearance reflect on us all, and speaking of, can I convince you to not brandish around that piece of blasphemy?"

She pointed at the corner, and James turned to see his Eclipsed Steel Staff propped against the tent wall, its black metal wrapped in a white sheet and bound with wooden sealing charms.

"I could feel its dark presence from outside the tent," his new mother said, wrinkling her nose. "Please tell me you'll get rid of it. It's not proper for a Claw Born."

"I'll find a way to be rid of it in Bastion," James promised, taking another bite of fish. "I have lots of proper weapons and armor in the bank that I can use to replace this stuff, assuming the bank is still okay." At her alarmed look, he quickly added, "It's all Naturalist gear, nothing you'd disapprove of."

"Just make sure to wear our crest when you're in Bastion," she said sternly. "Never forget that you're representing Windy Lake and the pride of the Claw Born." She tapped her foot while he took one more bite of fish, then she leaned down to whisk the plate away. "That's enough! There'll be time for more later. Now go to the main lodge! Gray Fang is already waiting for you, and don't forget to greet your sister, Lilac, as well! She needs a chance to thank you before you leave."

James's stomach was still growling, but she'd already shoved his things into his hands and hurried him out of the Claw Borns' large yurt, closing the flap with as much finality as heavy hide could manage. Gripping his bag and wrapped staff with a sigh, James turned and started toward the lodge. Elder Gray Fang was waiting when he got there, standing in the doorway with her gray tail lashing in annoyance.

"You're late," she said as he climbed the stairs.

"Sorry, um..." James trailed off. "What should I call you now? Teacher? Sensei? Elder?" The correct address was important. Propriety was clearly a huge thing among the jubatus, and he didn't want to give more offense than he already had, especially since Gray Fang already looked mad enough to spit nails.

"It doesn't matter," she growled. "This whole apprenticeship idea is ridiculous. You probably know more about magic than I do."

James flicked an ear in surprise. That was not what he'd expected her to be angry about. "Not at all," he said respectfully. "You're a master of nature magic. I only know a dozen or so very specific spells."

"You're joking," Gray Fang said scornfully. "No one with your power can possibly be that ignorant."

"Sadly, I'm dead serious," James replied. "Player power is highly specialized. I'd love to learn more about how magic actually works from someone as revered and wise as you."

He finished with a smile, hoping that Gray Fang wasn't immune to flattery. Hopes that were rewarded when her gray ears pricked up.

"I can show you a few things," she said, her voice less gruff. "So long as you remember who's the student around here. Honestly, it'll be nice to have someone who can do the mana-heavy work. I'm getting too old for the really exhausting stuff." She tilted her head at James, then she gave him something close to a smile. "I'll begin your training once you return from Bastion. For now, though, you should go inside. I told Lilac you'd visit her this morning, but don't take long. The peace talks are starting soon, and after all the work you did terrifying us into accepting them, I'm sure you won't want to be late."

James promised to hurry and ducked into the empty lodge. After a minute of poking around, he found a cot in one of the side rooms, and lying on top of it was the young cheetah-girl who'd been poisoned a few days ago. His new sister, Scout Lilac.

"Are you James?" she asked, opening her eyes, which were the same golden as Acacia's.

"I am. Hi." James twisted his hands, not sure what to actually say. "I'm...I suppose I'm your new brother. Big family, right?"

She smiled weakly, and James glanced down at the magic running through her lifelines. As expected given what she'd been through, the glow was weak, but he saw no traces of necromancy or the ghostfire, and he exhaled with relief.

Her smile widened at the sound. "I'm all right now, thanks to you and Fangs," she said, lifting her arm to show him the healing arrow wound. "Grandmother says I'll be able to go back to work in a few more days. Thank you so much for saving me."

James was about to say it was nothing when her head suddenly shot up.

"Was that the last time I have to do this?"

The fear in her voice made him wince. "Yes," he said firmly. "You got caught in the last of the Nightmare's momentum. But the lich is dead now, and the gnolls are free. You'll never be poisoned again."

"Thank the wind and grass," Lilac said, flopping back on her cot. "Ever since I was cured, I've been lying here terrified that I'd just wake up in the canyon where they always ambush me and everything would start again. I've suffered that poison for eighty years. Sometimes players would save me, and I'd get a few hours of relief. Other times…"

Her thin hands flew up to her face, but she couldn't hide the tears that trickled down her mottled tan fur. "In the beginning, it wasn't so bad," she whispered. "I was almost always saved. These last few decades, though, the players stopped coming. More often than not, I would die burning and turn undead, killing everyone until the next dawn, when it would start all over again. I knew every minute by heart, but I couldn't do anything differently. I couldn't save myself."

James had no idea what to say. He couldn't imagine going through what she'd suffered even once, let alone thousands of times. Outside, a pair of crows cawed loudly, highlighting the awkward quiet as his sister wept. He was desperately struggling for some way to comfort her when she reached up to grab his arm.

He jumped at the touch. Her hand was terrifyingly thin, and her skin felt papery beneath the fur, but her eyes were intense as she stared up at him. "You have to listen to me," she said, her weak voice urgent. "I know better than anyone here what the ghostfire does. It doesn't just burn. It fills you with the voice of the Once King. Fills you with his *hate*."

Her hand began to shake, and James grabbed it with his. "It's okay now," he said. "We broke the orb in Red Canyon for good. You'll never

397

have to feel that again."

"And I can't tell you how grateful I am for that," Lilac said. "But there's still something I must tell you."

She pulled him closer. James allowed it reluctantly, worried this had something to do with Rend's engagement nonsense. When they were almost whisker to whisker, though, he realized she was afraid.

"Every time I turned and was forced to attack my family and friends, I heard the Once King in my head," she whispered. "During the Nightmare, no one could talk. Not freely, anyway. I couldn't say anything but my quest text while I was being poisoned, but once the ghostfire consumed me, I could hear his voice. I don't know how, but the Once King could *talk* to me. Actually talk in words not bound by the game."

James hunched closer, awkwardness forgotten. "What did he say?"

"Madness, mostly," Lilac said sadly. "Sometimes he would recite poetry. Other times he ordered us around, telling us to go here or there, do this or that. I couldn't, of course, and that enraged him. He kept thinking I was a new recruit every time, and he'd always be angry that I wasn't following orders. But once, only once, he said something amazing."

Another tear rolled down her cheek, and James clutched her hand. "What?"

"Ten years ago, he said, 'I will save you. I will save us all.'"

James shivered. Lilac repeated the words with utter reverence, as if the Once King's promise was sacred to her. "Do you know what he meant?"

"I have no idea," she said. "But they were the only words I ever heard him say in love. Everything else he spoke was madness and despair, but not that. They were also his last."

James straightened up in surprise. "What do you mean 'his last'? I'm sure he's still around." Tina's raiders had wiped on him for three nights straight just last week, but Lilac was shaking her head.

"After those words, he never spoke to my undead self properly ever again. There were no more poems, no more orders. Just the same ravings over and over again. 'Death to the living,' 'I will have my revenge,' that sort of thing."

James nodded, thinking fast. The idea that there was a being out there who'd been in FFO while it was a game but hadn't been enslaved to the Nightmare was huge. He wasn't sure what it meant yet, but his instincts said that the exception was an incredible clue. He wished he could ask some of his more lore-savvy friends about it, like SilentBlayde. The Assassin had a ridiculously in-depth knowledge of FFO's setting and history. He dimly remembered a rumor that some players had reported hearing a weird voice during the roll-out of the Deadlands expansion a year ago. Tina's Roughnecks had been online twenty-four, seven that whole week, so maybe they'd heard something firsthand. He was scrambling to think of a way he could verify that when he realized Lilac was still crying.

"I'm sorry," he said, feeling like a horrible brother. "What's wrong? Do you hurt from the poison still?"

"No," she said, scrubbing angrily at her eyes. "I'm the one who's sorry. I promise I'm not normally this weak, but lying here all day and night with the poison eating me while everyone else walked around free was…bitter. Now we're talking about the Once King, and it makes me so upset. I can't handle it."

"Why?" James asked, realizing belatedly that maybe that wasn't the kindest response.

"Because I'm so sad for him," came the surprising answer. "I don't know what was done to him, but I'm sure someone hurt him deeply long ago." She looked down at her hands, almost as if she was ashamed. "I know he's the enemy of every living thing, but I…I don't think the Once King is actually a bad person. He recites poems to his minions to comfort them, like a father at his sick child's bedside. I think that those words I heard ten years ago were his last. I don't know what happened after that, but I think he chose to give us his hope at the end rather than his anger." She wiped her eyes again. "I know it's foolish, but I'm almost worried about him. Isn't that stupid?"

"I don't think it's stupid at all," James said quietly, squeezing her hand. "Thank you for telling me, Lilac. I know this might be hard to believe, but my sister from my world, Tina, is a player, too. She's been to the Deadlands, and she saw the Once King with her own eyes not even a week ago. I'm pretty sure she's there now, just like I'm here, so I'm going to find her and tell her what you've told me."

He left off any promises of further action because he had no idea what to do beyond that, but that promise was enough to make Lilac nod.

"Thank you, James," she said, lying back in her cot. "I'm happy

Father adopted you. You're already a great brother."

James flushed, wishing his real sister felt the same way. Being reminded of Tina and being called a good brother was enough to make his throat close up. Lilac didn't need his baggage, though, so he kept his worries to himself, rising to his feet instead. "Get well soon, sister," he said, summoning up a gleaming smile for her. She gave him a fanged grin back before closing her eyes for sleep.

The moment she wasn't looking, James rushed out of the lodge, blowing past Gray Fang as he rushed into the village toward the gnolls' encampment.

■ ■

The festival grounds were on the north side of the village. Looking at the large patch of barren soil, James felt that "ground" was about all this area could be called. The first thing James noticed when he entered was the improvised border complete with guard tent and checkpoint that the jubatus had set up between the gnolls and the town. On the other side, beyond the stern line of cat-warriors, lay what could only be termed Fort Thunder Paw.

James slowed down, jaw falling open in amazement. The gnolls had only arrived last night, but they'd already created an impressive structure, circling their wagons to create a walled ring complete with elevated shooting positions and controlled access. Inside, a ring of barracks-tents surrounded a larger, more formal tent that housed Thunder Paw and his emissaries. Gnolls were everywhere, marching in groups of six or more as they patrolled the grassy area between Windy Lake and its new neighbor.

"This is like the Korean border," James muttered, holding up his hands as the jubatus guards came forward to search him. Once they saw the Claw Born insignia on his armor, though, he was waved through with only minimal growling.

The guards on both sides eyed him warily as he walked across the no-man's land between village and camp. Thankfully, once he got inside the ringwall of wagons, getting to see Thunder Paw was relatively easy. He was still challenged at three different checkpoints, but the gnolls snickered and yipped happily at him once he announced his name, motioning for him to go on through.

Thunder Paw's tent was a lavish three-room affair made from canvas and woven grass rugs. Inside, he found another grim gathering. Ar'Bati, Rend, and Thunder Paw were all sitting on small wooden benches, scowling down at a large hide with a map of the entire savanna painted across it. The map was covered in various bits of glass, wooden tokens, and colored rocks that Thunder Paw was moving around like game pieces. Everyone looked up when the guard announced him, and the expressions on their faces were enough to make his fur stand on end.

"What happened?" he asked.

Ar'Bati, newly equipped in his own set of Claw Born-branded leather armor, turned back to the map with a dark look. "We have a problem. One of our scout patrols says that something called the Waterhole Bandits Event just started at one of the oases. I've never heard of it, and it wasn't in the list of threats you gave us last night."

"That's because it's not supposed to be happening," James replied in a worried voice. "The Waterhole Bandits are a one-off seasonal event that only happens on April First as part of the Spring Cleaning of the savanna series. The nightmare broke on April twenty-eighth, so those guys should be already be beaten and done for the year."

"Well, clearly no one told *them* that," Fangs snapped. "They are pillaging and plundering their way across the entire northern savanna as we speak! It's going to be too dangerous for us to travel to Bastion with things like this, so I'm taking a force of warriors to meet one of Red Canyon's chiefs. We're going to fight together to drive the bandits out once and for all."

Despite the grim looks, that announcement was enough to make James grin from ear to ear. They didn't even have a treaty yet, but if they were already fighting together, then this was already going better than he'd hoped. It would have been nice if it hadn't taken the threat of mutually assured destruction to ensure peace, of course, but James was ready to take what he could get at this point. That said, there was still one problem.

"I'm not going to tell you not to go," he said, "but I can't come with you. I have to get these scrolls to Bastion as soon as possible. It's only a matter of time before the lich's spies realize he's dead, and we have no idea how many of the Once King's other commanders are still active. Red Canyon was only a tiny part of the 'portal an undead army into

Bastion' plan. If the invasion goes down, and we fail to warn the king in time, Bastion's defeat will be on our heads."

Fangs growled deep in his throat, clearly torn between his duty here in the savanna and the jubatus' allegiance to the king. His tail was still lashing when Rend stood up and put a hand on James's shoulder. Like his son, the old jubatus was almost a foot taller than James. He was broader as well, towering over him as the old warrior looked him in the eyes.

"I know the honor we owe to the king," he said. "But even if you run straight there, you boys will never get to Bastion. There are hundreds of bandits between you and the border, and they're empowered by strange magics we don't understand. Duty is well and good, but I won't risk both my sons cutting through that alone. Is there any way the other players in Bastion already know about this invasion and can warn the king in your stead?"

James was so touched by his new father's concern for his safety, it took him a while to properly process the question. "Maybe," he said at last. "But I don't think there's anyone out there who has the whole picture like I do. The Bastion spy quests are spread out over many levels, and other than a few mandatory ones, most players just skip them. Even if they did complete the line, most max-level players haven't done those quests in years. The only reason *I* remembered them is because I was standing on top of the letters."

For emphasis, he took off his backpack and opened it to pull out a letter. He'd just meant to use the folded paper as a prop, but as he dug around inside the heavy cloth sack, his hand brushed a scroll that tingled with magic.

James froze, mind going blank. "Oh my god, I'm an idiot," he said, face splitting into a grin as he grabbed the scroll and thrust it triumphantly into the air. "We can use this!"

Rend frowned. "What's that?" His nose wrinkled. "Smells like necromancy."

"That's only because it's been inside a lich's desk for eighty years," James said quickly. "This is a portal scroll. The lich was going to use it to open a gateway for his army of undead to march into Bastion after he'd conquered Windy Lake, but there's no reason *we* can't use it to get there instead! I've got tons of other correspondence, so I don't even need it for proof." His grin widened. "We can turn the undead's own plan against them! We can use this scroll to teleport into Bastion and warn the king about what's coming! Forget walking through bandits. With this, we can be in the Room of Arrivals in five minutes!"

Thunder Paw and Rend were still eyeing the scroll fearfully, but Ar'Bati had already risen to his feet.

"Let's go, then," he said, grabbing a pack from the corner of the tent.

The agreement happened so fast, James was caught off guard. "Are you sure?" he asked nervously. "Do we need to arrange anything or—"

"What's to arrange?" Fangs said with a shrug. "You *said* it was important." He smiled at Rend. "Father will handle the bandits. He was going to be in charge of our warriors while I was gone, anyway."

"That's right," Rend said proudly, nodding to Thunder Paw. "We'll crush these fools who think they can take the grasslands from us." He stood up then stepped forward to grab Ar'Bati and James in a crushing hug. "You boys go. The Four Clans are the king's oldest allies. We can't let him down now! I'll take care of everything while you're away. This isn't my first stampede."

"Thank you, Father," Fangs said, lowering his head respectfully as Rend let them go. "I swear we will not disappoint you."

"And I promise to get us home safe," James added. "I have plenty of gold in the bank at Bastion. It should be more than enough to buy us safe passage back to Windy Lake when this is over."

Rend waved as though sending his sons through a one-way portal to an enormous city that might soon be under siege were a trivial matter, but Thunder Paw caught James's eye.

"Be careful," the old gnoll warned. "The undead are relentless. Even if you foil their plans, they will never stop. Me know this."

He touched the collar at his neck, and James nodded.

"We'll be careful," he promised. "Thank you, Thunder Paw."

The gnoll nodded, turning back to the map with Rend at his side. Satisfied the savanna was in good hands, James let Ar'Bati pull him out of the tent, through the gnolls' checkpoints, and to the edge of the festival grounds outside.

Once he'd located a suitably flat stretch of grass, James unrolled the scroll and started reading. Spell scrolls had been a pretty common mechanic back when FFO was a game, and most only needed to be read aloud to activate. That said, James almost screwed this one up immediately, because the scroll was written in elven, not the Language of Wind and Grass. Pronouncing the unfamiliar words was a challenge, but the spell had its own momentum once started, and soon James was caught up in it like a leaf in a stream, reciting the strange words in a ringing voice.

As he read them, the magical letters peeled off the page, forming huge glowing streams of blue mana exponentially larger than the ones he normally worked with. The ribbons of mana shot out into the land, seeking all the elements, even ones James couldn't see, like fire and light. Once it had gathered all the magics, the spell scroll wound them together to form a spinning mosaic of power. It was incredibly beautiful, but James couldn't appreciate it, because now that he'd reached the end of the spell, his guts were suddenly wrenched inside his body as the world twisted to form a blazing-white circle six feet in diameter shining like a tiny sun in front of them.

"Cooooooool," James said, lowering the now-blank scroll.

Portals in game hadn't been anything special. They were just spinning doorways, easy paths to other parts of the game world. Now, though, being near the portal was nothing short of incredible. The magic coming off the shining circle made his skin tingle, and he could actually smell the smoky city scent of Bastion wafting through from the other side. It was absolutely stunning, but as much as James wanted to study the spinning ring of interwoven magic in front of him, there was no time. As the glowing portal stabilized, the gleaming-white light inside the circle cleared to reveal a huge, empty stone room lined with pillars. The Room of Arrivals.

"We gotta move," he said, swinging his bag onto his shoulder and sliding his wrapped staff between the straps. "These things don't last long!"

"Then let us go," Ar'Bati said, offering James his hand. "Brother."

James grabbed the offered paw with a grin and jumped through, pulling his brother through the magic and into the great city on the other side.

■ ■

Thirty minutes earlier, on the other side of the world, Tina was sleeping in.

She woke to a dim gray glow, which was as bright as it got in the Deadlands. She rolled over on one of the barracks' stonekin-sized cots, then lay still a moment longer, listening to the noise of the Order outside. Given how many times she'd logged out here, the hustle and bustle of the fort felt oddly nostalgic. As much as she was enjoying lazing in bed, though, today was the day they were supposed to go to Bastion, so after a brief few minutes, Tina hoisted herself up and went to check on her guild.

After fourteen hours of fatigue-induced slumber, most of the other players were busy sorting themselves out as well. There were attempts at ordinary morning-routine stuff. People laughed at the new racial differences as the feline jubatus stretched their spines and the ichthyians discovered they had slept with their eyes open. NekoBaby and a few others with the his-her problem were pondering which gender's bathroom they were supposed to use before discovering that the Order's facilities made no such distinctions.

Tina poked her head outside to discover that breakfast had already arrived for them in the form of multiple baskets. When she brought them inside and opened them up, the smell of fresh baked bread roused everyone who wasn't already awake. Tina looked forlornly at the delicious golden loaves while she and GneissGuy crunched their rocks. Idly, she wondered if there were stonekin chefs out there somewhere who could make them different flavors of magical rock to eat.

She was still steadily crunching away when Tina felt a twisting in the air. Everyone stopped eating as their stomachs flip-flopped, looking around in confusion. Breakfast had just resumed when Commander Garrond, looking as disapproving as ever and still wearing his armor from yesterday, barged into the barracks.

"Morning, Commander," Tina said respectfully, angling to keep her good footing from yesterday. "All quiet on the western front?"

She was trying for friendly, but the prickly paladin was all scowls, glaring at the raid from beneath his bushy eyebrows. "The portal to Bastion is up," he snapped. "Finish your food and get out."

Tina sighed. So much for getting along. "We'll be out in fifteen," she assured him, rising from her reinforced stool. "Thanks for keeping your end of the bargain."

The commander nodded brusquely and left, his aides trailing after him in a flurry. When he was gone, Tina turned to her raiders. "You

405

heard the man! Stuff your bellies then your armor, 'cause we're leaving for Bastion in fifteen minutes!"

There were no cheers this time. Just the gulps, coughs, and slurps of rapid eating. When she was satisfied they were hustling properly, Tina returned to her bunk to put her boots back on. Nothing could get her out of her armor, but even she hadn't been willing to sleep with shoes on.

She grabbed the huge metal boots from under her bed, grimacing in disgust at how much of her silvery blood still coated the insides. From the clammy way her breastplate kept sticking to her skin, she suspected the rest of her suit wasn't much better. She really should have cleaned it last night, but eating and sleeping had taken priority.

She was regretting that decision now. Roxxy's main profession was Blacksmith, and just like her Knight skills, the smith's knowledge was waiting in her brain when she reached for it, informing her of just how impossible it was to get blood out of armor padding once it had a chance to set. Between that and all the dents she'd collected during Grel's beating, her gear was in serious need of maintenance. Hopefully, she could find somewhere to do that in Bastion. For now, though, there was nothing for it but to swallow her disgust and shove her bare stone feet back into her clammy, metallic-smelling footwear. She was pulling the leather straps tight when SilentBlayde walked over.

"Hey," he said brightly, jumping up on the stonekin-sized bunk to sit beside her.

"Hey yourself," Tina replied, smiling down at him. Like everyone else, he looked much better this morning. Magical healing could fix their bodies, but there were some things that only real sleep could cure. Now, though, the dark shadows that had been under his eyes since he'd died and been raised were finally gone, making her smile with relief.

"So," SB said, lowering his voice so the others wouldn't hear. "What's the plan when we hit Bastion?"

"It's less of a plan and more of a list," Tina replied. "First item is to get to the bank and get our stuff. Money, gear, pets, crafting materials, mounts, anything we might be able to use. After that, I'd like to talk to the portal keepers. In the game, it was their job to deal with all the multiple timelines, alternate dimensions, and other bullshit the developers came up with to fill the game with content, so I figure if anyone knows how we can get back home, it's them."

SB nodded and glanced pointedly at the rest of the raid. "What about the Roughnecks?"

Tina shrugged. "I've done everything I can to make us a guild, but there's no way to know for sure until people have a chance to leave without dying. We held together yesterday, and I want to think that's going to last, but once the heat's off, I wouldn't be surprised if things got messy." They both looked grim at the possibility, then Tina added, "I'm counting on you to help me. You're a lot better with people than I am."

He smiled at that. Or at least, she thought he did. It was impossible to tell when his mouth was hidden by his ever-present mask, and the more Tina thought about that, the more it bothered her.

"Hey, 'Blayde," she said wistfully, reaching out a hand toward the dark cloth that covered the bottom half of his face. "Do you have to wear this thing all the time?"

She felt him tense as she hooked a finger over the top of the fabric, but his voice was light when he answered.

"Of course. It's a crucial part of my cool ninja motif."

"That's a pity," Tina said as she began inching the mask down. "People around here might appreciate seeing your expressions." *She really wanted to see him smile again*, but as she pushed his mask lower, SB vanished out from under her fingers. He reappeared a few feet away, reaching up to push his mask back into place.

"Sorry," he said quietly. "I'm not comfortable keeping it open yet."

Tina stared at him, genuinely confused. "But... I thought you liked how your character looked. You did that whole beautiful-elf-prince reveal on me yesterday, remember?"

SilentBlayde's face reddened. "You needed that then," he explained. "But I need this now. Please, Roxxy, let it be."

The desperation in his voice caused an instant knot in her stomach. In all their years together, SilentBlayde had only shut her down this hard once before, and it had been one of the worst experiences of Tina's life. She never wanted to feel that way again, and she dropped the subject like a radioactive hot potato.

"Sure, man, no worries," she said quickly, struggling to keep her voice casual. "Sorry. Didn't know it was a thing."

"Thank you," SB said quietly. Then he was forced to duck to the side as NekoBaby bounced into their conversation.

"Oooooooo!" the cat-girl said, tail swishing. "It's getting steamy over here! What's the gossip?!"

SB gave NekoBaby the best death glare Tina had ever seen and left to grab his backpack. Neko shrugged at his back and turned to badger Tina instead, but Tina had already stood up, and she used her vastly superior height to look straight over the petulant cat-girl's head.

"Time's up, peeps!" she yelled, drowning out the rest of Neko's questions. "Let's move!"

■ ■

Standing in front of the portal to Bastion, Tina had to admit the magical doorway was much more impressive than she'd given it credit for.

Inside the Order's white stone portal shrine were five crystal columns. These had been dark when she'd checked the portal room yesterday. Now, though, each one contained a maelstrom of a different element. After days of the Deadlands' endless gray, the rainbow collage of colors was the loveliest thing Tina could imagine, but it was the massive hole in the world surrounded by crackling energy that really took the cake.

It was so crazy looking, Tina couldn't help reaching out to touch the swirling edges, and she got a nasty shock for her trouble. Other players were walking around the floating portal in circles, enjoying the bizarre optical illusions it created as it warped space and time. There was much oohing and aahhing and heated discussion among the Sorcerers as they tried to figure out how the Order had pulled off the one spell they could no longer manage. It might have gone on forever if Commander Garrond hadn't been waiting in the doorway, tapping his metal boot impatiently on the stone.

Rolling her eyes, Tina stepped up to the portal's edge. Through the swirling magic, she could see the Room of Arrivals, the giant pale-pink stone chamber lined with columns that served as the receiving room for all portals to Bastion and the game's central transportation hub with permanent portals to every major city and raiding zone, including the Deadlands by way of the Order Fort. All that crisscrossing normally made it the busiest place in the game, so Tina was surprised when she didn't see any other players—or any other portals—waiting inside. She was about to ask someone else what they thought when Garrond's tapping got more insistent, his boot clanging on the stone like someone bashing a frying pan against a rock.

"Okay, okay, we're going," she growled, giving the commander a poisonous look before raising her hand. "Roughnecks, *in!*"

With that command, she leaped through the portal. There was a brief moment of disorientation, like she was doing a backflip underwater, then her feet landed on solid stone again, and Tina moved out of the way as SilentBlayde came through right behind her.

Now that she was through, it was obvious that what she'd seen through the portal hadn't been an illusion. The Room of Arrivals really was completely empty. But that was a worry for later. She met SB's eyes with a knowing look, then the two of them took up position on either side of the portal, watching carefully as the rest of the raid jumped through one player at a time. Zen brought up the rear, crossing with a graceful leap, but even after she walked away, Tina and SilentBlayde didn't move. Then faster than Tina could blink, SilentBlayde's hand shot out to grab something out of the empty air.

The momentum of whatever it was nearly took him off his feet. Tina was at his side at once, putting a hand on his shoulder to steady him while she reached out to grab his struggling target with the other.

"*Ho bag!*" KuroKawaii yelled, her body flickering out of the shadows as she fought Tina's iron grasp. "Let me go, or I'll stab you!"

She reached for her daggers, but Tina just gave her a shake, knocking the small elf around like a doll before lifting the Assassin up until she was dangling two feet off the ground with her back less than an inch from the swirling magic of the portal.

"You dirty little traitor," Tina growled. "This portal is for Roughnecks only. You know, the people who actually *earned* it."

Kuro kicked Tina only to wince when her foot banged into a metal plate. "Screw you! I never said I'd join your guild! I don't owe you shit!"

"Zero was forced to hide inside an undead boar because of you!" Tina shouted in her face. "SilentBlayde almost *died*. We *all* almost died, because of *you!*" She leaned to the side so KuroKawaii could see the faces of the players behind her, and the elf went still as she realized all that anger was directed at her this time.

When she was sure Kuro had gotten the point, Tina pulled the short elf in close. "Guild or not, you don't sign up for a fight and bail," she said, her voice low and deadly. "We were counting on you, and you left us to die. The only reason you were able to use this portal is because we were awesome enough to pull victory out of the bag anyway." Her eyes narrowed. "I should throw you back to Garrond and make you hike your sorry ass through that damn swamp alone for the shit you put us through."

Kuro was shaking by the time she finished, her normally tan face drained of color as she looked backward through the portal at the four-skull commander waiting on other side. "You wouldn't," she whimpered.

Tina wasn't above letting her sweat over that for a moment. In the end, though, she pulled her arm back. "You're right," she said, placing Kuro back on the ground. "I wouldn't. I said I was going to get everyone to Bastion alive, and I meant it. That includes you, even though you don't deserve it."

She let the Assassin's expression of terror relax just a fraction before adding, "But this isn't just *my* guild anymore."

Her eyes grew wide again as Tina turned them around to address the other players.

"Roughnecks! Time for a vote. All in favor of throwing KuroKawaii back, raise your hands."

Kuro went stock-still as a scattering of hands went up. All around the room, people were glaring at the elf, some murderously so. ZeroDarkness wouldn't even look at her, but despite his obvious anger, the Assassin's hand stayed down. When it was clear the majority of the guild was with him, Tina released her grip on Kuro's shoulder. "You're a lucky one, KuroKawaii. Turns out we're decent folks after all."

"Thank you," Kuro said in a voice Tina could barely hear. Then she vanished into the shadows, flickering away before their eyes.

"Should I go after her?" SB asked quietly, hand on his sword.

"Nah," Tina said. "She's too embarrassed to be a threat right now. Maybe she'll come back. Maybe she won't. Either way, not my proble—" Her reply was cut off as that gut-twisting, world-moving feeling hit them all again. Tina's first thought was that Garrond had closed the door behind them, but then the whole room flashed as another portal suddenly opened right next to theirs.

Tina put her shield up instinctively then relaxed when she saw that the portal was for the low-level savanna zone. On the other side, she could see an odd collection of gnolls and jubatus standing in a sunny field, but only two jubatus actually jumped through. One of them was definitely a player. There was just no way an NPC would be carrying a raid-level caster weapon with that bizarre mismatch of Agility and Strength armor. The other she wasn't sure about, but the player-jubatus made it through first, landing in the Room of Arrivals as gracefully as the cat he resembled. He flinched back when he looked up to see the raid staring back at him. Then he spotted Tina, and his feline face split into an ecstatic smile.

"*Tina!*" he cried, waving his arms. "It's me! James!"

The moment she heard his name, Tina broke into a huge grin of her own. "*James!*" she cried, grabbing her brother in a huge hug. "I'm so glad you're alive! I was worried sick about you!"

James slapped his hands against her arms. "Not for much longer," he choked out. "Mercy! Mercy!"

Realizing she was crushing him, Tina let go at once, dropping James on the ground in her haste. Much to the alarm of his brother's strange companion, who rushed to his side.

"Sorry," Tina said sheepishly. "But how'd you know it was me?" She certainly hadn't recognized his character.

James arched an eyebrow at her as the other jubatus helped him up. "Uh, you might be the only female stonekin tank with that shield. You're kind of hard to miss."

Behind them, SilentBlayde burst out laughing. Tina just rolled her eyes and turned her attention to the tragedy that was his gear. "Dude, what are you wearing? You look like a broke Renaissance Festival cosplayer."

"I know," James said with a sigh. "It's the best I could manage. All my good stuff was in my bags."

Tina winced. That explained everything. "I *told* you it was stupid to take your armor off when you logged out," she snapped, eyes flicking to the scowling jubatus behind him, whom she was now certain was not a player. "Who's this?" she asked, returning the other jubatus's angry glare with a stone-cold glower of her own. "Your new pet?"

James winced. "Umm…Tina, this is my new brother, Fangs in the Grass, Ar'Bati of the Four Clans."

That was not what she'd expected to hear, but it seemed to please the jubatus. He straightened up with a smirk, almost going up to his tiptoes in an effort to minimize the difference between his normal height and Roxxy's towering one.

"And who are *you?*" he asked in heavily accented English. "Why do you speak so familiarly with James?" His eyes narrowed. "Also, *what* are you?"

"Wow, rude," Tina said, glancing at James, who looked like he was going to pop. She didn't know how he'd ended up with a cat for a "brother," but it was clearly important to him, so she stomped down on the overwhelming urge to punch the impolite jubatus in the face and put out her hand instead. "The name's Tina, and I'm James's little sister."

Fangs in Grass stumbled back at that one. "You said you were human!" he cried, turning back to James, who put his hands up helplessly.

"He is," Tina said. "And so am I. Or I was before this happened." Then just to freak him out, she flashed the cat a marble-toothed smile. "Have you never seen a stonekin before?"

"I've heard of them, but I never knew—" He cut off with a jump as NekoBaby bounced into their conversation.

"Oh! Em! Gee!" she said, flouncing right into Ar'Bati's face. "I know you! You're *Angry Cat!*" She whirled back to the raid. "Guys, guys! It's Angry Cat! You know, the NPC cat-dude from the old meme!" She turned around again, bursting into the song from the animation that had been all over the FFO parts of the internet a few years ago. "*Angry Cat eats your taaaaaaco!*"

Several other players laughed and joined in, and Tina dragged a hand over her face as James's new maybe-brother's face turned crimson.

"Neko," Tina said warningly, putting out a hand to shut the healer down before this turned violent.

Behind the poor taunted Ar'Bati, James reached out a hand of his own, but Fangs-in-the-whatever stiffly turned around before James could reach him.

"Typical players," he said, his voice dripping with disgust.

Normally, Tina would have taken offense at that. This time, though, she had nothing but sympathy. "Guys!" she bellowed, banging her shield. "Knock it off!"

The singing stopped, but the chuckles and snickering remained.

412

She was about to yell again when a loud snapping, fizzling noise made them all jump. Tina whirled around, but it was just the portal James had come through collapsing, showering their feet with rainbow-colored sparks as it vanished.

"Wow," Tina said. "Hope you didn't need to go back."

"It's okay," James said. "This is where we need to be. I need to get to—"

"The bank, I know," Tina said. "We're headed that way, too." She turned to the rest of the raid. "All right, everyone, let's get our asses to the bank and pick up our loot! Once we're loaded up, what do you say we hit the bar behind—"

A loud clatter interrupted her, and everyone whipped around to see a guard in Bastion's royal livery standing in the entrance of the chamber, his dropped sword still wobbling on the marble floor. Cursing under her breath, Tina stepped forward to tell him everything was cool when the man whirled around and shot back out of the room at a dead run.

"*Players!*" he shouted at the top of his lungs. "It's a raid! More players are attacking!"

"Crap," Tina said as the man whipped around the corner. "SB! Zero!"

The two Assassins vanished in the blink of an eye. A second later, there was a loud *thud* from the hallway, then they reappeared, dragging the now-unconscious guard to Tina's feet. She was scowling down at the NPC, trying to decide what to do, when she felt that weird warping sensation again.

Her head whipped around just in time to see Commander Garrond flash her a knowing smile from the other side of the Order's portal. Then he brought his hand down in a chopping motion, and the portal to the Order's fortress collapsed, vanishing with a brilliant flash that left her blinded.

Tina looked back down at the unconscious guard, his face still frozen in terror, then she glanced at the hall that led outside. Now that she was closer, she could smell smoke from outside. Not woodsmoke, but the thick, oily, ashy scent of burning flesh.

"Heads up, guys," she said, drawing her sword. "I think we're in trouble."

The raid moved closer together as she finished, getting in

formation behind Tina as she led them cautiously down the hall, out of the Room of Arrivals, and into the glorious—and now burning—city of Bastion.

THE END
Book 1 of 3

Thank you for reading *Forever Fantasy Online*! If you enjoyed the story, or even if you didn't, we hope you'll consider leaving a review. Reviews, good and bad, are vital to any author's career, and Travis and I would be extremely grateful if you'd consider writing one for us.

Not ready for the ride to end? The second book in the FFO trilogy, Last Bastion, comes out Fall 2018! You can also follow us on Twitter **@Rachel_Aaron** and **@TravBach** or like Rachel's Facebook page, **facebook.com/RachelAaronAuthor**.

If late 2018 is too long to wait, why not check out one of Rachel's other completed series? Just visit **www.rachelaaron.net** for the full list of Rachel's novels complete with their beautiful covers, links to reviews, and free sample chapters!

Thank you again for reading, and we hope you'll be back soon!

Yours sincerely,
Rachel Aaron and Travis Bach

GLOSSARY OF TERMS

Forever Fantasy Online is a full-immersion Virtual Reality game. It uses the proprietary Sensorium Engine to hijack players' senses and convey a fake world to them. For safety and health reasons, players can still feel about 10% of their normal senses (sans sight) while in VR.

FFO is a massively multi-player game set in a high-fantasy world involving millions of players across the globe. Though once the unrivaled juggernaut of VR gaming, eight years after its launch populations have declined in favor of newer full sensory VR games. The active player-base of FFO is now estimated to be around 5 million with about 200,000+ players online at any one time.

Unlike some MMOs, FFO doesn't have its player community divided up across multiple servers. Instead, it favors a dynamic zone-based system. Whenever there are too many people in a zone (like the Deadlands), the game will load another zone-server and start assigning newcomers to that version of the zone instead. So a million players could all be in the Deadlands at the same time, but the game would split them across 10,000 different servers to keep the load down.

GAME TERMS

HP & MP – Health Pool and Mana Pool, aka Hit Points and Mana Points. Damaging attacks reduce the health pool. If HP hits 0, the character is killed and must either be raised by an allied healer's spell or they must relinquish their current location in favor of respawning at a safe graveyard or shrine. No matter where they pop up, dead players always respawn with all of their gear and inventory.

Mana points are used to fuel magical abilities and are only possessed by the spell-casting classes (*Sorcerers, Naturalists, and Clerics. See below.*) Casting spells uses up mana. When a character is out-of-mana (aka OOM), they must wait to recover before casting any more.

Character Class – All players in Forever Fantasy Online must choose from one of seven classes: Knight, Berserker, Assassin, Ranger, Sorcerer, Cleric, and Naturalist.

Each class has a fixed set of abilities and equipment they have access to. For example, all Berserkers have the same stun abilities and use two-handed weapons, while spell-caster classes such as Sorcerers must wear cloth armor and use caster weapons such as staffs or wands.

While abilities and equipment vary, character classes all fit into the three general roles of FFO combat.

Tank (Role) – Heavily armored characters whose job it is to keep enemies from attacking less durable players. Tanks are not good at dealing damage, but they take it very well, making them hard to kill and easy to heal. To keep enemies on them, and not attacking the more vulnerable players, Tanks have abilities called "taunts"—such as *Roxxy's Ground Stomp*—which force monsters to attack them.

Healer (Role) – A magical character who specializes in healing spells. They can also remove status effects such as poisons, curses, diseases,

417

bindings, and even bring players back from the dead. Healers do have some damage-dealing abilities so that they can quest and level on their own, but while they aren't completely helpless, they will never do as much damage as the specialized damage-dealing classes.

Damage / DPS (Role) – Damage dealers are the most numerous classes of character in FFO. Berserkers, Sorcerers, Assassins, and Rangers are all high-damage classes. Tanks can keep monsters at bay while healers heal them, but it is the damage dealer's job to actually kill the attacking enemy.

Group / Party – a small team of two to five players. Used by friends to play together or strangers to tackle challenges too great for a solo player to handle. There are many dungeons and quests in Forever Fantasy Online which require five players to beat. (Ex: The Red Canyon's Lich Lab dungeon.)

Raid – a group of up to fifty players. Typically subdivided into ten parties of five, raids are basically player "armies" created to fight massively epic battles against foes no small party could hope to handle.

Raiding is a big part of the FFO endgame since the coordination required to get fifty players together and to fight well together is very hard. Because of all that work, the rewards for killing raid bosses are among the best in the game.

NPC – non-player character. Any computer-controlled character in the game. NPCs can be friendly or hostile and are generally humanoid and/or intelligent. Note that this term is not usually applied to monsters.

PVE – Players vs. Environment. PVE content is any gameplay that involves the players fighting computer-generated enemies. Completing quests, fighting through a dungeon, and participating in a raid are all examples of PVE content.

PVP – Player vs Player. Some players consider fighting computer opponents too easy. They prefer to fight other real human players in specialized combat called "PVP." FFO has a couple of options for those who wish to only fight human-controlled opponents, including dueling, and participating in ranked gladiatorial combat leagues for special PVP equipment. (There's also an opt-in system for conducting PVP in quest zones.)

Dungeon / Instance – Dedicated group content is often arranged in self-contained areas called dungeons or instances. When a party or raid enters such an area, usually marked by a portal, the game will create a unique instance of that dungeon just for them. So 1000 groups can all be in the Red Canyon dungeon, but it will be a fresh storyline and battle for each and no group can see another in there. The same goes for the Dead Mountain Fortress and other raids.

Aggro – A term used to mean "a monster's attention." When a monster is attacking a player, that player is said to have aggro. Tanks have special abilities to draw monsters' aggro, or attention, to themselves to prevent the monsters from attacking more vulnerable classes.

Levels – Every monster and character in FFO has a power level. Player characters can range from level 1 to level 80 depending on how much they've played the game. Some monsters can be above level 80, such as the skeleton knights of the Dead Mountain Fortress and other monsters in the Deadlands. This is to provide a stiff challenge for powerful veteran players.

Skull Ratings – In addition to levels, all monsters and NPCs in FFO have a skull rating. The number of skulls a monster has beside their level shows how many players the developers think it will take to kill that monster. All beings in FFO are one-skull by default, meaning they can be killed with moderate ease by one same-level player, but there are many harder enemies that require coordinated player effort to take down. For example:

- Two-skull monsters are designed to be a challenge for two players.
- Three-skull monsters are designed to be a challenge for five players.
- Four-skull monsters are designed to be a challenge for ten-player raids.
- Five-skull monsters are for fifty-player raids only.

Two-skull monsters are often called bosses or sub-bosses. Four and five skull monsters are called raid bosses since any group larger than five players is considered a raid.

Gear / Loot – To help them master the world of FFO, player characters have magical equipment, which gives them about 90% of their power. Gear can be looted off the corpses of defeated enemy monsters, earned through completing quests, or won from defeating dungeons or raids. Magical equipment comes in the form of rings, amulets, weapons, and armor. Armor is broken down into nine different "slots" - head, shoulders, chest, belt, legs, feet, bracers, hands, and cloak. Player characters can equip one of each type of gear, but they can't wear more than one piece in the same slot at a time.

Enjoyed Forever Fantasy Online?

Need a new book right now?!

Try one of Rachel's other completed series!
Just keep going to see the list on your eReader, or visit

www.rachelaaron.net

for full sample chapters,
links to reviews,
and lovely covers in high resolution!

The Heartstrikers Series

As the smallest dragon in the Heartstriker clan, Julius survives by a simple code: stay quiet, don't cause trouble, and keep out of the way of bigger dragons. But this meek behavior doesn't cut it in a family of ambitious predators, and his mother, Bethesda the Heartstriker, has finally reached the end of her patience.

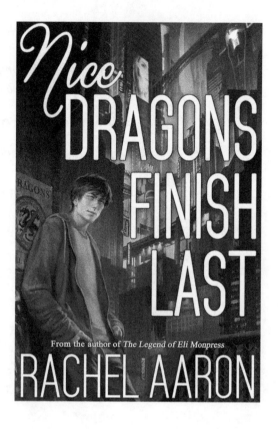

Now, sealed in human form and banished to the DFZ--a vertical metropolis built on the ruins of Old Detroit--Julius has one month to prove to his mother that he can be a ruthless dragon or lose his true shape forever. But in a city of modern mages and vengeful spirits where dragons are seen as monsters to be exterminated, he's going to need some serious help to survive this test.

He just hopes humans are more trustworthy than dragons.

"Super fun, fast paced, urban fantasy full of heart, and plenty of magic, charm and humor to spare, this self published gem was one of my favorite discoveries this year!" - **The Midnight Garden**

"A deliriously smart and funny beginning to a new urban fantasy series about dragons in the ruins of Detroit...inventive, uproariously clever, and completely un-put-down-able!" - **SF Signal**

Want to know more?
Visit **rachelaaron.net** for free sample chapters.

The Legend of Eli Monpress

Eli Monpress is talented. He's charming. And he's the greatest thief in the world.

He's also a wizard, and with the help of his partners in crime—a swordsman with the world's most powerful magic sword (but no magical ability of his own) and a demonseed who can step through shadows and punch through walls—he's getting ready to pull off the heist of his career. To start, though, he'll just steal something small. Something no one will miss.

Something like… a king.

"I cannot be less than 110% in love with this book. I loved it. I love it still. Already I sort of want to read it again. Considering my fairly epic Godzilla-sized To Read list, that's just about the highest compliment I can give a book" - **CSI: Librarian**

"Fast and fun, The Spirit Thief introduces a fascinating new world and a complex magical system based on cooperation with the spirits who reside in all living objects. Aaron's characters are fully fleshed and possess complex personalities, motivations, and backstories that are only gradually revealed. Fans of Scott Lynch's Lies of Locke Lamora (2006) will be thrilled with Eli Monpress. Highly recommended for all fantasy readers." - **Booklist, Starred Review**

The Paradox Trilogy

(written as Rachel Bach)

Devi Morris isn't your average mercenary. She has plans. Big ones. And a ton of ambition. It's a combination that's going to get her killed one day - but not just yet.

That is, until she just gets a job on a tiny trade ship with a nasty reputation for surprises. The Glorious Fool isn't misnamed: it likes to get into trouble, so much so that one year of security work under its captain is equal to five years everywhere else. With odds like that, Devi knows she's found the perfect way to get the jump on the next part of her Plan. But the Fool doesn't give up its secrets without a fight, and one year on this ship might be more than even Devi can handle.

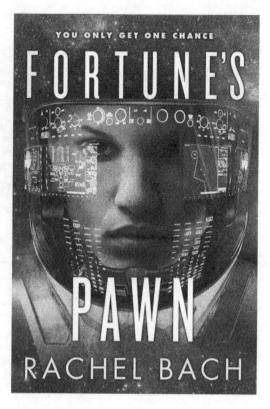

"Firefly-esque in its concept of a rogue-ish spaceship family... The narrative never quite goes where you expect it to, in a good way... Devi is a badass with a heart." - **Locus Magazine**

"If you liked Star Wars, if you like our books, and if you are waiting for Guardians of the Galaxy to hit the theaters, this is your book." - **Ilona Andrews**

"I JUST LOVED IT! Perfect light sci-fi. If you like space stuff that isn't that complicated but highly entertaining, I give two thumbs up!" - **Felicia Day**

2,000 to 10,000: Writing Better, Writing Faster, and Writing More of What You Love

(nonfiction)

"Have you ever wanted to double your daily word counts? Do you sometimes feel like you're crawling through your story? Do you want to write more every day without increasing the time you spend writing or sacrificing quality? It's not impossible; it's not even that hard. This is the book explaining how, with a few simple changes, I boosted my daily writing from 2000 words to over 10k a day, and how you can too."

Expanding on Rachel's viral blog post about how she doubled her daily word counts, this book offers practical writing advice for anyone who's ever longed to increase their daily writing output. In addition to updated information for the popular 2k to 10k writing efficiency process, 5 step plotting method, and easy editing tips, the book includes all new chapters on creating characters who write their own stories, plot structure, and learning to love your daily writing. Full of easy to follow, practical advice from a professional author who doesn't eat if she doesn't produce good books on a regular basis, 2k to 10k focuses not just on writing faster, but writing better, and having more fun while you do it!

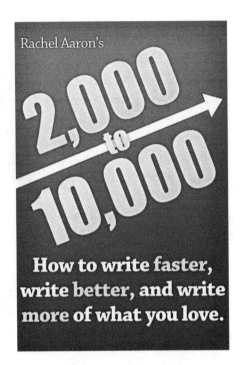

Rachel Aaron's

2,000 to 10,000

How to write faster, write better, and write more of what you love.

"I loved this book! So helpful!" - **Courtney Milan, NYT Bestselling Author**

"This. Is. Amazing. You are telling my story RIGHT NOW. Book is due in 2 weeks, and I'm behind--woefully, painfully behind--because I've been stuck... writing in circles and unenthused. Yet here--here is a FANTASTIC solution. I am printing this post out, and I'm setting out to make my triangle. Thank you, thank you, THANK YOU!" - **Bestselling YA Author Susan Dennard**

ABOUT THE AUTHORS

Rachel Aaron and ***Travis Bach*** are two giant nerds who love gaming, reading, writing, and hiking through the great outdoors while talking about gaming, reading, and writing! When they're not terrifying the wildlife, Rachel and Travis enjoy anime, manga, MMOs, table top gaming, cooking, pampering their old lady dog, and helping their son build secret bases in Minecraft.

Rachel and Travis currently live in Athens, GA, but dream of moving out west where the humidity isn't 90% all year long. If you love gaming and manga as much as we do, hit us up on twitter at:

@Rachel_Aaron

@TravBach

or send us a note at:

www.rachelaaron.net

As always, this book would not have been nearly as good
without my amazing beta readers! Thank you so, so much
to Kevin Swearingen, Eva Bunge, Beth Bisgaard, Christina
Vlinder, Hisham El-far, and the ever amazing Laligin.
Y'all are the BEST!

CPSIA information can be obtained
at www.ICGtesting.com
Printed in the USA
LVHW090001180719
624466LV00001B/353/P